# Fortune Is
# a Woman

# Fortune Is a Woman

## ELIZABETH ADLER

**Delacorte
Press**

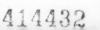

Published by
Delacorte Press
Bantam Doubleday Dell Publishing Group, Inc.
666 Fifth Avenue
New York, New York 10103

Library of Congress Cataloging in Publication Data

Adler, Elizabeth (Elizabeth A.)
Fortune is a woman / Elizabeth Adler.
p.   cm.
ISBN 0-385-30529-X : $20.00 ($25.00 Can.)
I. Title.
PR6051.D56F67 1992
823'.914–dc20              91-24977   CIP

Manufactured in the United States of America
Published simultaneously in Canada

February 1992

10  9  8  7  6  5  4  3  2  1

RRH

*For my lovely Mom,
the one and only Annie Louisa*

"Fortune is a woman, and it is necessary,
if you wish to master her, to conquer her by force."

—Niccolò Machiavelli
*The Prince,* 1513

# PROLOGUE

◆

## *1937*

When Lysandra's grandfather, the Mandarin Lai Tsin, knew he had very little time left on this earth, he took her to visit Hong Kong. He was seventy years old, or maybe more, small and thin and very dignified with parchment skin, high cheekbones, and lacquer-black, almond-shaped eyes. Lysandra was seven, her golden hair spiraled past her shoulders in a thousand energetic curls. She had round, sapphire eyes and a delicate creamy complexion, but she didn't think it strange that she belonged to him. He was Grandfather and she was Lysandra, it was as simple as that.

The journey from San Francisco took six days by flying boat with overnight stops at grand hotels in different cities en route and in that time he talked to her about his business and about China while Lysandra listened interestedly.

"I am an old man," he said as the flying boat lifted sluggishly from Manila Bay on the last leg of its journey. "I shall not have the honor of knowing you on your long journey through life into womanhood. I am giving you everything you could wish for on this earth—riches, power, and success—in the hope that your life will be blessed with happiness. I have told you everything, Lysandra, with the exception of one Truth. This Truth is my secret. This Truth is written down and locked away in my private safe in my office in Hong Kong. Only if despair overtakes you and your path in life seems unclear must you read it. And if that day should come, Granddaughter, then I pray you will forgive me and that my Truth will help you choose the right road to happiness."

Lysandra nodded wonderingly; sometimes the Mandarin was very confusing, but she loved him so much that "truths" didn't seem nearly as important as the fact that he had chosen her as his companion.

When they arrived in Hong Kong they drove immediately to the white, treasure-filled mansion overlooking Repulse Bay, where many soft-footed Chinese servants met them, exclaiming at the extraordinary blond hair and blue eyes of the child and the frailty of the old man.

After they had refreshed themselves with baths and food, the Mandarin called for his automobile, a long, elegant, jade-green Rolls-Royce, and drove with Lysandra to the Lai Tsin headquarters, a towering pillared building spanning the block between Queens and Des Voeux roads.

Taking the child by the hand, the Mandarin showed her the bronze lions flanking the entrance, the magnificent reception hall with the walls and floors paved in different colored marbles, the tall columns in his favorite malachite, the jade sculptures, the mosaics, and the carvings. Then he walked with her to each office, introducing her to every member of the staff from the lowliest cleaner to the highest taipan in the powerful Lai Tsin empire. Lysandra bowed respectfully to each one, saying nothing and listening carefully, as she had been instructed by her grandfather.

At the end of the day her eyes were blank with fatigue, but all was not yet finished. Ignoring his chauffeur the Mandarin summoned a rickshaw, and followed slowly by the elegant automobile, they jolted through the busy streets. The rickshaw man wound his way expertly through a labyrinth of narrow alleys to a seedy waterfront area, leaving the chauffeur and the car stranded far behind. Finally, after what seemed an eternity to the tired Lysandra, he stopped in front of a faded wooden shack roofed in corrugated tin. She looked questioningly at her grandfather as he stepped from the rickshaw and held out his hand to her.

"Come, little granddaughter," he said calmly. "This is what I have brought you all this way to see. This is where the Lai Tsin fortune began."

She held his hand tightly as he walked to the scarred wooden door, noticing that though it seemed flimsy, it was held by thick metal hinges and fastened with strong locks. The structure had been shored up with bricks and repaired with newer wood and there were spiked metal grilles across the small, high-set windows.

"Only fire could destroy the Lai Tsin godown," the Mandarin said, his soft voice full of confidence, "and that will never happen." Lysandra knew he believed the old warehouse would never burn because the fortune-teller, whom he consulted every week, had told him long ago that though there would be fire, nothing of his would ever be harmed again.

The Mandarin rapped twice on the wooden door. After a few seconds there was the sound of strong bolts being drawn and the door was pulled slowly back. A smiling Chinese man of about forty years bowed low as he bid them enter.

"Honorable Father, please enter with Little Granddaughter," he said in Chinese.

The Mandarin's face lit with a smile as he embraced the man, then they stood back and looked searchingly at each other.

"It's good to see you," the Mandarin said, but from the sadness in his eyes they both knew it would be for the last time. "This is my son, Philip Chen," he told Lysandra. "I call him my son because he came into our household when he was even younger than you. He was an orphan and still young and unformed and he became like my own child. Now he is my comprador. He takes care of all the Lai Tsin business here in Hong Kong and he is the only man in the world I trust."

Lysandra's blue eyes widened and she stared interestedly back at the man as the Mandarin took her hand and walked with her through the long, narrow warehouse. Its shelves were dusty and empty, lit by a single naked lightbulb swinging gently on the end of a long flex. Lysandra peered nervously into the shadowy corners, jumping back suddenly as her eyes met another's; but it wasn't the rat or fierce dragon she had been expecting, it was a young Chinese boy.

Philip Chen said proudly, "Sir, may I have the honor to present my son, Robert."

The boy bowed low as the old man inspected him.

"When I last saw you, you were three years old," the Mandarin said quietly, "and now you are ten—almost a young man. Your eyes are steady and your brow is broad. You will do well to inherit the trust we place in your father."

Lysandra stared curiously at him: he was small and stockily built with strongly muscled arms and legs and he was dressed western-style in cream twill shorts, a white shirt, and a gray blazer with a school crest on it. As the Mandarin turned away, the boy's curious eyes, half-hidden behind round wire spectacles, met hers for a long moment. Then he bowed formally and turned to follow his father and the Mandarin to the door.

"I was hoping to entertain you at my home," Philip said sadly, "but you are so tired."

"To see you for these few moments was enough," Lai Tsin replied as Philip's head rested for a moment against his shoulder in a farewell embrace. "So that I could thank you for being my good son. And to ask you to guard the Lai Tsin family and their businesses the way you have always done, even though I will not be here."

"You have my word, Honorable Father." Philip stepped back, his face stern with the strain of holding back his emotion.

"Then I can die in peace," the Mandarin replied quietly, and taking Lysandra's hand he walked slowly to the waiting rickshaw.

As they rode down the narrow street he commanded her to look back at the old wooden godown. "We must never forget our humble beginnings," he told her softly. "If we forget, we may believe we are too clever, or too rich, or too important. And that would bring bad joss, bad luck to the family."

A small treasure trove of gifts from the Mandarin's many business associates awaited Lysandra back at the mansion on Repulse Bay. As she opened the packages, exclaiming with delight over perfect pearl necklaces and exquisitely carved jade figurines, silken robes and painted fans, he cautioned her again. "Remember, the gifts are not because these people are your friends, but because you are a Lai Tsin."

Many years later Lysandra had cause to remember his words.

At the end, when the Mandarin lay dying on a cool October day in San Francisco, only Francie, the beautiful western woman known as his concubine, was allowed at his bedside. She bathed his fevered brow with cool cloths, held his hand and whispered words of comfort. He opened his eyes and gazed at her tenderly.

"You know what to do?" he whispered.

She nodded. "I know."

A look of peace crossed his face and then he was gone.

The Mandarin Lai Tsin's bones were not sent back to China to be buried with his ancestors, as was the custom. Instead, Francie hired a splendid white yacht, and decked it with festive red bunting, and, accompanied only by Lysandra and wearing beautiful white mourning clothes, she scattered his ashes far across San Francisco Bay.

It was what the Mandarin had wished.

# Part I

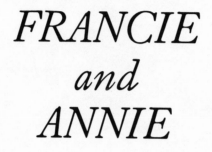

# FRANCIE
## and
# ANNIE

# CHAPTER 1

◆

## *1937*

*Tuesday, October 3rd*

Annie Aysgarth was a small, plump woman with large, expressive brown eyes, shiny conker-brown hair cut in a fashionable bob, and a permanent furrow between her brows. "Put there by years of worry" she always said. She was fifty-seven years old and had been Francie Harrison's friend for almost thirty years, and she knew all there was to know about her.

Annie owned and ran the luxurious Aysgarth Arms Hotel on Union Square. She was as snappy as a Jack Russell terrier, as stubborn as a mule, and as soft-hearted as a chocolate cream. She was also president of Aysgarth Hotels International, a subsidiary of the Lai Tsin Corporation, with hotels in six countries. Annie Aysgarth had come a long way for a Yorkshire lass.

She walked briskly through the thickly carpeted corridors of her San Francisco hotel, looking in at the oak-paneled Dales Lounge to see that the fire was glowing in the huge Elizabethan stone fireplace, as it did every day, summer and winter alike, and that the waiters in scarlet hunt-jackets and breeches stood ready to fulfill the guests' requests for brandy or coffee. She checked the malachite-and-chrome cocktail bar, nodding to the five busy barmen, pleased that, as usual, it was crowded with the city's rich and glamorous young people. She then sauntered through the opulent, gilt-mirrored dining room, pausing here and there to exchange pleasantries with a regular diner or nod to a familiar face. She smiled as she overheard the familiar whispers that of course she must be the famous Annie Aysgarth, that this had been her first hotel and was her favorite. She was a damned fine-looking woman and worth millions, they said.

Her antennae were so tuned after all these years that she would have noticed a rug an inch out of place, an ashtray unemptied or a guest waiting too long for his order. She loved her hotel; she had practically built it with her own hands from ten rooms to two hundred. She knew every inch of the place and exactly how it worked, from the miles of electrical wiring to the intricacies of the steam-heating system. She could have told you exactly how many Irish linen sheets were in the linen rooms on each floor and how many pounds of prime Chicago beef the chef had ordered that week, how many room-service waiters were on duty that night and the names of the guests checking in or out tomorrow.

She had told the laundry workers in the basement exactly how much starch should be used on the pink damask table cloths and she had been known to show the chambermaids how to properly clean a bathtub. She personally had decided the color schemes, fabrics, and furnishings for each of the twenty suites, and supervised the decoration of the entire hotel, choosing the English country-house look for the public rooms and the modern art deco green-and-silver mirrored decor for the cocktail bar. She always supervised the menus and the buying of the wines, and the coffee was specially blended to her taste. Nothing at the Aysgarth Arms was ever left to chance or in charge of a mere manager. Annie was a stickler for cleanliness and quality and she ran her smart hotel the same way she had run her father's house in Yorkshire, all those wasted years.

Satisfied that everything was as it should be, she strolled back to the marble hallway and with a little gold key opened the door to the private golden bird-cage elevator that took her directly up to the penthouse. She sighed pleasurably as it whooshed silently upward, and wondered why people preached that it was wrong to enjoy luxury. The lift stopped, the door slid open, and she was in her own world. Dropping her velvet coat onto a chair she walked straight to the windows, as she always did.

The penthouse was twenty stories high, the floor-to-ceiling windows ran the full forty feet of her drawing room and the view over the nighttime city was magical. Traffic roared through the streets below, but up here all was silent and the city unrolled before her in a million sparkling points of light. She sighed with satisfaction, pleased that it still gave her the same thrill it had when she had first seen it, then turned and looked around her, smiling. She had wanted her home to be completely different from everything she had ever known, and therefore she had consulted a famous interior decorator.

The decorator was shrewd, talented, successful, thin, and ugly, and

Annie was shrewd, talented, successful, and plumply pretty, and they had taken to each other immediately. "Look at me," Annie had demanded, taking up a dramatic pose in the center of the huge, empty room. "You may be looking at a short, plump, brown-haired Yorkshirewoman of a certain age, but inside I'm tall and blond and glamorous. And ten years younger. That's the woman I want you to design this apartment for."

The decorator had laughed and said she knew exactly what Annie meant and then she had gone ahead and created a white and silver, silk and satin, lacquer and crystal apartment just like a Hollywood film set. The floors were laid with costly white marble and covered with velvety cream rugs, the enormous windows were hung with hundreds of yards of billowing cream silk taffeta, the walls were mirrored and lit with filigree silver sconces, the opulent sofas were white brocade, and there were little glass tables and alabaster, chrome, and crystal lamps with pleated silk shades. Annie's huge bed was canopied in creamy satin and topped with a silver corona, and it looked, Annie said fondly, like a tart's boudoir.

The chests and cabinets were lacquered white and dotted with the tall vases she kept filled with fresh long-stemmed white roses, whatever the season. The designer had told her she had used at least fifty different shades of white to create her effect, and the apartment cocooned Annie in a feeling of lightness and luxury and well-being, far away from the brown oilcloth and threadbare Turkish carpets of her youth. And she knew she would not have any of it if it were not for the Mandarin and Francie. And of course, Josh—who was the beginning of it all. It was all due to fate, or happenchance, as they would have called it in Yorkshire, and nothing seemed so far away as the place that had been her home for the first twenty-six years of her life.

But tonight her mind wasn't on her past, nor the sumptuous decor and the sparkling nighttime view; it was on Francie. Picking up the copy of the *San Francisco Chronicle* she sank into a sofa, rereading the gossip column she had already read half a dozen times that day. It was headed DEATH OF THE MANDARIN, LAI TSIN.

The Mandarin Lai Tsin, a notoriously mysterious businessman, died yesterday at the estimated age of seventy, though no one knew his age for certain. He was said to have been born in a small village on the banks of the Yangtze River in China, and no one knows how he came to the United States, only that he ar-

rived in San Francisco before the turn of the century and quickly
made his first fortune as a merchant, using the old Chinese loan
system of rotating credit.

But it was his scandalous liaison with Francesca Harrison,
daughter of Nob Hill millionaire Harmon Harrison, the Yankee
founder of one of our most important banks and top San Francisco socialite, that enabled the Mandarin to move into areas
impenetrable to the Chinese in those early days. It was Francie
Harrison who fronted all Lai Tsin's business dealings here in the
U.S. and also in Hong Kong, and it's said by many that she was
the guiding force that turned the Mandarin into a billionaire.

Lai Tsin was generous with his fortune, creating foundations
to finance schools for Chinese children, endowing scholarships
at the nation's top colleges and universities, as well as building
hospitals and orphanages. It was said that he was trying to make
up for his own deprived childhood and lack of education. If so,
then he did not succeed, for not one of the colleges he endowed
ever gave him an honorary degree, and he was never a member
of the board of any of his schools, orphanages, or hospitals.

The Mandarin was a private man whose life—apart from his
very public liaison with his so-called concubine—remained a
secret. But the biggest secret of all now is whether the ever-
youthful and still beautiful Francesca Harrison will inherit his
fortune—and how much it is worth.

San Francisco waits with baited breath to hear the latest episode in the saga of San Francisco's most mysterious, most notorious, and richest man.

Annie wondered if Francie had read the piece, and how much the
gossip still hurt her. Annie hadn't attended the Mandarin's funeral at
sea, even though she had known and loved him as long as Francie;
she had understood Francie was carrying out the old man's last
wishes and saying a special, private good-bye.

Impatiently throwing the newspaper to the floor, she picked up the
phone, called reception and ordered her little dark-green Packard to
be brought to the front. She threw the soft fur-collared velvet coat
over her shoulders, stuffed the copy of the *Chronicle* into her pocket
and took the elevator back down to the lobby.

She stopped in the lobby for a quick word with the duty manager.

"Have Senator and Mrs. Wingate already left?" she asked casually, pulling on her gloves.

"Yes, ma'am, about a half hour ago."

As she swept through the tall glass doors, she nodded good evening to the top-hatted doorman, then climbed behind the wheel of the little green Packard. She knew one thing for certain: she wasn't going to mention to her friend Francie that Buck Wingate was in town with his wife, Maryanne, and that they were dining with Francie's hated brother, Harry.

Ah Fong, the Chinese houseboy who had been with Francie for more than twenty years, opened the door to Annie and told her that Francie was upstairs, comforting Lysandra.

"Tell her not to hurry. I'll wait," Annie said, crossing the hall to Francie's small sitting room.

She poured herself a large brandy, took a seat, and glanced around appreciatively. There were three other large reception rooms in the house, as well as a library stocked with more than twenty thousand books, and the Mandarin's study, which was as bare and austere as a monk's cell. But Francie's own small room was feminine and cosy. The paintings she had collected from all over the world jostled for space on the walls, a collection of precious white jade filled a tulip-wood Sheraton display cabinet, and books and magazines spilled from shelves onto chairs and tables. The pale rugs were Turkish Ottoman Empire, the amber sofas were deep and draped with soft paisley throws, and the heavy gold-silk curtains were drawn against the cold misty San Francisco night.

She glanced up questioningly as the door opened and Francie came in.

"Lysandra is sleeping at last," she said with a sigh. "She's going to miss him, Annie."

"Aren't we all?" Annie said sadly. "And I can think of hundreds more who had cause to be grateful to him. He was a great man."

She tossed the newspaper over to Francie. "Did you read this? It's the *Chronicle*—but it's the same in all the others."

"I've read it." Annie watched her anxiously; she looked calm and composed, but her beautiful heart-shaped face had lost its color and she noticed that Francie's hand shook as she carefully folded the newspaper and placed it on the table. She thought Francie was still as lovely as the day she had met her; her blue eyes were dark with sadness, but they still had that same sapphire intensity of youth. Her long, smooth blond hair was swept up at the sides with sparkling jeweled combs and coiled into a chignon at the back, and her white fine-wool crepe dress emphasized her slender, graceful figure.

"Better have a glass of brandy," Annie suggested, adding bluntly, "you look ill."

Francie shrugged. Refusing the brandy, she sank back into the soft cushions of the sofa.

"I asked him not to leave his money to me," she said. "I have more than enough, as well as this house and the ranch. There were many bequests, a substantial amount—ten million dollars—to the Chen family in Hong Kong, but he left the bulk of it to Lysandra. A personal fortune of three hundred million dollars and a business worth at least three times as much." She fingered the single strand of enormous pearls at her neck worriedly. "The mansion on Repulse Bay and all his art treasures and priceless antiques were donated to Hong Kong as an art museum, with an endowment for future acquisitions. And, of course, the Mandarin Foundation is already autonomous."

Annie looked at her, stunned. "I didn't realize how *much* money he had. I mean I knew he was rich . . . but . . ."

"Oh, Annie," Francie exclaimed, her blue eyes full of pain, "the sad thing is that it couldn't buy him the things he really wanted. An education, culture—and acceptance. He was forced to get his learning from the streets and he acquired culture by his instinct for beauty. But he was never accepted. I blame myself for that. If it were not for me, then at least the Chinese would have accepted him."

"That may be true, but San Francisco society never would. And that's what he wanted. For your sake."

Francie took a parchment scroll tied with red tape from the pretty little Empire desk by the window and as she unrolled it Annie saw the Lai Tsin chop, the great gold seal.

"He wrote his will himself in Chinese," Francie told her. "I want you to hear what he says."

The Mandarin had written each fine brushstroke of the Chinese characters as exquisitely precise as a miniature painting.

"It is my decree that no male heir of the Lai Tsin family shall ever occupy the highest position in the corporation. Instead they will be compensated with money with which to start up their own companies, to pursue their own business interests and to make their own way in the world, as men should.

"Through the years it has been proven to me many times that women are more worthy than men. Therefore I decree that women shall always carry the fortunes of the Lai Tsin family. The Lai Tsin women will be as powerful as the great dowager empresses of the Chinese dynasties. But they will always be modest, they will never allow the Lai Tsins to lose face, and they will never bring disgrace to the family, either in business or in their personal lives. Those who do will be banished from the family without delay and shall never be reinstated. So, when she is eighteen, I decree that Lysandra Lai Tsin will become owner and taipan of the Lai Tsin Corporation. And until she attains eighteen years, Francesca Harrison shall control the corporation and have total power and final say in any major decision."

"It's not right to burden a girl with all that responsibility," Annie exclaimed. "Lysandra's still a child, we don't even know if she will be clever enough, or strong enough—or if she'll even *want* to run the Lai Tsin Corporation. Francie, it'll just be the past all over again, she'll be a woman in a man's world. And you, of all people, know how hard that is."

Francie closed her eyes, unwilling to remember. "Believe me, Annie, I didn't want Lysandra to be the Lai Tsin heiress. You'll see, as soon as the newspapers get hold of the story she'll be branded the 'Richest Little Girl in the World.' They'll make a freak out of her! I just wanted her to have a normal childhood, to get married, have children . . . *be happy.* This is what *the Mandarin* wanted. He planned her destiny. When she finishes her schooling she will leave San Francisco and go to Hong Kong. She will live with the comprador's family and begin to learn about Lai Tsin and how the business is run. She will learn how to be taipan of one of the world's major trading companies."

Annie's mouth tightened. "You can't let her go to Hong Kong. And besides, when are you going to tell her the truth?"

Francie didn't answer. She walked across to the window and pulled back the heavy silk curtain, staring out into the night. The lights of San Francisco twinkled below in the mist, but she didn't see them; instead she saw the Mandarin's face as he lay on his deathbed and asked her to repeat her promise to him.

"Annie," she said slowly, "even you don't know the whole truth."

Annie stood up, smoothing her skirt over her ample hips. "Francie Harrison," she said angrily, "we've been friends all these years and there's not a secret in my life you don't know. And now you tell me you've been keeping things from me. Not that it matters—except if it concerns Lysandra, then I have a right to know."

The thin parchment crackled as Francie waved the Mandarin's will under her nose. "You know everything there is to know about Lysandra. Here, read it for yourself—"

"You know I can't read Chinese . . . and anyway, that's not what I meant."

"Then there's nothing more to say. The Mandarin guided our lives and we know he was right. Now he will guide Lysandra's and it is my duty to see that what he wished is done."

Grabbing her coat, Annie settled the big fur collar around her throat. "I don't want to quarrel with you, Francie Harrison, but I don't approve of it and I never will. And I'll make sure Lysandra knows where she can come when things go wrong—to her god-mother, her aunt Annie, that's where!"

She flounced to the door, then hesitated, her hand on the knob. "Oh, Francie." She sighed remorsefully. "I came to comfort you and all I'm doing is upsetting you. What kind of woman am I?"

Francie smiled through her tears as they hugged each other. "You're just the same woman you always are, Annie Aysgarth, and I wouldn't want you any different."

"Just remember that the past is over, Francie. It's the future that counts."

Francie shook her head. "For the Chinese the past is still part of life."

"More's the pity," Annie Aysgarth muttered under her breath as they walked to the door.

Francie watched the taillights of her Packard disappear into the misty night. It was only nine o'clock, but California Street was deserted. Up the hill she could see the lights shining on the sidewalk outside her childhood home. Of course, it wasn't the same house, because that had been destroyed in the great earthquake in 1906, but her brother, Harry Harrison, had rebuilt the mansion immediately, "To show San Francisco and America that nothing—not even an act of God, could defeat the Harrisons," he had said. *Only Francie had ever been able to do that.*

She looked down the hill at the blurred lights of San Francisco, thinking of the happy people going out to dinner or dancing or to a show, and loneliness enveloped her like the cold gray mist, chilling her very bones and making her shiver. Hurrying back inside she threw another log on the fire and curled up on the sofa, wrapping the soft paisley blanket around her. Silence settled about her like the fog; the logs crackled and the clock ticked, but there was not another sound. She might have been the last person on earth.

It was the way she always used to feel when she was a child, alone in her room in the big Harrison mansion on Nob Hill.

The lonely minutes were dragging past and she glanced at her watch. It was small and gold and simple and it had been bought for her years ago by Buck Wingate—and that was another name from the past she shouldn't be thinking of tonight. But she was. His dark, lean, handsome face swam into view in her mind as clearly as a photograph. Eight years had passed and she still thought of him every day and every night. The little portrait of the child he had given her one Christmas was still on her bedside table, his watch was on her wrist and his brand on her body. She was helpless with love for him and she hoped she would never see him again.

Hadn't the Mandarin told her before he died that she must put all that had happened behind her and go on? That she should never look back? She shook her head—it was easy to say but not easy to put into practice.

She stood up, smoothing her soft white dress over her hips and stretching. Then she walked restlessly to the window and pulled back the curtains.

Down the road every window of her brother's house blazed with light and a row of smart, chauffeured automobiles waited outside. Harry was giving another of his famous parties. She knew that despite his rumored financial troubles no expense would have been spared to achieve the perfection he demanded. The food would have been prepared by his French chef; the wines and champagnes would no doubt be the greatest vintages, the best hothouses would have been stripped of their choicest blooms and fashioned into breathtaking bouquets by a dozen fashionable florists. The footmen would be wearing the burgundy Harrison livery and the English butler, who had once worked for a duke and who was said to be more snobbish even than Harry, would announce the guests as they arrived. She knew there would be well-bred women wearing satin and lace gowns from Mainbocher and jewels from Cartier, and the men would look distinguished in black tie and tailcoats. And no doubt Harry would have the latest hopeful movie starlet by his side. And no doubt she would be working hard to please him, because even with two divorces and a reputation for being as chauvinistic as their father, her brother, with his social position and his depleted millions, was still a catch.

She closed the curtains, thinking bitterly that his timing was perfect. It almost seemed as if he were celebrating because at long last the Mandarin, Lai Tsin, was dead and could no longer tarnish the Harrison name.

# CHAPTER 2

At eleven-thirty Harry Harrison said good night to his dinner guests. He gratefully watched them go, all except for Buck Wingate and his wife, Maryanne, whom he personally escorted down the marble steps to their car. The Wingates were an old California family, rich for decades from the likes of grain and property, railroads and banking. But Maryanne's family, the Brattles, were old mainline Philadelphia and they had their money so long, no one even thought about where it came from anymore. Old money was always just there.

Buck's father had been at Princeton with Harry's father, the Wingate law practice had handled their business for years, and Buck and Harry had had a passing acquaintance all their lives, though they could never have been called friends.

He kissed Maryanne's scented cheek lightly as she stepped into the chauffeur-driven limousine, and she gave him the cool little smile that never reached her beautiful green eyes. Her blond hair lay in smooth, sculpted waves, her lips were a perfect glossy red, and her midnight-blue silk gown was uncreased. She looked as though she were just starting out the evening instead of ending it.

Harry knew Maryanne Brattle had not married Buck Wingate because he was handsome and charming and nice—and a good catch; she had married him because he was a man with his feet firmly fixed on the political road and she adored the world of politics. Her family lived and breathed politics. They had been in and out of Congress and cabinet posts for generations, though no one had ever yet made it to the presidency. And that was where Maryanne's hopes for Buck lay. He had been senator for the state of California for the past twelve years, and had held official posts under two Republican presidents. Now he was being spoken of as a future presidential candidate.

It was exactly as Maryanne had planned. She had used all her power as a member of an influential political family, and all her plentiful wiles and scheming to get what she wanted.

They had a house on K Street in Georgetown, the Wingate family house outside Sacramento, a vast apartment on Park Avenue, and the imposing country estate, Broadlands, in New Jersey hunting country, which had been left to her by her grandfather. She had two polite, good-looking children, a stable full of Thoroughbred horses, garages full of expensive cars, and acres of shady lawns for taking tea and playing croquet. Maryanne Brattle Wingate had it all. There was only one man who could stop Buck's ultimate progress to the White House, and that was Harry Harrison. Maryanne knew it and she hated him for it.

She said coldly, "Good night, Harry. I can't say I enjoyed myself. I'm afraid film folk make poor conversationalists." Glancing maliciously at the platinum-blond in the clinging silver dress waiting for him in the hall, she added, "Though I suppose Gretchen has her redeeming qualities."

"Greta," Harry corrected her, smiling and thinking what a superbitch she was. But she was smart, he had to hand her that. Just look at the way she had handled Buck's career. He could have used a wife like Maryanne instead of the two losers he had ended up with.

"Good night, Harry," Buck said, climbing thankfully into the limousine and wondering why in hell he'd just had dinner at Harry Harrison's. He was a busy man, his time was not his own and Maryanne took care of their "social" arrangements, all of which were connected with politics because there was nothing else in their lives. He glared at Maryanne as they edged from the curb. "Can you explain to me exactly *why* we spent the evening at Harry's," he said angrily. "I can't stand the man, you know that."

"I told you earlier, darling, his name still counts for a lot in San Francisco, and he had some very influential money men there tonight."

"I don't give a damn about Harry or his money men," he said coldly. "Just don't ever do that to me again."

"After all, darling, your office still takes care of his legal business. I thought it wasn't right just to ignore him," she said soothingly. "But if you dislike him that much, we won't do it again."

As they drove past Francesca Harrison's house, she noticed he turned his head to look at the lighted windows, but she made no comment.

Harry waved his hand in salute, watching as their car drove down California Street heading for the Aysgarth Arms, where they had taken the Royal Suite because Maryanne thought it bad taste to take the Presidential Suite prematurely. Down the street, lights glowed at the Fairmont and the Pacific Union Club, and at the windows of the only other private house on California Street, his sister, Francie's.

He thought of the report of the Mandarin Lai Tsin's death he'd read in the *San Francisco Examiner* earlier that day, and the speculation about the amount of his fortune. "Lai Tsin a Millionaire" it had said, and then naturally they had mentioned the old scandal about Francie and her Chinaman. The Harrison family name had been dragged through the mud one more time and he had wanted to kill her all over again. He thought bitterly that if Lai Tsin had planned to destroy him he couldn't have chosen a better time to do it, because his death was raking up the old scandal just when Harry needed to stay out of the public eye, at least until he had pulled off this coup with the oil wells.

He walked slowly up the steps, glancing briefly at Greta, the pretty young movie actress waiting in the hallway. She smiled appealingly at him, but he didn't even break his stride. "Ask Huffkins to get out the car and drive Miss Wolfe back to her hotel," he told the butler carelessly over his shoulder as he strode past her. She stared blankly after him; they had been together for three passionate weeks and she had a right to expect at least a civil good-bye, but by the time he reached his study and closed his door he had already forgotten her. Greta Wolfe was in the past.

Harry sank into the buttoned leather chair and put his feet up on the mahogany partners' desk. He was boiling with anger against his sister, Francie, and at Maryanne Brattle Wingate; one because she was a slut who had dragged his name in the dust and the other because she was snooty and unobtainable, and tonight she had let him know she still had the edge on him, despite the liveried footmen, the showy dinner, and the sumptuous flowers. And despite their complex "relationship."

Harry was a handsome man, tall, broad-shouldered, and bearded like his father. He had piercing light-blue eyes, sleek dark-blond hair that was beginning to recede, and a calculated social charm. He also had a great attraction for the opposite sex, but tonight Maryanne had sat on his right in the place of honor, ignoring the fine wines and toying with the delicious food, condescending to listen every now and again to Hollywood's most important movie-maker and owner of Magic Studios, Zev Abrams, as he engaged her in conversation.

She had turned her cool green gaze on Harry and said, "Buck and I are cutting back on our entertaining. We are going in for simple little dinners and smaller, more intimate parties. One feels, in our position, it's just a little bit in bad taste to flaunt one's wealth with the terrible Depression still so close in all our minds." And she had smiled that superior little smile. Maryanne had known the flamboyant dinner party was meant to impress her and Buck as well as the monied guests he hoped to persuade to invest in his oil wells, and she wanted to let him know she wasn't buying it. She knew he was using her and that without her he didn't stand a chance of getting his investors. And, goddamit, she was right.

Harry poured himself a brandy, swilling the rich amber liquid around the thin Baccarat crystal balloon glass.

He rested his head on the cool leather of the chair, remembering the shock of the stock market crash that had halved what was left of his assets overnight, and decimated them again a few days later. And after that had come the Depression and it had been touch and go whether his bank would survive. Oh, he hadn't been reduced to hurling himself from a Wall Street window or selling apples for ten cents on the sidewalks, but the Harrison fortune was no more. Some money still flowed in—thanks to a little stroke of luck he'd had a few years ago, *and* his own cleverness in exploiting it—but it flowed right out again into his various faltering enterprises. This time it was the oil wells; he'd been drilling for over a year day and night with no return. Money and time were running out and he needed more. And that was the reason for the fancy dinner tonight.

He gulped down his brandy, remembering the story of his grandfather and the nuggets of gold accumulating in the vaults of the California Bank and thought wryly that the old trader had been right. Gold was the only safe investment in times of trouble. But now he needed a little help. He needed capital to finance a new company prospecting for oil off the California coast and he had invited Buck Wingate to dinner to soften the other guys up for the kill. He wanted to show them that he didn't really *need* the money, he just wanted to count his old friends in on a sure thing. But Maryanne hadn't played the game properly tonight. She had acted cold and superior, like she didn't quite know what she and Buck were doing here with these inferior people. Maryanne was a bitch and he wished he had one like her.

Harry poured another brandy. He needed an alliance, not a marriage. It was time he found himself a woman with money and power and ambition. After all, look what it had done for Buck. And if his wife were as cold as Maryanne, then, like Buck, he could always take his pleasures elsewhere. He was sure women like Maryanne didn't mind that sort of thing. In fact, they probably welcomed it since it saved them the trouble of having to accommodate their husbands when they had so many other important things to do—like the children and the houses to run, and the servants, and the charity lunches, and the dressmakers, and the political meetings and functions, the fund-raising dinners and the full calendar of events on Washington's social circuit. But the bitch had given him the cold shoulder tonight when by right she should have been gazing gratefully into his eyes and telling everyone to invest in his oil wells.

He downed another brandy thinking of the women in his life, the endless train of mistresses and one-night stands, his two worthless wives, and Francie. God, he could remember like it was yesterday; his father telling him, when he was still only a kid, that his sister was crazy and that she did not deserve to have the Harrison name. It was at their mother's funeral when he realized that he was the important one. He was the son and heir. She was a mere girl and she just didn't count.

# CHAPTER 3

◆

Francie couldn't sleep. She heard the cars and voices as Harry's guests left and quiet settled over the city. Her mind cast back where it didn't want to go.

Her first memory was of the week her brother was born. The year was 1891. She was three years old and she climbed from her bed in the third floor nursery and tiptoed down the stairs to the landing to see what all the noise was about. The grand hall, with its dark oak paneling, its stained-glass dome and Italian marble pillars, was lit as bright as day. Menservants wearing the burgundy Harrison livery were hurrying back and forth to the dining room carrying platters of food under the supervision of Maitland, the English butler.

Clinging to the banisters, she watched with fascination a world she had never seen before. Snatches of conversation and laughter came from the dining room and she could hear her father's booming voice barking an order at Maitland. The butler emerged into the hall, his face impassive as he repeated the order to one of the servants and she shrank back into a corner as the man hurried past her up the stairs.

A few minutes later he returned carrying a tightly wrapped bundle. It was her new baby brother, who she knew slept in a crib by her mother's bed, and whom she had only been allowed to see once for a few minutes when her father was out. "Because he's afraid of the germs, dear," her mother had said. The servant disappeared toward the kitchen with the baby, and Francie's hand flew to her mouth in horror. Were they going to put him in the oven and cook him for supper?

She clung terrified to the banisters and a few minutes later Maitland strode across the hall bearing an enormous silver platter covered with a large silver dome.

Fear lent wings to Francie's feet as she sped down the richly carpeted stairs, tripping over the brass stair-rods and almost landing on her nose on the black-and-white checkered floor. The marble felt cold under her bare feet as she ran to the dining room and through the half-open doors.

The long table was aglitter with candlelight, silver, and crystal. Wine glowed ruby red in decanters and fragrant blue cigar smoke wreathed the air. Her father, Harmon Harrison, was seated at the head. He was tall, bearded, and heavily built. He exuded the power and confidence of his wealth and position. His eyes were fixed on Maitland carrying the platter toward him. He tapped on his glass and the twenty-three men around the table fell obediently silent.

"Gentlemen," Harmon boomed, "I have invited you here tonight not just for your company, and not only to discuss how we can bring San Francisco into the glory she deserves by strengthening her links to the east coast. No, sirs! You have partaken of the best the house of Harrison has to offer, but now there is something else I have to show you. Something special." Pushing back his chair, he rose to his feet, and with a flourish removed the silver dome. "Gentlemen," he said proudly, "may I introduce my son and heir—Harmon Lloyd Harrison, Junior."

The tiny baby, naked but for a cotton diaper, lay sleeping on a bed of green ferns oblivious to the laughter and applause. Grabbing the silver platter Harmon Harrison held it aloft. "A toast, gentlemen, to my son," he called, and the baby's health was solemnly drunk in the finest vintage port wine.

Francie stood unnoticed by the door as the silver platter with its tiny human burden was passed from hand to hand around the table. The baby was as still and silent as her rag doll. A scream forced itself from her throat as she launched herself suddenly at her father.

"Stop them, Papa, stop them," she screamed, throwing her arms tightly around his legs. "Don't let them eat him!"

"Francesca!" The depth of anger in her father's voice froze her screams into instant silence. With a gesture he indicated she should be removed and a servant pulled her clinging arms from his immaculate gray pinstriped trousers.

"I shall deal with you in the morning," he said quietly in a tone that changed her blood to ice as they bore her away. It was then that Francie first realized her father did not love her.

* * *

*Hate* was too strong a word to describe Harmon Harrison's attitude toward his daughter; for him she simply did not exist. His son was what he had desired above anything else and all his energy, all his ambition, all his life force went into grooming him to take over his position as head of the Harrison Mercantile and Savings Bank, as well as the myriad other Harrison business enterprises that fueled his lavish lifestyle and his ever-growing fortune.

Harmon had always claimed that his father came from old Yankee stock, from Philadelphia, and that his mother's ancestors had come over on the *Mayflower*. Nothing could have been further from the truth. His father, Lloyd Harrison, was a Yankee all right, but he was an itinerant trader whose life had been devoted to making a fast buck when and wherever he could, legal or otherwise, and to pleasuring any attractive woman who fell for his rough, dark good looks and practiced line of patter.

Lloyd had arrived in San Francisco, a town of tents and shanties, with twenty thousand dollars in his pocket earned selling guns and ammunition to settlers in the middle west. He was quick to take his talents out to the goldfields, where he bartered, dealt, and traded in everything from canvas tents to picks and shovels, candles, tea, liquor, barroom fittings, bibles, and brass beds for bordellos. Sometimes he was paid in cash, sometimes in still-worthless gold stock, and it was the stock that ultimately made him a rich man. With his fickle, fly-by-night nature, Lloyd never hung onto his stock; when it rose from worthless to lucky strike and hit a thousand dollars a share, he sold, and then he bought up real estate in San Francisco, cheap sandy lots that within a year were selling for small fortunes. Though he never put his shoulder to the pick and shovel in the gold mines everything Lloyd touched turned to pure eighteen-carat nuggets sitting snugly in a vault in the California Bank.

Within two years he was a millionaire, within five a multimillionaire, but he still preferred the rough-and-tumble atmosphere of the shantytowns near the gold mines to the urban pleasures of a growing San Francisco.

One day he had found himself with a shipment of fancy gowns and feathered hats direct from Paris. There was a shortage of women in San Francisco, so he took them to the only place where there were both women and money. The bordellos of the boom silver mining town, Virginia City.

He sold half a dozen fashionable dresses and some delicious silk underwear to Bessie Maloney, the buxom, dark-haired proprietress of Maloney's Cat House, consummating the transaction a little more personally later that night. Bessie was a nice woman, she ran a fair establishment, and he'd made a good profit on his shipment; it was nothing more than that to either of them. Except a couple of months later when he found himself back in Virginia City and Bessie told him she was pregnant.

She was thirty-four years old, she had never had a child, and she intended to have this one. Lloyd shrugged, passed a couple of thousand dollars across the bar and promised casually to "see her all right." Then he thought nothing more of it.

When he returned to Virginia City a year later he was told Bessie had died in childbirth and the baby—a boy—was being looked after by the whores. He stared at the infant sleeping in a Moses basket on top of the mahogany bar while blue cigar smoke and even bluer language floated around him.

Picking up the basket, he walked to the door. "This is my boy," he said firmly. "My son. He's coming home with me."

But first he had to build that home. He chose his lot carefully on top of the almost empty California hill and built the first of its grand mansions. Later it would be called "Nob Hill," because the men who lived there were like the nabobs of the east, the most powerful in San Francisco and rich beyond the dreams of avarice. He spent over a million dollars creating a palace for his son and he made sure that everything was the best. While it was being built, he took a suite at the lavish Oriental Hotel, where he left his son in the care of three nursemaids and returned to his old stamping grounds at the silvermines.

When the house was finally finished it occupied a full city block. It had more than sixty rooms including a drawing room with painted wall paneling brought from a French château, a ballroom with mirrors copied from those at Versailles, and floors and bathrooms of marble imported from Italy. There were three hundred silver wall sconces and forty crystal chandeliers from Venice, as well as forests of oak paneling and a great staircase from a Jacobean mansion in England. The tall windows were hung with satin and velvet drapes imported from Lyons in France, and the floors covered with magnificent rugs from Persia. The stables in back of the house rivaled it in luxury, with polished rosewood stalls embellished with silver, mosaic tiled floors, Brussels rugs, and elaborate chandeliers. The mansion was the talk of San Francisco, as was Lloyd's flamboyant lifestyle.

His son, Harmon, was brought up by nursemaids and governesses and by the age of seven already ruled the household like a tyrant; his word was law. "You tell 'em, son," his father would chuckle, watching young Harmon giving orders to the maids. "You show 'em who's the man of the house."

When he was ten Lloyd sent him back east to a smart prep school to teach him how to behave in men's company. "You've been around namby-pamby women too long," he told him. Harmon was of average intelligence, tall, fair, and good-looking, and he had a great deal of money to throw about. He quickly acquired a coterie of hangers-on and he enjoyed his school years and the new masculine company. At eighteen he went to Princeton, returning home at age twenty-one with a diploma and a sense of his own importance. He had become an overnight aristocrat.

It was a dreadful shock, therefore, when one night Lloyd, slightly the worse for drink, told him the truth about his mother, Bessie Maloney of Maloney's Cat House. Devastated, Harmon nursed the secret in his heart and his hatred for his "mother" grew into a burning hatred for all women.

For a handsome young man, Harmon sowed few wild oats. He preferred masculine company and sporting events and considered women a secondary breed, put there for a man's entertainment—and not worth the money he had to spend on them.

Lloyd died when Harmon was twenty-two and he found himself the sole inheritor of an estate calculated in excess of eighty-five million dollars. He buried his father with tremendous pomp, hosting a reception afterward at the Harrison mansion attended by every one of San Francisco's notables, most of whom had made their money the same way his father had. With that done he set about reshaping the family image by covering up Lloyd's wild reputation and the facts of his own birth, and throwing himself wholeheartedly into running the business. He did both very well and in ten years he had become a pillar of San Francisco society and had tripled his assets. He was discreet about his personal life and sexual predilictions and his public life was a model of propriety.

By this time he was thirty-two years old and still a bachelor, but he wanted a son and heir to carry on the Harrison name and tradition, and so he began to look around for a suitable wife.

He met Dolores de Soto at a dance at a neighboring Nob Hill mansion. As he whirled her around in a waltz, his hand tightly clamped on her tiny waist, her white skirts flowing, he was thinking less of her dark, sapphire-eyed beauty than her pedigree, because the de Sotos were decendants of Spanish aristocrats and they also were known for breeding sons. And he, the son of an itinerant Yankee trader and a whore, wanted to be socially well-connected as much as he wanted a son and heir. He knew the de Soto family had once been rich, owning many thousands of acres from the Spanish land grants, but generations of bad business deals had reduced their assets to a small ranch in the Sonoma Valley. They might not have money—but their breeding could be traced back to Queen Isabella of Spain.

He requested a meeting with Dolores's father; an agreement was reached and a marriage contract signed. The de Sotos left the ranch and planned to move back to Mexico, and within a matter of weeks the girl found herself walking down the aisle of St. Mary's Cathedral in front of a crowd of three hundred hand-picked guests as Harmon Harrison's bride. At that moment her father became a rich man again and Dolores became her husband's chattel, to be used whenever he desired, to be a vessel to breed his sons, and to be present on those public occasions when a wife's presence was required.

Dolores knew why he had married her and she breathed a sigh of relief when she knew she was pregnant. Harmon sent the best doctor in San Francisco to examine her; he watched over her health like a hawk, but she became weak and thin, her eyes were huge pools of blue in her pale face and her black hair lost its luster. Deciding that San Francisco's hills and fog were dangerous for a pregnant woman, he sent her up north to her family's old ranch in the Sonoma Valley, where he left her in the care of a nurse. He stocked the ranch with special Jersey cows to provide her with fresh milk and cream; he ordered San Francisco's best butcher to prepare prime cuts of meat, had them packed in ice and dispatched them daily to the ranch; and he hired a special cook to supervise his wife's diet and prepare her meals.

Dolores was still only nineteen and she felt like a prize calf being reared for the kill. She was a well-brought-up girl, soft-spoken and timid, and she was afraid of her husband's coldness and terrified of his anger. Everything she did was to please him; the way she wore her smooth black hair, wound into an elegant chignon; the way she dressed, quietly but expensively as befitted a rich man's wife; the way she behaved, smiling by his side in public or supervising his dinner table. But whenever they were alone she kept to her rooms and out of his sight. Because that's the way he wanted things. And she knew for a fact that he cared for his dogs, the Great Danes, King and Prince, more than he did for her.

When she was seven months pregnant he brought her back to San Francisco, worried that the baby might decide to make an early appearance, and Dolores, plumper and sleeker, was installed in a newly converted suite of rooms on the ground floor so that she should not have the trouble of walking up the stairs. She was not permitted to set foot out of bed until noon and she was taken on a short, sober carriage ride each day at three. She was dying of boredom and terrified that she might not bear her husband the son he so confidently expected.

She had no one to confide in; her mother was dead and she had no sisters. Her father and brothers had taken Harmon's marriage settlement and bought themselves a large estate on Lake Chapala in Jalisco, Mexico, and she no longer had young friends of her own. Depression settled over her like a heavy blanket; she wished the baby would never be born. She felt no emotion toward the child; if it were a boy it would be Harmon's child and she would have little to do with it; if it were a girl he would hate her for it. Either way she could only lose.

When she finally went into labor on a sultry September night, Harmon was summoned from the Pacific Club, where he dined more often with his friends than he did at home with his wife. His voice quivering with excitement, he promised Dolores everything would be all right, the best doctors were on hand—three of them, and when it was all over he would buy her a yacht even bigger than the Vanderbilt's *North Star*. In the spring, when she was better and the baby old enough to be left, they would sail to Europe for a vacation. He promised he would buy her dresses and furs from Worth in Paris, a diamond tiara from the royal jewelers in London, a palazzo in Venice, anything she wanted. But Harmon's pale blue eyes were hard as they looked into hers. "When I have my son," he added with a smile. Then he patted her hand and left her in charge of the three eminent doctors.

The labor lasted thirty-six agonizing hours and in the end, when the child was born, the doctors looked at each other and shook their heads gravely. It was decided that the eldest amongst them should be the one to tell the husband.

"I'm afraid it's a girl, sir," white-haired Doctor Benson said, noting that it was the first time in his long career that he'd ever apologized for a baby's birth.

Harmon said nothing. He walked to the window and stared silently out at the Mark Hopkins mansion opposite. After a while he said, "How long . . . ?"

Remembering his conversation about taking his wife to Europe, the doctor said, "How long before she can travel? Well, she's had a hard time. Let's say four or five months."

"No, you fool," Harmon growled, walking from the window and towering arrogantly over him. "I mean, how long before she can conceive again?"

The doctor looked him in the eye. "Mr. Harrison," he said icily, "your wife has just given birth. And though you have not inquired about her, she is exhausted and in pain. There are many years yet for childbearing and no doubt one day you will have your son. Meanwhile a little more seemly conduct might be in order."

Harmon shrugged. "I'm sorry, doctor. Having a son means a lot to me."

"And so," said the doctor, "I hope, does a daughter."

Harmon did not come to see her, and Dolores wanted to die. Her milk dried up and a wet nurse was hastily summoned. Whenever the child was brought to see Dolores she would turn her face to the wall; the baby was a living symbol of her failure.

Three days later Harmon knocked on her bedroom door. He brought her no gift, not even flowers, and he strode to her bedside and stared coldly down at her. "You are pale," he observed. "I think when you are well enough you should return to the ranch. You can rebuild your strength there."

Her fingers plucked nervously at the linen sheet and she nodded mutely.

He said, "Your family and mine are both known for breeding sons. The fact that this first one is a girl is not important. The next child will be a boy."

She asked tentatively, "Would you like to see her?"

He barely glanced at the pink-wrapped bundle proffered by the waiting nurse.

"I thought I might like to name her Francesca," Dolores said, "for my mother. Unless, of course, you prefer your own mother's name," she added hurriedly.

"Francesca is a suitable name," he replied, walking to the door. "But the christening will be a private one."

Dolores nodded. She understood that there were to be no great celebrations for the birth of this daughter, and that her life as Harmon Harrison's wife depended on her providing him with a son. And he was a very impatient man.

Harmon packed Dolores and her baby off to the ranch and then he consulted a new doctor about when he might reestablish his marital relations, bearing in mind Dolores's delicate condition and his own urgent desire for a son and heir. He never went to see his wife and child in the six months the doctor prescribed he must wait, but on the very day the enforced abstinence ended he sent for them to return to San Francisco.

Dolores looked back regretfully as the carriage pulled away from the ranch. It was just a simple wooden structure nestled in a fold of the hills, with grassy paddocks, post-and-rail fences and tall rustling poplar trees, but it was more like home than the great mansion on Nob Hill. Here she had found simple comforts instead of great luxury, she had found peace of mind away from the perpetual fear of her husband, and she had got to know her baby daughter.

Francesca had thrived in the fresh country air and at six months was a pink-cheeked, robust baby with her father's blond hair and her mother's sapphire eyes that sparkled with intelligence and happiness. Dolores dreaded their return to the huge, overstuffed house; she wished they could stay at the ranch forever. And besides, she knew exactly why she had been summoned back.

As soon as they arrived Francie was installed with a nursemaid in the third-floor nursery—well away from her parents' rooms. Dolores took her place beside her husband at the necessary social events— and in his bed.

When Harmon was at the bank or at the Pacific Club or his own business and social gatherings, she managed to spend time with Francie. Her little daughter continued to thrive and Dolores hoped her love made up for her father's neglect.

The nursery had originally been decked out for the expected son and heir and it was light and bright and cheerful with blue carpets and crisp white curtains and a pretty, lacy crib, and Francie was taken for daily walks by a uniformed nurse up and down the hills in a specially made wicker perambulator imported from London.

Dolores knew Harmon didn't love her; he treated her courteously if distantly, but now she didn't feel lonely because she had Francie. But six months passed and despite his nightly invasions on her body she still wasn't pregnant and she knew he was losing patience. After a year he took her to a specialist in New York, who declared she was exhausted.

"You're trying too hard," he told Harmon. "Forget about producing children and just let nature take its course. Woo her a little bit, pay her more attention, relax her . . ."

Harmon thought about what the doctor had said, then he telegraphed his offices and told them he would be away for some time. After booking the honeymoon suite on the S.S. *America,* he informed Dolores that he was taking her to Europe.

Sure that a romantic voyage would put Dolores in the right mood to conceive, he swept her across the Atlantic to Paris, London, Rome, and Venice, but after eight months he had to concede defeat. Dolores was still not pregnant and his business needed him in San Francisco. Then, on the return voyage to New York, the miracle happened. Dolores knew it immediately—she could just tell, the way women can—but she said nothing to Harmon until a few weeks later at breakfast.

He stared at her, his bearded face pink with surprise and pleasure. "Are you sure?" he demanded.

She nodded demurely. "Quite sure. I've already seen Dr. Benson and he confirmed it."

"Are you well? Is everything all right?"

She sighed as she met his anxious, pale-blue eyes. "Everything is quite normal, Harmon. I just pray that this time it will be the son you want."

"It will be," he said, confident that fate would not dare to deal Harmon Harrison a bad card a second time.

Francie and Dolores were sent to the ranch again for six months of blissful solitude and peace, but the time passed too quickly, and plump as a fatted calf, Dolores was once again installed in her downstairs suite and Francie was banished to the third-floor nursery.

Behind three-year-old Francie's doll-like prettiness lay a very sharp mind. Dolores had taught her the alphabet on their stay at the ranch and she could already string together letters and read some of the words in her little rag storybooks. She could count to ten and she could lace her own boots, though she did not always get them on the right feet. Her eyes were the deep sparkling blue of her mother's, her small face was heart-shaped, and her long white-blond hair was rolled in rags nightly and brushed out into fat ringlets again each morning by Clara, the young nursemaid. But her father only saw her when Clara took her downstairs at six o'clock to say good night.

She would be freshly bathed, her curls would shine, and she'd wear a starched cotton frock with row upon row of lace ruffles. Dolores would take her in her arms and hug and kiss her and then the child would approach her father's chair. "Good night, Papa," she would say in her clear piping little voice, dropping a wobbly curtsy.

"Good night, Francesca," he would reply, glancing up briefly from the evening edition of the *San Francisco Chronicle.* And then the nursemaid would take her hand and lead her from the vast opulent room back to the safety of the nursery.

# CHAPTER 4

From the day her brother was born Francie's life changed. Her father ordered her to be removed immediately to a small room on the fourth floor back, right by the servants' stairs, while the pretty nursery was repainted and decorated with new curtains and rugs and a wonderful new crib fashioned from solid silver.

Francie saw the baby in the crib when he was brought down to the drawing room for the christening party and her eyes grew round with amazement as she looked at the yards of cream lace draping the gleaming silver, at the proud blue ribbon on top and the tiny pink-faced baby crying lustily from his swaths of silk.

Somehow, after the nursery was finished, she was never returned there and the baby, Harmon Harrison, Jr., or Harry, as his father called his son, reigned over it in solitude—except for the half dozen nurses and under-nurses and nursery maids hired to pamper and fuss over him, while Francie kept her little room at the top of the servants' staircase.

The room faced north and was small and dark but she didn't mind too much because the window overlooked the stables and she could watch the horses being groomed, ready to be hitched to the carriages, and listen to the servants gossiping in the courtyard as they hung out washing or smoked an illicit cigarette.

When Clara, her young nursemaid, found her hanging halfway out the window, she was shocked into action.

"I must protest about the little girl being kept in that back room, sir," she said, bearding the master in his den.

"And why is that?" he asked distantly, barely glancing up from his desk.

"Why, it's too small. It's dark and pokey and just today she almost

fell out of that window. That's a servants' room," she said with all
the pride of position where a nurse was considered above the servants, "and it's not a fit place for the daughter of the house."

"I will be the judge of that," Harmon replied icily. "I will instruct
Maitland to pay your wages to the end of the month and you will
leave immediately."

"Leave?" Clara was stunned. "But I . . . I can't leave. . . .
Who will look after Francie?"

"I think the servants are quite capable of dealing with a three-year-
old child. I've discovered lately that she has become far too impudent
under your care. Please close the door quietly on your way out."

Francie waved good-bye forlornly from the library window as
Clara, her straw bags clutched in her gloved hands, stumped off
down the hill in tears. And the very next day a workman installed
iron bars on her small window. "For Francesca's safety," her father
said.

Dolores's confinement had been a difficult one and in the next year
she never left her rooms, so she was never really aware of what was
going on. When her father was away Francie would lurk nearby,
watching as doctors and nurses bustled in and out. And when she
knew her mother was alone she would slip through the door and run
to her bedside. Most times Dolores would have her eyes closed, lying
as still as Francie's rag doll. But at others she would lift her head
from the banks of embroidered linen pillows and smile at Francie.

"Come here, darling," she would say softly, patting the empty side
of the bed where Harmon used to sleep, though since she had been ill
he slept in his own room down the hall. "How are you, baby?" she
would ask, ruffling Francie's blond hair that hung straight now since
there was no Clara to tie it in rags and make ringlets. Nor was it as
clean as it should be because the servants were all too busy; they had
their appointed tasks to do and being nursemaid and washing
Francie's hair was not one of them.

Francie thought her mother's room smelled of flowers and red
medicine and her favorite scent—lily of the valley—and she felt
warm and secure, snuggled next to her under the cream silk com-
forter. "Are you better, Mama?" she asked anxiously.

"Of course I am, darling, I'll be up and about in no time," her
mother replied, smiling, only Francie thought her eyes weren't smiling so much.

"Mama, what's consumption?" she asked, suddenly.

"Wherever did you hear that word?" Her mother's voice had sharpened and Francie shrank back nervously. "The doctors said it, Mama. Is it a bad word?"

Dolores smiled ruefully. "No, it's not a bad word. It's just the name of an illness."

"Is that what you've got then, Mama?" Francie asked, leaning closer and staring at her worriedly.

"Well . . . yes, I suppose so. Just a little bit, anyway." Dolores smiled again to make it seem unimportant. "But it's not too dreadful, you know, it's just like having a really bad cold. And you know how weak and silly that makes you feel."

"Oh, good." Francie sighed with relief. "Then you'll soon be better and we can go to the ranch again."

"Of course we can, Francie."

"When, Mama? When?" she asked, bouncing on the bed in excitement.

"Oh, some day . . ." Dolores replied, with that familiar half-promise given to children that meant "maybe never."

Two more years passed before Francie went to the ranch again, and then it was because her mother was dying.

The doctors never told her, but Dolores could see the truth in their eyes as she became weaker each month. And every night as she lay awake, soaked in sweat and struggling for breath, her thoughts would turn to the months spent on the ranch with her baby daughter, and she knew they had been the happiest times of her married life.

One afternoon Harmon came to visit her. He had gained weight over the past few years and with his commanding height, his striped vest buttoned over his solid stomach, his dark blond beard and side whiskers and the two enormous dogs by his side, he was an intimidating figure. Dolores looked worriedly at him. She was still afraid of his anger and she had to screw up all her courage to tell him that she wanted to return to the ranch.

She stared at him, astonished, when he agreed immediately. But then he added, "It will be better for the boy. It is not good for him having a sick woman in the house—"

"But Harry's only three," she protested, tears stinging her eyes at his uncaring cruelty. "Besides, he's too young to mind that I'm always here, in bed—"

"Of course he minds. No boy wants to linger in a sick room.

Anyway, you are not dying, Dolores. The doctors say you just need to keep taking the new medicine. Go to the ranch, the fresh air will do you good. Your nurse can go with you and I'll send Dr. Benson out once a week to check on you. I'll tell Maitland to arrange the move."

"I'd like to take Harry with me," she said, meeting his eyes defiantly. "The fresh air at the ranch will be good for him, too, and besides, it may not be for long—"

"Take my boy?" He was astounded that she had even suggested such a thing. "Of course you cannot. The girl can keep you company. Harry stays here with me."

"Harmon, please, I'm begging you." She took his hand in her cold ones. "Please, oh, please let me have my son, just for a little while."

"I'll bring him to visit you," he promised hurriedly. "Later, when you're settled. Yes, that's right, later." He pulled the heavy gold half-hunter quickly from the fob-pocket of his vest and checked the time. "I have an appointment. I won't be home till late, so don't expect me. I'll tell Maitland to instruct the maids to pack your things."

Francie had the best time at the ranch. Away from the overstuffed mansion her mother seemed instantly better; there was a bloom of bright color on her cheeks, her blue eyes sparkled, and her black hair regained its luster.

Francie had promised she would look after her. She was six years old now, tall for her age and too thin because at home she never got enough to eat. The Harrison's chef had cooked elaborate meals for her father and his guests and he had prepared delicate dishes to tempt her mother's appetite; the nurserymaids fixed her three-year-old brother's food and the servants had their own cook who prepared meals for the staff dining room. But Francie didn't fit into any of those categories. She was an in-between, a nowhere child in a busy household that ran on oiled wheels without her. The chef shooed her out of his kitchen, thinking she was fed in the nursery, and the nursery banned her from their meals because her father said she was supposed to eat downstairs. So often, after a miserly supper of bread and milk, she was so hungry she would sneak into the kitchen and just steal whatever she could.

It was different at the ranch. The cook made a fuss over her and fixed her favorite—chicken and ice cream, the nurse bathed her and washed her hair and let it dry in the sun so that it shone like blond satin, and she was free to take off her tight boots and run barefoot in the grass, and shout and holler just as loudly as she liked instead of having to behave like a quiet little mouse. Because she just wasn't cut out to be a mouse, not even if she tried for ever and ever.

She pushed her mother around the grassy paths in her cumbersome wheelchair, chatting nonstop about the rabbits dashing away from under their feet and the flock of starlings in the hedgerow and the tall leafy poplars rustling in the breeze with a sound like a rushing mountain brook. And in the evening after supper she would take the heavy silver brush from the dresser and stand behind her mother's chair. She would unpin her long black hair and brush it gently with long, even strokes until it shone like a raven's wing and the furrow of pain between her mother's brows disappeared.

The days were long and the sun hot and life was carefree and easy, but the best thing of all was when Dr. Benson arrived one morning with the Great Dane puppy.

"It's one of Prince's pups," he told Dolores. "His mate had a litter of six. This was the only female and Mr. Harrison said she's damaged —something about a crooked ear. He thought she should live out here on the ranch, keep you company."

He placed the big puppy on the wooden floor of the porch and Francie exclaimed excitedly. "Oh, she's not crooked at all. She's just beautiful." Then she stepped shyly back, putting her hands behind her back.

"Don't you want to pick her up?" Dr. Benson asked, puzzled.

She stared down at the floor, trailing her bare toe along the line where two wooden planks met. "She's Mama's dog," she explained quietly. "Papa said it was for her."

"Then I give her to you, Francie," Dolores said quickly. "Now she's your dog."

"Really? Can I really have her, Mama?"

Her face was alive with happiness, and Dolores felt suddenly sad. She thought that poor little Francie never had anything, and she wondered, whatever would happen to her when she was gone. "Of course she's yours, darling. And now a dog must have a name, so what are you going to call her?"

"Why, Princess, of course," Francie said proudly. "After all, she's the daughter of a prince." And they all laughed.

She had never had anyone of her own to love before and Princess fulfilled all her needs. She was a big, shambling, sand-colored puppy with huge paws, intelligent amber eyes, and a very large wet tongue that she used lavishly on Francie's face every morning when she awoke. She slept on Francie's bed, made pools on her floor and sometimes, when no one was looking, ate from the same bowl. It was a mutual love affair; Francie adored her and Princess adored Francie and they were inseparable.

The De Soto Ranch was not really a working one; it was just forty acres with a few cattle, the Jersey cows and a dozen chickens scratching in the sandy backyard. Each morning Francie would take her basket and search eagerly for the eggs they laid in odd places, behind the rain barrel or in the hedgerows, and carry them triumphantly back for breakfast. There were geese by the pond that cackled and flapped their wings ferociously at them whenever she and Princess came near, and there were half a dozen horses in the paddock which she would eye longingly, leaning on the rough post fence, her chin on her arms, watching Zocco and Pepe, the Mexican ranch-hands, as they saddled up and galloped off toward the distant hills to fix fences and clear the scrub and check for stray cattle in the arroyos.

Then one day Zocco lifted her onto the bare back of the small chestnut mare called Blaize. Francie just sat there, her legs sticking out, her hands resting on the animal's neck. She felt the mare quiver in anticipation and the warm smoothness of her coat under her bare thighs and when Zocco guided her forward a few steps, she laughed in delight.

"You learn ride bareback," the Mexican told her. "Is better this way. Then you never fall off, ever."

Zocco held the mare on a leading rein and for fifteen wonderful minutes they paced slowly around the paddock, the big puppy ambling at their heels. Francie thought it was the best thing that had ever happened in her whole life, except for Princess, of course. She made Zocco promise he would teach her every day and then she ran excitedly back to the ranch house to tell her mother and to fetch a piece of sugar for the mare.

In a few weeks she could control Blaize herself, and holding the reins loosely so she wouldn't damage the little mare's tender mouth, she trotted proudly around and around the paddock for her mother to see.

"Wonderful, darling," Dolores called from her chair. "I learned the same way when I was a child."

Francie reined in her horse. *"When you were a child,* Mama?" she said, amazed at the very idea. "Were you like me then?"

Dolores shook her head and laughed. "I was a well-brought-up girl in a dozen petticoats and starched pinafores and high-button boots. And you are a ragged little tomboy, running around barefoot with not even a governess to teach you your lessons." She sighed. "I must speak to your father about that."

"Oh, Mama, *don't. Please."* Francie slid from the horse and through the fence and flung her arms around her mother. "It's so lovely here, just the two of us together. *Please, please,* Mama, let's not spoil it with silly governesses."

Dolores stroked her blond hair thoughtfully. "Well, I suppose there will be plenty of time for lessons later," she said quietly. "And I confess I like having you all to myself, Francie."

They beamed at each other and Francie slid back through the fence. Dragging over a wooden crate, she stepped up on it to unfasten the bridle. Then she slid the bit from the mare's mouth and slapped her on the rump the way she saw Zocco do, laughing as Blaize whinnied and kicked up her heels, galloping madly across the paddock to join the other horses under a shady stand of oaks.

They were a quiet little group at the ranch, just the three women: Dolores, her nurse, the cook-housekeeper, the child, and the dog. The months passed and still Harmon did not bring her son to visit her. Dolores's energy waned, she no longer rode in her wheelchair and instead lay on a rattan chaise longue on the porch, watching Francie in the distant paddock putting Blaize through her paces, sadly counting the final sun-filled days of her last summer.

As fall approached the days grew misty and there was a sharp tang of winter in the cold wind. The nurse wrapped warmer blankets around her and kept her on the porch in the hope that the crisp weather would do her good. And all the time Dolores was waiting, her eyes fixed anxiously on the curve of the sandy drive where one day Harmon would bring her son to visit her, just as he had promised.

Fall moved quickly into winter. The rains came, turning the sun-bleached clapboard ranch to a damp gray. The leafless poplars no longer rustled in the icy wind and Dolores took to her bed. Dr. Benson still came once a week, bringing with him hampers of special foods and bottles of port wine with messages from her husband saying he was too busy to come to see her personally, but that he hoped she would enjoy the California hothouse fruits, the plump chickens, and the port wine that would enrich her blood and make her stronger.

The doctor knew better; his patient was dying not only of tuberculosis but of a broken heart. "Did you see my son Harry?" she would ask each time he came, her eyes sparkling with fever and her cheeks burning red. "Tell me, is he well? He must be growing taller, stronger. He's almost four now, you know. Maybe Harmon will find time to bring him to see me on his birthday."

Dr. Benson answered all her questions about the boy except the one she really wanted to know . . . when was Harmon bringing the child to see her?

Just before Christmas she said to him, "There's not much time left, doctor. Please, *please* tell my husband I *beg* him to let me see my boy. Just once. That's all I ask."

Replacing his stethoscope, the doctor quickly snapped his black leather bag shut. "I'll tell him, my dear," he promised, trying not to show his contempt for Harmon Harrison. The man was a monster, leaving his wife to die alone in the middle of nowhere, in a place that was little more than a wooden shack, while he lived like a lord in his mansion, giving dinners and attending the theater and parties as though nothing were wrong. If it were not for the Hippocratic oath of confidence that forbade a doctor to discuss his patients, he would have made sure that San Francisco knew of his conduct, and sure, too, that poor Dolores Harrison saw her little boy for the last time.

Raging at his own helplessness he said good-bye to Dolores and almost fell over Francie and Princess, who were waiting outside her door.

"Is Mama better?" Francie asked, clutching anxiously at his hand. "She looks so pretty now, her eyes are sparkly and her cheeks are pinker than mine. That means she's better, doesn't it?"

Dr. Benson sighed. He looked at her thoughtfully. It had been ten months since they had come to live at the ranch and Francie had grown. Her simple cambric smock was clean, but it was way too small. She wore no stockings despite the cold and her clumsy boots must have been purchased at the local store and were more nails than leather. But Francie had bloomed at the ranch while her mother lay dying. She had a sort of golden glow of health about her and she brimmed with vitality. And she was surely pretty, with her heart-shaped face and eager expression, her shiny pale-blond hair and those deep sapphire eyes, so like her poor mother's.

Patting her head, he said gently, "Your mother's just fine, little one. Now, you just have a happy Christmas together and I'll come to see you again next week."

She fixed him with those round blue eyes. "Papa is never going to come, is he? He'll never bring my brother Harry."

Out of the mouths of babes and sucklings always came the truth, the doctor thought. "Mr. Harrison's a very busy man," he lied, "and it's a long journey for the little boy."

"Harry's almost four now. I came here when I was only three."

He had no answer. "Happy Christmas, Francie," he said, feeling like Scrooge as he left. "There's a present on the table for you. Mrs. Benson and I surely hope you enjoy it. Oh, and there's one for Princess too. She's getting to be a big dog now."

Francie held Princess's collar so she wouldn't run after Dr. Benson. The dog was big and strong and stood as tall as she did, but it sat quietly at her side as she watched the carriage bouncing over the potholes down the rain-soaked drive, water spraying from under its wheels.

The weather turned icy that night, but the pot-bellied iron stove, fueled with apple logs, glowed with heat and the old wooden house was cosy. A fire burned brightly in Dolores's room and Francie stretched out on the hearth rug with Princess beside her. Propped on one elbow, her chin in her hand, she stared deep into the flames, listening to her mother's labored breathing. Dolores slept fitfully, waking every now and then to cough. Then the nurse would put down her knitting and hurry from her chair in the corner to gently wipe away the blood that trickled from the corner of her mouth, as darkly red as the port wine Harmon had sent.

Francie said quietly, "Mama's not better, is she? I can hear the noise in her chest, that rattling sound—"

"She's all right dear," the nurse said, looking up from her patient. But a worried frown appeared between her eyes and her jaw tightened. "Perhaps you and Princess should go to bed now, Francie," she said, smoothing Dolores's pillows. "Tomorrow's Christmas and we'll have a fine old time. Cook's fixing a goose and there's presents to be opened. Best you and your Mama get some rest now."

Francie bent to kiss her mother as she left, and then she said, "I'll pray to the baby Jesus tonight to help Mama get better."

"You do that, Francie," the nurse replied.

She woke early next morning. Her room was cold as ice, and pushing Princess from her feet, she flung back her blankets and rushed to the window. A light fall of snow covered the entire valley and the distant mountain tops sparkled in the pale sunshine. Snow dappled the branches of the trees and icicles hung from the gutter over the rainbutt.

"Oh, Princess," she cried, flinging her arms around the dog, "look what we got for Christmas." And with a great whoop of delight, she flung her coat over her nightie, pulled on her boots, grabbed the egg-basket and ran laughing down the corridor and out onto the porch.

The sun was already melting the snow into little pools that would turn to ice later that night. Francie ran around in excited little circles, making footprints while Princess jumped around her, barking madly. Then she half-ran, half-slid to the henhut, rooting out the chilly disgruntled birds and seizing their eggs, laid for once in their nests. Next she skidded down to the frozen pond, laughing at the attempts of the bewildered geese to paddle on the ice, and from there to the stables to feed Blaize some oats and to wish her a Merry Christmas.

Carrying her egg basket carefully, she hurried back to the house and tiptoed to her mother's room. The curtains were still drawn and though the embers in the grate still glowed faintly orange, it felt cold. The nurse was asleep in her corner chair, her chin sunk on her chest and her knitting still clasped in her hands. Francie tiptoed past her to the bed.

"Mama," she whispered, "look what the hens have sent you for Christmas. A beautiful, perfect brown egg." She held it up for her mother to see, but there was no reply. *Of course,* she thought, *it's too dark, she can't see it.* She went quickly to the window and drew back the curtain. "Here, Mama, look, it's specially for you—" And then she saw the great red stain that covered the sheets. It covered her mother's white lace nightdress, it stained her face and matted her beautiful black hair. And though Francie did not know what death was, she knew this must be it.

*"Oh, Mama,"* she cried despairingly, taking Dolores's icy hand in hers and pressing it to her face, her tears mingling with her mother's blood. "Oh, Mama. This isn't what I prayed to the baby Jesus for for Christmas."

# CHAPTER 5

◆

## *1895*

The same snowy Christmas Day that Francie found her mother dead, six thousand miles away in Yorkshire, England, Annie Aysgarth, aged sixteen, placed the bouquet of tightly curled bronze crysanthemums beneath the granite angel on her mother's grave. Her three young brothers stood beside her, buttoned into warm overcoats and wrapped in woolen mufflers, their noses red with cold and their eyes watering in the bitter wind.

Martha Aysgarth had been dead for nearly four years now, but Frank Aysgarth still brought his family to pay their respects every Christmas Day, snow or shine. And it was mostly snow, Annie thought, shivering mournfully, wishing her father would make his annual pilgrimage in the summer; she just knew her mother would not have wanted them standing about in the cold and likely catching their deaths too.

The boys stamped their numb feet, the nails in their heavy boots ringing on the icy path, while their father stood, his black bowler clasped in both hands, thinking of Martha. Annie thought worriedly of the goose cooking slowly in the oven at home, afraid that the fire she had banked with coal before they left might have gone out. It wasn't that she was disrespectful to her mother—she came every week to care for her grave—but if dinner were late then her father would be angry and Frank Aysgarth's displeasure would put a blight on the whole of Christmas Day.

Just when she thought she could bear the cold no longer her father stepped back, placed his bowler hat firmly on his head and said, "Right, we'll be off home, then. Dinner's at one o'clock." He strode briskly through the cemetery gate, his youngest son, Josh, walking beside him with Annie behind and Bertie and Ted bringing up the rear. Annie almost tripped over her feet in her eagerness to get back home to the two up, two down row house in Leeds with the attic room that was hers and the cold cellar where on rainy days the family wash hung to dry amid the jars of homemade preserves and sacks of flour and potatoes. But she dared not run until they had reached the Horse and Groom on the corner of Montgomery Lane and her father said, "I'll just stop in for a pint with the lads. I'll be home at five minutes to one, Annie."

She nodded, wondering as she always did what her mother had found to love in him. Frank Aysgarth was a burly, gray-haired man with a bristling gray moustache, wind-reddened cheeks, and a dour disposition. He was a man of habit who had risen at the same hour, eaten at the same hour and gone to bed at the same hour every day for as long as Annie could remember. He liked his house clean, his children quiet, and his meals properly prepared and served on time. He brooked no argument and his word was law.

Sometimes when she was alone in the house on Montgomery Terrace, Annie would look at the brass-framed wedding photograph and marvel at how her pretty, laughing, brown-eyed little mother had ever married such an old stick-in-the-mud, because even on his wedding day Frank Aysgarth looked unjoyful, full of the importance of the occasion and his new responsibilities.

Her mother had told her the story of how, when he met her, Frank already had several jobs. He had left school at the age of twelve to work at the rope factory in Burmantofts, then at the brewery in Wakefield and at a printing works in Eastgate, but none of these had suited him. Beneath his solid facade lay the heart of an entrepreneur and one thing he noticed wherever he worked was that factories always needed cardboard boxes to ship their goods in. With a few pounds in his pocket he rented his own "factory," a small draughty room in the arches beneath the Leeds railway bridge. Then he arranged to buy a quantity of cardboard and set himself up as "Aysgarth's Cardboard Box Manufacturers."

When he met Martha he was making a living—just, but there was very little money left over for courting. Still, he couldn't resist her laughing brown eyes and found himself calling at her house several nights a week.

Annie's mother always said that Frank never actually went down on bended knee and *asked* her to marry him, but one evening he came to her house carrying a mahogany mantel-clock she had admired in a shop window in the Calls. It had cost him ten shillings, more money than he had earned that week. He said, "Here, lass, it's for you. I saw how you admired it and it'll look good on our mantel shelf." Martha said she just assumed from that that they were to wed and went ahead with her plans, accumulating a small pile of cotton sheets and towels in her bottom drawer, sewing a simple trousseau and her wedding dress of soft white voile trimmed with satin ribbons and hand-crocheted lace.

Everyone said how pretty Martha was and how lucky Frank Aysgarth was when she finally walked down the aisle on his arm, clutching a sheaf of tall lillies and smiling her dazzling smile. They spent their two-day honeymoon at a draughty boardinghouse on Scarborough's south side, which cost Frank his last fifteen shillings, returning, subdued, to their rented room on Marsh Lane. And the very next day Martha started work at her husband's side.

They worked hard, cutting and sticking the cardboard boxes to order. Then Frank would stack them up on his homemade delivery truck—a wooden crate on a set of wheels, dragging his heavy load through Leeds, sometimes for miles, to its destination.

When Martha fell pregnant she worked right up until the final week because they needed the money so badly, and a week after Annie was born she was back at the factory with the new baby wrapped in a blanket sleeping in a cardboard box at her side.

Business grew worse and money became even tighter and the poor cold rented room seemed even smaller. Sometimes there would be no wages on a Friday night and just bread on their dinner table. Frank spoke less and less and the baby seemed to cry more and more. Finally Frank said it was no good, they just couldn't make ends meet. He had to do something about it. He borrowed a few pounds and sent Martha and the child back to her family while he went off to seek his fortune in America.

Martha didn't realize she was pregnant again until he had been gone a month and again she worked until the final week, but this time there was no Frank around for his son's birth.

In five years Martha never heard a word from him. He never sent home a penny and everybody laughed at her, stuck with two kids and no husband. She found herself a job cleaning at a big house up at Lawnswood and many a time she had to walk there because the children needed new boots or winter jackets and she didn't have the tramfare. There was no room for her and two kids at her folks' house and now they were crammed into one cheap rented room on a mean little back street.

Then one spring day she was sitting on the doorstep shelling peas into a bowl and getting a breath of fresh air when she saw a man walking down the street toward her. He was smartly dressed in a brown suit and polished brown boots with a bowler hat on his gray head and he had a full beard and moustache. At first she didn't recognize him. Then, as he came closer she stood up, staring at him. She said, "It's Frank, isn't it?"

"Aye, lass, it is." He looked down at the children clinging to her apron and he said, "And these are my bairns."

Martha told Annie she held up the boy to him, but Frank never so much as touched him because he wasn't one to show his feelings, though she could tell he was pleased.

Over a meager tea of bread and cheese Frank told how he had started out in New York working as a laborer erecting steel girders for a lofty new skyscraper. The work was hard and dangerous, but the pay had been too good to turn down and for months he had clambered over scaffolding high above the streets of Manhattan, until the harsh freezing winter and a bout of pneumonia had put a stop to it. When he recovered his health he determined to find himself a better climate and with a few dollars in his pocket headed west "To seek my fortune, same as all the others," he'd said, with a rare smile at Martha.

Annie had stood by her mother's chair, her round brown eyes as big as saucers, excitedly twisting her clean pinafore in her chapped red hands, while Bertie leaned against his father's knee, listening raptly as he told them stories of San Francisco. "A city of hills above the most beautiful bay in the world," he said. He told them of the blue-gray winter skies and unexpected white fogs that rolled over them without warning; and about how rich the people were, "From mining gold and silver," he said as they "oohd" and "aahd" in wonder, thinking of the piles of precious golden coins the rich must have.

"There was allus plenty of building going on," Frank said. "I started at the bottom again, but I soon worked my way up. I learned how to build houses for the rich and houses for the working folks. Now I know what they want and I know how to give it to them at the right price."

Looking Martha in the eye, he took a thick wad of notes from his inside pocket and laid it on the table in front of her. "That's all my wages for the past five years," he said. "Less living expenses, of course, and the boat fare back home again. There's enough there to buy our bairns what they need and something pretty for yerself. I reckon you've earned it," he added with a glance at her worn dress.

Martha's eyes filled with tears and Annie slid her arms comfortingly around her neck. "It's just that I'm so happy," Martha sniffed, mopping her eyes on a corner of her flowered apron.

"No need to take on so," Frank muttered, clearing his throat, embarassed as he always was by any show of emotion. "We'll be out of this place and into something better tomorrer. But that's only temporary—I've enough money now to start up in the building business for meself, and I promise the first house will be for you, Martha."

He was as good as his word. They moved to a small rented workman's cottage and then a year later, the next baby, Ted, was born. Just a couple of months after that, true to his promise, Frank moved them all into number one, Montgomery Street, the first in a row of houses he built and only the first of many he was to erect over the years.

Martha and Frank Aysgarth were a happy enough couple, folks said knowingly; they kept to themselves and didn't try to live above their station now that Frank was making money, though there was a good deal of speculation as to exactly how much he was making with half of Harehills disappearing under Frank's terraces of small, identical redbrick, slate-roofed houses. He had been right; he knew the business, he knew what people wanted, and he knew how to sell it to them at the right price. He was getting rich.

A third son, Josh, was born, but this time Martha did not regain her health and vitality so quickly. She was weak and tired, and Josh was raised on the best Ostermilk money could buy rather than at his mother's breast. Everyone said he was the most beautiful baby in the world, and plump, brown-eyed, twelve-year-old Annie doted on him. It was she who gave him his bottles, changed his nappies, and washed and ironed his little dresses and bonnets. It was she who pushed his pram down the street, stopping to let the neighbors admire his blond, gray-eyed beauty. And it was she who shopped and cooked and kept the house clean, because Martha no longer was able to do so.

Annie would often pop next door to talk with Mrs. Morris about babies, because Sally Morris had a son just a few weeks older than Josh. They would place the two infants side by side in front of the fire on the clean rag rug made by Mrs. Morris from their old clothes and blankets, watching them crawl around together. "Just look at little Sammy," Mrs. Morris would say, beaming admiringly at her sturdy, dark-haired boy. "Why, he just dotes on Josh." Then she laughed. "Listen to me talk," she exclaimed, "like you're his mother, Annie, not his sister."

Three months later, when Martha Aysgarth faded from life, Annie became "mother" to her whole family. Her father told her she was finished with school for good and she would take her mother's place. "Your mam taught you well enough," he said gruffly, "and I'll not have any other woman coming into my house and telling me what to do."

Mrs. Morris felt sorry for Annie, having so much responsibility and still only a child. She often minded Josh while Annie struggled to keep up with the housework and the washing, the marketing and cooking and baking, because Frank Aysgarth expected it all to be just the same as it was when his wife was alive. And Frank became more silent and taciturn; he never ever embraced his children or showed them any affection, but he never took a strap to them either.

The years moved slowly by with scarcely time for Annie to take a breath, let alone think of herself. Josh and Sammy Morris were such close friends now, they practically lived in each other's pockets. They started Back Road Council School on the same day and moved slowly upward through the classes together, and they were constantly in mischief and constantly in and out of each other's houses, cadging a slice of fresh-baked bread slathered with delicious beef drippings from Annie, and sitting on the steps watching the world go by on Montgomery Street while they ate it. They stole burning-hot jam tarts from the wire tray where Mrs. Morris had left them to cool, or a hunk of feather-light Yorkshire pudding, fresh from the roasting tin. And they were always together for Annie's huge, tasty Sunday dinners of roast pork with crackling and roast potatoes, crisp and golden on the outside and soft as pillows on the inside, and her hot treacle pudding with creamy custard that was enough to melt the coldest heart. She was the best cook on Montgomery Street bar none, though Frank Aysgarth grumbled about her all the time.

"Treats her just the way he did his wife—like a slave," Sammy's mother said with a disparaging sniff. She didn't like Frank and he didn't like her; she thought he was a selfish old tyrant and he thought she was a lazy slattern who kept a rough-and-ready house and was too often at the Red Lion drinking port and lemon and keeping her husband poor, when she should have been home looking after her bairns.

"Frank Aysgarth's allus been a man's man," her husband commented. "He's got no time for women."

"Aye, not even his own daughter," she retorted bitterly. She'd heard him often enough through the adjoining wall, berating the poor girl, and God knows Annie did her best. She was always working. She would be outside first thing in the morning, scrubbing the front steps, rubbing on the bright yellow scouring stone and rinsing down the flagstones with buckets of water so that when Frank stepped out his front door it was as clean outside under his good leather boots as it was inside. She blacked the cast-iron range until it shone and you could fairly see your own face in the fireback. There was always something appetizing in the oven when the boys came home from school at dinnertime, and when she sent them back again in the afternoon, they were clean and with full bellies. Annie's wash would be strung across the street and blowing in the wind before anyone else had even got started, and at six o'clock every evening when Frank Aysgarth came home the table was set with a clean, starched white cloth with his dinner ready and steaming on the plate. As soon as he sat down Annie would take a jug and hurry to the Red Lion on the corner and fetch him a foaming pint of best Yorkshire bitter and then she'd sit quietly in the corner while he ate silently.

When he was finished, Frank would walk from the table without so much as a "thank-you" and sit himself down in the big burgundy plush armchair in front of the fire. He would pick up his copy of the *Yorkshire Evening Post* she'd bought for him and say, "Where's our lads, then?"

"Out," she'd reply, briskly clearing the table, "playing in't street." Or if it was raining, "Next door with t'other little lads."

And then she'd go quietly to the scullery and wash the dishes before calling the boys in and getting them ready for bed.

"Bloody hard labor, that's what Annie Aysgarth's doing," Mrs. Morris grumbled to her husband. "*And* she's only sixteen. She's a better mother to those lads than anybody on this street—and a better wife to her father too."

"In all ways except one," her husband replied darkly, sucking on his pipe and filling the poorly furnished room with sickly-sweet tobacco fumes.

Mrs. Morris glared at him, indicating the listening boys. "Little pitchers have big ears," she reminded him sharply. "But still, if you ask me she's nothing but a slave for the man. He'd have to pay two servants ten pounds a month to do what she does—and then he'd not get it done as well!"

Annie knew her father was a hard taskmaster, but she put up with it because she had never known anything else, and because she loved her brothers. It was true, as Bertie and Ted grew up they grew away from her, becoming like their father, shutting her out from their masculine lives and expecting their dinners on the plate as soon as they walked in the door, their Friday night bathwater hot and ready in the tub that was kept under the wooden slab in the scullery, and their shirts perfectly starched and neatly ironed with all the buttons sewed on for Sunday church. But young Josh was like her own son.

# CHAPTER 6

◆

## *1895*

For her mother's funeral Francie wore an expensive new black silk dress with a white lace collar purchased from the smart Paris House store on Market Street. She had new black boots made of the finest kid leather, a black velvet cape lined with ermine and her long blond hair was brushed to shining perfection and tucked into a black silk bonnet. She rode with her father and her brother Harry in a black satin-lined carriage behind six black-plumed horses at the head of a procession of sixty carriages of mourners and civic dignitaries, and she stood pale and trembling by the graveside as Dolores's coffin was lowered into it.

Her little brother, Harry, in black velvet knickerbockers and jacket, his cap held respectfully to his chest, sobbed loudly, and her father, handsome and sartorially correct in striped trousers and black jacket, dabbed at his eyes with an immaculate white linen handkerchief. But Francie never shed a tear. She stared straight in front of her, gritting her teeth together and willing herself not to scream. She wanted to cry out how unfair it was that her mother should die, that she was so young, so beautiful, so sweet and gentle and so kind-hearted. She wanted to tell the three hundred mourners who had also been guests at Dolores's wedding that she loved her mother, that she missed her dreadfully, and that she would just die, too, without her. But she knew they would not have understood, so she just locked the emotions deep inside her, refusing to let a single tear drip down her cheek onto her new black silk dress.

It was a raw January day and a cold mist lingered around the gravestones. Moisture dripped from the naked trees, turning the grass into a sea of brown mud. The elaborate floral tributes bound with purple ribbons, and piled around the open grave, looked garish in the gray light. The largest was from Dolores's family. They had sent their respects but claimed the journey was too far from Jalisco and were sorry they could not be present. They sent their condolences to Harmon and a magnificent four-foot wreath of scarlet roses.

As soon as the last prayer was said over the grave the mourners hurriedly sought the warmth of their waiting carriages. The two gravediggers leaned on their shovels like gray ghosts in the mist, stamping their feet to get the blood moving, coughing harshly as they prepared to fill in the earth, and Francie turned away quickly, unable to bear any more.

Back at the house she sat alone on a spindly, gilt loveseat in the mirrored ballroom watching the guests devour the lavish buffet. The women smiled and chatted in low tones about a dance that was being held next week, about who had been invited and what they would wear. The men clustered together in groups, drinks in hand, talking business. And her brother, Harry, stood quietly at his father's side as the guests filed past to shake his hand and offer their condolences.

"How odd that girl is," she heard the women murmuring to each other, "just sitting there alone when she should be at her father's side like the brother—only four years old and he knows how to behave like a little man . . . and she never shed a tear at the graveside either. . . . Why doesn't the child show some grief for her mother? It's not normal. . . . Harmon had better keep an eye on her, I'd say she might be troublesome. . . ."

Francie's cheeks burned scarlet and she stared hard at the blue swirls on the rug covering the polished parquet floor, praying she wouldn't cry. What did any of them know about her mother? Oh, they had probably smiled and chatted with her when they were guests in her house, and they had sent gifts of flowers and fruit when it was first known she was ill. But none of them had ever come to see her and she'd bet they didn't even know she had been away at the ranch this past year. Her heart clenched tight as a fist with grief. She wanted to shout at them that they didn't even care about her mother, that they wouldn't even miss her, that no one loved her the way she did. . . .

She caught her father's eye across the room and he gestured angrily for her to come and stand beside him. Sliding reluctantly from the velvet seat she threaded her way through the crowd to where he was standing.

"Why weren't you here?" he demanded, keeping his voice low, but she heard his fiery tone and shrank back from him. "People are talking," he muttered. "Stand next to your brother and remember your manners."

Standing stiff as a ramrod next to Harry, Francie thought the day would never end. The long line of guests filed past and she remembered to curtsy and speak when she was spoken to. She was aware of the women's eyes as they watched her father. "A fine figure of a man," she heard them whisper speculatively, thinking of their unmarried daughters and the Harrison millions. Then at last the nursemaid came to fetch Harry for his tea and she was reprieved.

She was back in her old room and somehow it looked dingier and more unwelcoming than ever. The white paint had chipped from the iron bedstead and the narrow straw-filled mattress was lumpy. The flimsy flowered curtains failed to stop the chill coming off the icy barred windowpanes, and though the house had the very best steam heating, somehow by the time it reached the servants' rooms it was diluted to a mere whisper of warmth. She huddled on the narrow bed, shivering and clutching a blanket around her as the tears finally flowed freely. She cried for her lost mother, and she cried for Princess, who had been banished to the stables, and she cried for her own loneliness, until she finally fell asleep exhausted, still wearing her smart black silk mourning dress and her soft little kid boots.

The day after the funeral Harmon telegraphed his final bid on a steam yacht he was negotiating to purchase in London. His offer was accepted and the following week he and his son traveled to New York in his sumptuous private railcar on the Southern Pacific Line, of which he was also a director. From there they sailed on the French steamship, the S.S. *Aquitaine* for Cherbourg, and from there by rail to Deauville, where he was to take delivery of his new yacht. They planned to be away for several months, so dust sheets were thrown over the furniture at the mansion, just as though no member of the family was still in residence. The only person who shared Francie's quarters was a German governess who had been hired to instruct her in deportment and some book-learning.

Francie's heart sank when she saw her. Fräulein Hassler was a strong-willed middle-aged spinster with coarse gray hair parted down the middle, then braided and curled into snails over her ears. She was tall and shapeless, her skin was sallow and her expression stern. She had large, protruding yellow teeth and she wore small steel-rimmed glasses that reflected the light, so Francie could not see her eyes. But the fräulein knew a rich household when she saw one and she knew how to take command of a situation.

"I am not a servant, Herr Harrison," she had told him firmly at the interview. "*Natürlich* I do not expect to be on the same floor with the family, but my rooms should be on the third floor *front.*"

"*Natürlich,*" Harmon agreed, glad to unload the problem of his daughter. So the fräulein had a large bedroom and sitting room of her own on the third floor front with a schoolroom down the hall, and Francie still had her cold little room at the back. And she ate her meals alone at the scrubbed pine kitchen table, while the fräulein had hers sent up on a tray to her room.

The first morning Fräulein Hassler sent a maid to fetch Francie on the dot of eight o'clock.

"You will report to me every day at this time," she told her, looking her up and down critically.

There was a long silence while Francie shifted nervously from foot to foot, desperately wishing she could see the fräulein's eyes behind the glasses.

"You are untidy," the fräulein said sternly at last. "Your boots are dirty, there is a stain on your pinafore, and your hair is a mess. You will go back to your room and clean yourself up. I will not tolerate slovenliness."

Scared, Francie rushed to do as she was told, then hurried back to the schoolroom.

Fräulein Hassler eyed her again carefully and then said, "You will come to the schoolroom each morning at eight precisely. You will be clean and tidy. You will knock at the door and wait until I bid you to enter. You will say, 'Good morning, Fräulein Hassler,' except on Wednesdays, when we shall speak only in German and then you will say, '*Guten Morgen, Fräulein Hassler,*' and on Saturdays when we shall speak only in French and you will say, '*Bonjour, Mademoiselle Hassler.*'

"From eight until nine you will learn arithmetic, from nine until ten, English. Then I will take a half-hour rest while you learn a piece of poetry which you will repeat for me after the break. From eleven to twelve you will learn history and geography.

"Then I will take my lunch and rest and at two we shall go for an hour's walk. You will learn to sew in the afternoons and at four o'clock, when I take my tea, you will finish the tasks I have set you. After that you may go to the kitchen for your supper and then to bed. Do you understand, Francesca?"

Francie nodded, her head swimming, thinking anxiously of Princess waiting for her in the stables. She didn't like Fräulein Hassler and she did not like her plans.

"What happens on Sundays?" she asked suddenly.

"You mean, 'Please, what happens on Sundays, *Fräulein Hassler?*'" the woman corrected her sharply. "We must do something about your manners, child. But since you ask, I shall reply. Sunday is my day off. No doubt the servants will take care of you and I suppose you will go to church in the morning and again in the evening. Your father left no instructions about that."

Francie nodded. "I suppose so," she said, a dismal vision of her future life passing quickly through her mind. But even Fräulein Hassler was better than having Papa around, so she guessed she'd just make the best of it. And hopefully, one day, Papa would send her back to the ranch again.

There was another compensation now that Papa was away; the fräulein never stirred from her rooms after supper and Francie was able to sneak Princess up to her room. She would save the dog something from her supper and at seven o'clock, when she knew the servants would be in their own quarters, she would take Princess for a walk down the hill. The winter evenings were cold and dark, but wrapped in her velvet-and-ermine cloak she didn't feel the cold, and with the huge dog beside her she had no fear of the dark. At first she only went a little way, but as her days with Fräulein Hassler became more and more tedious the evening walks became longer and more adventurous.

She and Princess wandered around the city streets, peering curiously into the lighted windows of houses, sniffing the beery smells coming from noisy saloons and watching the people, listening enviously to their laughter. She was eavesdropping on a world different from her own, where people sang and danced and laughed together and were happy.

Much later she and Princess would sneak back through the side door which she always left unlocked, knowing no one would check because they did not expect it to be open. She would hurry up the back stairs, making Princess walk on the carpet so that her claws made no noise on the wooden surround. She would lock her door carefully, pour the glass of milk she'd taken earlier from the kitchen into Princess's bowl and watch her eagerly lap it up. Then she would climb into bed and huddle under the chilly sheets with Princess curled up on her feet, and soon she would fall asleep to dream of life and freedom on the ranch, and of Blaize, her little chestnut mare, of fried chicken and roaring log fires and her mother, rosy-cheeked and smiling, sitting quietly beside her in the firelight's glow.

She began to stay out later and later, lingering outside the saloon at the bottom of Jones Street, loathe to leave the bright lights and the happy music and laughter for her own cold, dark little room. The people going in and out stared at her, laughing at the sight of the small girl in the black velvet cloak with the dog that was bigger than she was, but their glances became more curious as they noticed her there night after night.

"What is it, darlin'?" a red-haired man called out to her one night. "Lost your father to the demon drink, have ya?"

Francie blushed and shook her head. Grabbing Princess's lead even tighter she hurried away up the hill.

"You ought to do sum'n about that girl outside," the man told the saloonkeeper. "It's not good for business having kids waitin' on their drunken fathers. Throw the bastard into the street and tell him to take his kid home where she belongs."

"She's no child of any of my customers," the saloonkeeper replied indignantly. "Next time you see her, tell me and I'll call the police."

But Francie was scared and she avoided the saloon, roaming farther and farther through the dark city, inventing lonely make-believe scenarios for the families she saw behind the lighted windows and in the cafés.

It was a few weeks before she passed the saloon again. It was a clear, cold night and she shivered as she stopped to sniff the hot, spicy smells of cooked ham and corned-beef hash and the earthy aroma of rich dark ale mingled with the stinging smell of whiskey.

The red-haired man eyed her guardedly as he hurried into the bar. "Better send the lad around for the police," he told the saloonkeeper. "That little girl's out there again and the streets are no place for a young kid like that, she can't be more than seven or eight. She must've run away from home or sum'n."

"I'll get her this time," the saloonkeeper replied, calling over the boy.

Francie watched the uniformed police officer approaching the saloon curiously. She felt so invisible in her nighttime world that she almost jumped out of her skin when he called out to her.

"Hey, little girl? Lost your way, have ya?"

"No! Oh no!" She tugged urgently on Princess's lead as the police officer came closer, but Princess stood firm, her fur bristling, her teeth bared, growling softly. The policeman took a wary step backward. "I'd like to talk to you, young lady. It looks to me like you need a spot of help . . . you and your nice dog."

Francie tugged hard on the lead as Princess growled menacingly again. "Oh no, thank you, sir. I don't need any help. We're just on our way home, that's all." With a final desperate tug on the lead she dragged the big dog around and hurried back up the hill.

The policeman followed at a distance, watching to see where she would go. He was out of breath when he reached the top of Jones Street and surprised when she turned into the courtyard of one of Nob Hill's grandest mansions and let herself in by a side door. He wondered if she was one of the Harrison's servants' kids, and then he thought of the velvet cloak with the expensive ermine collar. Of course, he should have realized; she was the daughter of the house. He turned away thoughtfully; this was a matter for his superiors to deal with.

Captain O'Connor knocked on the door of the Harrison mansion at eight o'clock the next morning and was told by Maitland, the butler, that Mr. Harrison was away on an extended trip to Europe.

"Then I'd best have a private word with you, Mr. Maitland," he replied.

Half an hour later, fortified by a dram of Harrison's best malt whiskey, he emerged into the cold morning sunshine. "I'll leave it in your hands, sir," he said, smiling at Maitland.

Maitland returned to his rooms, drafted a lengthy cable to his employer on his yacht in the middle of the Atlantic Ocean and walked to the telegraph office to send it personally.

His reply came the very next morning and within a matter of hours Fräulein Hassler was packed and on her way out of the house, Princess was shut away in the stables, and Francie was locked in her room.

And there she stayed for more than two weeks, awaiting her father's return. She could hear Princess's pathetic howls from the stables and she pressed her nose against the windowpane, hoping for a glimpse of her. Her meals were brought up on a tray by a Mexican maid who spoke no English; she had no books, no writing paper and pencils, not even the detested needlework. She was alone with her thoughts and the time dragged by interminably. At first she paced the floor of the small room like a caged animal, sobbing with despair, flailing her thin arms and stamping her feet in anger, but as time passed she just huddled on the bed, shivering with foreboding as she contemplated her father's return.

The trays of food were returned to the kitchen untouched and in the end Maitland himself came to see her. He looked at her pityingly; she was only eight years old and so very thin; she was barefoot, her uncombed blond hair hung in dank strands about her shoulders and her blue eyes were wide with fear.

None of the servants had had much time for Miss Francie, mostly because they were kept too busy even to think about her, and anyway she was not considered their responsibility—that was a nurse's job or a governess's. But even though she had been naughty, none of them liked the idea of shutting a child up and leaving her for days on end. "It's not human," they had told each other angrily over supper in the servants' dining room. "It's barbaric, cruel." It was Maitland's job to control the staff and stop any gossip about the family, and he had been forced to tell them it was no business of theirs and that the master would deal with his daughter when he got home. But he had said it with dread in his heart. He had worked for Harmon Harrison for ten years and he knew his coldness and his anger only too well.

Francie looked up as he knocked on her door and came in. She knew what he had come to tell her. "Papa's back," she said.

Maitland nodded. "He wishes to see you right away, Miss Francie. Why don't you wash your face and brush your hair quickly, and I'll take you down to the study myself." He watched sadly as she dipped her hands into the pitcher, dabbed cold water on her face, then hurriedly dragged a brush through her tangled locks.

He held the door for her and they walked silently down the servants' stairs and through the green baize door to the main house. At the door of her father's study their eyes met. "Courage, miss," he whispered as he knocked on the door.

"Enter."

The sound of her father's deep booming voice turned her knees to jelly. Maitland opened the door and gave her a little push inside and said, "Miss Francesca, sir."

"Thank you, Maitland." He was sitting behind his big desk and he glanced up at his daughter hovering just inside the door. He said, "Come here, Francesca."

Taking a deep breath, she walked reluctantly toward him.

"Closer," he commanded. "I want you to hear clearly what I have to say to you. And I want you to remember it, because you will not get a second chance." She was at the desk now, her hands clasped tightly behind her back, her terrified eyes fixed on his like a rabbit in front of a ferret.

He looked her up and down contemptuously, taking in her dirt-streaked face and tear-reddened eyes, her grubby pinafore and bare legs. "You are disgusting," he said contemptuously. "You are not fit to bear the Harrison name. It's a good thing your mother is not here to see you and to hear about your escapades. Well, young lady, what have you to say for yourself?"

She shook her head, fighting back the tears. "Mama would never have left me alone," she cried. "She would never have locked me up—"

"Your mother," he said icily, "would have done as I said. And so will you."

He leaned back in his comfortable leather chair, his hands folded across his stomach, watching her. There was a long silence and she shifted nervously from foot to foot, avoiding his eyes.

Finally he said, "I am waiting for you to apologize, Francesca. Or can it be that you are not sorry for all the scandal you caused."

She hung her head. "I'm sorry, Papa," she whispered.

He nodded. Standing up, he took off his jacket and hung it carefully over the back of his chair. He picked up a strong leather dog lead from the desk, pointing to a low stool. "Bend over," he commanded.

"But that's Princess's lead," Francie exclaimed, puzzled.

He nodded. "It is. And if you behave like an errant bitch then you must expect to be treated like one. Bend over the stool and lift your skirts."

"But, Papa . . ." she protested as he grabbed her roughly by the arm.

"Bend over," he roared, and she dropped, terrified, onto the stool, lifting her skirts obediently.

She screamed as the first lash cut her flesh, and she screamed even louder as more blows rained down. Her tender rump burned like fire and the blood flowed free, staining her underclothes.

Outside in the hall, five-year-old Harry Harrison stuffed his fingers in his ears, screwing up his face as he imagined what was taking place behind the study door. But he knew his sister deserved her punishment, his father had told him so. He had told him that she was worthless and wicked, that she had brought disgrace to their name and she must suffer for that because nothing mattered more than their name and their breeding.

After a few minutes he took his fingers out of his ears. The screaming had stopped and he could hear Francie sobbing and his father telling her to stand up. He heard the sound of a drawer opening and shutting and then Francie screamed again, but it was different this time. It was a scream of mortal terror.

Then the study door was flung open and his father stood there, a pistol in his hand. "And now I will take care of the other bitch," he said, striding across the hall.

Francie gasped, she had thought he was going to shoot her, but now she knew what he meant to do. "No, no," she screamed, hurtling through the hall after him, "not Princess, please, Papa, no . . ."

Harry ran after Francie down the long marble corridor. His father already had the door open and was striding across the yard toward the stables. The busy grooms looked up from their work, stepping back and lifting their caps respectfully, making no attempt to stop the screaming child.

Francie heard Princess's joyful bark as the bolt was pulled back, then the dog leapt from the stall toward her. She flung her arms protectively around her; she could feel Princess's warm tongue on her face, licking away her salt tears. "I'll never let you kill Princess, never, never," she screamed at her father. "You can kill *me* first."

He signaled to a groom to remove her, watching as the man prized her clinging arms from the dog. Then he calmly walked over, grabbed Princess by the collar, and placed the pistol against her massive head.

"No, Papa, No. No," Francie screamed. "I'm sorry, I'll do anything you say, I'll never be wicked again, I promise . . . just please, please, please, don't kill her. . . ."

Harry Harrison covered his ears as the noise of the single shot ricocheted from the stone walls of the courtyard. He watched as the big sand-colored dog sank slowly to the ground, a puzzled expression in its amber eyes. There was very little blood, but he felt sick. Still, he knew his father had been right—he had explained it all to him on board ship as they paced the decks together recrossing the Atlantic. He glanced at his sister—a sobbing heap, her arms around the dead dog—and he felt no pity for her. His father had said she deserved it and he believed him.

The Harrison servants gossiped, and it had soon become common knowledge in smart San Francisco drawing rooms that millionaire Harmon Harrison kept his daughter in a maid's room with bars on the windows; that he had shot her dog to punish her; that he beat her when she was naughty, which was often; and that he had hired a strict governess to teach her French and sewing and Bible Studies, and to instill some moral principles in her.

"Every family has its cross to bear," they had whispered to each other over their teacups. "But young Harry Harrison is a different matter, so handsome like his father, such aristocratic bearing and splendid manners. He will go far—and one day he will inherit his father's millions."

Francie Harrison was soon forgotten and for the next ten years she lived in a twilight world on the fourth floor, studying French, embroidering neat flowers on traycloths that were never used and taking decorous walks each afternoon with her jailer.

Each week the governess reported on her conduct to her father, and if the demerits were too many she was summoned to his study and beaten with Princess's old lead.

Harry was sent to his father's prep school back East and she saw him occasionally when he returned for vacations. He acted rude and avoided her whenever possible. He behaved arrogantly with the servants and was as smooth as silk in society. Harry, she decided, was a worm and not worthy of her attention. He was just like his father.

A prisoner in her own home, Francie yearned for her mother and for Princess, dreaming of the days on the old ranch when she had been happy.

# CHAPTER 7

◆

Josh Aysgarth was a dreamy little lad with dark blond hair and solemn, clear gray eyes and a smile that would melt anybody's heart. He and Sammy Morris were as different as chalk and cheese; Sammy was as dark as Josh was fair and as stocky as Josh was slender. Sammy was quick-tempered, brooding, and moody, and Josh was slow to anger and saw no malice in anybody. He lived in a dreamworld of his own. But Mrs. Morris always claimed Josh led Sammy into trouble at school and Annie said it was Sammy who was the bad'n. Still, she treated Sammy like Josh's own brother and gave him whatever section of her heart was left over from Josh.

That's why it was such a blow when Frank Aysgarth decided to move up in the world and built himself a four-square, four-bedroomed redbrick house off on its own atop a leafy hill. He added a wooden front porch and a thick surround of laurel shrubs and called it Ivy Cottage, though there was not a scrap of ivy anywhere near it. He moved all their old furniture as well as a new three-piece suite upholstered in dark green velvet, a heavily carved oak sideboard with a mirrored overmantel, a matching table and six solid oak chairs into his new house along with his family.

When Josh first told him of the move Sammy was devastated. "We've lived next door to each other all our lives and now you're moving a mile away. It might as well be fifty," he raged, red-faced with the effort of keeping back his angry tears. "We'll never get to see each other again."

"Course we will," Josh said, putting a comforting arm around Sammy's shoulders. "We're best friends, ain't we? Nothing'll keep us apart."

And nothing much did, because Josh spent much of the week at

Sammy's place, saving him the long walk to school in bad weather, for there were no trams up top of Aysgarth's Hill, as it came to be known. And weekends Sammy was always at Josh's house.

"Now I know he's soft in the head over him," Mrs. Morris said laughingly to Annie. "Sometimes I think if Josh said jump over the moon, Sammy would do it."

Annie smiled back, but Mrs. Morris could see she was tired. She was twenty now, small and well-rounded with lovely brown eyes and shiny, rich brown hair, but everybody said how she had no life of her own. Sometimes, of a warm Saturday, she might escape for an hour or two, but always on her own because she had no friends, having left school and become a grown-up "mother" so young. She would take the tram to the end of the line and then go for a walk out in the woods, or if she felt more adventurous and had a little more time she might take a train out to Ilkley or Knaresborough and wander around the village and have tea in one of the small bow-windowed teashops. But Annie liked it best when she took Josh and Sammy out for the day to the moors or the dales, letting them run and clamber and shout from the top of the windy crags with no one to hear them and complain.

"I don't know which I like better, Mrs. Morris," she would say when she returned Sammy home, her cheeks pink from the fresh air, her brown hair windtossed and her eyes asparkle. "The dales in springtime when the rivers are rushing and trees bright with young yellow leaves the way they are now. And all the new lambs kicking up their heels in the sunshine and the calves hiding under their mothers' bellies from the rainshowers, and the trout jumping in the beck at Durnsell's Fell. Aye, it's a grand sight, Mrs. Morris. But then I think of the moors in autumn and standing atop the crags with nothing for miles but gorse and heather and windy gray-blue skies thick with scudding white clouds like sailships." She stopped and smiled at Mrs. Morris over her cup of tea. "Well, enough of dreaming," she said briskly. "I've me dad's tea to think of. He'll have been all right of course, with the cold dinner I left him, but you know how fussy he is . . ."

"Aye, I know," Sally Morris retorted crisply. "If you ask me, Annie Aysgarth, you should spend a bit more time thinking of yourself and less of your dad. It's time you found yourself a nice young man. After all, lass, you're a 'catch,' with your rich dad and your talents as a housekeeper. And pretty with it," she added as an after-thought.

Annie smiled, embarrassed, throwing her woolen cape over her shoulders and gathering her things together. "Mebbe I will one day. When Josh is all grown up and ready for off."

"When Josh is grown up and ready for off will be too late," Mrs. Morris said bluntly. "You'll be an old maid, Annie. A spinster. On the shelf."

Annie blushed. "Mebbe that's the way it's meant to be, Mrs. Morris," she said as she hurried to the door. "It's just God's will, that's all."

Sally Morris watched her go. It was a long uphill walk to Ivy Cottage and Frank Aysgarth wouldn't dream of spending money on a pony trap for his daughter. "She's got young legs and she'd best use 'em," he always said. It was true enough, but it was also true that Annie's youth was disappearing fast under the workload he imposed on her. She was lonely and she'd bet Frank was lonely too. She'd always said he regretted the move to Ivy Cottage and if it were not for his damned stupid masculine pride he would have sold up long ago and moved them all back again into Montgomery Street where they belonged. And then Annie might have a chance of meeting someone and having a life of her own. But it was no good, everybody knew Annie would never marry now because that would mean Frank Aysgarth would lose a good housekeeper and he was too selfish to stand for that.

When Annie got home that evening, her father was sitting at the oak table, smoking his pipe, waiting for her.

"Sorry I'm late, Dad," she said, flinging her cape over the brass hook on the back of the kitchen door, hurrying to bank up the fire and put the big tin kettle on the hob to boil. "I'll have your tea ready in a jiffy though. I left a lamb hotpot to cook slow in the oven, seeing as you only had cold meats dinnertime."

"Stop chattering and sit down, Annie," he said suddenly.

She lifted her head, surprised. She stared warily at him, wondering what she had done wrong. True, she was a bit late, but he knew she'd been off to the dales so it couldn't be that, and his shirts were all clean and ironed in the drawer, his socks were darned and the house was immaculate . . . unless something had happened to one of the lads. "Is it our Josh?" she asked, worriedly wiping her hands on her apron and sitting opposite him.

"Nay, it's not the lads. It's Aunt Jessie. Your mother's cousin, you met her once at the funeral. She went to live up Northumberland way and now she's died and left you a small fortune. Though I can't think why she left it to you and not the lads," he added, tamping the tobacco down in his pipe and puffing out pungent jets of smoke.

"A fortune?" she repeated, stunned.

"Aye, lass. A hundred pounds she's left you. In memory of your mother. That's what it said in the will anyway. And that's a sight more than a workingman makes in a year, so you'll not go squandering it on frocks and fur tippets and fancy bits of jewelry. No, it'll go in't bank wi' the rest."

Annie's round brown eyes grew even rounder as she said slowly, "But that's my money. Aunt Jessie has left it to me."

Frank puffed consideringly on his pipe; he wasn't used to his daughter speaking up against him. "Aye, so it is," he agreed, "but lasses don't have bank accounts of their own. So it'll go along with mine, until you have good need of it, that is."

Annie met his eyes angrily. A hundred pounds was more money than she had ever dreamed of seeing and now it was hers and she desperately wanted to see it. "Aunt Jessie left it to me, Dad," she repeated. "I have the right to do what I want with it."

Frank pushed back his chair, placed his pipe carefully in the big glass ashtray and said coldly, "You don't have any rights, Annie Aysgarth, and don't you forget that. You'll do as you're told and that's that."

Annie's head drooped. She stared miserably down at her hands, red from housework, with ragged, bitten nails. "Poor Aunt Jessie," she said, blinking away tears of anger at her own helplessness. "Barely in her grave and we're quarreling over her money already."

She looked up and met her father's eyes. "Please, Dad?" she begged. "I've never asked you for anything before." She watched his set, implacable face with a sinking heart; the money had suddenly become a symbol of the freedom she might decide to buy with it one day. . . . When Josh was a grown man and had fallen in love with some pretty lass and left her to get married. She caught her breath as she saw a flicker of indecision on her dad's face. She sighed again as he coughed and picked up his pipe. He sat down at the table and began slowly repacking it with fresh tobacco.

"Well," he muttered, "it is in memory of your mother. Aunt Jessie

said so . . . though you best keep it somewhere safe, Annie. I'll not
be responsible if it goes missing."

She sprang to her feet, her eyes shining with gratitude. She wanted
to throw her arms around him, but it was impossible, she had never
embraced him in her whole life, and instead she said, "Thank you,
Dad, and I'll thank our aunt Jessie in Church tomorrow for remembering me. And don't worry, I'll keep the hundred pounds under my
mattress, where nobody will ever find it."

She bustled excitedly about, setting the table. The lads would be
home any minute, six prompt, the way their dad liked it on a Saturday, so she knew she had better be quick. But this time she hummed
a little song to herself as she hurried about her tasks, telling herself
that she would save her unexpected fortune for a rainy day.

The disastrous year that changed all their lives was 1906. Annie's
Josh was nineteen and he wasn't just handsome—he was beautiful.
He had dark-lashed gray eyes, a cap of thick dark-blond hair and
perfect features. He was tall, lean, and well-muscled. He looked like a
classical Greek statue, but it was his wide, level gaze and his gentle
smile and the sweetness of his expression that made people call him
"beautiful."

"Josh Aysgarth is wild," they agreed, "but he would help any lame
dog, and he'd never hurt anyone." They called Josh "one of life's
innocents."

Sammy Morris could remember perfectly the day he realized Josh
was beautiful and he was ugly. It was the same day he knew he loved
him.

They had gone walking in the dales with a crowd of other lads.
Josh, tall and athletic, strode easily at the head of the group, his head
held high and a little smile on his face as he stared at the wonders of
nature around him. He did not need the applewood stick he swung in
his hand to help him over the hills and boulders, he sprang up them
like a deer. Sammy, bringing up the rear, watched jealously while the
other boys crowded admiringly around him, laughing at each other's
quips and slapping each other affectionately on the shoulder. He
wasn't used to sharing Josh with anyone. It had always been just the
two of them.

By the time they reached the river he had sunk into a sullen, tired
stupor, straggling well behind the others. When he caught up they
were already stripped off and skinny-dipping in a sheltered pool by

the bank of the fast-flowing river. Josh was standing on top of the rock, naked as the day he was born, smilingly surveying the dark, still pool. An admiring silence fell on the merry group as he stretched his arms over his head, ready to dive, and Sammy caught his breath at the sight of his slim-hipped, tautly muscled young body and his carelessly displayed manhood. Flinging back his head Josh stood there in a moment of perfect stillness. And then in a pale, flashing arc he dived with scarcely a ripple into the chilly dark water. He rose to the surface almost instantly and climbed laughing onto the rocks, shaking his blond head with a shower of crystal droplets and throwing a friendly arm around Murphy, a brawny Irish lad who lived in the next street.

Jealousy struck Sammy's heart like a blow, it burned his stomach and churned in his guts. Josh was *his* friend. He *belonged* to him. But Josh was wayward, he liked the other lads' company as much as he liked Sammy's, and now Murphy was his best friend.

Sammy undressed, wrapping his arms about himself, shivering in the chill northeast wind that always seemed to blow even on the hottest summer day. He glanced down at his body, comparing his stocky, powerful torso and short, bulkily muscled legs with Josh's grace, and his own heavy, bulging masculinity with Josh's, and he felt uglier than the hunchback of Notre Dame.

Josh and Murphy were dunking each other's heads under the water, jumping in and out on top of each other while the other boys splashed around, and after a while Sammy ventured cautiously in, too, but he was always on the outside of the group, always the observer. That was why it was so odd when later he claimed he didn't know what happened next that afternoon.

Sammy told his mother they had all been frolicking in the river and Josh and Murphy were daring each other on to even bigger and better dives, slapping each other on the back and laughing all the time. After a while the others grew tired and climbed out and were drying off on the bank. He said Murphy must have swum out from the pool into the river, mebbe to show off a bit more. Next thing they knew he was missing. It was two days before they found his body, tangled in the slimy green weeds on the opposite bank. His head was bashed in and they said he must have hit a rock when he dived.

When Annie asked Josh what happened he just shrugged without answering, but his gray eyes looked faraway and she could not read them. She told herself he was grieving and patted his shoulder comfortingly. "It's all right, Josh," she said, "there's nothing you could have done to help him, else you would have done it. I know."

Sammy and Josh had both worked for Frank Aysgarth since they had left school at fourteen. They had started at the bottom the way Frank had, climbing the scaffolding with a hod full of bricks, mixing cement and learning how to lay the bricks evenly. They had learned how to measure up, to put in a window frame, tile a roof, and plaster a wall.

Sammy loved the rough work, but Josh hated it, though he never dared complain to his father. But he had told Annie. Next to Sammy, she was the only one he confided in. His brothers were both married now with homes of their own and it was just Annie and Frank and Josh at home.

Annie's brown eyes were worried as she said, "Well, what do you want to do, Josh?"

He shrugged. "Mebbe I'd like to be a gamekeeper," he said lazily, "on a fancy estate. Or a farmer, looking after the cows and bringing in the harvest."

"Eh lad, you're a dreamer," she replied, laughing. "What do you know about gamekeeping and harvests?"

Sammy knew Annie worried about Josh. "Sometimes I don't know where he is," she confided to him, "or what he's doing. He just disappears."

"Don't you worry," Sammy reassured her, "I'll allus look after him."

He remembered how they had sworn when they were seven years old that they would always be best friends, always watch out for each other no matter what happened. And they had pledged their promise in blood, cutting their thumbs and squeezing them messily together, swearing their vow solemnly. He had kept his promise even though Josh had put him to the test a few times, ganging up with the others and leaving him on his own. But he had put Josh to the test, too, many a time, daring him on to things he would never do alone, like balancing on the parapet of the railway bridge or running across in front of the big thundering steam engine with seconds between them and certain death under its churning iron wheels. But what Sammy really could not stand was when Josh got interested in girls.

"Leave the lasses alone," he would say disgustedly as Josh smiled at a passing pair of pretty young ladies. And, "Why do you want to walk out with *her*?" when Josh picked up a rough, eager girl outside the Maypole grocery shop in Kirkgate. He felt that same jealousy burning him again, churning his guts till he thought he would die of the pain, and he told himself again it had always been just him and Josh and that's the way it was always going to be, no matter what.

Annie could not understand why it was that Josh suddenly became so moody. Each evening he would come home from work, wash himself and sit silently down to his tea, just the way his father did. Except that wasn't like Josh at all. And for a whole week he did not go out and Sammy didn't come to see him. She supposed they must have quarreled, but whatever it was he wasn't telling her and she sat with her knitting, noting how he jumped each time there was a knock on the door, or how he just stared silently into the fire, not even bothering to read the *Yorkshire Evening Post* she had placed on the table beside him. Mind you, with the story of that horrible murder, she wasn't surprised. The second one it was; each time a young girl and each time when the moon was full. "Moon murders," the papers were calling them, and no young woman in Leeds felt safe.

The clock on the mantle—the same mahogany clock her dad had bought for her mam before they were married—chimed its sweet Westminster chimes and then struck nine, and with a sigh she put away her knitting and began to tidy up.

"Would you like a cup of tea before I go up?" she asked, stopping by Josh's chair on her way to the scullery, but he just shook his head. She walked to the stairs, hesitated and then came back again. "Something's the matter," she said quietly. "Why don't you tell me? After all, it can't be that bad. I'll bet you're just in love or something." She smiled. "Go on, tell us about her. Maybe I can help."

But he just shook his head again, leaning back in the big green plush chair, his eyes closed. "Nobody can help," he said bleakly. "Just leave me alone, Annie, will yer?"

The night was bitter, frost had formed scratchy patterns on the windowpane and a blast of icy wind sneaked through the dark velvet winter curtains. Annie undressed quickly, hurrying into her pink flannel nightdress and adding a warm bedjacket she had knitted herself. She washed her face and dragged the harsh-bristled brush through her long brown hair for the hundred strokes required to keep it shiny, and then she inspected herself in the mirror. She did not like what she saw.

Sally Morris had told her what everyone was saying about her.

They said she looked less bright and perky than she used to, that there were tired lines on her face and a weariness in her walk that told her old neighbors that Frank Aysgarth pushed her too hard. They said she was twenty-six now and never been courted. They said that when Josh got married that would be the end of Annie Aysgarth because then she would be stuck with old Frank, knitting away her winter evenings and her life until he died and she was finally alone. She would be the spinster, the nuisance maiden aunt forgotten by her brothers with no young 'uns of her own to bless her declining years. *She would be a lonely old maid.*

She sank down onto the bed, her head in her hands, tears trickling between her fingers. She was only twenty-six and life was over and she had never even had a chance.

After a while she slid to the floor, put her hands together and closed her eyes. She prayed for her dead mother and she prayed for her brothers, Bertie and Ted, and for Josh, whose sadness had only served to bring out her own misery. And then she prayed for herself. "Oh God," she begged, "please let me know *life*. Let me know what it feels like to be loved. Let me taste adventure and excitement. Let me have children of my own so I can let go of our Josh when the time comes. . . ."

The hot stone wrapped in a bit of flannel sheeting had warmed a tiny patch of the bed and she pushed her cold feet gratefully against it. But when she finally fell asleep she was still worrying about Josh, and still wondering how life would ever catch up to her.

It was a few weeks later that it happened. Things had drifted slowly back to normal, Josh was back with Sammy and they were always out somewhere together. Frank was coughing over his pipe and grumbling about his dinner, like usual, and Annie didn't know how she was going to stand it all much longer. She had sacrificed her youth to her father's selfish demands and now she was losing Josh, too, to his own world. Resentment choked her.

The winter evenings became long, silent, desperate hours by the fire with her father in the chair opposite. Her fingers fumbled clumsily with the knitting she had always been able to do automatically over endless years of pullovers and mittens, as she dreamed restlessly of a different world, like the one she read about in the newspapers where ladies wore satin ball gowns and danced with tall, distinguished men, or sailed away to foreign countries on fabulous steam yachts and married counts and princes who loaded them with enormous jewels and love. *Living,* she told herself enviously, *that's what they were doing.*

Josh had still not come home by the time she went wearily to bed and she left the door on the latch so he could let himself in. She was up again at five the next morning as usual, wrapping her woolen dressing gown around her, shivering as she hurried noiselessly downstairs to bank up the coal fire. She was filling the kettle from the tap in the scullery when she heard a noise at the window.

"Sammy," she cried, flinging open the door, "whatever brings you here at this hour?"

"Shhh," he whispered, a finger on his lips, "not so loud, Annie."

She stared at him open-mouthed, taking in his disheveled appearance, his torn jacket and muddy boots. His face was a colorless gray and his dark eyes wild with panic. "It's Josh," she said, fear suddenly clutching her heart. "Something's happened to him?"

He nodded reluctantly, and she clutched at his arm. "Is he hurt?"

Sammy shook his head. "Josh isn't harmed," he said hurriedly. "Don't ask me what happened, Annie. But he's in bad trouble. As bad as any man can get. He sent me to see you. He said if you love him you'll help him. You know there's no harm in Josh, Annie, not really—"

"Whatever do you mean?" she gasped. "What trouble, what harm . . . *what are you talking about, Sammy?*"

He took in a deep, shuddering breath and said, "Josh is in police trouble, Annie, they'll be after him this time. He told me you had your aunt Jessie's money hidden under the mattress. He said to tell you he needs it to escape." He grabbed her by the shoulders, suddenly desperate. "He has to get away, Annie, a long way away. Out of the country. He said mebbe we would go to San Francisco where your dad went, we'll make our fortunes there . . . if only we can leave this mess behind us. Don't ask any more questions, Annie, just give me the money. I'll go with him. I promise I'll look after him with my own life. Only I beg you not to ask me why."

His wild, dark eyes met hers and she knew he was talking about something too terrible to put into words, but she still could not understand how it could relate to Josh. He was such a good lad, he always had been . . . what could he have done to be in trouble with the police, such bad trouble to make him run away, all the way to San Francisco?

"Annie, for God's sake, there's no time to lose."

Pulling herself together she ran swiftly up the stairs and dragged back the heavy flock mattress, rummaging underneath for the thin sheaf of ten-pound notes. She ran back downstairs and thrust them into his trembling hands, too shocked to question him further.

"Thanks, Annie, you're a grand lass," he said, stuffing them quietly into his pocket, and without another word he ran off down the path. She called after him. "Did Josh say anything else, a message for me or anything . . . ?"

Sammy shook his head. "I've got to rush, lass," he said, glancing nervously up and down the lane.

She nodded, tears squeezing from her eyes. "Tell him I love him, no matter what," she called. "And I'll never believe he did anything bad." Sammy's fathomless black eyes met hers for a moment and then he was gone.

The neighborhood was in an uproar when the police announced they were looking to arrest Josh Aysgarth for the murder of three young women.

"Josh Aysgarth?" they cried disbelievingly. "Why, he'd never hurt a fly. He's one of life's innocents, that lad, allus in a world of his own. And he didn't have no time for lasses either. He was allus just with Sammy Morris."

But Mrs. Morris told everybody how her Sammy had found Josh standing over the girl's body down by Durrent's Beck, half-in and half-out of the water, it was. She said Josh told Sammy he hadn't done it and Sammy—who had always been daft in the head where his friend was concerned, believed him. He had run to Ivy Cottage to ask Annie Aysgarth for help. How could she refuse? She had been a mother to Josh since their proper Mam died when he was a little lad and she were nothing but a girl herself. Annie had said she knew their Josh would never do such a thing and she had given Sammy the hundred pounds her Aunt Jessie had left her that she was saving for a rainy day. Then Sammy had run home to tell his mother what had happened and that he was running away with Josh and now Mrs. Morris didn't know where they had gone.

"I'll never forgive Josh Aysgarth for leading my son astray," she told the awestruck neighbors, wiping her eye on a corner of her clean, flowered apron. "My Sammy's gone and likely I'll never see him again."

And if Annie Aysgarth knew where they had gone, she wasn't telling. But everyone who saw her, shopping at the Maypole or hurrying to catch the tram or buying ale for her father's dinner just like normal, said she had aged overnight from a girl of twenty-six to a woman of forty. Poor Annie Aysgarth, they said, she had loved that boy like her own son and she would never tell on him, not in a thousand years.

As for Frank Aysgarth, after those first headlines hit the newstands he never left Ivy Cottage again. His hair turned white and he retreated into total seclusion and silence, looked after by his faithful daughter, Annie.

# CHAPTER 8

◆

## *1905*

Francie's difficult childhood years slowly passed and one morning she awoke and remembered it was her eighteenth birthday. She leapt from her bed, the same lumpy, chipped iron bed she had slept in for fourteen years, and ran to the mirror eager to see if she looked any different. But the face that stared back at her was not one bit changed, not one bit more grown-up.

That afternoon her father summoned her to his study. She stood dutifully before him, her hands clasped together, eyes lowered, hating him with every fiber of her being.

His brow furrowed as he looked at her. She was eighteen, no longer a child, and she was virtually unmarriageable. Of course, if he gave her a good enough dowry he could find someone to take her off his hands, but he could not allow her to marry just anybody, she would have children—his grandchildren, and they would have to be a credit to the Harrison name. He frowned, wondering how he could make her more presentable. She must be taught how to behave so that she could redeem herself in the eyes of society and make a decent marriage. If his plan failed, then he would simply claim her health had broken, like her mother's, and banish her to the ranch.

Francie stood quietly, eyes downcast, and he suddenly noticed how tall she was. Her spine was straight, her complexion clear and soft, and her blond hair shiny. Her breasts under the stiff wool of her dress were small but nicely rounded and with a bit of grooming he could see she might be made into an attractive marriage proposition. With the right dowry, of course. And in return he would demand an aristocratic title. Nothing less would do.

He said, "So. You are eighteen today, Francesca."

She lifted her head and looked at him, surprised. He had never mentioned her birthdays before and she thought he had forgotten.

He said, "Please ask Miss James to come to my study at three o'clock. Tell her I have a great deal to discuss with her."

"Yes, Father." She waited, head bowed again until he dismissed her.

His eyes narrowed speculatively as she walked to the door. He was pleased with his plan, he could unburden himself of her very satisfactorily, *and* add the gloss of a title to the Harrison name, but he knew he would need some help. Picking up the phone he called Mrs. Brice Leland, one of San Francisco's grandest matrons, told her he needed her help, and was invited to stop by to take afternoon tea. He explained his problem to her: a difficult, unsociable daughter. He had done his best to bring her up properly but without a mother she knew how hard it had been. Francesca was a shy girl and now that she was eighteen she must be brought out into society. She needed a woman's touch. . . .

Mrs. Brice Leland smiled, thrilled to be of help, thinking of the opportunities it would offer to present her own eligible nieces to the oh-so-rich Harmon Harrison, still a widower after ten years, though not for want of San Francisco's young ladies trying.

And later that day Miss James told Francie she was to make her debut in society.

"But why?" she gasped, bewildered. "I don't know a single member of San Francisco society. What do they care about *me*?"

"It is your father's wish," the governess replied, leafing through the lists of dressmakers, hairdressers, shoe and glovemakers, the dance academy and deportment classes Mrs. Brice Leland had given her. "Your father is planning to give a ball for you in two months time. We must begin immediately."

The following day Francie was swept off to the ultrasmart City of Paris store to be outfitted from head to toe for every conceivable social occasion. On Mrs. Brice Leland's instructions, she bought daytime skirts of light wool with matching tailored jackets, ruffled lace blouses and silk afternoon dresses, chiffon tea gowns and a beautiful lace ballgown with a velvet opera cape. Each outfit had matching shoes, stockings, and gloves and the appropriate accessories—a ruffled parasol, a flowered straw hat, a plumed hair ornament. All her life she had worn plain, starched cotton and drab woolens and it was intoxicating to feel the swirl of beribboned taffeta petticoats and the strangeness of the narrow, pointed satin evening slippers. But her heart sank when she looked at herself in the mirror dressed in her new finery. She knew that next to the other girls at the ball, she would be like a clumsy carthorse decked out in festive ribbons in a stable of sleek, knowledgeable, well-groomed Thoroughbreds.

Still, there was hardly time to worry; her days were too full. She dashed nervously between fittings and deportment classes, where she was taught how to sit like a lady with her ankles crossed and feet tucked in, how to use a fan, and how to walk in a dress with a train. She learned the proper ritual of a ladies' tea party and how to converse politely at the dinner table, and at the dance classes she learned how to waltz and polka. After six weeks she was considered ready and was summoned to tea to meet the society ladies who had advised her father.

Wearing a blue silk georgette tea gown that exactly matched her eyes she trailed reluctantly down the big oak staircase toward her father's study, wondering for the hundredth time why, after all these years of ignoring her he now seemed determined she should become a star of San Francisco society. She hesitated outside his door with the old familiar feeling of foreboding. Then, with a sigh, she straightened her spine, lifted her chin, and knocked.

"Enter," he said, and her heart sank to the soles of her new kid shoes as she obeyed.

His critical gaze swept her from head to foot. "Turn around," he commanded and she swung around obediently. "For once you look presentable," he said finally. "You will thank Mrs. Brice Leland for her help and you will behave like a lady. I expect you to be a credit to the Harrisons. Do you understand?"

She nodded. "Yes, Papa."

"Then you may go."

She felt his critical eyes watching her as she walked away and heard his exasperated sigh as she tripped nervously.

"For God's sake, Francesca, haven't they taught you to walk like a lady?" he exclaimed angrily.

"Yes, Papa," she murmured again, biting her lip, convinced more than ever that she would make a fool of herself at this tea party.

Mrs. Brice Leland's home was an Italian-style stone palace a couple of blocks away on California Street between Mason and Taylor. Inside was dark with lots of carved oak paneling, and satin and gilt Louis XIV furniture and hundreds of potted palms. Half a dozen ladies perched on small overstuffed brocade chairs around their hostess, presiding like a queen over the silver teapot. Mrs. Brice Leland was a bosomy lady, regal in purple lace and her pink "afternoon" diamonds. She possessed much larger and grander diamonds for evenings, which she claimed were inherited from her ancestors, though everyone suspected that, like her husband, she hadn't possessed beans—let alone diamonds—until he'd made a killing in gold stocks. But they were used to glossing over pedigrees—as long as there was enough money in the bank to cover the lie. The ladies wore elaborate silk tea gowns sparkling with jewels, and there was a buzz of genteel laughter and conversation as they sipped China tea from fragile Wedgwood cups and nibbled delicacies prepared by the French chef. When the butler announced Francie they swung around, staring at her, their feathered hats quivering like a flock of birds.

Mrs. Brice Leland smiled and said in a loud whisper, "Well, well, the skeleton in the Harrison closet." Putting her lorgnette to her eye she looked the waiting Francie up and down. "And a rather pretty skeleton at that," she acknowledged.

"Come here, girl," she called, waving an imperious arm and frowning as Francie tripped over the fringed Turkish rug. She introduced her to the ladies and said, "Sit here by me, Francesca, we would like to get to know you a little. After all, your father asked us to help him and we have done our best. I must say you look a credit to the Harrison name and I shall tell your father so."

"Thank you, ma'am." Francie blushed, clutching her cup and saucer and refusing a wafer-thin cucumber sandwich because she was afraid she might drop it, and besides she was so nervous she knew it would choke her.

She had no idea how she got through the next forty-five minutes of polite questions and answers, but she supposed she must have because they smiled at her as she left and one lady said, "I'm having a little tea for my daughter tomorrow, dear. Why don't you come along and meet some other girls your age?" It was kindly said but the thought of meeting girls her own age filled Francie's heart with dread and she knew it would be awful.

It was worse. Oh, she looked like them in her rose-pink silk dress with the puff sleeves and the bows on her shoulders; like them, she sat with her ankles neatly crossed; like them, she spoke quietly and politely. But she didn't know what they knew, she just had no idea of what or *who* they were talking about so merrily. She didn't know

about the schools, the resorts, the houses, the friends, the parties. She
felt like a visitor from another planet and she knew they thought so
too; she could see it in their surreptitious glances and their half-
hidden, supercilious smiles and she burned with humiliation at the
secret whispers whenever two young, shining, well-coiffed heads bent
together.

Still, there were no refusals to the supper and dance given by
Harmon Harrison for his daughter Francesca a week later, because
by then the whole of San Francisco, except Francie, knew that the
millionaire was looking for a husband for his errant daughter.

The house had been in a turmoil of preparation for days; the parquet ballroom floor had been polished a dozen times and scattered
with French chalk, the enormous crystal chandeliers had been
cleaned and their hundreds of candles lit, garlands of pink roses were
looped around the marble pillars and walls and piled in great bouquets on every possible surface. Buffet tables groaned beneath carved
ice swans mounded with glistening black caviar, and giant ice cornu-
copias were filled with fresh pink lobster. There were dozens of shiny
silver platters of baked meats, small mountains of fresh asparagus,
towers of enormous hothouse grapes, peaches, and figs, and tier upon
tier of *gâteaux,* tortes, pastries, wobbling iced soufflés, and colorful
jellies. There was a champagne fountain eight feet high and dozens of
extra waiters to supplement the normal household staff.

Fifteen-year-old Harry had been summoned home and he stood
next to his father and Francie as they waited to greet their guests in
the domed marble hall. He was already as tall as Francie, broad
shouldered and a younger version of his father. And, like his father,
he did not speak to her.

Francie's dress was made from yards and yards of fragile white
lace over half a dozen swirling pink taffeta petticoats threaded with
narrow pink velvet ribbon. Her stockings were pure white silk, her
shoes embroidered white satin, and her gloves the very softest white
kidskin fastened with dozens of tiny satin buttons. Her blond hair
was piled on top and fixed with a glittering diamond tiara and she
wore a corsage of pink roses.

Josh Aysgarth thought she looked like a princess in a fairytale. He
was one of the extra waiters hired specially for the night and his job
was to offer the guests champagne, but he couldn't take his eyes off
Miss Francesca Harrison. She was an unobtainable dream for a lad

like himself, fresh off the boat from England without a penny in his pocket.

He and Sammy had been lucky to get this waiting job tonight because without it they would have gone hungry, and that wasn't something either of them liked. He just couldn't take his eyes off the girl, though, and he was puzzled because he could swear she was frightened; her face was so pale and her blue eyes enormous. He wondered what she'd got to be scared of—she had everything anyone could ever wish for: beauty, wealth, a wonderful home, and a devoted family.

"Better get your eyes off her," Sammy Morris whispered jealously as he walked past balancing a silver tray laden with glasses. "She's too rich for your blood."

"A cat can look at a queen, can't he?" Josh retorted, but he knew Sammy was right.

Those who attended the Harrison ball remembered it to their dying days. Later, they spoke of it in shocked whispers, telling each other that it was obvious even then that Francie Harrison was no good.

She stood there between her powerful father and her handsome brother, looking as pretty as any girl could in white lace and roses and her mother's diamond tiara. She greeted her guests without so much as a smile on her pale face. She sat, frozen with nerves, at the top table and not a morsel of food or drink passed her lips. She looked terrified as she led the dancing with her father and then old Count von Wurtheim danced with her. In fact, the count monopolized her—Mrs. Brice Leland saw to that. Of course, he was old enough to be her grandfather and everybody knew he had no money, but he had an ancient title and vast estates in Bavaria. There was a lot of cynical laughter and raised eyebrows—it was so obvious that Mrs. Brice Leland was matchmaking. Everyone was talking about it. Then someone commented on it a little too loudly. "Everybody knows Harrison's trying to marry off his crazy daughter," he said, "giving her away with a million dollars just to be rid of her."

The color drained from Francie's face; she turned absolutely chalk white and then an ashen gray, and with a cry of distress she picked up her skirts and fled from the ballroom. People parted in front of her like the waters of the Red Sea, staring astonished at her as she ran past. Her father went after her and Mrs. Brice Leland went after him, but they soon came back. It seemed they hadn't been able to find her. The dance went on as normal with everyone pretending nothing was wrong, but they were all watching and waiting to see what would happen next.

Then her brother came rushing in and they watched as he spoke to his father. It was Harmon Harrison's turn to go pale, only this time they all knew it was from anger. He strode from the room trying to keep his dignity, but he looked fit to kill someone. And that's what he almost did when he found her on the balcony, sobbing her eyes out. In the arms of a handsome young waiter.

And while the ball to celebrate her debut continued downstairs Francie was locked in her room again. She flung herself across the bed, her cheeks burning with humiliation, pounding the pillows with anger. After a while she got up and stood in front of the mirror and looked at herself, "the crazy daughter," dressed in her foolish finery with an invisible label pinned to her shoulder that said "One million dollars." Her father had humiliated her in front of the whole world. Everybody but she had known he wanted to be rid of her, everybody knew he thought she was crazy, wicked, unfit to be in society. And she had just proven him right.

With a wail of despair she tugged off the beautiful diamond tiara and flung it against the wall. She tore off the fabulous lacy dress and ripped away the rustling silk petticoats and stomped on them. She flung off the fine kid gloves, the embroidered satin shoes, the achingly tight corset, and sobbing and cursing her father, she looked at herself again in the mirror, half-naked, her long blond hair in disarray, her face pale with anger and her eyelids swollen from crying.

"This *is who I am,*" she told herself, *"this real person in the mirror. Not a dressed-up doll to be given away to an old man with a title who doesn't want* me—*only my father's money."* And then she flung herself on the bed again and cried some more.

When all the tears were finished and the first pain and anger had subsided she remembered the poor waiter who had helped her. He had grabbed her arm as she had run blindly through the hall, pulling her onto the terrace. She had been shaking so badly her teeth had chattered, and he had taken off his jacket and flung it over her shoulders. Then he'd put his arms around her and held her tight.

"It's all right," he'd said soothingly. "It's all right, miss. Nothing can be this bad. I know, because I've been through it too. It only hurts for a while and then things get better again. Come on now, miss, stop crying and tell me about it. Maybe I can help you."

But she just shook her head, too choked with tears and humiliation to speak. He kept on holding her, stroking her hair and talking to her reassuringly until the tears ceased to flow and she looked up at him and saw him properly for the first time.

His hair was as blond as hers and his eyes were dark and long lashed. His nose was as fine and straight as a Greek statue and his brow was broad. He was so beautiful and his expression and smile were so sweet, she thought she must be looking into the face of an angel.

"Who are you?" she whispered, leaning back in his arms.

"I'm nobody," he replied. "Just a waiter."

Tears of sympathy spilled from her eyes as she said bitterly, "I'm a nobody too."

"Francesca!" She turned and saw Mrs. Brice Leland and her father's shocked faces and then she was dragged from her savior's arms and her father was punching him and that beautiful good angel was covered in blood. He was on the ground and her father was kicking and cursing him and then he turned on her. He grabbed her arm, dragging her through the servants' entrance and up the back stairs to her room. With a thrust that sent her sprawling to the floor he said in an icy whisper, "You are not fit for decent society. You are insane, a slut, a whore . . . I'll see to it you are locked away forever."

Then he slammed the door and turned the key and she realized what he intended to do. Oh, he wouldn't lock her up here, to be forever the skeleton in the closet in the Harrison house. No, he would commit her to the state insane asylum near San Jose, where they locked up the *real* crazy people. And then he and Harry need never see her again. No one would see her. She might as well be dead.

Petrified, she ran to the barred window and peered out into the night. The moon was pushing through the mist and faint strains of music still came from the ballroom. A few servants lingered in the courtyard for a surreptitious cigarette, and a horse whinnied in the stables. She remembered Princess's sad puzzled eyes when her father put the gun to her head, and she wished he would just shoot her too. But she knew he wouldn't. He would beat her. And from that there was no escape.

She was summoned to her father's study at seven the next morning. He was as immaculately dressed as ever, freshly shaved, and smelling faintly of bay rum cologne. He was standing by his desk, waiting, the old leather dog lead in his hand.

His eyes were chips of ice as he said, "You know what to do."

Francie stood straight and absolutely still by the door. She had bathed her red swollen eyes, brushed her hair and tied it back with a ribbon, and she wore her old, sensible dark dress. She had prepared what she had to say very carefully, but now that the time had come to say it she was terrified. She took a deep breath—it was now or never.

"No, Father," she said quietly. "I am not a child anymore. You will not beat me again."

His implacable expression did not change. "Bend over the stool, Francesca," he said.

She stared at him as he flexed the leather strap across his palm; it was as though she had never spoken.

"No," she said loudly. "I told you, you will never beat me again."

He closed his eyes as if trying to control himself, then his face dissolved into a mask of hatred and rage, and seizing her by the hair he dragged her across the room. He hurled her across the stool and lifted the strap and brought it down on her with all his strength. She screamed but he whipped her again and again, each lash harder than the last in a frenzy of anger until her screams stopped and she slid, stunned with pain and shock, to the floor.

He stood over her breathing heavily, the bloody strap clutched in his hand, his face full of contempt. Then he walked back to his desk, put the strap in a drawer, straightened his cravat, smoothed back his hair, and strode to the door. Maitland was waiting in the hall. He looked expressionlessly at his master as he told him to fetch Miss James and help her take Miss Francesca to her room; he was leaving for his office.

The governess's face turned pale as she looked at Francie lying half-conscious on the rug—her dress in ribbons and her naked back covered in blood. Her shocked eyes met Maitland's and she said, "I've never seen anything like this. The girl needs a doctor."

Maitland said, "He's insane with anger. Next time he'll likely kill her. We'll take her to the convent. The Little Sisters of Mercy will look after her and she'll be safe from him there. I'm telling them about this in the servants' hall and then I'm leaving, and them that wants to come with me can. I'll not work any longer for a man as cruel as Harmon Harrison, no matter how important he is and how good wages he pays."

Miss James nodded in agreement. "I'll get a blanket for her, Mr. Maitland, and after we've taken her to the convent, I'm leaving too. I'm not staying on here to face his anger."

# CHAPTER 9

◆

A couple of weeks after the Harrison's ball, Maitland dropped into the Barbary Saloon on Pacific Street, where Josh was working. He was wearing a tweed jacket and trousers and at first Josh didn't recognize him out of his formal butler's pinstripe and black. But Maitland recognized Josh by his battered face.

"Looks like Harmon Harrison did a pretty thorough job on you," he said, eyeing the plaster on his head, his black eye and swollen mouth.

Josh placed a pint of ale on the stained wooden counter in front of him, shrugging indifferently.

"He damned near killed his daughter too," Maitland added, taking a long swallow of the beer.

"His daughter? But she's just a girl and she weren't doing nothing wrong . . . just crying, that's all . . ."

"I know you were just helping her, son, but she shamed him in front of the cream of San Francisco society. He hates all women, and her more than the rest. She's been shut away for years and the story got about that it was because she was difficult, a bit crazy. But he polished up her manners, dressed her up, and let it be known she had a million-dollar dowry and he was willing to give her away to any taker with an aristocratic title. She heard some fool talking about it and naturally she was upset and ran off. And now everybody knows she was found in a waiter's arms. *And* they know the rumor that Harrison was so angry he beat his daughter to a bloody pulp and that even now she's at death's door."

Josh stared at him, shocked. "It can't be true, no father would do that."

Maitland nodded. "It's true, all right. I took her myself to the

Convent of Mercy. The sisters are looking after her, but they don't hold out much hope. Harrison donated them a little money, but he's never been to see her. And I heard him telling his son that she'll never be allowed to set foot inside his door again. If she lives, that is."

"If she dies, the bastard should swing for her," Josh exploded, banging his fist on the bar counter.

Maitland looked cynically at him as he drained his glass and he shook his head. "Not in this town, young man. Harmon Harrison is rich and powerful and he runs San Francisco. Men like him make the rules. It's folks like us who have to obey them."

"It's all my fault," Josh said, putting on his jacket. "I'll go see her right now . . . the Convent of Mercy, you said. . . ."

"They'll not let you in, lad," Maitland warned, but he was already swinging through the saloon doors and on his way.

The Sisters of Mercy was a nursing order dedicated to caring for the poor and the sick, and the convent was a small, arched white stucco building set back from Dolores Street. The walls surrounding it were high and the heavy wooden gates were firmly closed against the world, but that didn't stop Josh. He tugged urgently on the iron bell-pull, stamping his feet against the cold, waiting impatiently for someone to answer. He tugged again, hearing it ring in some far-off place. There was the sound of sandaled feet on flagstones and then a panel in the door was drawn back and a nun, half-hidden by her starched white wimple, looked out at him.

"I'm here to see Francesca Harrison," he told her. "I must see her."

"Miss Harrison is not allowed any visitors," the nun said, her quiet voice barely a whisper.

"But she'll want to see me," he cried urgently.

"Are you a relative?"

"A relative? Yes, of course," he lied desperately.

"No relatives are allowed to see her," she said firmly, beginning to close the little flap.

"No, no, please wait." He pushed the flap open again. "You don't understand. I'm—I'm her *fiancé*. I love her, you see, and she loves me. She *can't* die, *I won't let her die*. Not without seeing me, please Sister, I'm begging you. . . ."

He saw the indecision on her face and added quickly, "The lass was going to be my wife. How can you forbid me to see her?"

"Please wait a minute," she said, turning away. He listened to the soft slap of her sandaled feet on the flagstones as she disappeared, then paced up and down, swinging his arms. The February night was raw and he had no overcoat. His jacket of good Yorkshire tweed was almost threadbare, newspapers were stuffed into the soles of his boots to keep out the cold and wet and he had exactly five dollars to his name. But none of it mattered; beautiful Francie was dying and he knew he had to save her.

He heard the nun returning and peered anxiously through the flap. "Reverend Mother says you may come in," she told him, unlocking the massive gates. "She wishes to speak to you."

Pulling off his cap he followed her across a flagged courtyard and through a door into an anteroom.

"The Reverend Mother asks if you will wait here. She will be with you as soon as possible."

The nun disappeared through a second door and Josh paced the room anxiously. It was small with rough plaster walls and uneven terra-cotta tiled floors; there was a plain oak table and two straight-backed wooden chairs. On one wall hung a beautifully carved wooden figure of Christ on the Cross. The single window was placed high so that no one could see either out or in, and the room was as cold as the icy night outside. He groaned, thinking of Francie Harrison in this cold place; a girl like her needed to be where there was warmth, life, color. And it was all his fault. He thought of his sister, Annie, at home in Yorkshire, and wished she were here. Aye, Annie would have looked after her properly. She would have fed her nourishing soups, she would have banked up the fire and plumped up the pillows. Annie would have had her right in no time.

"Good evening."

He turned, startled; he hadn't heard the Reverend Mother enter. Like the other nun, she was wearing a long, gray robe and a stiff white linen wimple that hid her face. From the rope belt around her waist dangled an ebony rosary and a bunch of silver keys, and a large simple gold cross hung from a chain around her neck.

"You wish to see Miss Harrison?" she said, in a voice so soft he had to strain to hear it.

"Yes, ma'am—Reverend Mother. You see, I know what happened, what she has been through. I love her, Reverend Mother, and I believe I can help her."

"I'm sorry to tell you, but Miss Harrison is dying. We think it only right to let her do so in peace. Even her father is refused admittance."

"Her father!" Josh exploded, his face twisted in a sneer of contempt. "Why, he's the one who almost killed her."

There was silence while she regarded him from beneath the shadowy wimple, then she said, "Why do you think you can help her, Mr. . . . ?"

"Aysgarth. Josh Aysgarth." Then he said urgently, "With love. Pure love. Just like the Lord gave to us."

Silence fell again. He stared down at his hands, blue with cold. Then she said, "Very well, Mr. Aysgarth. The Lord gave us love. I accept that it must have its chance. Please follow me."

He paced anxiously behind her as she glided along the dim tiled corridors to a room lined with gray hospital beds covered in bright scarlet blankets. Only two were occupied; in one an old lady who was sleeping, and in the other a boy of about twelve, his face red with fever and his eyes wide and dark with pain. A large screen partitioned off a section of the ward from the rest and the Reverend Mother beckoned him behind it. And there, pale and still as death in the middle of the little iron cot, lay Francesca Harrison.

A young nun, her head bowed over her rosary, kept silent watch by the bedside and the only sound in the room was Francie's labored breathing. Josh sank instinctively to his knees and folded his hands together in silent prayer, hardly daring to look at Francie, but when he did he saw that the ravages of death were already tearing at her. They had cut her beautiful blond hair to defeat the fever, there were dark, bluish-gray shadows beneath her eyes, her cheeks were sunken, and her bloodless lips parted as she struggled for breath. And her bony, lifeless hands were folded across her breasts as though she were already laid out for her coffin.

Impulsively Josh reached out and took her thin hand in his; it was icy cold but he could feel the slow uncertain beat of her pulse and knew she was still clinging to life. "Francie," he whispered, as though afraid of disturbing her sleep. "Francie. I'm here to help you. I'm sorry they hurt you, Francie, but I promise you, on my honor, nobody will ever hurt you again. I will look after you now, I give you my solemn word." He stayed for a long time, talking to her, but there was no response, and after an hour or so, he left her to her sleep.

He went to see her every day, twice a day when he could, hurrying over in the early mornings before the bar opened and returning again before his evening shift. But it was always the same. She lay still as death, her eyes firmly closed against the world that hated her, her lips sealed to a world that did not understand her, and her body longing to escape from a place that did not want her. Josh knew that Francie wanted to die, he felt her longing for release and he didn't know what to do, so he talked to her, holding her hands, stroking her face gently as he whispered in her ear, telling her about himself.

"When you are better, Francie, I'll take you back to my home. You've never seen anything as beautiful as the Yorkshire moors, my little lass, and the sheep in the dales; the best wool in the world, they have, and all woven in our Yorkshire mills. . . ."

He stopped, remembering suddenly the reason he had come to San Francisco, then he sighed deeply and added, "Aye, mebbe one day, Francie, I'll be able to take you there. When I can go home again."

Sammy told him every night that he was a fool. "You hardly know her," he said, drinking deeply on his beer and leaning angrily over the counter so Josh could better hear what he had to say. "She's trouble, that lass. She's already cost you your job and a beating. Ain't that enough for you? If she dies her father will be there to claim the body, and if she lives—which is unlikely, he'll be there to take her home and make sure she causes him no more trouble. *You* are the one who's looking for trouble, Josh Aysgarth, just the way you always do."

Sammy slammed his empty beer glass threateningly on the counter, glaring at Josh as he buttoned his jacket, ready to face the cold rainy night. "You'd best take heed of me this time, Josh Aysgarth, because you know what happens when you don't. Remember the last time?"

Josh watched as he walked angrily away, wondering as he always did how it was, when the two of them were so different, they had been best friends all their lives. He loved Sammy all right, but there were things about him that, friend or not, Sammy would never understand, and a part of Sammy he would never understand.

Still, Sammy was right, he thought, gloomily wiping the beer stains from the counter; there was no way Mr. Harrison would let his daughter go, even if she didn't die.

"Daydreamin' again, are ya, Josh?" the saloonkeeper shouted irritably across the room. "Well, I'm telling ya, this'll be the last time. Get movin' and serve them customers or you'll be back out on the street where y'came from."

Spurred on by the threat, Josh jolted into action, but Sammy's words haunted him and he remembered what had happened last time he had ignored his advice and gone his own way. He shuddered as he thought about their escape, running through the dark, rainy night, running and running, terrified. And Sammy promising to help him. If it weren't for Sammy he wouldn't be here now, he wouldn't even be alive. And he would never have met Francie. He owed everything to his best friend, Sammy Morris.

Francie knew it was impossible to open her eyes. She seemed to be hovering in a haze of white light, filled with soft rustlings and the soothing murmur of quiet voices, like the wind in the poplar trees on the ranch. She thought maybe that's where she was, back at the ranch with her mother and the pretty chestnut mare and Princess. It was so peaceful, except when she moved and then she exploded into fragments of pain, each one sharp as a knife blade. Then she would hear someone screaming and she knew it was herself. As the pain eased she remained suspended in time, her eyes tightly closed, safe in her own peaceful, private white world.

She heard gentle voices calling her name. "Francie, dear," they said, "open your eyes. It's such a lovely day, Francie. Look at the sunshine." And often she would hear voices praying for her, asking the good Lord to give her strength and courage to face life again. But she did not want to face her old life; she liked this one. There were no harsh voices in her private world, no cruelty or hatred or pain. It was a peaceful dream and she wanted to stay there forever. Then one day, instead of the soft feminine whispering voices, she recognized a man's voice.

"Francie," it said, "it's Josh. I'm the waiter who helped you. I've come to see you. Just open your eyes, Francie, and look at me."

Josh, Josh, Josh . . . the name echoed through her mind. Then she stopped herself from thinking any further, she didn't want to remember what had happened.

Her eyelids felt so heavy, as though they had already been weighted with pennies—the way they did when people died. Maybe she was dead and she would never open them again . . . but then she would never see Josh.

The weight suddenly removed itself from her eyelids and she lifted them slowly. It was like raising the curtain in a theater. Daylight struck her like a blow; there were only vague shapes, unconnected voices. Then gradually her vision cleared and a face swam into view. The beautiful face of the good angel. "Josh?" she whispered.

"There you are, lass," he said, smiling at her, relieved. "I thought I'd lost you." And he took her hand in his and kissed it.

# CHAPTER 10

◆

Francie began to get better; the color returned to her cheeks and the flesh to her bones and each day she grew stronger. The nuns smiled when they saw her eager eyes as she waited for the young man and the way she reached out for his hand—the hand that had been her lifeline, bringing her back from the brink when no one else, not even the doctors, could. "The young man was right," they whispered. "It was the love the Lord gave us that worked the miracle."

Josh came every day. When he had been paid he would bring her a present, a bunch of violets, a single perfect hothouse peach, fresh-made chocolates. "You must not spend your money on me," she reproved him, "you need it for yourself." But he just smiled that sweet smile of his and took her hand and kissed it gently.

The innocent kiss sent tremors through Francie's body; in all the years since her mother died no one had ever kissed her and she had forgotten the warm feelings of loving and being loved. She wanted to throw her arms around Josh and hug him like she used to hug Princess, to stroke his face the way she stroked her chestnut mare, Blaize, because they were the only experiences of affection in her love-starved life and she knew no others.

But when he had gone a worried frown appeared between her brows; the nuns had said that in a week's time she would be well enough to leave. But where would she go? What would she do? She had no home and no money. Her only friend in the whole world was Josh and she knew how hard he was struggling just to make ends meet.

The next day as they walked slowly through the cloisters she said determinedly, "I'll be leaving here soon. I must get a job."

He shook his head, "Women like you don't work, Francie. They've

not been brought up to it." He smiled at the thought. "I'll bet you've
never even boiled an egg."

"I can learn, can't I?" she retorted. "I could be a kitchenmaid,
learn to cook, serve at table . . . anything. . . ."

"Not here in San Francisco you couldn't. Nobody would give Harmon Harrison's daughter a job."

"Well, I could train to be a nurse, like the nuns—"

"And then I'd never see you, Francie."

"At least I can sew and embroider, that's all I've ever done in my
life—"

"No wife of mine's going to work in a sweatshop," he said with a
flash of anger.

Francie's heart skipped a beat and she stopped and looked at him.
"Your *wife?*"

"Aye, lass, that's what I said."

She pulled herself together and said with quiet dignity, "You don't
have to feel responsible for me, Josh. I can manage on my own."

He took her by the shoulders, looking deep into her eyes. "But I've
never loved anyone before, Francie. I want to look after you and
make you happy."

She suddenly brimmed with happiness; she felt like she had when
she was just a kid turned loose on the ranch, ready to whoop and
holler and turn cartwheels. She had never loved anyone since her
mother died, but this was different, it left her breathless and trembling inside. And when Josh bent forward and kissed her gently on
the lips all she wanted was for the kiss to last forever.

When Josh came to fetch Francie home the following week she was
wearing a brown woolen dress and jacket donated by the civic charity
and she carried a little bundle with a few more cast-offs. The only
thing she had of her own were the boots she had worn when she had
first gone there. She had covered her head with a plaid woolen shawl
and Josh told her she looked like a Yorkshire mill girl on her way to
work.

The Reverend Mother bestowed a blessing on them and then she
pressed a soft leather purse containing a few dollars into Francie's
hand. "Please take this with our blessing, and may the Lord guide
you and help you on your way," she murmured.

As the great wooden convent doors closed behind her Francie
stared down at the purse, her humiliation complete. She possessed
nothing, not even her own clothes. She was filled with a deep, burn-

ing anger as she vowed to herself that one day she would see the Harrisons humiliated just the way she was. And she knew she would hate her father till the day he died, and even beyond the grave, into eternity.

The Barbary Saloon and Rooming House was a four-story brick-and-timber building on Pacific Avenue, at the foot of Telegraph Hill. It was sandwiched between the trashy Venus Dance Hall on the left and the notorious Goldrush Bordello on the right, and the saloon did good business, catching customers either on their way into the dance hall, or on their way out of the bordello. Either way, the men were hungry and thirsty, and with the workers from the produce market a couple of blocks to the south the long scarred mahogany bar was always crowded.

Francie smiled as she waited on the sidewalk while Josh paid the cab, remembering her secret nocturnal walks when she had lingered enviously outside the saloons; now she would get to see what they were really like. Josh had got her a room next to his and he had paid for it too. She meant to pay him back from the money from her charity purse, and then, no matter what he said, she would look for a job, because she just couldn't go on living on other people's charity forever.

"You must be Francie Harrison."

Surprised, she looked at the dark, stocky young man leaning against the door. He wore a threadbare jacket with a brown muffler knotted at his throat and a flat, checked cap that he made no attempt to remove. Francie smiled shyly and said, "And you must be Josh's best friend, Sammy Morris. He told me all about you."

"Mebbe he did and mebbe he didn't," he replied, unsmiling.

She thought he didn't seem very friendly, but Josh put his arm around her and said, "I see you've met Sammy," and she could tell by the way his eyes lit up that he was pleased, so she smiled politely and said, "I'm very happy to meet you at last, Sammy."

He wrinkled his nose disdainfully, mocking her educated tones. "Oh, very grand, aren't we? Well, you're gonna have to come down to earth a bit now, Miss Francesca Harrison. It ain't exactly Nob Hill around here."

"Francie knows that and she don't want Nob Hill," Josh said, pushing past Sammy into the house. The hallway smelled of years of stale cooking and grime and Francie wrinkled her nose as they walked up the uncarpeted stairs. She was out of breath by the time they reached the fourth floor and Josh put his arm around her waist as they climbed the last five steps together. He flung open the door proudly.

She stared at the tiny room squashed under the eaves, the ceilings sloped almost to the ground; but it was still bigger than her old room at home and there were no bars on the big window that filled the room with gray March light. She looked at the sagging brass double bed covered with a thin white cotton quilt, at the battered dresser with one drawer missing, at the worn brown oilcloth on the floor and the old rug, at the red plush armchair with the stuffing hanging out and the rickety gate-legged table with a jar of anemones placed carefully in the middle.

And she thought it was perfect. It was light and airy and Josh's flowers made it feel like home. She felt dizzy from love and happiness and the long climb up the stairs.

He was looking anxiously at her. "Is it all right? I know you're used to a grand house, but it's the best I could do. At least it's away from the noise of the saloon. And I'm just at the foot of these little stairs, so you need never be afraid."

Francie laughed as she took his hand. "I'll never be afraid with you around, Josh."

Sammy Morris eyed them dourly from the bottom of the steps. "I'm off to work now, Josh," he said, tightening his muffler around his neck and buttoning his jacket. "I'll see you later." And without a glance at Francie he stumped off down the stairs.

Francie watched him go and she knew for sure he didn't like her, but Josh told her not to worry, it was just Sammy's way. "He's used to there being just the two of us, you see. That's the way it's always been since we were kids. He's never met someone like you before, but once he gets to know you, he'll love you too."

Francie wasn't so sure he would, but she smiled as she walked around her new home. "We'll have tea here," she said, running a hand over the rough tabletop. "And just look at the view. Why, you can see practically all of San Francisco from here."

They stared together at the white sea birds circling the iron-gray March sky and at the busy sprawling streets, and she said, "You never told me why you came to San Francisco." Josh turned away, not answering, and she added hurriedly, "I didn't mean to pry, it just seems a long way from your home, that's all."

After a few moments he said, "I came here to seek my fortune, like my father before me."

"Your father?"

"Aye. Frank Aysgarth. He came here thirty years ago, for that same purpose. They were poor, my mam and dad. There had never been much money in the Aysgarth family, except for Aunt Jessie, and she was only by marriage. It was Aunt Jessie that left a hundred pounds to my sister, Annie, and Annie gave it to me and Sammy to come out here."

Josh told her the story of his mother and father, about their poverty and how his father had come to San Francisco and learned how to make his fortune.

"Anyway," he concluded, "that's the way our Annie tells the story. And she should know, she was there. She's a good lass," he said warmly. "She was better than any mother."

Francie uncurled herself from the bed where she had been listening to him. She flung her arms around him and said, "You've told me all about yourself, so now I really know you and you know me. We have no secrets from each other." She laughed. "We shall be just like your mam and dad, working hard so that one day we can have kids of our own to raise, and a house like Ivy Cottage."

Francie's days soon fell into a pattern; Josh would run upstairs and wake her at ten o'clock with a kiss and a cup of coffee and a hunk of crusty bread fresh from a neighboring Italian bakery. He insisted she stay in her room and rest until he had finished his long lunchtime stint at the bar, but he always appeared at her door again at noon bearing a plate of Irish stew or corned beef hash, depending on what free lunch the saloon was serving that day. And when his shift finished at three she would be ready and waiting for him. He had bought her a long silky scarf in a pretty blue to cover her shorn hair and she wrapped her plaid shawl tightly around her against the cold early spring winds as they explored San Francisco, but they were careful never to go anywhere Francie might be recognized.

He showed her a city she had lived in all her life and never seen; they climbed Telegraph Hill and watched the fog lift itself in a white mass from the ocean and roll toward them, engulfing them in a clinging white shroud; laughing, they covered their ears as every boat afloat sounded a warning horn or bell or whistle. They rode the cable cars and the ferries and laughed at the seals frolicking on the rocks near the Cliff House, and watched the waves roll in along Ocean Beach. And they admired the magnificent Palace Hotel, America's largest, with a soaring seven-story atrium, seven thousand bay windows overlooking the city, and a sumptuous, thirty-foot-long bar.

Sometimes Josh would smile as he listened to Francie chatter about their discoveries, but at others he would stride silently by her side, his eyes fixed on the ground, lost in a world of his own. "Is anything the matter?" she would ask anxiously, but he would just shrug his shoulders and say, "Nothing's wrong, lass," as though it was a great effort for him even to speak. And sometimes when they were in her room he would stare silently out the window for ages, his eyes as opaque as the gray sky outside. But there were other times when he would hold her in his arms and kiss her and her whole being would just fill with joy.

Still, there was no doubt about it, Sammy Morris did not like her. Sammy worked on a construction site carrying bricks up and down scaffolding all day and he spent his evenings in the bar downstairs with Josh. He had not been near her since she met him on the sidewalk that first day, and then one night he came to her door. She was standing at the window looking down at San Francisco's twinkling lights and at the pale spring moon when she heard the knock.

She ran eagerly to open the door, stepping back, surprised when she saw Sammy.

His dark, glowering eyes met hers. He took off his cap and said, "I've come straight from work. I've got to talk to you, Miss Harrison."

She smiled shyly. "Please come in. Won't you call me Francie?"

"I've not come here to make small talk," he said abruptly. "I'm here to tell you about Josh."

"I think I understand, I know how important your friendship with Josh is."

"More important than *you*," he said with a sudden venomous glance. "And more important than you'll *ever* know, *Miss Francie Harrison*."

His dark eyes filled with hatred. He stepped closer; she could smell the sweat on his work shirt and see the cement dust like powder on his skin, and she pressed herself against the door, away from him. She wished Josh were here, but Sammy had chosen his moment well —Josh wouldn't be home for another hour.

"Josh and I are in love, we are going to be married," she said nervously. "But we can all stay friends. . . ."

Sammy gripped his cloth cap so tight, his knuckles gleamed white. He wanted to hit her smiling face.

"What have you done to count yourself *his friend?*" he snarled. "You don't even know him. Not *really* know him, the way I do. He doesn't *need you.* He doesn't need any weak woman leeching onto him. He needs a friend who'll look out for him, who'll help him, who'll be there for him, whatever happens. Josh has got nothing to give you."

"But he saved my life—"

"And bloody near lost his own doing it. He didn't tell you what your father did to him, did he? No, of course he didn't. He's probably forgotten about it already. Josh always conveniently forgets anything *unpleasant.* Just ask him and watch his eyes go blank. 'No,' he'll say, 'I didn't do that, Sammy,' and all the time you know bloody-well he did."

"I don't know what you are talking about," she whispered, frightened. "I love Josh and he loves me and we're going to get married and that's all there is to it."

He took a step closer and his voice dropped to a menacing whisper. "All right, you've asked for it. Why d'ya think Josh ran away from home? Why d'ya think he's here, in San Francisco? You think you know all about him, but I'll bet he's never told you that. Well, now *I* will. *He's running from the police.*"

His boots clomped heavily on the bare wooden boards as he paced the room. His fists were clenched and his brow knotted in anguish. Francie's knees turned to jelly with fear as she watched him and she sank into the chair. "But *why* is Josh running from the police?" she asked.

Sammy flung back his head. He closed his eyes and said slowly, *"Because Josh Aysgarth is a killer."*

Terrified, Francie stared at him. She told herself he just wanted to frighten her and she knew he had succeeded. She said tremulously, "You're just jealous, that's all."

He looked consideringly at her. "I'm here to warn you. He's already killed three women, all young and pretty like you. Stabbed them to death." He reached out and put a finger on her neck. "In the throat . . . just where the pulse beats. That's what he told me, he said it's the best place." He glanced out the window at the big round moon. "And it always happens when the moon is full. You'd better believe me, Miss Harrison. You'd better get out of here, out of his way. You've no time to lose."

Francie knew he must be crazy and she said, "What kind of a friend would say a terrible thing like that?"

"A *true* friend," he said bitterly. "That's what you will never understand."

She was so frightened of him now, she thought she might faint, but she said, "I'll never believe you. And I'll never leave Josh. *Never.*" She sank back in the chair, flinching as he took a step toward her; his fists were clenched and he boiled with anger. Then he seemed to pull himself together. He walked past her and out the door. "Don't say I didn't warn you," he called over his shoulder.

Francie quickly locked the door, leaning against it, her heart thudding, then she ran to the window and stared out at the great pale moon lighting up the city, thinking about what he had said. She ran her fingers along the smooth curve of her throat, letting them rest on the fluttering pulse at the base. He stabbed them there, Sammy had said, *it was the best place.*

She sat on the bed and wrapped the blanket around her, cold with fear, waiting for Josh.

The minutes ticked slowly by until eleven, and when at last she heard his footsteps on the stairs, she ran to the door and flung it open and hurled herself into his arms.

"What's the matter, lass?" he asked, holding her close. "You're shaking like a leaf." Francie looked into his gentle gray eyes and at his good, familiar face and she knew what Sammy had said was impossible, but she still could not stop crying.

Josh picked her up and carried her to the bed; he lay down beside her and held her close. He stroked her short silken blond hair and kissed the tears from her eyes and then he kissed her mouth, drawing her even closer to him until she forgot all about evil Sammy Morris. She just wanted to stay in his arms forever.

His hand found her breast and her heart turned over. She trembled as he slowly unfastened the buttons and kissed her naked body and she was filled with happiness. He was holding her so close that they were almost one and at last she knew what it felt like to be loved.

It seemed such a natural thing to be in his arms, to share their bodies the way they shared their thoughts. She was young and innocent and happier than any woman ever could be, to be clasped in the arms of a man who loved her.

The next day Josh bounded eagerly up the stairs to Francie's room, his arms full of daffodils. He knocked impatiently on the door. "Hurry up, Francie, it's me," he called, smiling as he heard her quick footsteps.

She flung open the door and for a long moment they just looked at each other. He thought he had never seen anyone so lovely—her blond helmet of hair shone, her sapphire eyes sparkled, and she was smiling at him, half-hesitant, half-shy. And she thought she had never seen love in anyone's eyes like that, so warm and gentle and beautiful.

"Surprise," he said, thrusting the bouquet into her arms.

"Daffodils!" She buried her nose delightedly in them, inhaling their delicate fragrance. "The flowers of spring." She threw her arms around him. "Thank you, thank you so much for loving me!"

Their lips met in a long kiss and as he drew his mouth away she glanced shyly up at him. "I'll never forget last night."

Tilting her chin with his finger he kissed her again. "Aye. And nor will I. But I can't stay, I'm on my way to work and I'm already late."

She leaned over the banister, watching as he ran lightly down the stairs. He paused on the landing to wave and the sunlight filtering through the dirt-encrusted sash window turned his blond hair into a halo, and she thought how beautiful he was, and how good, and she knew Sammy Morris was the evil one. She smiled as she turned back into her room and saw the daffodils and thought how rich her life was even though they were so poor.

Through the open window she could hear the clatter of horses' hooves and the rattle of the trolley cars and the cries of newspaper boys with the early evening editions. The street vendors were loudly hawking their roasted peanuts and pretzels, and music wafted gaily from the Venus Dance Hall next door.

She sewed buttons onto Josh's shirt, waiting for the hours to pass until she saw him again, thinking about her long imprisoned childhood and her brutal father. She had wished him dead and she did not regret her words one bit. He had locked her away from life, he'd stolen her childhood and her youth and she hated him just as passionately as she loved Josh Aysgarth.

\* \* \*

Josh was late. The round tin alarm clock with its twin bells showed four o'clock, then five, and still he didn't come. Francie watched the minutes ticking away until six and then she could bear it no longer. Wrapping her shawl over her head, she hurried down the stairs to the saloon.

The bar was crowded with groups of men in dark suits and derby hats drinking whisky with beer chasers and reading the evening newspapers by the light of the hissing gas lamps. Cigarette smoke wreathed around the raftered ceiling and there was an earthy smell of male sweat and sawdust and ale. A group of women from the bordello next door were seated at one of the little marble-topped tables, flamboyant in big feathered hats and bright dresses. As she walked past they called for more gin, laughing raucously, and a buxom woman with impossibly red hair looked her up and down and called mockingly, "What have we got here, then? The orphan of the storm?"

The men at the bar turned to look at her, laughing, and Francie clasped her shawl tighter, looking desperately for Josh. A burly man in shirt sleeves and apron called to her from behind the counter. "Yeah?" he said. "What d'ya want?"

"Pardon me," she said in a small voice, "but I was looking for Josh."

"Speak up," he cried, "I can't hear ya' in this racket."

She repeated it loudly. "I'm looking for Josh Aysgarth."

The customers stared interestedly at her and the bartender smiled knowingly. "Josh Aysgarth, is it? Well, you've missed him. He finished a couple of hours ago."

"Finished?" she asked, bewildered.

"That's right. His friend Sammy came for him and they went off together." He went back to serving his customers and Francie turned away uncertainly.

"Stood you up, has he?" the raucous red-haired woman yelled. "Can't say I blame him, looking like that. Get yourself a new dress, honey, and some new . . ." she put her hand over her mouth and said something to the other women and they burst into shrill shrieks of laughter.

The red-faced man leaning against the counter tossed back his drink, watching thoughtfully, as, averting her eyes from the group of women, Francie hurried across the sawdust-covered floor to the door.

Then he picked up his newspaper, flung the barman a few coins and quickly followed her.

Francie ran back upstairs to the room Josh shared with Sammy and tapped on the door. There was no reply. She knocked again, waiting worriedly, wondering if Josh was sleeping, or if maybe he was ill. She was sure he wouldn't just go away without telling her. Not now. The door was unlocked and she pushed it open and peered in. The two beds were made up, and Sammy's brown wool muffler lay across a chair. Francie shivered. The empty room felt chilly and impersonal; it didn't feel like Josh at all. She walked slowly back to her own room. She had no idea where Josh was or even if he would be coming back.

The hours ticked slowly by, evening changed to night, but still he did not return. She heard the drunken shouts of revelers on the streets and the strains of music from the dance hall and remembered how happy and alive it had made her feel only that morning. The moon shone brilliant as a spotlight through her window and she could see the clock said three A.M.

The endless night was worse than any she had spent alone in her old room on Nob Hill because then she had not been in love. In the moonlight the pretty daffodils Josh had given her looked like stage props in a play that had taken place years ago, instead of just that morning. She closed her eyes and lay perfectly still; her life was suspended until Josh came back, and if he didn't come back, she knew she would just die.

The moon faded, the sun took its place, and the street was suddenly filled with noise and life again. And still Josh did not come.

Francie lay still as death on her bed, so drained of emotion she couldn't even cry. It was two o'clock in the afternoon and outside the call newsboys were shouting, "Extra, Extra." She heard another noise, a faint rustling outside her door. She leapt up and flung it open, but no one was there. Just a copy of the Extra the newsboys were crying in the street. The huge black banner headline shouted the news: WOMAN MURDERED—STABBED TO DEATH IN BARBARY COAST ALLEY.

Francie closed her eyes, afraid to read anymore. She dropped the newspaper and sank down onto the bed, but her eyes were drawn back to the terrible headlines. And across the top of the paper she saw scrawled in pencil: *Don't say I didn't warn you.*

The words danced before her eyes as she read about the girl . . .
"only twenty-one . . . brutally stabbed, her throat slashed . . ."

Her hand stole to her own throat and she groaned out loud as she
remembered Josh's gentle smiling face as he had waved good-bye to
her only yesterday. But Josh had not been home last night. And it
had all happened exactly as Sammy had said it would.

# CHAPTER 11

◆

## *1906*

A thin, dank fog rolled in from the bay, shrouding the wharfside tenements, and fingering the windows of the grand houses on Nob Hill. Its chilly tendrils touched the soft cheeks of the women hurrying home along lonely nighttime streets, making them shudder and glance nervously over their shoulders, as if they already felt the murderer's touch.

But Francie slept the sleep of the exhausted. She did not hear the door open, did not even know Josh was there until she felt his hand on hers and his breath against her cheek.

"So cold," he murmured, "you are so cold, little lass."

Too frightened to move, she watched him cross the room and turn up the gas lamp. He walked to the window and stared out at the fog, his brow furrowed, and then he turned to look at her. He picked up the newspaper and read the bold, black, terrible headlines.

"Sammy told me about you," she sobbed. "I said he was just jealous, that it was all a lie, I wouldn't believe him. But it happened, just the way he said it would."

He sat next to her on the bed and put his hand under her chin. "Do you believe him, Francie?"

She looked at the face of the man she loved, the man who had saved her life, not threatened it. Goodness radiated from him, even the nuns had said so. Yet Sammy had known a girl would be murdered and Josh had been out all night. . . .

He said quietly, "What if I told you I would never kill any living creature, not even the lowliest moth."

"But Sammy was so plausable."

"Aye, Sammy is always that. And many's the time I've regretted it. We swore when we were little lads we would never let each other down. 'Thick and thin' was what we said. And we've both kept that promise."

He stared sadly at her and then said, "He told you how we ran from the police? I didn't want to believe it was Sammy, my friend who had done those murders, but now I know it's true. He came to the bar yesterday afternoon full of wild talk, he told me what he'd said to you and I was afraid for you. I followed him from bar to bar, dance hall to dance hall. I saw him with a girl, but then I lost him, he just disappeared. And now this. He's insane," he said, his gray eyes full of bitter disillusionment. He held out his hand and said, "Please believe me, Francie. Sammy is the killer, not me."

"Oh, of course I believe you, Josh. I'll always believe you," she cried, her young face glowing with love.

He put his arms around her, kissing her hair, her eyes, her lips. "You look exhausted," he said tenderly, "and I'll bet you've not eaten. Let's go to a café."

As she walked down the stairs on Josh's arm all thoughts of Sammy and the murder disappeared into the back of her mind like a bad dream. She was so relieved and happy she didn't even notice the burly, red-faced man in the derby hat detach himself from the crowd outside the Venus Dance Hall and follow them at a discreet distance down Pacific Avenue.

And she didn't know either that Sammy Morris heard them leave. He waited, his ear against the door of his room, until their footsteps disappeared. Then he ran quickly up the half dozen steps into Francie's room. A look of bitterness and despair crossed his face and he put his hands to his eyes to shut out the sight of the rumpled bed where they had lain together, and at the newspaper with its terrible headline tossed carelessly on the floor as though it didn't even matter. He fingered the bowie knife in his pocket, thinking of them lying together in the bed, his sick mind inflamed with rage and jealousy, and then he turned and stalked from the room.

Harmon Harrison and his handsome young son, Harry, walked up the steps into the Grand Opera House near Mission Street. The season had started badly, but tonight the Metropolitan was redeeming itself with a performance of *Carmen* featuring the legendary tenor Enrico Caruso as Don José, and everyone who was anyone in San Francisco was there. Harmon waved and nodded to their friends as he and Harry took their places in their box. The orchestra struck up the overture, the enormous crystal chandeliers dimmed, and the curtain slowly rose. With a rustle of anticipation the glittering audience settled down to hear the voice of the century in one of his most famous roles.

But even though the performance was magical, Harmon could not concentrate. He could not get his daughter out of his mind. He told himself that all women were the same, that Francie was just like his own whore of a mother, the woman from Maloney's Cat House, Virginia City. The memory of her burned him like hot coals; his doctors had told him he had developed ulcers and that his blood pressure was too high. They said he should relax and forget all about his worries but he could not. His fingers drummed nervously on the burgundy velvet of the chair arm while his eyes darted restlessly to and fro across the shadowy audience looking to see if people were watching him, if they were gossiping about him and his slut of a daughter.

He stared at his son. Harry was leaning forward in his chair, his chin in his hands, listening to the great tenor, and Harmon vowed that nothing would ever sully his boy's reputation. He would not rest until he had locked Francesca behind the bars of the state asylum, where she could never ever tarnish the Harrison name again.

After the performance he took Harry to Signóre Caruso's champagne reception at the Palace Hotel and then on to a late supper party, and it was after four o'clock when they finally returned home. The footmen had the door open before the expensive new Stanley Steamer automobile had even stopped, and the butler said a gentleman was waiting to see him. "I told him you would be very late, sir, but he insisted on waiting. He said you would be expecting him."

The red-faced man hovered in the background, his derby hat clutched to his beefy chest, and Harmon said, "Take him to my study, I'll be with him in a few moments."

"Who is it, Father?" Harry stared, surprised, at the odd, late-night visitor.

"Go to your room, son. What he has to tell me is not for your ears."

When his father went to his study and the butler had disappeared into the servants' quarters Harry tiptoed back down the hall and put his ear to the door.

"I noticed the girl when she came into the Barbary Saloon," the man was saying. "I saw right away she fitted the description, sir. She looked pale and nervous and even though she had a shawl over her head I could see her hair was blond. She asked the bartender for a man called Josh Aysgarth. He told her he wasn't there but I understand that Aysgarth works at the saloon. Naturally I followed her and saw that she went up the stairs into the Barbary Rooming House —it's over the top of the saloon, you understand."

"Yes, yes, yes," Harmon snarled impatiently.

"The bartender later established that Aysgarth also has a room there, and that he was paying the rental on the woman's room." Harry heard his father's quick indrawn breath and the sound of his fist slamming on his desk as he cursed her.

"Tonight, sir, I finally saw them together. They walked arm in arm down Pacific Avenue to a café. And afterward, they returned to that same rooming house. The man's arm was around her waist, sir, and they both went into her room. I waited for some time, but the man did not emerge. They are there now, sir."

"I'll kill her," Harmon roared. "This time I'll kill her. . . ."

Harry jumped back from the door. He ran back down the hall and waited by the foot of the stairs. A few moments later he saw the man come from the study, a wad of notes on his hand and a satisfied smirk on his face as the night-footman hurried him out through the servants' door.

His father strode into the hall. His face was a dark purple-red and contorted with fury. There was a pistol in his hand and Harry knew what he meant to do and he knew that even Harmon Harrison could not get away with that. He caught his arm urgently. "Father, no . . . *No.*"

"I'll kill her," Harmon raged. "You don't know what she's done—"

"Yes, yes I do," Harry cried. "I heard it all. But *you can't kill her,* Father. You'll only cause more scandal. Horsewhip them. Put her away in the state asylum the way you planned. It's only what she deserves, and no one will blame you for it."

Harry took the pistol from his father's hand. He ran to the study and carefully put it back in the top drawer of his father's desk, locked it and pocketed the key. Then he picked up the old dog lead and returned to the hall and gave it to his father. "Use this on them both," he said savagely, "and then we'll make sure she never bothers the Harrisons again."

Harmon strode to the door. He turned to look proudly at his tall, handsome, clear-thinking son. He said, "Harry, you just saved me from doing something very foolish. You kept a cool head. Thank you, my boy."

Dawn was breaking. The early morning air was still and clear, promising a fine April day, and Old St. Mary's Church clock struck five as Harmon drove by. His mind was churning with thoughts of Francie and her lover and he barely noticed the dray turn onto Pacific Avenue, almost into his path. He stepped on the brakes, sounding his klaxon and the big shire horses reared in terror, overturning the dray and hurling the driver onto the road. The man lay motionless amongst his fallen load of cabbages and Harmon cursed him for a fool. Now the road was completely blocked.

Workmen came running from the nearby produce market, grabbing the leading reins and trying to quiet the kicking horses, bending urgently over the drayman, shaking their heads as a cry went up for a doctor.

"Damned fool," Harmon said angrily, "almost ran me down. He should be more careful, driving a heavy dray like that, he might have killed me."

"Looks like he killed himself instead, sir," a shirtsleeved workman said bitterly.

"Killed himself?" Harmon shrugged. "You can be thankful there's only one of us dead."

A crowd had gathered and Harmon felt their eyes boring into him, taking in his smart automobile, his white tie and tails and his richness. He picked up the leather dog lead and said curtly, "I shall send my chauffeur to pick up the car. If any of you touch it you will have Harmon Harrison to deal with."

Slapping the leather strap against his thigh as he strode away, he burned to take his revenge on all women. The street was full of drays on their way from the early-morning market and he cursed the drivers; it seemed none of them could control their horses, the beasts were rearing and whinnying, dancing sideways across the road as though they had gone mad. There was a sudden rumble and he glanced up, expecting thunder clouds, but the sky was blue and innocent. The noise grew louder like the roar of an express train, and he glanced around again, puzzled. Then suddenly the road was undulating toward him in a great wave—it rose under him and hurled him to the ground. He struggled to his feet and staggered to the doorway of an adjacent building, but the roar became even louder and the earth shook so violently he was thrown to the ground again. Steel girders shrieked as they were wrenched apart and bricks and masonry crashed past his terrified eyes into the street. Then with a final mighty heave the building collapsed, and bellowing with fear like a wild animal, Harmon was buried beneath a ton of bricks and masonry.

Francie jolted awake, filled with a sense of foreboding. Josh was sleeping peacefully, one arm flung protectively over her. She heard a great roaring noise and she pressed her hands over her ears and sat up. But the noise grew even louder and the room began to shake. The vase of daffodils crashed to the floor and Josh flung his arms around her, pulling her closer. The whole earth seemed to shake, the room trembled and shivered, and the window exploded into a thousand glittering fragments. With a scream of steel the whole building crumbled, and still in the bed in which they had so recently made love they plummeted from the fourth floor of the Barbary Saloon and Rooming House into the basement.

# Part II

◆

# THE MANDARIN

# CHAPTER 12

◆

## *1906*

Lai Tsin was tall for a Chinese, pale-skinned and clean-shaven with narrow, piercing dark eyes and glossy black hair. He wore a blue high-necked smock, wide black cotton trousers, and black cotton shoes. He carried his worldly possessions in a straw pannier on his back and he clutched a small boy of maybe four years tightly by the hand.

They walked slowly up Stockton Street with the other Chinese refugees, hundreds of them fleeing the earthquake and the flames. Whole families walked together, the father at the head, his wife two steps behind and a stream of gaily clad children following in single file, each clutching the queue, or pigtail, of the child in front so they would not stray. Everyone carried or pushed or pulled something: prams and trunks crammed with ancestral scrolls and pictures, pots and dishes, bedding and bird cages, chairs and chests; they staggered under their heavy loads, hurrying to save what they could from the flames.

Lai Tsin paused at the top of the hill on the corner of California Street and looked back at what was left of San Francisco. A pall of gray smoke covered the city lit from beneath by a sinister orange glow. The fires had already devoured many of the important buildings, licking up masonry and marble as though it were wood and demolishing mere wood to instant ashes. Whole areas of the city were already gone and the firefighters were dynamiting buildings in the path of the flames in a desperate effort to save what was left. But by now the inferno had a life of its own, leaping easily across roofs and streets. The retail district had been devoured; the monumental Palace Hotel was a smoking ruin, as was most of Market Street and the areas around Russian Hill and Telegraph Hill, and now it had jumped Kearny Street into Chinatown. Aftershocks rippled the city, shaking nerves already stretched to the limit, but people were behaving in an orderly fashion, sitting stunned atop the hills, resignedly watching their homes burn.

After the first chaotic hour the citizens had thrown themselves into the dreadful task of digging out the wounded and the dead, but City Hospital had been destroyed and the other hospitals were badly damaged and no one could hold back the flames. It seemed to Lai Tsin that the very sky was on fire and he knew that by midnight Chinatown, too, would be just a heap of ashes.

His face was expressionless as he walked with the boy along California Street. Workers were hurriedly carrying treasures and paintings out of the old Mark Hopkins mansion, which had been donated by the millionaire's widow as an art school and gallery. It and the other big Nob Hill houses still stood intact, but the flames were spreading threateningly closer as the firemen battled with an uncertain water supply.

Unsure where to go, he sat on the steps of the mansion and took the tired little boy onto his knee. The child was poorly dressed, his little blue cotton smock was torn and his dark eyes darted about in terror. Lai Tsin gave him a rice cake to eat but there was nothing to drink and the child began to cry soundlessly as though he were too afraid to make any noise. Tears squeezed between his tightly shut eyelids and Lai Tsin held him close, patting his back soothingly. "It's all right, Little Son," he told him. "Do not cry for your mother and father. I will look after you."

After a while the child fell asleep, his thumb tucked securely into his mouth and his gay little cap with the multicolored ribbons askew. It was then that Lai Tsin noticed the girl.

Her face was as gray as the ashes and he could see a bandage beneath the shawl she wore wrapped around her head. She was dressed poorly in an old skirt and blouse and her bruised eyes looked haunted as she stared fixedly at the door of the grand mansion opposite.

Francie was unaware of Lai Tsin's eyes on her. She shrank back as a small dray drove swiftly up California Street and stopped outside the mansion, watching as the men leaped down and hurriedly removed a stretcher from the back of the cart, tucking the red blanket more securely over the body it contained before they lifted it and carried it up the steps.

Her eyes grew even wider as the door was flung open and she saw Harry standing there. His face was white and tense and his pale blue eyes were hard with anger.

She shrank quickly back into the shadows as she heard him say, "Bring my father in here, please," and the men obeyed. They placed the stretcher on the great oaken hall table and a few minutes later emerged from the house, pleased smiles on their faces as they pocketed their gold pieces.

The doors were wide open and Francie could see the staff gathered in the hall as Harry drew back the blanket and looked at his father lying broken and bloodied, his dead eyes still staring angrily at the world he could no longer see. Harry raised his eyes to the great stained-glass dome that glowed like a jewel in the light of the flames.

"You did this, Francesca," he cried savagely. "If he hadn't gone after you he would have been safe at home. You killed him just as surely as if you had taken a knife to him. And by God, I'll see you dead, if it's the last thing I do."

Standing in the shadows, Francie shivered. She knew Harry meant what he said and that his hatred was even more powerful than her father's. If Harry ever found her, he would keep his promise.

Lai Tsin saw the rich black chariot of the undertakers arrive and a silver-handled ebony coffin hurriedly carried in, and he stared puzzled at the young girl crouched in the shadows, watching. She seemed unaware of the rapidly approaching flames even though a great heat radiated from the streets below and the evil crackle foretold their doom. Even as he looked he saw a wisp of black smoke coming from the Hopkins mansion and then the sinister lick of yellow flame along the wooden fretwork edging the roof.

Gathering the sleeping boy to him he stood up, watching and waiting. Firemen were running urgently along the street, ordering everyone to leave. They knew they had no hope of saving the houses of the wealthy and their treasures.

Francie felt the heat of the fire on her skin, her eyes burned from the smoke, but she still could not leave. She watched and waited, mesmerized. A few moments later Harry opened the door. He ushered out a stream of frightened servants clutching their bags and baggage, watching as the grooms led away the terrified horses. Finally the butler walked back up the steps with half a dozen of the men and she moved closer, still in the shadows until she could see into the house that had been her home.

"Shall we carry the coffin out, sir?" the butler asked as the men respectfully held their caps.

Harry surveyed them from the top of the steps. He looked back at the silver-handled coffin lying on the massive oaken hall table and then he shook his head. He said bitterly, "This house was built as my father's home. It is a monument to a great man. And now it will be his tomb."

Francie shivered as the hot wind soughed along the street. The window of the Fairmont Hotel suddenly exploded and flames shot from the empty sockets.

With one last long look at his father's coffin Harry closed the door and turned the key. Francie's eyes followed him as he walked down the steps and along California Street, followed by his retainers.

Lai Tsin watched him go and then walked over to her. She was staring at the house as though waiting for something to happen. "Come with me," he said in English, but she did not even turn her head. Puzzled, he looked across at the house. The whole street was burning now and there was not much time left.

Francie sighed deeply as the roof began to smoke. There was a hiss and a quick jet of flame and suddenly it was afire.

She turned slowly and looked at the Chinaman.

"Look," she said in a voice like a sigh. "It's burning. That terrible house is dying. I swore I would see him in his grave. And now he is."

And then without another word she fell into step beside him and they walked together down the street, away from the flames and the heat and into the unknown night.

# CHAPTER 13

It was a dark April morning and the gray clouds were so heavy with rain they were almost sitting on the roofs. Annie peered outside and thanked the Lord it was not Monday and a washday. Abandoning her plans to scrub the front steps, she slammed the door shut and contemplated what to do with the day.

The red Turkey-carpeted hallway was immaculate; the front-room, where no one ever sat except on highdays and holidays, was dust-free; and the kitchen, where they spent all their time, gleamed from endless hours of blacking and polish. Upstairs was cleaned to within an inch of its life. There was not a speck of dirt nor an unstarched shirt in the entire house. And it was Thursday, so tonight was shepherd's pie. Her father had always eaten the same meal on the same day each week, and Thursdays were always shepherd's pie.

A fire already burned brightly in the kitchen range and she lifted the kettle from the hob, took out the brown pot, spooned in some strong black tea and poured on the boiling water. Then she sank into her usual chair, waiting for the tea to brew.

It was early and her father was still in bed, the warm, shiny room that had been her world for the past ten years closed around her like a cosy trap. It looked the way it always had, the gleaming brass fender surrounding the dark-green tiled hearth, the wooden mantle with its red-velvet cover and the faded sepia family photos in silver frames, the circular brass vase holding the thin wooden spills her father used to light his pipe and the stuffed bird under the glass dome. She glanced around the room at the bronze gas jets with their fluted glass shades, at her father's favorite burgundy-velvet chair, sunken in the middle from years of sitting, and the embroidered white linen antimacassar over the back that she changed for a clean

112        ELIZABETH ADLER

one each morning. She looked at the shiny brown linoleum and the big fringed rug, faded and worn over the years to a muted maroon, and at the pine table covered in red-checkered oilcloth where she baked and prepared their meals. And at the wheelback Windsor chairs they sat on to eat; at the deep pot sink with its gleaming brass taps, the dresser stacked with blue and white dishes, and hanging over her head, the wooden clothes rack with its rope and pulley where every day of her life freshly washed or ironed clothes hung to air in the warmth from the fire. The big sash window looked out onto a paved backyard surrounded by drooping rhododendron and laurel bushes, and come summer she would fix up a window box with a few colorful petunias and busy-lizzies.

Annie closed her eyes and sighed. She had no need to look, it was all indelibly imprinted on her brain, as were the ticking of the mahogany clock and its sweet Westminster chimes, the faint whistle of the kettle perpetually steaming on the hob ready to brew a pot of tea for the visitors who nowadays never came, the hiss of the gas jets, and the blustering roar of the coal fire that was lit every day of the year, regardless of summer's warmth, to heat the big oven.

In her mind she could hear the click of her own knitting needles and see her father puffing on his eternal pipe as they sat silent evening after silent evening with the heavy velvet curtains drawn and the long hours stretching interminably ahead till bedtime and dawn and another identical day.

She sighed. It had been over a year now that Josh had been gone and hardly a minute went by that she did not think of him. The only communication she had from him was a picture-postcard of a saloon on San Francisco's Barbary Coast. It had arrived five months ago, carefully concealed in a brown manila envelope and said simply, "I am all right, do not worry about me. I did not do those terrible things. Please believe me. Your loving brother." She had read it and reread it a thousand times. Josh had been the one who brought life to this house and she had lived vicariously through him. When he had gone she had grieved like a mother for a lost son and she had never, never, believed what they said about him. Though most everyone else did. His brothers were so shamed they rarely came around anymore even to see their dad, and their wives kept his grandchildren firmly away, unwilling to be tainted by Josh's wickedness. Though they were not afraid to be tainted by Frank Aysgarth's money. In fact, it had got so that every time she saw Bertie or Ted coming up the path she knew what it was they were after.

"The old man's gone soft in the head," Bertie had told her. "It's best for us to get the business away from him or it'll go right down the hill. He'll not make decisions one way or t'other, and how can we build houses if he won't say yea or nay?"

She knew he was right, but she also knew they were taking over Frank's finances. Still, there was nothing she could do about it and her dad simply did not care, so she just went on knitting endless little jackets and bonnets in the finest, softest angora wool for the steady procession of babies that filled her brothers' households. And no one ever so much as mentioned the name Josh Aysgarth out loud.

She jumped up as she heard her father's footsteps on the stairs, quickly stirring fresh creamy milk into a saucepan of porridge oats and adding a pinch of salt the way he liked it. She put it on the hob to simmer while she sliced up the crusty white loaf she had baked yesterday, setting the jar of strawberry jam and the morning paper next to his plate as she always did, though he had never glanced at another newspaper since those first terrible headlines about his son. But she still took the *Yorkshire Post* and read it herself later in the afternoon when she had finished her self-imposed chores.

"Morning, Dad," she called cheerily, pulling his chair out from the table and pouring his tea. "Your porridge'll be ready in a few minutes. How about a nice rasher or two this morning and maybe some scrambled eggs?"

He shook his grizzled head, sinking into the chair with a loud sigh. "Porridge will do," he said.

He stared silently at his plate and Annie sighed exasperatedly. How many times had she argued that he had two other sons, that he had grandchildren, that he had a business and money in the bank. That Josh was innocent. But to no avail. "When you have a lad who's done what our Josh has done, that's something God will never forgive. And nor will I," he had told her. And that was all he had ever said on the subject to this day.

But this morning was different. Frank pushed the newspaper to one side the way he always did, only this time something took his eye.

MASSIVE QUAKE DEMOLISHES SAN FRANCISCO, the headline blared. THOUSANDS FEARED DEAD IN RAGING INFERNO.

"I'll bet there's a few houses I helped build gone down in that," he commented, stirring strawberry jam into the steaming bowl of porridge.

"What's that then, Dad?" she asked, astonished he had passed a comment on something other than his food or the house.

"This 'ere earthquake," he said, pushing away the porridge untouched and spooning sugar into his tea instead.

Annie was kneeling on the hearthrug toasting bread over the glowing coals on a long brass fork. Two slices lay ready on the flannel-wrapped hot brick, and her cheeks were pink from the heat. She glanced over her shoulder exasperatedly. "What earthquake, Dad?"

"The earthquake in San Francisco, like it says here in t'paper. Read it for yourself."

"San Francisco? An earthquake?" Dropping the toasting fork she ran to the table and grabbed the newspaper, scanning the story rapidly. Her eyes grew round with horror, her face turned pale, and she clutched her hand to her heart. "Oh Dad," she whispered, "it can't be true."

"It'll be true enough," he replied, sipping his tea. "There was allus a rumbling going on under that city even when I was there."

"You don't understand." She sank into her chair, covering her face with her apron so he would not see her tears. She thought of Josh in San Francisco, maybe dead, maybe buried under a shattered building or burned in the inferno. What could she do? *Oh, what could she do?* Her beloved, beautiful, innocent Josh . . .

After a while she dried her tears and picked up the newspaper again. Her father was still sitting quietly over his cup of tea, his breakfast lay untouched and he was puffing on his old pipe, filling the room with smoke the way he did every morning. She wanted to scream at him to stop it, that his son might be lying maimed under a ton of rubble or burned to ashes. Instead she read the story again.

It said news reports were still sketchy because all communications had been cut by the massive quake. The state of California had already sent help and the major American cities were dispatching food, blankets, clothing, and money to aid the survivors. The fire chief had been killed in the first tremor when the firehouse collapsed around him, and the water mains had fractured so there was no water to fight the blaze. The whole city was alight, nothing could save it. The brand-new eight-million-dollar City Hall had crumbled to dust, the fantastic Palace Hotel, the world's largest, was reduced to ashes and Nob Hill's mansions were even now being devoured by the flames.

The famous opera star, Enrico Caruso, escaped with his company on a specially commissioned train before the fires took hold. He said the city was "a hell of a place," and swore he would never come back. After the first shock the citizens had run into the streets, wondering what to do. When things quieted down, most of them decided to cook themselves some breakfast, and with the many broken gas mains the city soon had a dozen fires burning. There was no proper fire-alarm system and no water, and the fires had spread quickly until by noon the same day fifty separate fires were burning, leaping from wooden building to wooden building, gathering strength until they became one raging inferno, generating an evil sucking wind so hot that it melted anything in its path. "San Francisco is doomed," the report concluded, "along with many of its citizens."

Annie did not know how she got through that day. At four o'clock she rushed down Aysgarth's Hill to the corner shop and bought a copy of the *Evening Post* late edition, hoping for better news, but it said things were worse, the whole city was alight. Tented refugee camps were being set up in San Francisco's parks and across the bay in Oakland, where many had escaped to on the ferries. They said the citizens were fleeing from the flames, that boundfoot Chinese women unable to walk were being carried through the streets, that terrified children were running by their parents' sides clutching their toys while their elders struggled with dogs and cats and caged birds, pictures and pianos—whatever they treasured most they lugged with them. "Though what will become of them or their possessions no one knows."

Annie walked slowly back up the hill. She thought of all the nights she had knelt by her bed and prayed for proof of Josh's innocence so that he might return to her, and for his health and happiness far away in San Francisco, and she knew without a shadow of a doubt what she had to do. She trudged slowly up the hill, her eyes on the toes of her shiny black boots, thinking of her plan.

That night after his supper when Frank Aysgarth had sunk into his chair, lit his pipe and was staring silently into the flames as usual, she said, "Dad, I need to talk to you. There is something I have to do."

"Hmmph," he growled, not even looking at her.

"I have to go away, Dad," she said loudly. His head swiveled and he took the pipe from his mouth, astonished. "Away? Are y'daft in the head or summat? Don't talk rubbish, Annie." That settled, he puffed on his pipe again and stared back into the flames.

"I mean it, Dad," she persisted. "I have to go find Josh. You see, Dad, he went to San Francisco and I just have to know whether he's alive or dead. And if he's dead, then—then I'll see he's buried properly, in consecrated ground."

"They'll never bury a *murderer* in consecrated ground!" Frank roared. His face had turned beet red and he puffed angrily on his pipe, filling the kitchen with the powerful scent of his tobacco.

"Josh is innocent," she retorted. "Sammy Morris had him run off so quick he never even had a chance to defend himself. And all the police knew was Mrs. Morris's story that Sammy had found him standing over the woman's body."

She looked at her father, but he just puffed on his pipe, staring silently into the fire like always. Suddenly she saw a tear slide down his cheek and lose itself in his bristly gray moustache. Then another and another . . .

"Oh, Dad," she said helplessly, not knowing how to comfort him because she couldn't just go and throw her arms around him like she would have with Josh. "Don't take on so. Your youngest son's no murderer, I'll guarantee that. No matter what Sally Morris says or doesn't say."

"He finished me, Annie," he said, ignoring the tears pouring down his face. "Our Josh finished me off. A man has a right to look to the future through his sons. And he was my favorite, you know that, though I tried never to show it, I allus treated 'em all the same. I never expected anything like this in our family. Never."

Annie looked away from him, she could not bear to see his crumpled face and his shaking hands and the unstoppable tears that must have been damned up in him since Josh left. Frank Aysgarth was allowing himself the luxury of emotion for the first time in his life and she knew it was the best thing that could happen to him. After a while she said, "Dad, I'm going to San Francisco to find him. I'm going to clear his name—*our* name. You'll not go to your grave thinking your son a murderer. I'm asking you for two things, Dad. One is the money I need to go with. And the other is secrecy. Nobody must know where I've gone or why."

He looked at her, his face quivering, and for the first time in her life she pitied him. "You'll do that?" he whispered.

She nodded. "I promise."

"Then you shall have the money tomorrow. And it'll just be between you and me, Annie. Nobody else will know."

She smiled gratefully. "And I promise you will have your honor back—whether your son is dead or alive."

The next morning Frank Aysgarth was seen walking down the street for the first time in over a year. The neighbors ran to the door to watch him pass, noticing his white hair and hesitant step, wondering out loud what he did with himself all alone with Annie atop Aysgarth Hill.

"For all his money and success he's nobbut an old man now," they said, disappointed.

And Sally Morris, older and more bitter, leaned from her doorway and yelled after him, "I'm surprised y'dare show yer face around here after what Josh did. And making our Sammy run off with him like that. It's you and your rich ways that corrupted my lad, Frank Aysgarth, and God will never forgive you for it."

The neighbors sucked in their breaths in alarm as he stumbled and almost fell, but then he righted himself and stepped quickly along the street, staring straight in front of him as though he had never heard a thing.

Two hours later they saw him come back up the street again and disappear homeward up Aysgarth's Hill. A while later Annie Aysgarth hurried past and this time all the heads were turning, wondering what she was up to in such a hurry. And they were even more surprised when the following week a cab came to take Annie and all her boxes and baggage to the railway station, and Bertie Aysgarth and his wife and bairns moved into Ivy Cottage to take care of the old man.

# CHAPTER 14

◆

Lai Tsin was puzzled. In the six days since he had found the girl she had not spoken another word. She was as trusting as the child; when he brought her food and said "eat this," she ate; when he said "follow me," she followed; when he said "wait here," she waited. And he knew if he failed to return she would wait forever. She showed no curiosity about her circumstances nor the plight of the other two hundred and fifty thousand homeless camping out in the city's parks. She simply sat with the child in her lap, staring into space, suspended in time.

He sighed feelingly. It was a dilemma. He had taken responsibility for her as he would a person wounded in battle, afraid she had gone crazy from shock and her injuries. But he could not go on looking after her. He was a poor Celestial with many problems of his own. And she was an American lady.

"Lady?" he said, leaning toward her, careful not to touch her, for that would have been impertinent and above his station. "Lady?" he repeated. Her sapphire eyes swiveled uncomprehendingly toward him. He could tell she was waiting for him to say what she should do next and he sighed again. "You must stay here with the other refugee American ladies," he said, taking five dollars from the secret pocket under his smock and putting it in her lap. "Good-bye, lady," he called, hoisting his straw pannier onto his shoulder, but she did not answer.

He and the child walked a few yards, then he turned to look at her. A big tear slid down her cheek. He stared doubtfully at her. The tears spilling from her eyes were big and shiny as crystals and there was an air of utter loneliness about her that struck a painful chord in his memory.

He walked back again and said, "All this time you not cry, and now you cry. Why?"

She shook her head. The big crystal tears flowed even faster, like a long-dry river after rain. "I thought you were my friend," she whispered desolately, "and now you are leaving me."

"It is not possible to be friends. I am a lowly Celestial, a poor Chinese and you"—he looked at her cheap dress, her shawl, her rough boots—"you are a lady."

She rubbed her eyes with her fists, trying to stem the tears, and he noticed the blue shadows beneath her eyes, the fragile pallor of her skin and the frailty of her narrow wrists. His heart stung with pity for her, but he knew he must leave her with her own kind.

The boy waiting at his side tugged at his trouser leg and began to cry too. He patted his head soothingly, still watching the girl.

"I would rather be your friend," she sighed.

He considered the matter carefully, aware that her eyes never left his face. "It will be very difficult," he said finally.

"Nothing can be more difficult than what I have already suffered."

Her voice rang with bitterness and Lai Tsin nodded. "Then let us go," he said, shouldering his straw pannier and taking the boy by the hand.

She scrambled to her feet and fell into step beside him, and somehow he knew that if he had said "We shall walk to the ends of the earth together," she would have gone with him. It was their fate.

After a mile or so he stopped to buy food at a makeshift roadside stall, taking money from the secret pocket under his smock to pay for it. He handed over fifteen cents, carefully replacing the few notes left and then he carried the hot soup and slabs of buttered bread to where she was sitting on a clump of fallen stones. The boy was on her lap and he had his arms around her neck. The gods had performed a miracle. She was smiling.

"Eat," Lai Tsin said, pressing the tin mug into her hand. "You must get strong."

He watched as she sipped the soup, closing her eyes and savoring it, thinking worriedly of the five dollars left in his pocket. It was all he had in the world. His precious book from the Chinese credit showed one hundred and three dollars and twenty cents in his name, but the money must surely have burned with the rest of San Francisco. He sighed. He had won that money gambling at mah-jongg; it was all he had from his past and it was to have been his stake in the future. It was very bad joss, but still, he was alive and unharmed.

There was a new pink glow to her cheeks as they walked on, her step was firmer and she took the child's hand, smiling down at him as he trotted to keep up. People turned to stare angrily after them and Lai Tsin knew they did not approve of the Western woman with the Chinese man. He realized they would not accept them together at the refugee camps in the park and he kept his eyes open for a shelter. They passed another stall by the road selling small canvas tents. "How much?" he asked. The man looked at him consideringly. "Ten bucks to Celestials," he said contemptuously, "and cheap at that price."

Lai Tsin turned away, aware of the man's angry speculative eyes following them as they walked down the road. It was getting dark and he knew he must find shelter soon. His eyes darted this way and that as they marched on. The boy grew tired and he picked him up. Just as darkness fell he saw the place. It was all that was left of a row of artisans' cottages and it had been sliced down the middle as cleanly as if by a knife. The walls of the upper rooms had fallen in but downstairs looked intact. The door was gone and he walked in and looked around. Checkered gingham curtains flapped at the glassless window and a wooden table with bulbous legs lay half-buried beneath a layer of grit. There was a black horsehair sofa in front of the fire grate and a heavy oak dresser stood upright with a row of dusty plates that had somehow survived unbroken. He inspected the ceiling carefully; there were a few big cracks but it seemed safe enough. It would do for the night.

He righted the sofa and brushed it off and said, "Please to sit down, lady."

Francie sank down thankfully and he lay the tired little boy beside her. He looked at her and said nervously, "Lady, I am Chinese. I enter America with no papers. I make a small living by gambling. I have no past, lady, and no future. Only *today*. It is the way I have always been forced to live, and my family before me. I can offer you nothing."

Francie thought carefully about what he had said and realized they were alike. She nodded. "Then we are lucky, you and I. The earthquake has buried my past and taken my future. I, too, have only today."

"Maybe it was good joss after all," he agreed.

While the little boy slept she helped him search the ruins for bedding or blankets, anything to cover them, for the night was cold and
it was forbidden to light fires. Then, exhausted, she curled up next to
the boy and fell asleep. Lai Tsin covered them gently with a ragged
pink quilt, and wrapped in an old curtain he kept watch until dawn
came.

He thought about her as she slept. He remembered the hatred in
her voice when she had watched the house burn and he knew she
must have suffered because he was no stranger to that emotion himself. He had lived all his life with brutality, loneliness, fear, and hate.
Yet when she awoke he did not ask her for an explanation. He knew
the time would come when she would want to unburden herself and
then she would tell him the truth.

The next day they moved on, leaving their temporary shelter without a backward glance. "Where are we going?" the child asked in
Cantonese, tugging at Francie's skirt.

"To the next place," Lai Tsin answered calmly. He had no idea
where that might be but it was enough to satisfy the boy and he
ambled uncomplainingly at his side.

After a while they came across a park filled with small white tents.
People were sitting on the grass in the morning sunshine, chatting or
reading newspapers while others stood in line for the free breakfast
being served from the backs of wooden carts. There was a smell of
hot coffee and bread and the boy tugged hungrily at Francie's skirt
again. She stood in line for the breakfast and an issue of blankets, and
they ate quickly, sitting away from the crowd. Then throwing their
blankets over their shoulders, Francie and the boy followed Lai Tsin
wherever he would take them.

For the next few days Lai Tsin looked after her like a little sister;
he found food for her, he sought nightly shelter for her, and he spent
all his money. He asked no questions and she barely spoke. Until one
night they were sitting by the fire he had built amongst the rubble.
The little boy was sleeping and the stark black smouldering ruins of
San Francisco were silhouetted against the ink-blue sky and Francie
said, "There is something I must tell you."

She hid her face in her hands and he waited patiently; he knew she
would go on. She needed to cleanse her soul.

He was right. The words spilled from her lips as she told him her
name—and her father's—Harmon Harrison. "I can see even you
have heard of him," she said bitterly as he reacted to the name.

"Everyone in San Francisco knows of him," he replied, his black eyes suddenly unfathomable.

She told him how he had hated her, and about her brother, Harry. "If he ever finds that I'm still alive he'll put me behind bars in the state asylum and then he'll kill me," she said, terrified. She told him how she had met Josh and fallen in love, and how he had saved her. She said how beautiful he was. "And good, like an angel," she said with a long sigh. "Even the nuns said so." She told him about Josh and Sammy and about the murders, and how Josh had not wanted to believe it was Sammy, but he knew it was. And she put her head despairingly in her hands, reliving the moment the earthquake struck.

"Suddenly we were plunging into an abyss and everything was falling on top of us," she said. "I thought I was dreaming, that it was a nightmare. There was a great weight on my chest and my mouth was full of dust. I was choking, gasping until I thought my lungs would burst. I opened my eyes and I was looking into Josh's face. We were still lying on the bed, our arms were around each other, and his body was the weight I felt on top of me. A little light was coming from a hole above us, there was a terrible rending noise and an enormous beam came crashing down onto Josh's back, pinning him down on top of me. I could hear him breathing, harsh, rasping breaths like a file on metal. I tried to pull myself from under him but he was too heavy, he was still trapped by the beam. I could feel the stickiness of blood and I did not know if it was my own or his and I knew I had to get help. I eased my body inch by inch from under him. I don't know how long it took, maybe minutes, maybe hours, but finally I was free and I scrambled to my feet."

"I could still hear his harsh breathing and I remembered it was the same sound I had heard when my mother was dying. He was moaning, and I put my hands over my ears. I couldn't just leave him there to die. I tried to lift the beam lying across his back but it wouldn't move and then I knelt beside him and put my arms under his shoulders, trying to tug him out from under it. For a moment I thought I was succeeding, then suddenly the earth shook again and the beam slipped. There was a rumble and out of the corner of my eye I saw the chunk of falling masonry. Without thinking I jumped back and put my hands over my head to save myself, and instead it fell on Josh. I knelt beside him. I didn't know what to do. He was as still as death. Suddenly he lifted his head and looked at me." She stared, trembling, at Lai Tsin, hardly daring to remember, then she said slowly, "That beautiful angel's face was just a mass of blood and bone."

Lai Tsin was silent. He made no effort to comfort her. He knew there were some things that could never be expiated by mere words, there were some burdens too terrible ever to be rid of and man was doomed to carry them with him to the grave.

"I couldn't move," she said in a voice like a sigh. "I waited beside him, his harsh breathing became slower and slower, smaller and smaller . . . and finally there was only silence and I knew he was dead. I pulled the blanket from the bed behind him and covered him with it. And then I walked away and left him alone in his tomb.

"I don't remember how, but I found myself on the street. Only there was no street anymore, just rubble. There was the glow of many fires and people were running, but I did not know where. I followed them . . . someone helped me . . . they bandaged my head and gave me clothes. They took me to the hospital on a horsecart, only the hospital was no longer there. There were so many people in the street, patients, doctors, nurses, so many people wounded and sick. I turned away. I knew I had to go home. I had to see what had happened. And in my heart I was wishing my father had died too."

She looked bleakly at Lai Tsin. "I went home," she said. "You were there. You saw what happened. I got my wish."

He said gravely, "Little Sister, my heart bursts with compassion for you. But it was not your wish that killed your father and destroyed your home. Your father stole your youth from you and gave everything to his son. You did not kill him, nor did you kill your lover. It was fate. Now it is time, Little Sister, to become your own person. You must forget youth and passion and control your own fortune so that fate will not treat you so contemptuously. It is time to pick up your life strings and go on."

Francie rubbed the tears from her eyes. She wrapped her arms around her knees, leaning forward, staring at him, really seeing him for the first time. Her savior was not a young man, though she could not have said his age. His oval face was delicately boned with deep, almond-set eyes, high cheekbones, and a wide, firm mouth. He was thin, with a look of deprivation, and an undefinable quality that had nothing to do with the shabbiness of his clothes nor how little money there was in his secret pocket. It was in his face; it had been passed down through generations and spoke of grinding hardship and endless sorrows and a depth of poverty she could not even begin to comprehend.

"You are very wise, Lai Tsin," she said quietly. "As wise as the Mandarins."

He bowed. "You must sleep now," he said. "You must forget your bad memories, forget the blows that have befallen you. Sleep like the child, Little Sister, and tomorrow you shall begin life anew. You will not forget, but you will bear your burden without looking back."

She lay obediently down beside the little boy and Lai Tsin placed a blanket carefully over them. And then he sat by the fire thinking for a long time of what he knew about Harmon Harrison. Then he put the bad thoughts behind him and turned to watch them as they slept. They were just two children, he thought pityingly. Fate had deprived them of their childhood, just the way it had him. Now it had united them and they would all face the future together. Tomorrow.

# CHAPTER 15

It was raining, a short sharp shower with heavy gray clouds scudding fast through the sky. Francie hurried up the hill to California Street, pausing near the top to catch her breath. Her cheeks were pink from the wind and raindrops glistened on the fringe of blond hair sticking out the front of her gray shawl. It was three weeks since the earthquake. Three weeks since Josh had died. And three weeks since her brother had committed her father's body to the flames.

Now she had to lay his ghost. She had read that morning in the *Chronicle* that there was to be a memorial service for Harmon Harrison. It said that his son, Harry, brave in the face of his personal tragedy, had declared that he would rebuild the family mansion on Nob Hill "to show the world that nothing, not even an act of God, could destroy the Harrisons."

The report had also said Harmon Harrison was the richest man in San Francisco and that he had left his entire estate to his son. There was just one small exception; a ranch in the Sonoma Valley belonging to his late wife had been deeded by her to the daughter, Francesca, but the girl had not been seen since the earthquake and was now presumed dead.

She walked slowly along California Street, skirting the blackened Fairmont Hotel, staring at the ruins. Workmen were sifting methodically through the debris, loading carts with rubble and putting aside anything that might have survived—a scrap of mosaic, a marble bust, a satin shoe.

Only the facade of the Harrison house remained. Francie walked between the scorched Doric columns, up the familiar white marble steps and into the hall. She stared upward. The great stained-glass dome was no more and the house stood open to the pouring rain.

With her foot she cleared a patch of dust from the black-and-white marble floor and saw it had cracked into a million tiny pieces. She shivered as she looked around her. Somewhere in that dust and rubble were the ashes of her father and she felt he was here, just as surely as if he were still alive.

She ran, shuddering, from the house, sprinting down the hill as fast as she could. She was glad she had no part of her father's inheritance. She would rather be poor and free.

By now she had become used to the scenes of ruin and desolation, yet down the hill the streets had an oddly festive air. Folks stood chatting in a neighborly fashion outside their makeshift dwellings, chairs and sofas lined the sidewalks, women cooked on outdoor stoves and men nailed orange crates into tables. Children ran through the ruins, dancing to the music of the organ-grinder, laughing at the antics of his monkey while street vendors hawked their wares to anyone who had money left to spend. The stricken city had an air of camaraderie and jollity as people made light of their hardship. "After all," they said to each other, "everyone is in the same boat."

Like the other two hundred and fifty thousand homeless refugees, Francie and Lai Tsin and the boy took whatever handouts the city gave them, dining for fifteen cents at the relief kitchens, or for free with Red Cross tickets when the money ran out. There was mush and hot biscuits and coffee for breakfast; soup and a plate of beef and vegetables for dinner; and Irish stew, bread, and tea for supper. They were living in their little shack on the edge of Chinatown and making do, like the others, as best they could.

Lai Tsin was sitting on an orange crate in their makeshift lean-to, showing the boy how to count on an old wooden abacus. He smiled at Francie. Taking some money from the secret pocket under his smock he offered it to her and said proudly, "See how much money I have."

She quickly counted it, then glanced at him astonished and said, "But Lai Tsin, this is more than a hundred dollars."

"One hundred and three dollars and twenty cents," he agreed, beaming. He held out a small black book and said, "The Chinese credit reopened today. All my money was not burned as I had thought. Today they pay me."

He beamed again and she laughed. "Why, Lai Tsin, you are rich after all."

"Tonight I play *pai-gow*," he said confidently, pocketing the money, "and I get richer."

She stared at him, shocked. "You mean, you are going to gamble all that money?"

His face was suddenly expressionless. "That is what I do," he said, turning away.

She looked wistfully after him as he wended his way through the crowded street past the sewing machines and wash tubs and strings of hanging laundry, past the chiffoniers and trestle-tables, the painted screens and red banners and the improvised cooking-stoves made from bits of scrap metal and bricks. And she thought of what the hundred and three dollars and twenty cents might have bought: shoes for the boy, bedrolls, candles, soap, food that they could pay for instead of receiving from charity. She shook her head. The money was not hers, it was Lai Tsin's and he must do what he wished with it. And she must think about getting a job.

She went back into the shack and began to prepare the boy's supper of bread and milk, looking up, surprised, as Lai Tsin flung the curtain aside. He pushed fifty dollars into her hand and said quickly, "Before, I was alone. Now I am a man of responsibility. I am not free to gamble away all the family money. We must buy Little Son some shoes and other things Little Sister needs." He bowed quickly and was gone.

She sat stunned on the orange crate, the fifty dollars clutched in her hand. The boy looked up from his abacus and smiled at her. "Little Son," Lai Tsin had called him. And she was "Little Sister." A warm feeling crept around Francie's heart. Lai Tsin and the boy were more of a family to her than her flesh and blood had ever been.

He returned very late that night and by the light of the guttering candle she could see that his face was long. He sighed as he sank onto the crate and put his head in his hands. "Joss forsook me tonight, Little Sister," he said in a mournful singsong. "*Aiee, aiee,* how it deserted me."

Her heart sank as she thought of his savings. "Oh, Lai Tsin, you lost all your money," she gasped.

He shook his head. "I am a very good gambler. I won, but the man I gambled with had no money to pay me. Instead he gave me this paper. He told me it was worth eighty dollars, maybe more. . . ."

Francie took the paper from him. It was written on thin parchment with Chinese lettering at the top and a red seal. Underneath was written in English:

"Leasehold for a term of nine hundred and ninety-nine years to a Parcel of Land in the Central District of Hong Kong, running between Des Voeux Road and Queens Road, the exact area and dimensions of which are defined in the map hereunder."

She stared at him, surprised. "But Lai Tsin, this is the deed to a piece of land in Hong Kong. It says the lease was sold by the Mon Wu Land Company to a Mr. Huang Wu.

He nodded. "Huang Wu was Chung Wu's grandfather. The land became Chung Wu's and now it is mine. Here is his letter saying it belongs to me."

He handed her a scrap of paper written in Chinese and she gave it back to him. "You must translate it for me," she said.

He held the paper at arm's length, clearing his throat and shifting his feet. Finally he shook his head. He stared at the floor, embarrassed, and said, "Little Sister, it is my eternal sorrow that I have never learned to read or write."

Francie blushed; she had caused him to lose face and by now she knew how important the facade of politeness and respect was to a Chinese. "I'm sorry," she said.

He shrugged, his thin face expressionless. "My family was poor, there were no scholars amongst us. There was no time and no money for learning. All I know are my numbers. From the age of four I worked in the mulberry fields, harvesting the leaves and packing them into hampers. I worked in the rice fields, helping plant the new shoots, or tended the ducks on the duck-farm owned by the village big lord. It has always been my wish to cultivate my mind instead of the fields, but it was not my fate. We were seven sons and one daughter and all had to work, for without our labor no one would eat." He sighed. "And now I am more than thirty years old and I am still as poor as when I was a child of four. Fate is my master, Little Sister. She has not destined Lai Tsin for scholarship and greatness."

"That is not true," Francie said earnestly. "You *can* be a great man, Lai Tsin, greater than your village lord. You *can* be a scholar. I will teach you myself to read and write."

He smiled sadly at her across the guttering candle. "I was like you when I was young," he said gently, "full of foolish hopes. Now I am older and wiser and I tell myself I am Lai Tsin, the unscholared gambler. It is my destiny."

He sat opposite her on the floor and said, "I am not like the other San Francisco Chinese, who come from Toishan. My village is in the province of Anhwei on the banks of the Yangtze, called by us 'Ta Chiang, The Great River,' because it is the highway of China. It rises in Tibet and circles around high mountains and through deep gorges, flowing eastward over the great plains to Shanghai and the China Sea. Each year after the monsoon rains, Ta Chiang rises and overflows its banks. Sometimes it would penetrate our village and ruin our crops and those years would be bad for everyone, for there would be no food and no money.

"My village was very poor. The village lord owned the land and the peasants farmed it. Our houses were made of yellow mud baked into bricks. There was a courtyard with wooden galleries linking the rooms and a cookroom on the ground floor where the women would gather to prepare food, and a deep well where they drew water. At each end of the roof were placed two carved wooden bats, lacquered red. They said they warded off misfortune, though why anyone still believed it after so many bad years I did not understand."

Lai Tsin paused. He took his waterpipe from the corner and lit it with a spill from the candle, inhaling luxuriously, while Francie waited for him to go on.

"The windows were made of thick rice paper," he said at last, "and I remember how they trembled in the ice winds of winter, blowing over us as we huddled on our bedmats around the little charcoal stove. And in summer we could barely breathe in the stillness and the moist heat. My family was large: there was my father and his Number Two wife, and also his concubine and ten children, though three of them died young. Two were infants who had barely breathed, but Little Chen, my younger brother, was three years old and my favorite. He had a face as round and flat as a pancake, with twinkling dark eyes, and he was always making me laugh. It was I who looked after him; I took him to the rice fields with me, I shared my food with him because he always had a hungry mouth and I was the one who snuggled up to him at night to keep warm. Then suddenly he fell ill with the fever that comes from the swamp lands near the river and within a day he lay dead.

My father informed the village elders, and the next night when it was still dark they came with a basket and took him away. It was forbidden, but I followed them. The tears for my beloved little brother were streaming down my face, though I dare not cry my sorrow out loud. Because Little Chen was so young they said his spirit was too unformed for a funeral and we were not allowed to mourn him. They left him in his little basket at the foot of a tree in the sacred *fung-shui* grove for the birds and the dogs to take.

"I knew the elders must be home before dawn and I waited until they had hurried away. Then I went to his basket, opened it, and kissed his sweet little face and said good-bye to him. I could hear the whirring of the wings of the big birds overhead and then the stirring in the reeds as the hungry dogs came in search of him, and I ran terrified back to the village. As was the custom, my family never spoke of him again."

Lai Tsin fell silent. He blew a long spur of ash from his pipe and looked across at Francie. "I have never spoken of this to anyone before," he said wonderingly. "My whole life is locked inside me, the words are inscribed on stone tablets around my heart and the memories are as cruel as a sharp sword." He shook his head. "It is better not to talk of such things, not to remember them."

In the candle glow he caught the glimmer of tears in her blue eyes and he reached across and took her hand. "You have a tender heart, Little Sister," he said quietly. "And a trusting one. Once I was like you, my wounds were as deep, my sorrows maybe even greater. I promise you that life goes on and one day all our ghosts will be laid."

"I tried to lay my father's ghost this morning," she whispered, clutching her blanket tighter, chilled by the thought of him. "But it was no good, Lai Tsin, his spirit was still there, still searching for me. . . ."

He put down his pipe and beckoned her closer. She leaned toward him and he took her face in his thin, narrow hands, turning it first to one side then the other, running his fingers across her temples and the lobes of her ears. Then he took her hands and placed them palm-up in his, inspecting the thumbs and peering at the minute whorls and lines.

"Your fortune is written here," he said at last. "Here is the line that says you were strong in your childhood, and here the jagged cross-lines that show illnesses and sorrows. And I see cleverness and ability in your face, you have the power to command other people and they will do as you wish. That power is there, in your head and in your hands. You will gain much money. It will encompass many lands and much travel and earn you great respect. There are hardships, yes, but these will be overcome because your will is strong and you are stronger than those who seek to curtail you. And I see children, maybe two—" He stopped and looked at her strangely.

"Oh, but I'll never marry," Francie cried passionately, "never."

His brown, almond eyes were mesmeric in the candle glow; she could not take hers away from them. "There will be men in your life," he said. "You are a beautiful girl and soon you will become a woman. Men will not ignore you, and men will love you. It is also your fate."

She dropped her eyes, staring down at her hands still lying in his, and he said gently, "There is violence in your fortune. Much violence. There will be times you will not avoid it and it will bring you great sorrow."

"Then my fortune is already decided," she whispered, looking at him, frightened.

He nodded again. "Fortune has made her plans. All we can do is try to fool her. There are many things I could tell you about myself and how to cheat fate."

She watched as he relit his bubble pipe. "Please, won't you tell me now?"

He shook his head and said, "Maybe one day, Little Sister."

Francie lay down on her bedmat in the corner next to the boy. She peered at his innocent sleeping face, marveling at the resiliency of children. The boy had lost his family and his home, he had gone through earthquake and fire and yet he slept the sleep of the angels. She covered herself with her blanket and lay down beside him, soothed by his gentle, even breathing and the soft bubbling of Lai Tsin's water pipe, and within minutes, like the boy, she slept.

Lai Tsin sat till dawn over his pipe and his memories. In the early morning light his face looked gray and careworn and his eyes were black with unnamed tragedies. He put away his pipe and lay down on his mat by the door, turning his face from the others, as though his memories might trouble their dreams. He thought of Francie and what was to come and he sighed. It was a long time before his eyes closed and he slept, the light sleep of a cat keeping watch for its enemies.

# CHAPTER 16

◆

Annie recognized the place from the postcard Josh had sent her. She stood on the sidewalk gazing at the pile of bricks and rubble that had once been the Barbary Coast Saloon and Rooming House, wishing she had never come to San Francisco. She had seen the list of missing and presumed dead and Josh's name had been among them. This had been his home and this was where he had died. Tears streamed unchecked down her face and people turned curiously to stare at her but she didn't notice.

Sorrow dragged like a lead weight on her heart as she remembered the sunny, beautiful baby, the mischievous boy, and the tall graceful young man. She remembered his gentleness and knew beyond a shadow of a doubt that he had never killed those women, no matter what Sammy had said. And if it were not for Sammy Morris, Josh would never have run away, he would never have come here to San Francisco, he would not have died alone and afraid in a shabby rooming house. She tried to imagine how he had felt when the earth shook and the walls fell in on him, burying him under the rubble. She thought of him trapped, choking for air, waiting and hoping for someone to save him and then the fire had come. She shuddered, putting her hands over her face. It was too terrible even to think about.

Francie hadn't wanted to go to the saloon that day, but somehow her feet just took her there. She walked slowly, holding the boy by the hand, staring silently down at the toes of her stiff old leather boots, thinking of Josh. Lai Tsin had told her that if she was to get on with her life she must lay his ghost to rest too.

She noticed the young woman from half a block away. She was wearing a blue woolen traveling suit and a large hat with a russet plume and Francie thought she looked different, sort of foreign. She saw her put her head in her hands and then her shoulders shook with sobs and Francie's heart went out to her. She hurried toward her and put a comforting arm around her shoulders.

"Believe me, I know how you feel," she said sympathetically. Annie sniffed back her tears and looked at her. "I lost my fiancé. He was badly injured, then the earth shook again, a great slab of mortar came flying down and struck him on the head." She closed her eyes as she said, "I had heard someone die before and I knew that sound. I knew he was dying."

Annie gazed into her sad face and said, "I'm sorry, lass. I know there must be thousands of others grieving as myself. But my brother was such a special lad and I've come such a long way, hoping to find him still alive."

Francie stared at her, puzzled. There was something familiar about the way she spoke . . . she had called her "lass," just the way Josh did, and she said she had come from a long way to find him. Her eyes widened as she looked at her. She was small and rounded, she had big brown eyes with a fringe of dark lashes and there was something eerily familiar about her smile. Suddenly she knew. She said, "You are Josh's sister."

Annie's jaw dropped, she clutched her arm, dazed. *"You knew Josh?"*

"It was Josh I was talking about, it was Josh I was with in the earthquake—"

Annie burst into tears again as she realized that Josh really was dead. She put her arms around Francie, and hugged her tightly. "I'm glad he met you," she said between sobs, "at least he was with somebody who loved him when he died. I had nightmares thinking of him all alone, just lying there waiting for the flames. Now I know what happened, and terrible though it is, it's not as bad as the unknown."

She took a step back, holding Francie at arm's length, seeing what Josh had seen in her. A thin, waiflike young girl with crazily cut pale blond hair, a sweet heart-shaped face with a jagged scar across her forehead, and huge sapphire-blue eyes. She mopped her tears and said, "So you were Josh's fiancée. That makes you almost an Aysgarth, doesn't it? I mean, if Josh had lived you would have been my sister-in-law. And I don't even know your name."

"It's Francie. Francie Harrison." The little boy lurking behind her tugged at her skirts, and Annie stared surprised at the little Chinese lad in his coarse blue smock and the funny little cap with bunches of colored ribbons on the earflaps. He had a round face and almond eyes and he looked about four years old. She scooped him into her arms. "And who are *you,* little fellow?" she asked, pulling his cap straight and smiling at him.

"The boy is an orphan," Francie explained. "Lai Tsin found him wandering in the street and now we are looking after him."

"And what's his name?" Annie gave his queue a friendly tug and he glanced shyly up at her and giggled.

Francie looked surprised, she had never thought about his name before. "Lai Tsin just calls him 'Little Son.' "

"Everybody is entitled to a name," Annie exclaimed indignantly. "What about Philip? That's a good Christian name for a little heathen like this one. And who is Lai Tsin anyway?"

"Lai Tsin is my Chinese friend," Francie said proudly, "and they are not heathens, Miss Aysgarth. Besides, Lai Tsin is a gentleman. He helped me after the earthquake."

Annie nodded. "Well, now I'm here to help—you were Josh's girl and he would have expected it." She sniffed back the threatening tears as she thought of her brother. "I'd best save my crying for my pillow," she added bravely. "And now at least I can write to our dad and tell him Josh was buried along with a hundred other San Franciscans. After all, it won't exactly be a lie, will it? I know it's not consecrated ground, but at least it saved our honor." Then she added quickly, "Josh did tell you, didn't he, lass? Why he ran away? Of course, it wasn't true and if it weren't for Sammy Morris he would have been home where he belonged and I know his name would have been cleared."

Francie had not thought of Sammy once since Josh had died; he had just gone from her head like he never existed. Now she said his name with a shiver of fear.

"Aye. Sammy Morris," Annie repeated bitterly. "Josh's friend, if you can call someone like that a friend." She shifted the child's weight from one hip to the other. "I'll check the 'missing' lists again tomorrow," she said, adding, "No doubt he'll turn up—just like a bad penny."

She straightened her russet-plumed hat, taking in Francie's shabbiness, her worn skirt and old gray shawl and her clumsy old boots, and she said briskly, "We can't have you walking around looking like this. You'll want some new clothes. But first we'll take young Philip back to your Chinaman." She threw her arm affectionately around her shoulders as they walked slowly down the street. "They say God allus sends something to compensate you in your sorrow," she said feelingly, "and now he has sent me you. Josh's chosen lass."

Lai Tsin was bent over the little charcoal stove, cooking vegetables in a round tin wok. He bowed respectfully to the small, pretty-faced woman with Francie and she called, approvingly, "Good morning, Mr. Lai Tsin. Francie told me how you helped her. She said you were a gentleman and I can see she was right." She sat on the orange crate, catching her breath, and said, "We've given the little orphan a good English name, Philip, though I expect his last name will have to be Chinese?"

Lai Tsin stared at her as she slipped off her jacket and rolled up the sleeves of her white cotton blouse and said, "My, it's a bit hot for top-grade eight-ounce Yorkshire woolens. What's that you're cooking, Mr. Lai Tsin? It smells good, though it's like nothing I've ever smelled before."

He was still thinking about the boy's name and remembering his little brother and he said, "Chen."

"Chen?"

"Little Son's other name is now Chen. It was my brother's name."

"Oh I see. Philip Chen. Mmm, yes, that's a good solid name, I like that. It's a very good choice, Mr. Lai Tsin. Now. Francie tells me you helped her, and I'm very grateful to you for that. She was my brother Josh's fiancée, you see. We just met each other by chance in the street where"—she bit her lip and then went on quickly—"at the Barbary Saloon. Francie told me she didn't intend to go there today but somehow she found herself there. I reckon it was fate, don't you? And since Francie would have been my brother's wife, now I will help her." Opening her purse she took out a sheaf of bills and said, "I expect you lost everything, too, Mr. Lai Tsin, and I daresay a bit of extra cash wouldn't go amiss."

Lai Tsin stared expressionlessly at the money. Francie recognized that blank-faced look and she knew he had lost face. She said quickly, "You don't understand. Lai Tsin and I have been through everything together. Now he and Little Son are my family. Thank you for your offer to help, Miss Aysgarth, but I will stay here with them."

Annie's jaw dropped in astonishment. She had never imagined the girl would want to stay with the Chinaman, but she surely admired her for it. She wished she had had as much spirit when she was eighteen and imagined how different her life might have been. She thought of her dreary routine, chained to Ivy Cottage, a slave to her father and quickly decided that she was never going back. Didn't they say it was never too late to start over?

She said briskly, "Well, if that's the case then I suppose I'd better just join you. Because I'm alone, too, now that Josh has gone. Oh yes, there's our dad and my brothers back in Yorkshire, but they've outgrown me long ago. All I was was a workhorse, the maiden aunt with no bairns of her own to tend. I spent my life looking after our dad and now it's somebody else's turn." She looked pleadingly at Francie. "Josh was like my own boy. I've got nothing left without him. At least here with you and the Chinaman and the Little Son there'd be a purpose to things. It's thanks to poor Josh that I'm here. And here I want to stay. With you."

Little Son suddenly ran toward her. He climbed onto her lap and she hugged him, smiling anxiously at them.

"Our home is the streets," Francie warned her. "We have no money, we eat what the relief kitchens give us. You don't know half my troubles, and you certainly don't know Lai Tsin's. He's Chinese, he has no papers, he lives outside the law. I must stay with him and help him the way he helped me. Together we will cheat our fate."

Annie nodded. They had each other, they didn't need her. She stood up and forlornly dusted off her skirt. "Mebbe that's what I've always wanted too," she said, putting on her hat. "To cheat my fate."

Her eyes met Francie's and there was a flicker of recognition, as though they sensed each other's bitter struggle to escape their pasts, and Francie smiled. "Then why don't you stay?" she said.

# CHAPTER 17

◆

Lai Tsin stood at the back of a small room in a narrow little alley in Chinatown, watching the gambling. The mah-jongg tiles crackled like gunfire, the players shouted and screamed excitedly and the languorous, sickly sweet smell of opium stole from the curtained-off back room. The place was a ruin, the crumbling walls were shored up with beams and the ceiling was a dangerous spiderweb of cracks, but games of chance had been going on there for years and not even an earthquake could put Chinese off their gambling.

He fingered the money in his pocket, counting it mentally: there was the twenty dollars won from Chung Wu along with the worthless paper for the land in Hong Kong, and ten dollars left from the sum he had started out with because it was his rule never to gamble down to his last cent, and almost five dollars in nickles and dimes scrimped and saved and stashed away in his straw pannier for a rainy day, which would have to be a monsoon because every day was a "rainy" one.

He stared at the men at the tables, despising them. They were gambling because they had the fever, not because they were clever like he was. His brain flew like a bird, chasing figures and permutations through his mind so fast, he could almost predict the outcome before it happened. The only trouble was the men he gambled with were as poor as he was, so he could never win enough money to join the really big games. It was, he thought sorrowfully, a case of the chicken or the egg. But tonight, because of the scarcity of gambling halls due to the earthquake, there were men playing he had only heard about, legendary gamblers whose skills were equal to his.

He thought of this thirty-five dollars and his new responsibilities. By rights, he should return to work in the fields, picking apples and plums or tending the crops, but that had barely fed him and certainly would not feed his new family. And he knew he had to make money for them or lose face. He must take his chances with the poorest gamblers.

He waited patiently until finally an old bearded man pushed back his chair with a curse of disgust at his bad joss, and then he quietly took his place. The worn bone tiles inscribed with red and green and white dragons, the east, south, and north winds, the flowers and the seasons, bamboos, circles, characters and numbers, were set out and the dice thrown, and he smiled with satisfaction as his "wall" was quickly built. Within five minutes his ten-dollar stake had become sixty, half an hour later it was three hundred, and with much angry shouting the other men abandoned his table.

Pocketing his winnings Lai Tsin wandered over to the table near the glassless window. An embroidered scarlet shawl was draped over the opening, protecting them from the gaze of passersby, and its deep fringes swung to and fro in the night breeze. Six men were playing a Chinese card game of immense complexity by the light of a guttering candle and the smoke from their pipes mingled with the opium fumes, filling the room with a blue haze.

He leaned against the wall, his face expressionless as he watched them. He knew the game, it called for a quick brain as well as skill and lightning responses, but he rarely had an opportunity to play it because his usual gambling partners were too slow and ignorant. He glanced discreetly at the faces of the players—they were solemn and hard-eyed and the amount of dollar bills lying on the table took his breath away. These were the notorious big gamblers from Toishan, but he reminded himself again that all the omens had been good that day. He thought of the money in his secret pocket and knew it was a chance in a lifetime, and when the next man dropped out he took his place.

His heart jumped when he picked up his first cards, double sixes and double eights, both fortuitous numbers, but he kept his eyes as blank as the glassless window and his face as still as a stagnant pool. His hand did not tremble as he placed his two hundred dollars on the table, though his stomach churned with tension and excitement. Numbers flashed through his brain as the cards were laid out and within seconds he had assessed the other men's hands, and thirty seconds later he was scooping up his winnings.

His face remained expressionless as he let his winnings ride on the next game, though inside he was seething with excitement, and his eyes glittered as he saw his next hand with three cards of number nine and two aces. They were the luckiest numbers of all, for "nine" was the largest number and signified fullness, and "one" meant "a beginning." All the omens had been good that day. Nothing could go wrong for him.

The gamblers who had inspected his poor clothing with sly eyes when he had first sat at the table looked at him with new respect when he won another hand. And then another. And all the time he let his winnings ride. The gods were with him and who was he to go against their wishes?

The other men gathered around, *oohing* and *aieeing* as they saw the amount of money on the table, gasping as time and again Lai Tsin tested his fate and played his hand and won, leaving all those dollars on the table, multiplying into thousands. "Joss will surely go against him," they muttered. "Lai Tsin is tempting fortune with so much money."

After an hour the other gamblers glanced at each other and pushed back their chairs. Lai Tsin stood up, bowing respectfully to them as they congratulated him on his good fortune, but their eyes were steely and he knew they were angry. Scooping up his winnings he sought out the poor men from whom he had won his first three hundred dollars and gave them back their money. "You brought me good joss," he explained. "Without you I could not have played."

He was a changed man as he walked from that room; for the first time in his life he saw respect in the eyes of the men watching him. He stood taller, holding himself with dignity, and he told himself that when fortune smiled a man surely knew he had been blessed by the gods. He had started the day a poor man and now he was rich.

It was almost dawn when he returned to the shack, and Francie and Little Son were sound asleep. As the first gray light stole through the curtain that served as their door Lai Tsin counted his winnings, gasping as he realized the amount. Almost twelve thousand dollars. He touched the pile of money, awestruck, and then he folded his arms and leaned back against the wooden boards, thinking.

He thought about his life, about the hardships, the beatings, the terror and the poverty, about the lack of education that had forced him into the servitude of a peasant when inside he knew he was different. He had worked hard all his life. As a child he had walked behind the water buffalo, dragging his bare feet through the cold mud of the ricefields and he had known there must be something more than just this. He had watched the poor white ducks squabbling endlessly in the village pond, understanding that, like his, their fate was sealed before they were even born. He had felt like a changeling, a prince among the paupers, a scholar among the ignorant. He had no words to describe it but he knew it was all there inside him. And now, with those American dollars won from the men from Toishan, at last he had his chance to become somebody. And he would never gamble again.

He waited impatiently for Francie to wake, wishing there were some magic that would take away the frown from between her brows and the sighs that, even as she slept, escaped her lips. He knew that her troubles were deep and there was gladness in his heart because now he knew he could help her.

When she finally began to stir he went outside and blew on the little charcoal stove until it glowed scarlet. He collected water from the standpipe at the end of the street and put it on to boil. Then he took the little blue-and-white pot with the wicker handle, spooned fragrant jasmine-scented leaves inside it and poured on the boiling water. When he finally went back inside she was sitting up, rubbing her eyes in astonishment at the pile of dollars. "Lai Tsin," she gasped, "what did you do? Rob a bank?"

He poured the tea and offered it to her. "I had good fortune last night," he said. "I beat the Toishan gamblers. I let my winnings ride until they had had enough and when I counted them, I had twelve thousand American dollars. It is a fortune, Francie. We are rich."

Francie stared at him, stunned. Though he had not slept his eyes were clear and alert and there was a new air of confidence about him. Lai Tsin looked like a different person. But twelve thousand dollars was a huge sum, it was more than just shoes for Little Son and candles and bedrolls. It was a stake to build his fortune on and she could not just stand by and see him gamble it away again. "You must start a business with the money," she told him. "Think of the opportunities the earthquake has made! Why, it's like the old goldrush days when my grandfather was a trader. He bought and sold anything that was needed and he made a fortune. Just think what is needed here in Chinatown, Lai Tsin. Chinese spices and special foods, oriental clothes, shoes, tobacco. They will buy everything you can imagine, because now they have nothing."

Lai Tsin lit his bubblepipe and she knew he was thinking about what she had said. After a long time he put away his pipe and took a square of scarlet silk from his straw pannier and wrapped the money carefully in it. He walked to the door carrying the money in the scarlet cloth under his arm, but he did not look back and Francie sighed. She had lost, and he was going back to the gambling den after all.

Lai Tsin wended his way through the ruins and knocked nervously on the door of one of Chinatown's few remaining buildings. The old man who lived there was one of the most powerful Chinese elders in San Francisco. He controlled most of the money loaned in the old southern Chinese system of rotating credit whereby members pooled their money and each member in turn had access to it. Lai Tsin knew that it operated on a system of honor, that each borrower pledged personally to repay the money, and that the Chinese sense of honor and their desire not to lose face was so strong, defaulters were rare. If their new businesses ran into trouble then their families helped repay the loan. But Lai Tsin had no family to help him. All he had was an idea, an opportunity, his honor, and twelve thousand dollars.

A woman opened the door and he told her he had come to see the Honorable Elder.

"Who is it wishes to see him?" she asked warily, half closing the door.

"Tell the Honorable Elder that Ke Lai Tsin from Anhwei Province wishes to speak with him on a matter of business." He used his family name "Ke" for the first time in many years and it felt strange on his tongue. The old woman closed the door abruptly in his face and Lai Tsin's new self-respect shriveled with every minute he waited. He reminded himself he had twelve thousand dollars wrapped in the red silk bandana under his arm, that he was a man of substance and responsibility now, and he pulled himself taller and lifted his chin higher.

At last the door opened again and the old woman reluctantly bade him follow her into a spacious downstairs room. He glanced around, marveling at the many treasures it contained, at the porcelain vases, the carved jade animals, the soft silken carpets and screens inlaid with mother-of-pearl. There were painted scrolls and calligraphy, tassled lanterns and ivory figurines. A carved altar table from the Ming Dynasty held a collection of Han bronze dressing mirrors, jade bowls, and Tang sculptures. Elegant blackwood chairs were crammed in between enameled chests and tables and a dozen Chinese clocks ticked away the passing of time. The darkened room was filled with the old man's earthly riches and Lai Tsin was afraid to move in case he knocked into something and broke one of the valuable pieces.

A man entered the room, wrapping his padded silk jacket closer around him, trying to keep the cold out of his old bones. His bald head gleamed in the lamplight, his eyebrows slanted ferociously upward and his long moustache drooped into his pointed white beard. Lai Tsin bowed quickly three times, seeking courage to speak to such an important and rich personage.

"Honorable Grandfather," he said nervously, calling him "Grandfather" as a sign of great respect for his venerable age, "I am here on a matter of business. Because of the earthquake there are many shortages in Chinatown. Our people do not have the things they need and the merchants who have lost everything are slow to return to their businesses. It is my wish to leave my lowly standing and become a merchant, importing things directly from China."

The old man's dark eyes bored into him, assessing his poor clothing, his thinness and his air of need. "And how do you propose to start this business, Ke Lai Tsin?" he asked.

Lai Tsin unwrapped the red silk bandana. "With my twelve thousand dollars, Honorable Grandfather. And, good joss be with me, also with an extra sum borrowed from the rotating credit and yourself as the Honorable Banker."

The old man's expression did not change as he looked at the bundle of money, but when he looked back at Lai Tsin, his eyes hardened. "And where does a poor coolie come across such a sum?"

Lai Tsin lifted himself taller and said proudly, "Just yesterday, Honorable Elder, the man you see before you was a gambler. Yesterday he won these many dollars and gained face as a man of substance. And today the peasant Lai Tsin will become a merchant and a man of respect."

The elder nodded, satisfied that he had not stolen his new wealth. "Tell me your ideas for your new business," he commanded, summoning the old woman to bring jasmine tea while he listened to Lai Tsin's tale.

"Honorable Grandfather, I will ask the Chinese themselves what it is they need most urgently. I will walk the streets and see what is lacking. I have not sufficient funds to rebuild their homes and businesses, but with the Honorable Elder's generous assistance I can provide the goods they will need in their new abodes. Foods and spices, ginger and ginseng, woks and teapots, bedmats and padded quilts, lanterns, chairs, rice-paper shades for the windows, shoes and clothing. I will find out immediately what ships are en route from the Orient and I will telegraph an order for their entire consignments, whether they dock at New York, Seattle, Los Angeles, or San Francisco. I will corner the market on all the next shipments into America. I will rent a warehouse and fill it with my goods. I will open a shop in a favorable location with good *fung shui,* where the crossroads meet and many people pass by. I will treat my customers with respect and give them good prices so when the other merchants are finally back in business it is Lai Tsin they will remember and return to." He picked up his red bandana with his twelve thousand dollars and held it out to the Elder. "All this I can do, if the Honorable Grandfather grants me his assistance. And if the gods are willing."

"And what makes you think that finally the gods are favorable to you?"

Lai Tsin thought over the old man's question carefully and he knew there was only one answer. "My fortune has changed since I met the *gwailo* woman," he said honestly. "She has much to teach an ignorant peasant like me. It was she who told me that I need no longer be a gambler. And it was she who showed me the way."

The Elder said angrily, "A *gwailo* woman, Lai Tsin? A 'foreign devil'?"

"Honorable Grandfather," Lai Tsin protested quickly, "she is an orphan of the earthquake. She has a good heart and a sad life and we have helped each other. And even though she is the daughter of foreign devils, she has been kind to this lowly Chinese peasant."

The Elder thought for a long while, sipping his tea and watching Lai Tsin. Finally he nodded. "I believe your story. And I see the cleverness of your plan depends upon its quickness. I am prepared to lend you an equal amount to your twelve thousand dollars. What guarantee do you give that you will repay the money?"

Lai Tsin sighed. "I have no guarantee, Honorable Grandfather. Just the knowledge that I will succeed."

The Elder nodded approvingly again. "There are many who come to me for money who are not as honest as you, Ke Lai Tsin," he said. "And for that you will have your chance. But in return for the risk, as well as repaying the money and lending an equal sum to the credit so others can benefit from the system, you will also pay five percent of your profits up to the sum of twenty-four thousand dollars into the association."

Lai Tsin bowed respectfully again. "Honorable Grandfather," he said solemnly, "the day I pay the five percent will be the happiest of my life."

Annie had found a tiny room and invited Francie to share it, but she preferred her new life on the street. Little Son was playing with friends and Francie was alone. She tidied the shack, swept the floor, and went to fetch more water. Then she lay down on her bedmat, suddenly tired. But the problem she was refusing to face would not go away and she sat up again.

She stared at Lai Tsin's straw pannier lying in the corner. She knew it contained his worldly possessions, and suddenly consumed with curiosity, she went to the pannier and opened it. His treasures were few: a pair of ivory chopsticks, the title deed from the Hong Kong land that he had won gambling, a long wooden box, and a dog-eared sepia photograph of a pretty girl in Chinese robes. The girl was sitting on a chair with a scalloped paper fan clutched in her hand and Francie looked at her for a long time. She had the same dark almond eyes and oval face as Lai Tsin and she knew it must be his sister. She picked up the wooden box. It was about eighteen inches long with a curved lid. She hesitated; she knew she shouldn't, but she couldn't resist. She lifted the lid and looked inside. On the bottom lay a silky braid of glossy black hair bound with scarlet yarn.

"The braid was my sister's," Lai Tsin said from the door, and Francie jumped guiltily. She said, blushing, "I didn't mean to pry. I just don't know what made me do it."

He shrugged. "Curiosity sometimes overcomes good sense and courtesy. The box is a 'treasure pillow.' We poor Chinese store our valuables and money in it. We place it under our heads at night, like a pillow, so no one can steal it." He looked sad as he said, "I kept my sister's hair to remember her by. She was young and pretty and too full of life. My mother would scold her, saying that such a noisy girl would attract the displeasure of the gods. And she was right, because soon the gods decided to take her away."

He replaced the box carefully in the straw pannier and Francie noticed he was no longer carrying the red bundle.

"Do not worry," he said, reading her mind. "I went to the most Honorable Chinese Elder. I showed him my twelve thousand dollars and told him I wanted to become a merchant, importing goods from China. He saw that the opportunity was right and agreed to lend me twelve thousand more dollars from the credit. The numbers are auspicious, two pairs of double sixes. Twenty-four thousand dollars in all." She smiled at him, thrilled, and Lai Tsin added, "I am not yet a rich man because the money is borrowed. And I am not yet a successful man because my stake was not earned and came from a game of chance. But because of your wisdom, Francie, today I became a man of respect."

His almond eyes were gentle as he looked at her. He said, "When I met you I recognized you. You were like the lost soul I had once been. Now we are turning fate around into fortune. From today I am no longer Lai Tsin, the peasant and the gambler. I am Lai Tsin, the merchant."

Lai Tsin immediately set about his work. He found out what ships were coming in from the Orient, telegraphing his orders to them in Seattle and New York and Los Angeles. He rented a small warehouse facing the harbor, which had barely been touched by the earthquake, to store his goods in when they arrived and he hung a mirror over its door to drive away the bad spirits and protect the good *fung-shui,* the good spirit of the place. He leased a small plot of land in Chinatown, just a tiny corner at the end of an alley where two roads met, but he knew that the two roads were favorable to his business because many people would walk by his store. Within a couple of weeks a makeshift wooden store was erected on it and the name, FAVORABLE TRADING COMPANY, was painted in black Chinese letters over the door. Long red banners printed with encouraging Chinese slogans; "Long Life," "Success," "Happiness" and "Filial Piety," were stuck on the windows and a sign calling for "The Five Blessings" to fall on it was stuck over the door. The Five Blessings were a long life, riches, a serene mind, a healthy body, and love of virtue.

A young man was installed to serve the customers and the Chinese population flocked to buy Lai Tsin's spices and dried mushrooms, preserved duck and ginger and sesame oil. They bought charcoal for their stoves and new stoves to put the charcoal in, they bought cooking pots to put on the stove and new rice bowls to serve the food in. Within weeks he was forced to expand his shop and as life drifted back to normal his customers returned to buy new bedmats, rice-paper screens, tea kettles, padded quilts, and wooden-soled shoes.

In two months a second store was opened and another warehouse rented where people could buy larger goods: tables and cabinets and sewing machines and chairs. There were racks of embroidered silk jackets and black cotton coolie smocks and trousers—anything and everything could be bought from Lai Tsin's Favorable Trading Company.

Annie and Francie moved into a small, hastily refurbished apartment on Kearny Street and Lai Tsin took a room next door. Francie began to teach Little Son to speak English and she was also helping Lai Tsin with his reading and writing. She was thin and pale and always tired and Lai Tsin knew she was in despair, yet he could not allow her to lose face by mentioning her problem first. He must wait for her to tell him.

They heard that the city's records had all been burned and thousands of Chinese rushed to claim they were American by birth. Lai Tsin went with the others to receive his papers. Good fortune was smiling on him; because of the earthquake he became a legal American citizen.

Time was passing, and Annie needed something to do. She was used to keeping busy, she had the money her father had given her, and she said to Francie, "All I know is how to cook and look after folk. I'm going to open a little rooming house. There's lots of people still homeless that'll be glad of a good, clean place to stay and a decent supper of an evening. I've got the money and I'm going to ask Lai Tsin to find me a place."

Lai Tsin came back to her a few days later and told her that the word was there was a nice piece of land near Union Square with the remains of a building still on it. The foundations were good and he could organize credit and also the necessary labor and supplies.

Francie watched their busy lives listlessly. It seemed good fortune was smiling on everyone but her, and her awful secret.

# CHAPTER 18

◆

*Josh.* The name sent vibrations through her entire body and she pressed her hands against her growing belly. She went to look in the long mirror Annie had installed in their shared bedroom, turning anxiously from side to side. There was no doubt her waist was thickening, but the bulge was still small enough to hide under her long Chinese smock. Her secret was safe.

She looked dispiritedly at her reflection. Her blond hair was dragged back into a knot, her small heart-shaped face looked gray and pinched, and there were lines of tension around her mouth and eyes. She thought of the girl of a few months ago in her white lace ball dress and sparkling tiara, and she looked again at the same eighteen-year-old girl, who was now a gray waif in her high-necked Chinese smock and black trousers. She belonged to a different world.

She walked tiredly back to the window, gazing out on the endless activity. The old Chinatown had been a dark, secretive ghetto, a hellhole of rat-infested tenements filled with crime of every sort: sing-song girls, slave-girls, gambling halls and sweatshops, opium dens and the bloody violence of the rival tongs who ran it all. The city fathers wanted to build a new Chinatown out at Hunters Point, but the Chinese ignored them and were busily rebuilding it exactly where it had always stood. Only this time the new buildings were in the old Chinese style with carved rafters and pierced screens at the windows, painted scarlet, green, and gold. They had green-tiled roofs with curved eaves and guardian lions at the red-lacquered doors. The streets smelled of incense and spices and rang with the sound of sawing and hammering. New buildings were rising up almost overnight as men worked round-the-clock shifts to restore their shattered homes and businesses.

Francie thought of Annie over at Union Square, supervising the rebuilding of her new boardinghouse and, no doubt, driving the workmen crazy. Annie had lived with the family building trade all her life, she knew what was what and she let the builders know it. Francie had been with her once when she had found the men shirking, drinking beer and standing around smoking. They stared sheepishly at the little battle-ax of a woman giving them a piece of her mind, reminding them it was her money and her time they were wasting, telling them they had better get on with it or they'd know about it. There had been black looks and grumbles as they'd straggled slowly back to work, but they knew Annie was fair as well as feisty, and that a hard worker always found a good bonus in his wage packet at the end of the week.

Just the other day, when the roof was finished, Annie had declared a party. Long trestle tables had been set up and covered with starched white cloths, because even amongst the dust and cement, Annie liked everything nice. She invited their families and there was as much beer and food as anyone wanted and they raised their glasses in a toast to her, laughing as they admitted she was a good employer even if she was a woman.

And Lai Tsin worked at his business more hours than Francie thought existed, yet he still found time to do the lessons she set him to. He pored avidly over the simple children's storybooks, reading each new word out loud, running his finger carefully along the letters. And he copied his lessons neatly into the exercise book he took with him everywhere. He absorbed her teaching like a sponge and he was so eager to learn that she almost had trouble keeping up with him.

Lai Tsin had decided it was proper for Little Son Philip Chen to be brought up with a Chinese family. "He must be like the other Chinese boys and learn their ways," he said. "When he is older and wiser he will learn Western ways, too, but now he must understand his heritage."

And that left only Francie with nothing except her bad memories of the past and her fear of the future. And she dare not even tell Lai Tsin or Annie about the baby, she was so ashamed.

There was a sudden tap at the door and she ran to open it. A small boy looked quickly up at her, pushed a piece of paper into her hand and darted back down the stairs.

She stared after him, puzzled, and then she closed the door and looked at the crumpled piece of paper. On it was written, *"If you still love me, come to Gai Pao's alley at nine o'clock tonight."* And it was signed, *"Josh."*

The blood rushed from Francie's face and her heart thudded in her chest. She told herself it couldn't be true, it must be some kind of cruel joke. But no one knew about Josh—only Lai Tsin and Annie, and they would never play tricks on her. There was a sudden flutter in her belly and she put her hand there, feeling her child for the first time. Maybe it was an omen and meant Josh was still alive after all. *If you still love me,* the note had said.

Panicked, she stared at it, wishing the others were there, but Lai Tsin would be working and Annie was at a meeting with the architect and wouldn't be back till late.

She paced to and fro, telling herself she wouldn't go, and then she thought of Josh lying in the ruins and thought maybe he really wasn't dead after all. And she knew she must.

She left a note telling Annie where she had gone and then she made her way through mean back streets, searching for Gai Pao's alley, and when she found it, it was just a dark deserted little dead-end. It was pitch-black with just a faint glimmer of light at the very end and she hesitated, frightened. She wanted to turn and run but the note was like bait, luring her on. She stepped nervously down the alley, hugging the broken walls and peering over her shoulder. A dim light burned over a curtained doorway and she hesitated again. She knew she should just turn around and run, but she couldn't. *If you love me,* the note had said, and it was love that made her pull back the curtain and step inside.

The cramped room was lit by a flickering kerosene lamp. It was noisy with the clatter of mah-jongg tiles and the shouts of the gamblers and it reeked of tobacco, paraffin, opium fumes, and sweat. The Chinese at the gambling tables turned to stare at her, muttering angrily, and she shrank timidly against the wall. At a counter on the left a man was serving rice wine in gourd-shaped pots. He beckoned to her and said quickly, "Come with me, missee. Hurry. This way."

She followed him through another curtained doorway, stumbling after him down an endless labyrinth of ruined passageways until they came to a small square room. Only half the walls remained standing, there was no roof and the moon glimmered from behind the clouds, silhouetting the empty doorway and blank windows. Francie suddenly realized that her guide had gone and she was alone. A thrill of fear shot up her spine as she stared around her. She could just make out a shape in the middle of the floor—it was a chair. And there was someone sitting on it. The blood sang in her ears and her heart was thudding so hard against her ribs, she thought it would burst.

"Josh?" she whispered.

"I thought you wouldn't be able to stay away from him," a familiar voice said. A lamp shone in her eyes, dazzling her, and she froze. It wasn't Josh's voice she was hearing, it was Sammy Morris's.

"Aye, it's me," Sammy said, holding the lantern higher so she could see his face. Terrified, Francie stared at him. She had walked right into his trap. "Then it was you who wrote that note," she whispered.

"Aye, of course it was me. Josh here can't write anymore, y'see. So I thought I'd just tell you he still loves you." His dark eyes glowered at her the way they always had and he smiled a small, triumphant smile. He lifted the lamp so it shone on the chair. A blond-haired man was sitting on it. Francie felt faint, she knew it couldn't be true. She had heard Josh die. She had watched him die. Had he come back from the grave to find her?

Sammy grabbed her arms. He twisted them behind her back and dragged her across to the chair. "Take a look at him, Francie," he said savagely. "Just look at your lover. See how handsome he is now?" And then he lifted the lantern high so the light fell on the man's face. Only it wasn't a face anymore, it was just a lump of puckered blueish-red flesh. Supperating sores marked the wounds, the mouth was a grotesque grimace, and the blank eyes stared sightlessly upward.

Francie screamed with horror and Sammy twisted her arm even tighter. He pressed her closer to the monster on the chair. "Go on, kiss him, Francie, why don't you? After all, *you* did this to him." She screamed again, a high, thin, keening sound. Terror gave her strength and she twisted from Sammy's grasp. With an oath he dropped the lantern and the light flickered and went out, leaving them in darkness.

He cursed again as Francie ran for the patch of lighter gray where the door had once been. Then she was out in the alley, running and running. She heard him pounding behind her, he was gaining on her, getting closer and closer. She could see a light where the alley joined the street and she ran even quicker. Then suddenly she tripped. He grabbed her. She smelled his sweat and heard his rasping breath and felt his hands on her throat. As though from a great distance she heard footsteps and someone shouting and then she remembered no more.

Lai Tsin felt for Francie's pulse; he chafed her icy hands, stroking back her hair, willing her to open her eyes. And he called silently to all the gods to help her; she was his friend, his helpmate, his child, his daughter, his love, and all his good fortune meant nothing without her. And when at last she opened her eyes again he carried her into a cab and brought her home.

Annie almost fainted herself when she saw them. She thanked God that at least Francie had had the sense to leave her the note and Lai Tsin had known where to find her. And when she looked at her, ashen-faced and trembling and barely able to speak with shock, she knew something terrible had happened.

"They're not dead," Francie whispered. "I saw both of them, Sammy and Josh. Oh, Annie, it's too terrible even to think about, his face was so hideous, all his sweetness and beauty gone. Sammy forced me to look . . . he had a knife—"

Annie clutched a hand to her heart as fear gave way to hope. "You can't mean Josh is alive!"

"Where did you see them?" Lai Tsin asked quietly.

"In the opium den on Gai Pao alley. The note said to meet him there . . . if I still loved him, it said." She uncurled her hand, and Annie took the crumpled note from her, and read out the message.

"That's not Josh's writing," Annie said. "I'll swear to that. It'll be Sammy Morris, just like she said."

Lai Tsin thought about the note and the message that had seemed to come from beyond the grave and knew that Francie was still in danger.

The half-ruined streets of Chinatown were quiet as Lai Tsin returned to the alley later. He knew the place, it was a notorious haunt of the tongs, the old Chinese secret societies that ruled the worlds of prostitution, gambling, opium, and violence. They had divided the town into territories and their wars were bloody, hachet-wielding affairs that left many dead.

He stole silently toward the glimmer of light at the end of the alley, pulled aside the heavy curtain and slid inside. No one noticed him in the noise and the gloom. Through a layer of smoke and opium fumes the flickering kerosene lamp shone on the mah-jongg tiles and the flasks of rice wine and the opium pipes piled in a heap. The man behind the bar was young and hard-faced, his flat eyes flickered from side to side as Lai Tsin asked him about the *gwailos,* the Westerners who had been there earlier.

"I don't know what you are talking about." He shrugged, but Lai Tsin could tell by his shifty demeanor that he knew all right.

"How much did they give you?" he asked, taking some dollars from his pocket and displaying them carelessly.

The man hesitated and Lai Tsin slid a ten-dollar bill across the splintered wooden counter. "They paid me twenty," the man said, reaching greedily for the money. Lai Tsin held another ten temptingly in front of him and said, "When you tell me all you know."

He shrugged. "One man came in. He was young, black hair and eyes, small and wide like this." He held his arms out from his shoulders like a gorilla and laughed. "He said he wanted a secret place to meet a *gwailo* woman, someone else's wife." He grinned, showing a row of brown-stained teeth. Lifting his shirt, he showed Lai Tsin the small hatchet strapped to his waist. "If she were a Chinese wife you know what would have happened to him," he boasted, patting the gleaming blade.

"So?" Lai Tsin prompted.

"So I showed him a place in the ruins and he told me she would come at nine o'clock and I should bring her there and leave her. And that is exactly what I did. No more, no less."

He held out his hand for the other ten dollars but Lai Tsin said, "First you show me the place." The man's eyes flickered dangerously, but he turned and picked up the lantern, and, grumbling, led the way out the back door and down the winding half-ruined passageways to the place. There was no need of a lantern now, the full moon was riding high in the night sky and in its light Lai Tsin could see it was empty. The man silently pocketed his extra ten dollars and disappeared the way he had come.

A broken chair lay overturned in the center of the room and Lai Tsin walked toward it and righted it. Something lay underneath and he picked it up. It was a blond wig and next to it was a Chinese "devil mask," the kind used in processions and festivals, only this had been altered to make it even more hideous. The moonlight showed the puckered red scars, the twisted mouth, and the hollow eyes, which were mere paint, but he could easily see how in the semidarkness and with fear they would have looked real and terrifying.

He thought hard as he walked back down the alley. A man like Sammy, intent on stalking his prey, would not be too far away. He would stay close to her, where he could watch, waiting for his chance. And a *gwailo* in Chinatown should not be hard to locate. Threading his way through the labryinth of alleys he emerged into a bigger street at the house of the Honorable Elder. He knocked on the door and waited. There was no reply, and picking up a handful of small stones he tossed them at the upstairs window. Immediately it was flung open and an irate voice exclaimed, "Who is that disturbing the sleep of the blessed?"

He stepped back and met the old man's angry gaze. His bald head gleamed in the moonlight, and his moustache drooped into his long, pointed white beard. He said, "Honorable Grandfather, it is Ke Lai Tsin. I must speak with you." He heard the old man muttering angrily, then his head disappeared and a few moments later the door was opened just wide enough for him to slide through.

The old man wrapped his blue kimono around himself to keep out the cold and said, "Has your business failed then, Ke Lai Tsin? Is it for this you wake me at such an hour?"

Lai Tsin shook his head. "No, Honorable Grandfather. My business goes well. It is a matter more difficult than mere business."

The old man listened carefully as he explained, then he said, "It is wrong to involve yourself with the *gwailos*. Especially a concubine. Has it not been proven to you? Leave the girl to her own people and find yourself a nice Chinese woman. I myself have a cousin of a suitable age with whom a marriage could be arranged. Although she is a little older, her parents would be generous to a prospective husband, they could do your business much good."

Lai Tsin replied patiently, "You do not understand. The girl is not my concubine. She is young, like a child. Even though she had deep troubles and sorrows of her own, she helped me. She brought me good fortune and it is my duty to help her."

"It is never the duty of a Chinese to aid *gwailo* women." The old man spoke sharply and Lai Tsin sighed. It was not going to be easy to convince him to do as he asked.

He nodded. "That is true, Honorable Grandfather. But is it not also true that we are bound to repay those who have showered us with blessings? And what I ask is very small. Just your help in locating a man." Keeping his voice low and his tone reasonable he pleaded his case for half an hour until the old man grudgingly agreed. "You are a good man, Lai Tsin," he said finally. "Your sinful association with the girl is talked of everywhere, but the way you explain it she is innocent. I will do as you ask. Come here tomorrow evening at seven and you will have your answer."

The Elder knew everyone, he had a finger in every pie in Chinatown and Lai Tsin knew he would be as good as his word. He hurried back home, satisfied. Even though it was dawn again and he had had no sleep he was filled with energy and his step was light as he ran back up the stairs. Annie was waiting for him.

"She's just lying there, gazing into space," she told him worriedly. "And she's cold even though I've wrapped her in all the padded quilts."

He went to look at her. He called her name and took her hand, but she did not respond and he was worried because he knew she was in deep shock. "I will fetch the healer," he said, hurrying away.

He returned fifteen minutes later accompanied by a broad-browed Chinese man carrying a black bag. As Annie watched in amazement, instead of listening to her heart and taking Francie's temperature, the Chinese doctor tested all the pulse points for their twenty-eight different qualities, and from this he made his diagnosis.

"She is in a state of shock," he confirmed, writing a prescription for Lai Tsin to take to the medicine shop. "She must drink this potion three times each day. She must be kept warm and fed only on boiled ricewater for two whole days. I can do nothing for the fear in her head, but this will be effective in curing her body." He looked angrily at Lai Tsin and said something in Chinese and Lai Tsin shrugged.

"What was he so angry about?" Annie demanded, after he had gone.

He met her eyes, he knew he must tell her now because he was afraid. Francie might do something foolish. "He told me what I already knew. That Francie is going to have a child. He was angry because he thought that I was the father, and he disapproved."

Annie stared blankly at him, her heart filled with pity as she thought of Francie worrying about her secret all alone. Realization slowly dawned on her and she said, "The child will be Josh's."

"That is so. I saw how she tried to hide it. I waited for her to speak because I did not want her to lose face. But now I am afraid for her.

She may do something very foolish. She will need your help, Annie. You must take her away from here, take her away from Chinatown, from San Francisco, from everything she knows and those who know her and seek to do her harm."

Annie looked at him bewildered, the news about the baby had driven everything else out of her head but now she remembered Sammy. She stared, shocked, at the mask Lai Tsin showed her and she nodded as he repeated the description the barman had given him. "That'll be Sammy all right," she said bitterly. "How could he do such a thing? He must be insane."

"He is insane with jealousy. His love for your brother is mixed up with his hatred for women. It is not uncommon for a man to love another man, but it does not usually lead to such violence."

Annie blushed, he was talking about things she had barely heard of except in the Bible. "But Josh wasn't like that."

"That was Sammy's tragedy. Maybe if Josh had loved him, too, this would not have happened. Now you must take Francie away," he repeated wearily. "It is not good for her to live here. The Chinese do not like it. They believe she is my concubine. When she has her child they will think it is mine. I cannot allow them to say such things about her. She will be treated with contempt and indifference by my people and by her own. She would live in a no-man's land, neither one thing or the other. And her child would suffer the same fate. Take her away, start a new life with her. You are my family and I will take care of you and send you money. It is only right."

Annie heard the sadness in his voice and she pitied him his loneliness, because she knew he loved Francie dearly. Nevertheless she felt the stirrings of a happiness in her own heart as she thought about Josh's child. She would take Francie far away from here. She still had money, they could buy another boardinghouse somewhere else and she could earn enough to raise the child properly. She couldn't wait to tell Francie that instead of despair her child would bring great happiness into the world.

Lai Tsin left her and went back to his room. It was the only room he had ever had of his own and this was the first time he had closed the door without a feeling of pleasure. He lit the incense taper in the painted tin holder, unrolled his bedmat and lay down. He put his hands behind his head and reran the events of the night in his mind. Tomorrow Sammy Morris would be found and he knew what he had to do. And in a few days' time, when she was feeling better, Francie would leave him.

A bitter feeling of loneliness swept over him. He had felt it many times before, only now it was worse. He told himself that when you are alone you have nothing and you have nothing to lose. But when you have savored the pleasure of companionship and love, then to lose it was the worst thing in the world. The gods had been good to him for a while and now they had taken their favors away. So be it.

# CHAPTER 19

◆

The next evening at seven o'clock, Lai Tsin went to see the Elder and get his answer. The old man bade him enter and he sat opposite him, stroking his white beard and eyeing him solemnly.

Lai Tsin waited. It would be disrespectful to ask the old man to hurry; he would speak in his own good time. "Before I tell you what you wish to know I must ask what your intentions are," he said at last.

"It is better that I keep my own counsel, Honorable Grandfather," he replied guardedly, but the old man refused to be deceived.

"It would not be seemly to bring violence and disgrace into the Chinese community."

"Honorable Grandfather, we are talking of a person who is more violent than the hatchet men of the tongs, a man who has killed many women and even now seeks to kill another—"

"Your *concubine.*" The elder's eyes were contemptuous and Lai Tsin hung his head. The old man thought for a long time while Lai Tsin stared at his shoes, waiting, until finally he made his decision.

"I have investigated your story," he said calmly. "What you said about the concubine was true. But I also know she is from a great family. Your passion must be strong for you to play such a dangerous game with such important personages. It would be better for all of us if you were to return her to her own."

"Then it would be better if I killed her!" Lai Tsin's eyes were angry and the old man knew he meant it. His eyebrows rose in surprise, but he nodded, thinking hard before he spoke again.

"If this murderer were Chinese we would deal with him in our own way. But if your decision is final then you shall have your answer. On these conditions: whatever happens to this man shall never be known, you will not tell me or anyone else. There must be not a whisper that would undermine the honor of the Chinese community."

Lai Tsin leaned forward in the slippery blackwood chair. He said, "I agree, Honorable Grandfather." Then he listened, surprised as the old man told him what he had found out.

He bowed to him as he left, thanking him, but the old man turned away, saying dismissively, "The words have already flown from my mind. I remember nothing of this conversation."

Lai Tsin walked slowly home and for once his mind was not on his business but on what he must do. Annie met him at the door. Her shirt sleeves were rolled up and the little room shone from polishing, but her brown eyes were very anxious. "She is awake," she said agitatedly. "She took the potion and a little of the boiled ricewater. Then I talked to her about the baby. She cried on my shoulder, she was so relieved. Then I told her we must go away but she just shook her head and said she would never leave you."

"I will speak with her."

Francie was lying stiffly in the narrow bed, her hands clenched into tight fists. Her eyes were closed but her face was not peaceful; tension seemed to radiate from her.

"Sammy Morris will never harm you again. This, Lai Tsin promises you. Do you believe me, Francie?" She nodded slowly, but her eyes remained tightly shut.

He crouched by her side and took her hand. "It is time to leave, Little Sister," he said. "Your life journey must continue without Lai Tsin. Like Little Son, Philip Chen, your child must be brought up among his own people, knowing their ways and understanding his heritage." She lay stiff and silent, but he continued talking in a soft persuasive voice, explaining that she must put her child first, that Annie would help her, that he would look after them because they would always be his family. But she must go.

She held his hand to her face. "You are my friend," she whispered. "I'll never leave you."

Their eyes met for a long moment and he said, "Then I must tell you a story so that you will understand your new responsibilities. Listen to me and you will know you have no choice." She clung to his hand, gazing trustingly at him as he began the story that was engraved on his soul. "My sister, Mayling, and I were born into a world of poverty, the children of the concubine, Lilin. Our father, Ke

Chungfen, was already an old man of sixty years, gray-haired and bent and cruel. His Number One wife had died after giving him five sons and he had married again quickly because more sons meant more comfort in his old age.

"His Number Two wife was young and pretty but she was also barren and lazy and he cursed the day he had married her. His house was dirty and it was said she smoked opium all day and took young lovers and made a fool of him, even though he beat her every night to teach her a lesson.

"He asked around the villages for a *mui-tsai,* a young girl whose family were willing to sell her into servitude. Lilin was thirteen years old and her family was so poor they were glad to let her go for the miserly sum of only forty *yuan,* just so they would not have to fill her rice bowl every night.

"She had a sweet oval face, long, shiny black hair to her waist, and big dark eyes. It was not long before the old man claimed more than he had paid for with his miserly forty *yuan* and young Lilin became his concubine. He treated her cruelly, beating her even though she worked hard to please him. She was forced to clean their poor rooms, to wash their clothes and prepare their food, and to wait on the wife and the arrogant young sons, who copied their father by berating her continually. And she would hang her head meekly and promise to try harder to please them, for she was only a paid-for *mui-tsai* and had no rights."

Lai Tsin's eyes met Francie's as he said, "When Lilin knew she was to have a child she prayed it would be a son so he might have a better chance in life than she had, for even though the son of a *mui-tsai* would be considered the lowest of the low, he would never be as low as a girl. She worked even harder, staying up half the night to sew the little flat cotton shoes that the eldest son, a boy of thirteen, would sell in the marketplace. The father tended the big white ducks on the flat, reedy ponds belonging to the village lord, and the other sons worked picking mulberry leaves or in the rice fields, depending on the season.

"Lilin was filling their wooden lunch boxes with boiled rice to take to the fields when the pains struck and she knew the child was finally coming. When the pains became too bad to continue her work, she went to lie on her bedmat. No one came near, even though the Number Two wife heard her screams, and when the child was born it was a girl. Lilin wept, but the baby resembled her and she was someone to love, an infant who one day would love her in return. She gave her a pretty name, Mayling, and took the family name, Ke.

"Now she had to work even harder, looking after her child as well as all the household tasks, and she was forced to keep the baby quiet and out of sight because nobody wanted to be disturbed by its crying.

"One night she heard Ke Chungfen quarreling with his Number Two wife. Their voices were raised in anger. She was laughing at him, mocking him. The stink of her opium pipe crept through the thin screens and the voices got louder and then suddenly there was just silence. The next morning the old man said that his wife had died in the night from smoking too much opium.

"Lilin had to help lay her out and she could not help noticing the bruises on her neck, though the old man quickly covered them, and she felt sure that he had killed her.

"Afterward Lilin was frightened and tried to keep out of his way as much as possible, but with the Number Two wife gone he became even more of a tyrant. Even his sons felt the lash of his tongue as well as the lash of the whip he used at the ponds. But he still claimed his rights with her, though with good joss she did not become with child until some years had passed. Her daughter was already three years old when the next child was born. A son whom she named Ke Lai Tsin."

" 'I have enough sons,' the man said coldly when she proudly showed him the child."

Lai Tsin stopped. He stared down at the floor, his brow furrowed as he remembered his mother. "She was still only seventeen," he continued. "She had no love for this man. He had taken her against her will and she had not wanted his children. But now she loved them. She still kept his house clean, she washed the clothes and prepared their meals, but she gave her love to Mayling and Lai Tsin. Even though she herself existed only on rice and a few morsels of vegetables, she tried to see there was a little fish or meat in her children's rice bowls at night. She taught them games, held them close, and told them she loved them. She called them by their milk-names, Mayling was 'Little Treasure,' and Lai Tsin, 'Little Plum.' They slept close to her at night on her bedmat and they would watch her combing her long black hair as she sang them to sleep.

"I was almost four years old when Chen was born and I remember laughing at his funny little pancake face. Mayling and I loved him and helped look after him, though we were already hard at work in the fields. But little Chen was not destined by the gods to grow to boyhood and the day he died was the saddest of my life. A year later our mother died. I was seven years and Mayling ten." Lai Tsin shook his head sadly. "Even now I do not know what happened, only that one morning our mother did not wake up. I remember looking at her, wondering why she did not answer when I said I was hungry, and I noticed that even in her death-sleep she looked tired. Ke Chungfen had worked her to death.

"Our mother was not given a proper ceremonial burial. After all, she was only a *mui-tsai*. Ke Chungfen claimed he was too poor to buy a coffin and she was wrapped in the straw mat in which she had been laid out, tied at the head and the feet, and buried quickly. The loss of face at such a burial is overwhelming and our shame was terrible. The family observed no mourning and we went immediately back to our work in the fields. Mayling and I were left alone to face our father's indifference and anger."

There was a long silence; Lai Tsin's face was drained of expression and emotion, and Francie forgot her own fears. She squeezed his hand. "Poor Lai Tsin. Your world was such a harsh one."

"Our worlds were the same, only your surroundings were rich and mine the poorest of the poor. But the neglect and cruelty of our fathers was the same. You see, Francie, it was only our mothers' love, brief though it was, that showed us life could be different. And that is why you must think of your child. You must give the baby love so that he will be strong inside. Remember it has no father, there is only you to teach it the meaning of love. And if you do not, then it will be damaged the way we were."

Annie listened, thinking of her own life, devoted to caring for her selfish father. He had never given her anything of himself, no word or gesture of affection had ever passed between them. She understood what Lai Tsin meant and knew he was right.

Francie nodded, her heart too full to speak. In his wisdom Lai Tsin had showed her the path out of her despair. She would no longer think only of herself, she would have her child to love and protect. And she would be eternally grateful to him, for she knew what it had cost him to speak of his past. But she also knew he still had not told her everything, and that the rest of his tragic story was still locked away inside him.

# CHAPTER 20

◆

Annie's heart sank as the hired gig jolted around the final bend in the long, rutted road and the de Soto Ranch came into view. It was even worse than she had expected. But Francie's face had lit up when she told her about it. She said it was a special place, that her only good memories were the times spent there with her mother. "Mama left it to me" she said stubbornly, "I read it in the newspapers when they published my father's will. I never went to the lawyers to claim it because I was afraid Harry would find out. But he never goes there, no one does! It's beautiful and it's mine and it's where I want to have my baby." And just two days later here they were. They hadn't passed another house in miles and the place looked as though it were about to fall down.

"Oh, Annie," Francie said with a contented sigh, "isn't it just the most beautiful house you've ever seen?"

Annie stared gloomily at the weatherbeaten gray clapboard house with its broken windows and sagging wooden porch. "I suppose we can fix it up all right," she said grudgingly.

Francie climbed from the gig and ran up the steps. She turned to look at the long valley view, at the green paddocks and low sun-dried hills. In the distance she could hear the cackle of geese and the whinny of a horse and she felt the soft breeze on her skin.

"It's just the same," she said happily. "I've always felt free here. And it's the only place that ever felt like a real home to me, all those long summer days spent with my mother and the cold winter evenings together by the fire."

The door was unlocked and she stepped inside, wandering slowly through the dust-covered rooms, smiling as it came back to life in her memory. She saw the parlor in the warm glow of the old pot-bellied stove and her mother lying in the chaise longue and herself sitting at her feet while Princess snoozed on the braided hearthrug. In her memory, the big kitchen with its long scrubbed pine table and its old cast iron pots and pans was full of the delicious aromas of baking bread and roasting chicken, of rosy, fresh-picked apples and green walnuts and black wine grapes.

There was no lingering sadness about her mother's room: the warm afternoon sunshine filtered through the broken windowpanes and she could see her now, rosy-cheeked and sparkling-eyed, lying on her embroidered white pillows in the carved wooden bed, bringing her the gift of love and happiness.

"It's just the same." She sighed, content. "It's just as perfect as it always was."

Annie raised a skeptical eyebrow. All she could see was a broken-down old house whose roof probably leaked. It was hard to tell what it might look like after twelve years of dust and grime had been removed. But at least now Francie was happy. "We'll have it fixed up again in no time," she said cheerily enough, but her heart sank as she wondered where to start. She glanced up, startled at the sound of horse's hooves on the drive.

"I know who it is," Francie yelled, racing for the door. The small, wiry nut-brown man hitching his horse to the porch rail turned to look at her in astonishment.

"Zocco," she cried, leaping down the steps toward him, "don't you remember me?"

"Francie?" he asked disbelievingly.

She laughed and flung her arms around him. "Oh, Zocco, yes, it's me, after all these years. I've come home again."

She looked into his face; Zocco was no longer the young man of her memories. He was in his forties now and there were a few more lines around his eyes and his skin was a bit more weather-beaten. His English was as faulty as ever.

"I tell Esmerelda," he said quickly, "she help clean up the place. No one is here for so many years, we not do nothin'. But now I fix her up. Right away, Miss Francie. And I'm real glad you are back, Miss Francie, real glad the de Soto Ranch comes alive again."

Annie watched as he unhitched his horse, leapt agilely into the saddle, and galloped away in a cloud of dust. "Who was that?" she demanded.

"That's Zocco. He's been here as long as I can remember. When I was six years old he taught me to ride bareback so I would never fall off. He is my friend," she added simply.

Zocco was back within half an hour with Esmerelda, his wife, at his side in the pony trap, laden with brooms and buckets, planks of wood, nails, saws, and hammers. And on her lap was a big basket of food.

"Am I glad to see you, Esmerelda," Annie said, thankfully unpacking fresh tamales, a pot of refried beans, cornbread, pickled chilies, and an enormous apple pie from the basket. Esmerelda, as brown and smiling as her husband, spoke no English but she nodded, understanding that Annie liked what she had brought. And then Annie sent Francie out for a walk while she and Esmerelda put on their aprons and began sweeping up the dust.

Forbidden to help, Francie strolled lazily down to the pond, laughing as the geese flapped their wings threateningly at her, remembering them skidding and slithering on the frozen pond that final winter of her mother's life. She found the old deserted chicken coop where she had searched for her mother's brown Christmas egg, and she promised herself that tomorrow she would buy more hens so they could have fresh eggs for their breakfast. She wandered through the empty stables, breathing in the sweet familiar scent of hay and strolled down the grassy paths remembering how she had pushed her mother's cumbersome wheelchair. With a sigh, she told herself firmly that this would not be just a house of the past, it was a house for the future, her own and her child's. There was just one thing missing. There was no dog trotting at her heels. And she made another promise that the very next day she would find another dog to take the place of her Princess.

After a week the old house sparkled with cleanliness. The wide-planked chestnut wood floors were scrubbed and waxed, there were glistening new panes in the windows, the sagging porch had been fixed and every piece of furniture had been polished until it gleamed in the sunlight. The braided rugs were washed and hung out to dry in the sun, the pine kitchen table was bleached and scrubbed, the old iron range cleaned and fired up. Once more the smell of applewood and Annie's baking hung in the air. The de Soto Ranch was a home again.

Sammy Morris scarcely noticed the fire-blackened buildings as he hurried, head down, along the narrow streets on the fringes of Chinatown. The wind blowing direct from the Pacific Ocean was damp and chill. It brought tears to his eyes and he shivered, tucking his bearded chin deeper into his woolen muffler. He turned left then right through a maze of streets and finally stopped outside a derelict building. Setting down the basket he was carrying, he turned and looked around him. He waited a few minutes, listening and watching until he was satisfied no one was following him, then he picked up his basket and hurried inside, past the charred wooden stairway leading to a nonexistent second floor, through the hallway full of rubble to a room at the back of the building. The doorless entry was covered with a piece of sacking and he glanced quickly around once again before he entered.

The room was freezing, not just the damp temporary cold of the ocean wind outside but the penetrating marrow-chilling cold of an abandoned place. Setting down his basket he hurried to the little stove, took a box of matches from his pocket and relit the charcoal. He had been gone longer than he intended because he had imagined he was being followed. He'd had that feeling in his bones; he had felt eyes on him, heard footsteps behind him, yet every time he turned around to confront his shadower there had been no one there. Sweating with fear he had led his imaginary followers a dance, dodging through alleys and racing down shadowy lanes, losing himself in the process. Eventually he had found himself back at the relief kitchen. He'd eaten a meal there, acting as though nothing was wrong, keeping an eye out all the time, but no one had shown any interest in him.

As he left he'd turned at the door to check. People were eating, drinking, talking, no one was looking at him, but still he kept a cautious lookout as he walked back home.

Wisps of smoke sprang from the freshly lit charcoal and he put his hands to his mouth and blew on it till it glowed red. Then he turned to look at Josh.

He was lying on the rough pallet bed exactly where he had left him. He thought bitterly that that wasn't surprising, since Josh was paralyzed. His blind eyes stared vacantly upward, and if he had heard Sammy come in he did not show it. Josh had not uttered a sound since the night Sammy had dragged him from the flames roaring along Pacific Avenue and carried him in his arms to the hospital.

Sammy put his strong arms around Josh now and lifted him to a sitting position, chafing his icy hands to get the circulation going. "I've got something that'll warm you up," he said cheerfully, taking his purchases from the basket. He uncovered the bowl of beef stew and held it under Josh's nose for him to savor the aroma. "Just like your Annie used to make," he said, putting a little broth in Josh's mouth.

"That's a good lad," he said, feeding him spoon by spoon, like a child. "Aye, that's good, Josh. You can't ever say your friend Sammy didn't look after you proper. And I'll keep right on looking after you till my dying breath, just like we promised each other. Right, Josh?"

Josh's head lolled sideways and Sammy put down the bowl and took his friend in his arms again, moving him into a more comfortable position.

"I'll get meself a job soon," he promised, sitting back and lighting a cigarette. "There are plenty, with all the new building going on. And then I'll find us a nice room—on the ground floor, so it'll be easy to get you in and out. And when I'm earning a bit we can buy you a wheelchair and I'll take you for walks. Mebbe down to the ocean? You'd like that, wouldn't you, lad?"

His black eyes burned with pain as he stared at Josh, remembering the vital golden boy he had once been. And now he was talking about pushing him around in a wheelchair, about showing him places he would never see, about taking him to an ocean he would never swim in.

He pulled the bottle of cheap whiskey from his pocket, opened it and drank deeply, shuddering as the harsh liquor hit his stomach. Then he leaned forward and tilted the bottle to Josh's mouth, nodding, satisfied, as Josh swallowed. "That's better, lad," he muttered. "It'll ease your pain for a while."

He sat drinking the whiskey, watching his friend and wishing he could turn back the clock.

"I'd put it right back, Josh," he said thickly after a while. "All the way back to when we were still lads at school. Them was the best times, Josh, weren't they? Just you and me, havin' a good time together?" He sipped the whiskey reflectively. "Aye," he added quietly, "I'd put the clock right back to before the day at the river when Murphy drowned." He sighed deeply. "I didn't mean to do it, you know, Josh, but it was like a rage took over my heart." He thumped his fist to his chest, tears stinging his eyes at the memory. "I just looked at you standing up there on that rock and I knew I loved you. And you were making such a fuss over Murphy, having such a good time together and ignoring me. *I felt like nothing.* Nobody even knew

if I was there or not, and nobody cared. Least of all you. I couldn't
let that happen, Josh, not after all we had been to each other all those
years, swearing friendship and loyalty in blood and all. It wasn't hard
to do what I did. It just seemed natural. I never knew if you realized.
Nobody else did."

He stared silently at Josh, half-expecting an answer, but Josh's face
was blank. He poured more whiskey into his slack mouth, brushing
away the dribble with his fingers, then he sat back again. "Are you
warmer now, lad?" he asked, anxiously checking the fire. "I know
it'll never be real warm in here, but the whiskey'll help. I hope it
takes away your pain, Josh, because it sure as hell will never take
away mine. After all I've done for you, and now look at you." His
eyes filled with tears again as he stared at him and he shook his head
slowly from side to side.

"Y'see Josh, if you'd never looked at those girls, I'd never have
had to kill 'em. I couldn't bear to think of you touching them, kissing
'em . . . it made me sick to my stomach, y'know that? And I had
that old burning feeling in my heart again. But after Murphy, I knew
what to do about it. I slipped up that last time though. I knew you
suspected me, but even so, you came through for me when I pleaded
with you to help me. 'They'll hang me, Josh,' I said to you. 'The
judge will put on his black cap and they'll hang me by the neck until
I'm dead. I didn't do it,' I said, 'You can't let them hang me, can
you?' Remember how I told you all I needed was a chance? And you
agreed, you sent me to Annie to get the money while you tried to
divert the police. But I made sure it was *your* muffler they found on
the body, and I made sure to tell my mam it was *you* who'd done
those murders, Josh, and as your good true friend I was helping *you*.
That way I knew you would have to run away with me. I knew you
could never go home again because it would be *you* they would hang.
I had you all to myself then. Oh yes, I had you all right. Until you
met Miss Francesca Harrison, that is."

He got up and walked drunkenly toward Josh. He knelt and
peered into his sightless eyes. "Can you hear what I'm telling you,
Josh? I'm tellin' you the truth, my friend. The whole truth and nothing but the truth. And Francie Harrison would have been next if I
hadn't lost her. I wanted her to *suffer* first, you see, Josh. *Suffer like
you have.* I thought it only fair."

He glanced at the empty bottle in his hand and then hurled it
viciously at the wall, flinching as it shattered noisily into a thousand

pieces. "If it weren't for her you wouldn't be lying here like this, Josh Aysgarth," he shouted, staring despairingly at him. "It's *Francie* who crippled you. *Francie* who blinded you. It's Francie who took your mind away and made you dumb. It's her who's put you through all these weeks of hell."

He slumped to the floor, his head in his hands. Tears cascaded down his cheeks as he sobbed. "I'll never forget when I came to look for you. The flames were burning all around but I *knew* you were there. I found you and carried you in my arms to the hospital all bloodied and broken. I watched over you while they did what they could. I stayed beside you all those weeks and when I knew you would live and there was nothing more they could do for you, I brought you home. Where you belong, Josh, lad. With me."

He reached for the second bottle of whiskey and unscrewed the lid with trembling hands. "You're mine all right now, Josh," he said, a touch of triumph in his voice, "and I'll never let you go again." Tipping back his head he drank deeply, coughing as the spirit hit his throat. "Aye," he said, wiping his mouth with the back of his hand, "and when the moment is right the woman who caused you all this pain will join the rest of 'em. In her grave."

Jimmy's Bar on Washington had been quickly patched up. It was back in business and doing a roaring trade and whenever Sammy couldn't stand Josh's silence another minute he took himself off there to drown his sorrows in his favorite Irish whiskey, sitting at the scarred wooden bar, staring into his glass, thinking about Josh.

Josh's silence filled their terrible derelict little room with menace. It was as though there were words locked inside him, things he wanted to say that he was struggling with all his might to express. And yet every time Sammy looked at him his eyes had that same vacant stare. Many a time Sammy had stood angrily over him after a few drinks and shouted, "Talk for God's sake, Josh. Come on, if you've got summat to say, then say it."

Tonight his anger had risen to boiling point. He'd picked him up by the collar and shaken him like a dog, screaming at him to speak, to walk, to act like he used to. "Even if you want to tell me you hate me, then say it, for God's sake." But Josh's head just lolled to one side and his horrifying ever-open eyes had stared sightlessly into his like a vision from a nightmare.

Sammy had dropped him back onto the pallet and covered him

quickly with the blankets. The room was cold, but he was soaked with sweat. Fear crawled over his skin and he'd run from the derelict house back to the bar. But he couldn't stay away for long—Josh's silent, sinister presence drew him back like a magnet.

He tossed back his drink and ordered another. Josh was neither alive nor dead. It was getting so Sammy was afraid to go back, afraid to see him lying on the filthy pallet, afraid of his own futile anger because Josh never moved and never spoke. He knew he couldn't take it much longer. He would have to do something about him even though it would break his heart. He slid his hand into his pocket and felt the cold steel of the bowie knife. It was waiting there for Josh. One day soon.

It was late when he finally stumbled from the bar. The night sky was black and the clouds so low they seemed to be sitting on the rooftops, but Sammy didn't need a moon to light his way, he knew the route like a homing pigeon. The knife clanked against the bottle of whiskey in his pocket at every step, but he was so lost in his thoughts he didn't even notice. It couldn't be tonight, he told himself. He would spare Josh one more night at least, give him a last chance. He'd pour some more whiskey down him to deaden his pain, though there was no way to even know whether Josh even felt any pain.

He stopped outside the entry, glancing automatically around, but it was too dark to see anything and he stepped inside and groped his way through to the back. The stove had gone out again and the room was in darkness. Grumbling, he stumbled across and put a match to it. Then he lit the candle on the floor and turned to look at Josh. *He wasn't there.*

Sammy blinked and looked again. Nothing. He held the candle aloft disbelievingly, but the blanket was tossed onto the floor and the pallet was empty. His spine crawled with fear as he tried desperately to clear his whiskey-fuddled head. Josh had gone, he had gotten up and walked away. *He had left him.* He dropped the candle and spun around, roaring like an enraged animal, but his roar turned into a terrified scream as two men leapt at him from the shadows. They threw him to the ground, twisting his arms behind him, forcing them back and up until he thought he would explode with pain.

"Let him go," a calm voice said. His arms were dropped, his captors stepped back and Sammy peered at them, breathing heavily and groaning with pain. They were Chinese and they had small, lethally sharp hatchets tucked into red sashes at their waists. They had just proven their strength and he knew he was no match for them.

"Sit down," the calm voice ordered and Sammy quickly obeyed, peering nervously into the shadows behind them.

"Who are you?" he demanded. "What do the Chinese want with me?"

Lai Tsin stepped forward, holding up a lantern. His words were icy. "A confession, Mr. Morris," he replied.

Sammy stared at him, frightened. He looked familiar, but he could have been any one of a thousand faces he saw every day in China-town. "What have you done with Josh?" he growled.

"You will never see him again," the man told him in his light singsong voice.

A red rage filled Sammy's brain. It was the kind of rage that made him lose control . . . they had taken Josh from him, they had hurt him . . . they had killed him. Snatching the knife from his pocket he suddenly hurled himself at the Chinese man.

Lai Tsin saw the flash of steel in the lamplight, he felt its sharpness split his cheek and then the warm trickle of blood. He stood un-moved as the two hired tongs grappled Sammy to the ground. Then he bent and picked up the knife. He said calmly, "And now you will do as I tell you."

Sammy was on his knees. One of the Chinese held his arms and the other had him by the neck, his hatchet at the ready. Lai Tsin put writing paper, pen, and ink on the floor in front of him. He said, "Pick up the pen and write what I say."

Sammy peered bewilderingly at him and then down at the pen. The man holding his neck jammed his knee painfully into his back and he quickly picked it up, waiting for what came next.

"Let him go," Lai Tsin ordered, and the man released him. He stood behind him and the other stood in front, and Sammy glanced fearfully at them. He shook his head. This was all wrong, it was a nightmare. What did they want from him? *A confession,* the Chinese had said. . . .

He looked up. Lai Tsin's eyes met his and he said, "You will write, 'I, Sammy Morris, confess to the murder of five innocent people.' "

"No," Sammy roared, throwing his pen to the ground. "You'll never get me to write that."

Lai Tsin nodded to the men and they grabbed him again. And this time Sammy felt cold steel against his own neck, sharp as a whisper against his flesh and the sudden warm ooze of his own blood.

"Now you know how your victims felt," Lai Tsin said. "You know their terror and their helplessness. Pick up the pen and write."

Trembling, Sammy did as he was told. "I confess to the murder of my schoolfriend, Murphy," Lai Tsin continued.

Sammy's head shot up and he looked around, panicked. Nobody knew about that, nobody—except Josh. He had confessed it all to blind, silent Josh . . . he was the only one who could possibly know about Murphy.

"Write!" Lai Tsin commanded. The knife touched his neck again and Sammy quickly scrawled the words, "I confess to the murder of the three women that my friend, Josh Aysgarth, was blamed for."

His breath came in short, frightened gasps. Josh must have been faking, he had heard all the time, he had told on him. . . .

Terrified, he stared at Lai Tsin. His jaw hung slackly and a strangled groan came from his throat. *Now* he knew who this man was. He was the Chinese who had befriended Francie Harrison. It was *she* who had told him all this, *she* who had sent them to make him confess, *she who had taken Josh away from him again.*

"Write," Lai Tsin commanded. His voice was cold. Terrified, Sammy bent over the paper and wrote what he said. "Sign it," Lai Tsin ordered.

"Where is Josh? What have you done with him?" Sammy screamed. "You can't take him away from me, we're brothers, we love each other. . . . I saved him, I looked after him, I always have—"

"Sign," Lai Tsin repeated stonily.

Sammy's hand trembled so much he could barely hold the pen and his signature scrawled unsteadily across the page.

"Sign again," Lai Tsin ordered, "so that we can read it." Sammy felt the hatchet blade threateningly on his neck as he wrote his name again.

Lai Tsin nodded to the men and they grabbed Sammy's arms, wrenching them behind him until he screamed with pain.

Lai Tsin calmly picked up the paper and read it. He nodded, satisfied. He stepped closer to Sammy and looked into his burning eyes for a long moment. They were the eyes of a murderer, a madman who killed without compunction. A man who would kill Francie if he could. "You know what to do with him," he told the two men, turning away.

"No!" Sammy screamed, lurching after him. "No." But Lai Tsin had already disappeared. And then Sammy felt a stinging blow on the back of his head and knew no more.

Later that night, when the darkness was the deepest, the men from the tong carried Sammy Morris in a covered dray to the waterfront and onto a China-bound vessel. The captain pocketed his fee and the crew looked the other way as they thrust him down the ladder into the hold. He was still alive, as Lai Tsin had commanded. But before they left they cut off his manhood.

# CHAPTER 21

# Six Months Later

It was midnight and Lai Tsin was in his warehouse, checking his stock and making notes for his new orders. Francie had taught him all the words for the goods he sold and he wrote them slowly and precisely.

He shook his head as he put away his notebook. He had been alone all his life—he was used to it and he had never expected more. But there was an emptiness without Francie. Everything had changed when he met her. He had become a person of respect in his own eyes as well as in others. And in return he wanted to take all her burdens onto his own shoulders; he wanted to give her back her youth and beauty; he wanted to give her the world. But first he had to earn it.

He locked the door of his warehouse and walked slowly homeward through San Francisco's dark, quiet streets, thinking about his life. He had never expected to have a future, there was only the present and that needed no planning. Now he knew if he was to achieve his goals he must look further than his shops and warehouses. He had to be more than a mere merchant. He had to become an entrepreneur. He must progress beyond San Francisco, to Hong Kong and China, to Hawaii, India, Russia, and the Orient.

He glanced at his image reflected in a shop window and saw an ordinary Chinese peasant. The educated, prosperous Chinese had all stayed home in China, it was only the poor who had fled to America to labor in railroad gangs and in the fields, in laundries and in restaurants. Those with sharper brains and a little money had become merchants like him, but even their lives were fraught with difficulties and dangers, and not just from the *gwailos,* the foreign devils. There was much jealousy and trickery, and the tongs were vicious and a constant threat. The other Chinese merchants were strong because they were heads of their own large families who helped them, but he had no family. Only Francie. He thought about her for a long time as he walked slowly homeward, and he suddenly realized that with Francie as his partner he was stronger than them all. With Francie as head of his company he could buy land and own businesses forbidden to Chinese, not just in Chinatown, but anywhere in America, anywhere in the world. With Francie at his side, he could be more powerful than any of the Chinese merchants.

Later that night as he tossed restlessly on his bedmat, he told himself that what he wanted most of all was to become a man of learning. Because only then, armed with the three great powers of success, money, and learning, could he return to his village on the banks of the Ta Chiang and show them how fine the child of the poor *mui-tsai* Lilin was now. He wanted to erect a temple to her memory and those of her dead children so that their spirits might have a home. And he wanted to bestow all his riches on Francie and her unborn child.

Meanwhile all he could give her was the dog she wanted. He had found two big, shambling sand-colored pups with amber eyes and now he must take them to her. He had told himself he'd put off going to see Francie because he did not want to disturb her, but there was another reason: he had been to that same valley years ago and was afraid of the bad memories that returning there would bring.

He bought himself some new clothes for the trip so that she would be proud of him: a long, dark blue silk robe, a padded black jacket, and a round hat with a silk button in the center. His hair had grown and he wore it braided in a queue; he carried his wicker pannier on his shoulder and held the two eager pups on leather leads. He walked downtown to the Ferry Building and nervously took the Contra-Costa ferry, unaware of the superior smiles his fellow-passengers gave his outlandish appearance.

His head was filled with old fears as Zocco drove him northward to the ranch. He reminded himself that he was a respected merchant and that soon he would have enough money to pay the Elders their full five percent. He told himself to forget the past, but his heart was like a lump of charcoal, burning with hot remembered pain as the long valley unrolled in front of him.

Francie ran eagerly onto the porch to greet him. She was big with the child and his eyes darkened with tenderness. He thought she looked like a child herself with her pink cheeks and her blond hair falling like a cape around her shoulders. She was laughing at the pups, tangled in their leads around his feet.

"*Two* puppies, Lai Tsin!" she exclaimed.

"One female and one male. In time you will have more Great Danes. I hoped they would please you."

She laughed again. "I shall call them Duke and Duchess—in memory of Princess. And now I have something to give you," she said proudly. "My house is your house, Lai Tsin. It is our home."

As she led him through the simple rooms he saw there were no things of great value, no precious silk rugs, no ornaments of nephrite jade, no paintings or carved blackwood chairs such as he had seen in the Elder's house. But the little ranch house glowed with warmth and welcome like no other place he had ever known.

Annie bustled, smiling, from the kitchen to greet him. She had prepared a feast for him and they sat at the long pine kitchen table and she served a tomato soup made from their own tomatoes, fish from the river, vegetables from the garden, a pie made with apples from their trees and cream from their own cow. And though he had never eaten such food in his life he smiled and said it was a wonderful *gwailo* feast.

After supper they sat by the fire and Annie looked curiously at him. His new clothes hung on his thin frame and his face, with its prominent cheekbones, looked gaunt, but Lai Tsin had the strength of steel and she guessed he had acquired it the hard way. Francie said she had been afraid to ask about his past but Annie's curiosity knew no such boundaries. Slipping off her shoes, she stretched her wool-stockinged toes toward the warmth of the fire. Wriggling them pleasurably in the heat, she said bluntly, "Tell us what brought you to America, Lai Tsin."

Lai Tsin was silent, wondering how he could tell them. It was dark outside and the cold night wind beat urgently at the windows. He stared around at the snug little room lit by the dancing flames of the log fire. He had never felt this before, the security of four walls and the company of friends, people he loved and who he knew cared about him. His heart was very full as he replied in his light, cool voice, "My dear friends. You have been free and frank about your own lives. I am the stranger, the foreigner in your midst and you are right to be curious. I will tell you why I came to America."

Their eyes were fixed on him, waiting for him to begin. A log fell in the grate amid a shower of vermilion sparks and the pups growled restlessly in their sleep. After a while he said, "Where I lived, in Anhwei Province on the banks of the Yangtze, the village lord owned everything: he owned the land and the houses on them, he owned the ponds with the ducks, the rice fields and the mulberry fields. He owned us all. My father was in charge of looking after the ducks, which were much prized for their meat. Every so often the village lord would send his ducks to Nanking to be killed and sold for food. My sister and I would be given the job of herding them from our village to the Great River, prodding them onward with long canes, though we were careful never to harm them. Mayling and I were sad for them and sometimes we wondered if the ducks knew their fate, because they would squawk and complain and try to fly away. But their clipped wings only fluttered uselessly and they would waddle tiredly on down the long road toward the Great River and their fate.

"Tenderhearted Mayling would be crying many tears as we reached the river. There was always one duck who seemed more special than the others. She would pick up the bird and stroke its feathers and whisper soothingly to it before setting it sadly with the rest on the yellow waters of the Yangtze.

"But worse was yet to come. Already exhausted from their long march, the ducks would then be forced to swim all the way to Nanking, one hundred miles. Both our eyes would be filled with tears as we watched them paddling frantically, trying to escape the big black junk sailing behind them forcing them on, and the men in sampans at each side keeping them together. The junk sailed almost faster than the ducks could paddle and they were allowed no rest. They were forced to keep going until nightfall, when they would be herded on shore. But at daybreak they would be back in the river again, paddling to Nanking and their doom.

"My father always went to Nanking alone. In all these years he had never even asked anyone to accompany him, but this time he told my sister that *we* were to go with him. I was nine years old and Mayling thirteen. She was pretty, like our mother, with long black hair to her waist, which she wore in the long pigtail of a child. Not until she was a woman could she put it up into a bun. She was still just a little girl and despite her hard life she was full of sparkle. She saw joy in the smallest of things; she was sweet-natured and tenderhearted, always laughing and teasing. She would laugh at the dogs chasing their tails in the courtyard; she would put a flower behind the water-buffalo's ear and stroke it comfortingly after its hard day's labor, and she would be filled with delight over a scrap of red yarn given to her by a kindly village woman to tie up her hair. Our smocks and trousers were of the very coarsest blue-and-white patterned cotton of the sort coolies wore, and to keep out the winter's cold we covered ourselves with the worn padded jackets our brothers had grown out of.

"When we took the ducks to Nanking we did not travel in the junk with Ke Chungfen but in a little sampan, taking turns with the paddle and making sure to keep the ducks together, thus avoiding our father's anger and a beating.

"There was much traffic on the Lower River and I was excited to see the huge white foreign steamers and the convoys of salt junks and the big wooden rafts where whole families lived. But Mayling's eyes were red from crying for the poor little ducks.

"All we knew was our little village. We had never seen a city before and we were amazed by the hundreds of ships lined up along the river at Nanking, and frightened by the bustling traffic on the narrow cobbled streets and the crowds of pushing, hurrying people. Mule-carts loaded with bundles twice their own size lumbered past us as we nervously herded our flock of ducks to their final destination. Coolies with great baskets slung on bamboo poles pushed us aside and sedan chairs carrying lordly merchants trotted by, the bearers shouting us out of their way.

"Mayling stopped to stare at a grand lady. Her face was rouged and painted and her black hair decorated with jade ornaments. She wore a dress of yellow brocade with a padded satin jacket and we knew she must be a member of the Emperor's family, for only they were allowed to wear the royal yellow. We gasped when we saw how tiny her bound feet were as she stepped from her chair and hobbled into a store selling bolts of expensive, colorful silks, emerald and indigo and scarlet and gold. And we jumped in fright as a man appeared around the corner beating a huge gong, while another man ran behind him. He was a thief and his arms were tied, and at each stroke of the gong another man struck his naked back with a bundle of thin bamboo rods, to punish him.

"We were stunned at the sight of stores spilling with foods such as we had never seen, bottles of *sam-shu* rice wine, pottery vessels of oil and aromatic spices and lotus-seed paste. And we stared awed at the temples painted in scarlet and jade, ornamented with gold lions and tasseled lanterns and at the many people kowtowing to the gods. We were overwhelmed by the scent of a thousand sticks of burning incense and we were silenced by our glimpse of such richness and the knowledge of our own poverty.

"Our simple country heads were filled with city sights and sounds and smells, but we still mourned the demise of our tired little ducks as we herded them into the wooden godown and left them to their fate. Ke Chungfen collected the money and then he turned to us and told us curtly to return to our sampan and wait there until he sent someone to fetch us.

"Mayling was still sobbing and I reminded him that we had not eaten since breakfast upriver at dawn and it was now five in the evening. Grudgingly he took a few coins from his pocket and told us to go to a teahouse and buy the smallest bowl of rice. I was excited as we ran back through the streets searching for a place that was cheap enough. We had never in our lives been in a teahouse. It was a great adventure and for once our hearts felt kindly toward our father for giving us this treat. But in the end all our few coins bought us was a single bowl of salty maize gruel.

"Still, it was enough to satisfy our hunger temporarily and we wandered back through the busy streets, hand in hand, gazing into alleys that sold only ironware, or silverware or vegetables or live fish. But we were frightened by the pushy, harsh-voiced city people. It was all too much for such young, unworldly country-bred peasant children and by the time we reached the river we were exhausted. We curled up in our little sampan and fell straight to sleep, dreaming of the ducks and their sad fate.

"I was awakened a couple of hours later by a coolie shouting in my ear and shaking me by the shoulder. 'Your father has ordered you to come now,' he said, prodding Mayling awake. I thought he looked strangely at us as we climbed from our little sampan, but we followed him anyway.

"Night had fallen and only an occasional oil lamp lit our way. We held hands for safety, glancing many times over our shoulders. Incense sticks, lit to appease the household god, burned outside every door and their powerful scent helped disguise the foul odors coming from the muddy drains as the sinister-looking coolie led us through a maze of dark alleys, until finally we came to a small square.

"A group of men were gathered in the corner under a flickering lantern and among them was our father in close conversation with a squat, swarthy-looking man wearing a black cheongsam and a round buttoned hat. He had a long, drooping moustache and narrow, slitted eyes and instinctively I did not trust him. My father said something to the bearded man and he turned to look at us. His eyes lingered a long time on Mayling, taking her in from the top of her shiny black pigtailed head to the tip of her worn cloth shoes and she shivered, blushing under his gaze. He shrugged and said something to my father, who flung out his arms and began to argue with him, and we stared at them puzzled.

"I noticed a little platform had been erected in the corner and half-hidden behind it cowered a frightened group of young girls. Men were crowding into the square, staring boldly at them, laughing and prodding their breasts and touching them intimately.

"I grasped Mayling's hand, terrified. She was just a little girl, barely thirteen, not yet even a woman. Even though she worked hard for our father he knew that one day, if he were ever to be rid of her, he would be forced to give her a dowry. His elder sons were soon to be married and he needed money to pay for their weddings. If he sold Mayling now he would not have the burden of filling her hungry mouth every night until she married, he would not have to provide a dowry, and he could also pay for the weddings.

"My eyes met Mayling's and I knew she understood. She had turned pale and her dark eyes were big and glassy with panic. I glanced quickly back at my father, still arguing over her price with the flesh-peddler. I grasped her hand tighter. I said, 'Run, Mayling. Run with me. Fast as you can.'

"We slid unnoticed out of the square, slipping on the evil-smelling mud and tripping over the cobblestones, weaving in and out of alleys, running and running until our hearts thudded in our chests and our throats burned like fire and we gasped for air. We stopped, leaning against a wall, listening intently, but the only sound was our own gasping breaths.

" 'Come,' I said, taking her hand and beginning to run again, though I did not know where, only away. Away from my evil father and the terrible man who wanted to barter my sister into slavery and prostitution.

"At last we emerged onto a broader street, one I recognized, and soon we were back at the river. We leapt like gazelles into our little sampan and pushed off, paddling fast down the river, like the little ducks pursued by the fateful junk. We did not know where we were going. We knew nothing except our home in our small village. We had no money and no idea of real life.

"We paddled all night and at dawn, exhausted as the ducks, we climbed onto the riverbank and slept. When we awoke a few hours later we were hungry and still exhausted. We hid our little sampan in the reeds and walked down a dusty track until we came to a village, but the peasants there turned their faces from us when we begged for rice. We walked on, not knowing what else to do, and then suddenly we came upon the banks of a clear flowing stream, and a small white-walled Taoist monastery.

"A young monk in saffron robes inclined his shaven head toward us in greeting and we quickly bowed in return as I explained our circumstances. His eyes filled with pity as he bade us come inside and share what food they had. It was not much because they had no money and lived only on what the peasants placed freely in their bowls, but the thin rice gruel tasted like heaven as it warmed our empty stomachs. And that night we slept on bedmats in a bare little cell and we felt safe with our friends. It was to be our last night of safety for many years.

"The next morning, with a little breakfast gruel in our bellies and their prayers for our safety and good fortune ringing in our ears, we went on our way.

"We had talked things over and decided we would return to the river and paddle our sampan to the next city, maybe even all the way to Shanghai, where we would find work. Night was already falling as we walked the last weary mile and we sighed in relief when we saw our sampan still there in the reeds where we had left it. What we did not see was the black-sailed junk waiting under cover of darkness around the bend in the river, nor the men who crept silently up on us, knives clenched between their teeth—not until they leapt on us, clasping their hands over our mouths so we had not time even to scream. They had known we could not get far and had found our sampan and lain in wait for us.

"Within minutes we were on board the junk and face-to-face with our father, Ke Chungfen, and the swarthy, narrow-eyed flesh-peddler. He laughed when he saw us. 'She has spirit,' he said admiringly to our father, pinching Mayling's little rump, testing her flesh before deciding how much she was worth. 'On the other hand,' he said consideringly, 'she has no breasts yet, only buds. This, of course, will bring down her price.'

"Mayling and I were standing side by side and I glanced at her. Her head was bowed onto her chest and she was blushing with shame as he discussed the intimate details of her body.

" 'How much?' Ke Chunfen demanded eagerly.

" 'The boy will make a good servant. I will give you three hundred *yuan* for both of them,' the man announced, folding his arms and walking around and around, inspecting us like cattle in a pen.

"I looked into my father's eyes and saw the greed for even more money.

" 'Take it or leave it,' the peddler said, turning away indifferently.

"Ke Chunfen sighed deeply and I knew he was thinking of the forty *yuan* he had paid for our mother, and regretting how little return he was getting on his money after all these years of feeding us, but he finally accepted and a deal was struck. And now Ke Mayling and Ke Lai Tsin belonged to the flesh-peddler.

"They put chains around our ankles so we could not escape and the junk took us back to Nanking, where we were to join the peddler's own ship. I looked back once as we stumbled down the gangplank onto the jetty, but there was no sign of our father.

"We were thrown into the evil-smelling hold of the peddler's junk and we huddled together in the darkness, listening to the scurrying of the rats, waiting for what was to come.

"A long time passed and then suddenly the hatch was lifted and we saw it was daylight. A coolie lowered a rope with a little basket containing a bowl of rice and a hunk of steamed bread and a flask of water. And despite our fears we ate the food like hungry little rabbits, scooping the rice into our mouths with our hands as fast as we could, afraid they might take it away. We took great gasps of the fresh morning air until the coolie came back and closed the hatch and left us in darkness again.

"After a few days of this a ladder was lowered and we were ordered on deck. Our chains cut cruelly into our ankles as we clambered up the narrow ladder and as we were accustomed only to darkness, the sunlight blinded us. To our surprise our chains were unlocked and we were told to go inside to the cabin and wash ourselves. We looked at each other doubtfully as we obeyed, wondering what was to come. But no one came to see us and we crouched on the floor of the cabin, waiting.

"A long time passed. At dusk the junk hove-to by the riverbank. Night fell and the moon came up and still we waited. Suddenly the flesh-peddler appeared. He laughed when he saw us, cross-legged on the floor in the moonlight. Then he grabbed Mayling's pigtail and pulled her to her feet. I leapt up to defend her, but he cuffed me away and a crewman sprang at me, holding me back as the peddler dragged her screaming to his cabin.

"The crewman stood over me, a knife in his hand, and I crouched helplessly back on the floor, the echo of Mayling's screams ringing in my ears. But they were not just an echo, or a memory. My little sister was still screaming, locked away in the cabin with the flesh-peddler."

Lai Tsin covered his face with his hands, hardly able to go on, but at last he continued. "I waited and waited, but Mayling did not return. Eventually, the crewman put me back in the hold. He replaced the hatch cover and I was alone in the darkness with my terrible thoughts. Days passed; occasionally rice and water were lowered to me but mostly I was just alone, hungry and frightened in the darkness.

"After an eternity passed I heard sounds outside and realized the junk was mooring in some big port and knew it must be Shanghai. Now at last maybe I would see Mayling again. The hatch was flung open and a coolie appeared, silhouetted against the gray sky. He let down the ladder and I climbed up, filling my lungs with the sharp, salty sea air, narrowing my eyes against the light, and looking quickly through my slitted lids for any signs of my sister. But the deck was full of crewmen busily taking down sails and tying thick ropes to the bollards on the jetty. The coolie slid the chains around my ankles again, but his eyes met mine and I must have stared so piteously that he hesitated—after all I was only a boy of nine years, and as poor as he was. What harm could I have done? He shrugged and took the chains off and hid them under a coil of rope, indicating that I should remain where I was. And then he left me.

"Minutes later I saw the flesh-peddler hurry down the gangplank and climb into a waiting rickshaw. I waited until he had gone, and keeping out of sight of the busy crew, I slipped into the masters' cabin to look for Mayling. But she was not there, nor was she in the tiny galley or the saloon. I ran around that little junk searching every corner, my heart gradually sinking into my shoes. I knew that after paying so much money for Mayling he would not have killed her and thrown her overboard, because then he would have lost his profit. I realized she must have been sent off the boat as soon as it docked, maybe to join the other girls he would have for sale. I ran back on deck, waiting until the crew hurried down the gangplank, heading for the city. Then I followed them, hoping they would lead me to the flesh-peddler and Mayling. But they made quickly for a malodorous alley filled with evil-smelling opium cribs, cheap singsong girls and noisy gambling dens, and there was no sign of the man or my sister.

"I wandered away, walking all day along the slippery granite-paved streets until my feet hurt. Every now and again I stopped someone and asked if they knew where the girls were being sold, but they just looked strangely at me and hurried by. Night fell and I was alone in the big terrifying city, hungry, penniless, desperate. Exhausted, I crouched in a dark corner of an alley and tears slid from my closed eyes. I knew I would never see Mayling again.

"Several days passed. I wandered the city begging for my food, grateful for every small morsel grudgingly given to me. I lurked like a hungry ghost on the edges of real life, haunting the teahouses longingly, listening to the talk of how hard life was in China and how rich the men were who had gone to work at the Gold Mountain in America. They said the men in America dug for gold and silver, they said they built railroads and opened their own businesses, that they lived like kings out there and still had enough left over to send home precious money to support their aged parents, their wives and children. 'The men of Toishan are becoming rich,' they muttered enviously as they savored fragrant pork dumplings and bean curd and all the delicious dim sum I could only long for. Riches to me meant food in my belly and a bedmat, but I thought about what they had said. I had lost Mayling, I had no family. Why should I not join the rich men of Toishan in America?

"I made my way back to the docks and by careful inquiry I found a ship that was leaving the next day for Seattle. It was a small, scabby-looking steam vessel and the villainous-looking crew leaning on the rails, spitting into the water and smoking, were dirty and unkempt. But it was the only ship leaving immediately for the Gold Mountain and I was determined to be on it. I marched boldly up the gangplank and asked to be taken on as a cabinboy. They laughed at me and showed me to the captain, a fat, bearded American in a grimy white naval uniform ornamented with much gold braid. He had on a peaked white cap with more gold and held a bottle of whiskey in his hand from which he took frequent gulps. He laughed as uproariously as the others when I nervously told him I wanted to join the ship.

" 'Sure, son,' he said, his fat belly shaking with laughter. 'One more won't make any difference. But you'll work hard for your keep.' Wages were never mentioned, but all I wanted was to keep from starving, and when I got to America I would work and earn money like the men from Toishan, in the Gold Mountain.

"The ship sailed on the dawn tide and as I scrambled about helping to coil ropes, I looked back at China disappearing on the horizon and I knelt on the splintery wooden deck and kowtowed, touching my head nine times to the floor in respectful memory of my mother, Lilin, and my sister, Mayling. And then I turned my face toward the open sea and America."

The fire had settled into a red glow, illuminating Francie and Annie's shocked faces, as Lai Tsin said with a sigh, "What happened next is another story."

He rose to his feet and bowed politely to them. "And now Lai Tsin begs your understanding, he is tired and must seek sleep. But before I go I wish to thank you for the gift of your friendship. I have never spent a night like this, in the warmth of a true home. Nor have I felt love and understanding from others. Tonight my life has been enriched by both emotions and I am grateful for your kindness."

Their eyes followed him as he bowed again and walked from the room, and they sat silently for a long time, each lost in her own thoughts. "I imagined my own life was hard and unfair," Annie said quietly at last. "Now I feel ashamed because compared with Lai Tsin's it was an earthly paradise. I always had a roof over my head, food, material things."

Francie nodded. "But like him, the one thing we never had was what money couldn't buy. Love and friendship."

Later that night as she tossed restlessly in bed, thinking of Lai Tsin and his story, Francie clasped her hands to the unborn child fluttering in her belly, and she vowed that the one thing in life her baby would never be short of was love.

# CHAPTER 22

◆

The very next morning Lai Tsin spoke to Francie about his idea. "Other merchants are already selling the same goods," he told her. "I must offer better prices, newer things, or lose my advantage. Therefore I must cut out the agents and the middlemen and buy direct from Shanghai and Hong Kong and ship the goods myself. And not just to San Francisco, but to New York, Chicago, Washington, all of America. And I will not buy just goods for the immigrant Chinese, but more important things that will appeal to the *gwailos:* silks from Hunan, carpets from Persia, ancient silver, bronze mirrors and antique ebony chests, fine paintings and screens and porcelain. My future as a merchant lies not only with my own countrymen but with the world. But *gwailos* will not do business with a Chinese. A company bearing the name of Lai Tsin is valueless. But with you as my Western partner, everything is possible."

Francie looked at him, puzzled. He was a man of mystery—she knew him and yet she didn't. Maybe she never would know the real Lai Tsin. Yet he had become her guide in life and she trusted him completely. She was so excited he'd asked her to be his business partner that she wanted to throw her arms around him and hug him, but Lai Tsin always kept a respectful distance between them and she knew she could never violate that code. "I am privileged to be your partner, Lai Tsin," she said simply.

And that night after supper, as the wind howled like a wolf outside the little wooden ranch house and the first flakes of snow flung themselves against their windows and the pups snored in front of the blazing fire, Lai Tsin continued his story.

He told them that they were only a couple of days out to sea when he realized that the ship's cargo was not tea, but men.

He said, "The hold was filled with coolies heading, like me, for the Gold Mountain. None of them had entry papers and all of them had paid the captain large sums to smuggle them into America. After a while they were allowed up on deck, and grateful to be out of the filthy, crowded hold, they spread out their worldly possessions: their grass bedmats, their padded quilts, and their treasure pillows, and immediately took out the cards and the maj-jongg tiles. They lit incense and kowtowed to the gods, and began to gamble, breaking off only to pick up their chopsticks and shovel rice into their mouths as fast as they could, or to smoke a pipe of opium, and occasionally, to sleep.

"In between my duties for the captain, endlessly running between the galley and the bridge carrying food, emptying his slops and scrubbing out his cabin, I assisted the cook, washed the dishes, helped stoke the big roaring boilers with coal, sluiced the decks and tried to keep out of the way of the drunken crew. And I watched the gambling. I already knew maj-jongg, but now I studied it intently. I watched the fan-tan, a game played with beans, and *pai gow,* which is Chinese dominoes, and many different complex card games, and soon knew I could win. But I had no money with which to play.

"When the ship suddenly ran into a typhoon it was every man for himself. The coolies were thrust into the hold and the hatches battened down. The captain stayed at the wheel, cursing and swigging whiskey as the ship lurched through mountainous green waves, tossing like a cork on the boiling foam at the top and sliding with a sickening lurch down a Niagara of water, only to be swamped at the bottom by the next enormous wave. The terrified crew hid themselves, waiting for their fate. Their cries were as loud as the coolies' wails coming from the hold, and the captain's curses grew even louder. I crouched behind him on the bridge, handing him a fresh bottle of whiskey as soon as the first one was finished. The crew had disappeared and he damned them all to hell. He smacked me fiercely across the head when the boat lurched and I dropped the next bottle, spilling half his precious whiskey. I was so frightened that I hardly felt the blow, all I knew was that the captain stood between me and death. But the captain knew different. He knew he had no say in the matter and that only the gods stood between us and death.

"The typhoon blew past us as night fell and we were once again on calm waters. The crew appeared from their hiding places and the hold was opened to let the coolies out from their prison and they were told to clean up their own vomit. The captain looked at me and I looked at him—he was roaring drunk by now. He took a silver dollar from his pocket and handed it to me. 'You've just earned yourself your first American dollar,' he said. 'And that's more than I can say for the other cowardly scum on board.' He strode the decks hurling curses and blows at whoever crossed his path and the crewmen glared murderously at me out of the corners of their eyes, muttering bad things.

"After that I kept as close to the captain as possible because they blamed me for his anger and I knew it would be easy enough to kill me and claim I had fallen overboard. Between the captain and the crew I scarcely slept; every menial job on the ship was mine. Dysentery broke out among the coolies and the ship stank and it was I who had to sluice down the hold and the decks, and help cast overboard the bodies of those who had died. The boilers were giving trouble and we limped from port to port, some of the crew absconded and new men had to be found, and still the coolies gambled. It took three weary months to reach California and as we sailed up the coast, the captain fell silent.

"We were hugging the cliffs off the coast north of San Francisco, heading for Seattle. It was a stormy, blustery night, nothing like the rage of the typhoon but enough to toss the rickety little ship around. The rain was lashing the decks, yet I saw we were sailing closer and closer to the shore, so close I could hear the boom of the surf on the rocks and the tolling of a buoy. Suddenly the captain roared an order for the hatches to be opened and I watched, bewildered, as the coolies were herded onto the decks. They huddled together, shivering in the rain, staring wonderingly at the captain pointing a rifle at them. Four of the crewmen stood by his side, also armed, and the coolies just stared dumbly back at them.

" 'This is America,' the captain roared suddenly in Chinese. 'The Gold Mountain. This is where you get off.' He waved the rifle menacingly at them, but they just stood there, too stupified with fright even to move. 'You have your choice,' he roared again. 'Jump and take your chances in the sea, it's only a couple of hundred yards to the shore. Or be shot and thrown into the sea already dead.' The crewmen let forth with a volley of shots, a couple of men fell dead and they kicked them contemptuously over the side.

"I stared at the captain, numb as the coolies. These poor men had scrimped and saved and borrowed money so they could go to America to make their fortune and return to take care of their poverty-stricken relatives in their old age. The captain had taken all their money. He had been their savior and now he was casting them overboard into the wild dark sea, uncaring whether they could even swim, for those who could not would be shot. He was a pirate and a murderer and I hated him as passionately as I hated the flesh-peddler.

"I watched, horrified as one by one they forced the terrified coolies to jump, laughing as they struggled in the icy waves. I took the captain's silver dollar from my pocket and spat on it and flung it contemptuously over the side. If this were America I wanted nothing to do with it, it was as evil as the place I had left behind.

"The captain saw my gesture, and with an oath he grabbed me by my queue and forced me to the rail. 'Join 'em, you miserable little Chinee bastard,' he roared, pushing me over the edge.

"I sank deep beneath the waves, kicking and struggling like a wild thing. I popped suddenly upward like a cork and my head was above the water. I had learned to swim in the Great River and struck out strongly toward the sound of the surf. All around me heads bobbed on the waves and my ears were filled with the cries of doomed men and the sound of rifle shots. I closed my eyes because I was too small and weak to help them and I could not bear to look into their faces. The swell was huge and I could tell from the roar of the surf there were great rocks in front. I swam on and on. A few others were swimming around me. I knew we were near the shore. But then a great wave engulfed us, enveloping us in icy darkness, hurling us forward with its momentum onto a rocky beach. I clung desperately to a rock as the wave surged out again, dragging men back out to sea with its force, and then I crawled over the rocks and up the shingle beyond the water line. I lay there, my arms flung out, my breath coming in shuddering gasps. I had arrived in America."

Lai Tsin looked at them watching him with horrified eyes. "The storm had worsened," he said. "The waves were huge, flinging themselves at the small scrap of shingle where I found myself. As they unfurled I would catch a glimpse of a head bobbing helplessly in the torrent, an outflung arm, and then nothing. Shivering with cold and fright, I waited for the others to make it to shore, but the only coolies from that terrible ship ever to set foot on America were dead ones."

\* \* \*

It was the third day of the Lai Tsin's visit and he still had not talked to them about Sammy. Even though it would bring gladness to their hearts he was afraid that talking about Josh would hurt Francie, and that mentioning the evil one's name would bring bad joss to the peaceful ranch.

When they had found Josh in the derelict house where Sammy kept him, they had placed him on a stretcher and carried him to a renowned Chinese doctor. The man had observed him for several days, and had taken innumerable tests. His examination was thorough and his verdict harsh. Josh Asysgarth would never walk or talk or see again. The blow had destroyed his mind, he knew nothing and no one. He was more dead than alive and the doctor gave him only a week or two at the most.

Lai Tsin had agonized over whether to tell Annie and Francie, but in the end he knew his decision was the right one. They already thought him dead, their grief had been spent, and now Francie was pregnant and it was time to look to the future. Even if they saw him Josh would not know them and it would only bring them terrible pain.

He took him to a nursing home on the cliffs just south of San Francisco. It was a pretty place with pastel buildings, set amid pines and sweet-flowering shrubs with the surf roaring on the rocks below. The sun shone and the sea breezes ruffled Josh's cap of blond hair as he lay in his bed. A week passed, two, then three. Lai Tsin went to visit him as often as he could and one day, Josh was lying there as usual, his head turned to the window. He took a deep breath, his sightless eyes turned to the sound of the roaring surf and the ocean he would never see again. And then with a faint sigh, he was gone.

It was a blessed release, the nurses told him when after a quiet service he buried him in the tiny churchyard nearby. His grassy plot was marked with a simple white cross bearing his name, and Lai Tsin also offered prayers for his spirit at a Chinese temple.

He had thought carefully about what to tell Francie and Annie and knew what he had done was for the best. But Sammy's written confession, kept safely into his secret pocket, was like an explosive firecracker waiting to be lit as the days slid peacefully on.

That evening Francie said she didn't feel like supper, she said her back ached and she was tired. Annie glanced at her with concern. The baby wasn't due for another few weeks, but the low backache suggested that it might be sooner. She settled Francie in the big chair by the fire, tucked plenty of cushions behind her, put her feet up on the footstool and then hurried to the kitchen to make her a cup of tea.

Francie sat quietly, her hands resting on her swollen belly, but tonight the child inside her was still. "Sometimes I wish he would never be born," she said sadly to Lai Tsin. "After all, what chance will he have? He'll be branded a bastard. And even though he is innocent and has done nothing to deserve it, he will always be an outcast." She looked wearily at him. "He will suffer all his life for my sin. And the sins of his father."

Lai Tsin said sharply, "The father's only sin was to love you."

He took the confession from his pocket and handed it to her. "Read this. And do not question it, for it is the truth."

Francie glanced at him, puzzled. Then she read the piece of paper and her eyes grew wide with shock. It was the confession of a madman, a murderer.

"You must not ask how I obtained this," Lai Tsin warned her, "only accept that it is the truth."

"But you know where Sammy is?"

Lai Tsin's eyes were suddenly blank and unreadable as he replied. "You need never fear Sammy Morris again. Do not ask me anymore. It is the confession you hold in your hand that is important—to you and your child. I cannot give you back the man you loved, Francie, but I have given you back his honor."

Francie suddenly felt as though a great weight had been lifted from her. She sighed, leaning her blond head back against the cushions, feeling the child move again under her hands. Josh's name would be cleared and at least her child would not have that terrible burden.

The child leapt again in her belly and then became still, a delicious drowsiness suddenly overcame her and her cares and worries seemed to drift away.

Lai Tsin smiled as her eyelids drooped and she slept. "The child will be born sooner than we thought," he said as Annie came in. "We must send Zocco to Santa Rosa for the doctor."

"It's a long way, more than thirty miles," Annie said doubtfully. "Maybe we should wait. After all, the baby's not due for another three weeks."

"The child will come within forty-eight hours," Lai Tsin said quietly. "It will be good to forewarn him."

Annie looked curiously at him. "You seem to know everything, Lai Tsin."

"I know something else," he said quietly. "I have brought a gift for you and for Francie. The gift of peace of mind." He handed her the paper and as she read it Annie's brown eyes filled with tears. "I knew it," she said simply. "I knew Josh didn't kill those girls. But why? Why did Sammy do such a terrible thing?"

"He did not think like a normal person. His felt only three basic emotions; jealousy, anger, and pleasure. There was a madness in him that made him feel free to destroy those who got in his way."

"And where is he now?"

Lai Tsin's eyes were inscrutable as he told her, "You will never see him again."

Annie looked into his enigmatic face and she shivered; she didn't know what he meant by that and she was afraid to ask.

Bitter tears rained down as she thought of Josh, but Lai Tsin offered no words of comfort for he knew none. And when her tears were finished he said, "Your family's honor will be vindicated. Now we must look to the future, to the child who will soon come into our lives."

And as she dried her eyes and blew her nose, Annie knew he was right that, thanks to Lai Tsin, her father would be able to hold his head up proudly again. She put the confession safely away to be mailed to the British police, and then she went to tell Zocco that he must ride to Santa Rosa and fetch the doctor.

A low, dragging pain woke Francie a short while later. She sat up quickly, her eyes wide with shock. "Oh, Annie," she said half-nervous, half-excited, "I think the baby's on his way."

Annie's worried eyes met Lai Tsin's. "Just as Lai Tsin predicted," she said, "he's already sent Zocco for the doctor." She walked to the window and looked doubtfully out into the night. The wind that had plagued them for three days had risen to gale force, the rain was lashing down and she prayed it wouldn't turn to snow again.

Francie lay in her mother's bed. Her face was pale and her blue eyes glittered with fear.

"Stay and keep me company," she begged. "And ask Lai Tsin to come too." She gasped as another pain hit her. Annie looked worriedly at her and then went to fetch Lai Tsin. The small paraffin lamp shed a soft light on their faces as they sat beside her and Francie thought of the Christmas night long ago when she had lain dreaming on the rug in front of the stove, while her mother slept her final sleep in the same bed she lay in now. And she wished with all her heart that her mother was here to help her.

Annie glanced anxiously out the window again. It was snowing and her heart sank. Lai Tsin's eyes met hers and she knew he understood what she was thinking; that the doctor would never get through such a storm. Squaring her shoulders, she told herself babies got born every day, there was nothing to it. She could cope.

Francie winced as the pain grabbed her again. "Talk to me," she begged. "Tell me the rest of your story, Lai Tsin. Please."

He looked worriedly at her. "It is not the right time to hear my cruel tale," he said.

"Yes, please, it will help take my mind off things."

He shook his head, wondering *what* to tell her . . . *how* to tell her. There was only one way.

"I did not know it then, but I was at a place they called Little River, notorious for the savagery of its seas and also for the pirate ships bringing in illegal Chinese immigrants. The tide was surging rapidly up the small beach and I knew I was in danger. I looked around and saw where cliffs ran into an inlet and I followed them, searching for a place to climb out of reach of the racing tide. At last, far above me on the bluff I saw a few scrubby bushes and beyond, clusters of pine trees. I clambered up the steep slope, clinging to the stones, scrabbling upward inch by painful inch. My hands were bleeding and my neck ached with the strain of always looking upward because I knew if I ever looked down at the tide, already swirling and crashing on the rocks below, my courage would fail me.

"At last I reached the scrub. I grasped the thorny, brittle branches, hauling myself ever up, and then I was amongst the trees; the slope was less steep and there was grass under my feet. I flung myself down, sobbing with fear and exhaustion and shivering with cold. After a while I plucked up my courage and began walking through the forest, but the trees clustered together so thickly, they cut out even the black night sky. I was left in total darkness. I could not walk any farther. I curled myself up as small as possible, praying there were no fierce tigers or dragons or poisonous snakes in this American forest, and exhausted, I fell asleep.

"I was awakened by a thin gray light filtering through the tall pines. My wet clothes clung to my body and my belly was hollow with the craving for food. I began to walk again, upward from the shore. The forest was changing; as well as the pines there were lofty redwoods with trunks vaster in circumference that the arms of two men. Somewhere in the distance I heard the whine of a saw and knew I must be near a mill.

"Panicked, I sat beneath a tree trying to think what I must do. I was a Chinese child, small and terrified. I spoke no English. I had no papers that allowed me to be in America and no money to pay for food, even if I knew how to ask for it. I thought if the Americans found me they would kill me and I decided I must wait until nightfall and try to steal some food. I would walk each night until I came to the city and the Gold Mountain and then I would get work with my countrymen from Toishan.

"I crept closer to the sounds coming from the sawmill and finally I saw it through the trees. It was a tall wooden building perched on a bluff overlooking a rushing river. There was a strong smell of resin in the air and all around lay great fallen trees and planks of wood piled high and bound with rope. Men brandishing axes were hacking the branches from the big fallen redwoods while others jumped agilely on the logs floating on the river. I knew the ax-brandishing men were the *gwailos,* the foreign devils, and I shrank back with fear.

"I circled behind the mill and saw a small wooden shanty. Smoke came from the chimney and a woman in a black dress and a flowered apron was throwing crumbs to the few stringy hens roaming by the door. My heart lifted, where there were hens, there were eggs. If I were clever and silent enough, I would have a meal that evening. Then it sank as I saw the shambling black dog sniffing in the bushes. He would be sure to bark and warn his mistress.

"As the sun set, the whining of the saw ceased and the *gwailos* drifted homeward, shouting and laughing. I waited until the woman had gathered her hens together and locked them in their pen for the night. She called her dog and went inside and closed the door. I saw the light of a lamp through the curtained windows and my heart ached for the lamplit security of my poor village near the Yangtze— until I remembered my father and what he had done to us, and I knew that I had no home. I steeled my heart and vowed to go on. Somehow I would survive and one day I would return to my village a rich man. And I would destroy him the way he had destroyed my mother and Mayling.

"As dusk fell, I crept closer and sat behind a tree waiting for darkness. The birds sought their nests and fell silent and the rustling in the forest stilled.

"I crept stealthily up to the pen. The hens squawked loudly and I stood there, trembling, letting them get used to me. Then I quickly searched their nests and found two warm eggs. I couldn't wait. I cracked them open and poured them into my gaping mouth. I was ravenous for more. I scooped up the scraps she had thrown down for the hens and ate them. I found the dog's dish and scraped up the remains of its dinner, licking the bowl. And then, still hungry, I started to walk again through the forest.

"I do not know how many days I walked, or how far. I lived on berries and roots. I caught a young rabbit and killed it, scraping off its fur with a stone. Then I ripped it limb from limb and devoured it with its blood still warm. The forest thinned until I was in an orchard, and I chewed the wizened fallen apples and drank water from the brook.

"The hot daytime sun had dried my clothes but the nights were cold and as dawn came I could see my breath on the icy air. That next night it grew even colder and though I walked even faster it was impossible to get warm. I still had only my cotton trousers and smock and my thin cloth shoes were now full of holes. I saw a path and followed it and soon came across a long wooden building with a bell on top in a little tower. The door was open and I crept in. In the moonlight, I saw rows of long wooden benches and an altar table with a cross such as I had seen at the mission in Nanking. I realized it must be the *gwailos'* holy place and I prostrated myself and kowtowed to the foreigner's god, touching my head respectfully to the floor so that he would not mind my intrusion.

"It was a cold place but at least I was out of the freezing wind and I stretched out on one of the wooden benches and closed my eyes. It was the first time I had felt four walls around me since I left China. I felt strangely peaceful and secure, and I slept.

"I awoke suddenly. Sunlight was streaming in through a tall window and someone was shaking me by the shoulder. It was a man, dressed all in black, red-faced, with hard eyes of a pale water-blue such as I never saw in China."

Lai Tsin paused. He stared down at the floor, unwilling to go on, and Francie said comfortingly, "It's all right, you don't have to tell us."

He shrugged, "It is nothing. The man was a preacher. I did not understand what he was saying but I knew I was his prisoner. I looked wildly about me for an escape and the man laughed, a big booming laugh, like his deep voice. And holding me by the shoulder he marched me out of the chapel and along a path until we came to a small village. There were a dozen two-story houses and stores strung along a straggling road. It was early morning and people were about, women dressed like the one I had seen with the hens, in long, full-skirted dresses and flowered aprons. Some wore bonnets and capes, and I envied the men their warm woolen shirts and jackets. Like him, they were bleak, silent, hard-eyed men and women and they stared open-mouthed at the pastor and his strange captive.

"I did not understand his language but I knew what he was telling them. 'Found him in the chapel,' the pastor said, 'a young Celestial, *a heathen boy*. God has sent him to our little community to test us, and I shall take up the challenge. *I* shall teach this heathen boy the ways of our Lord.'

"The pastor's house was dark and musty. I had never been in a *gwailo* house before and it frightened me. It was so different from what I knew, full of ticking clocks and paintings of more hard-eyed men, with heavy, dark furniture and velvet curtains at the many-paned windows. But a big fire burned in the grate and as the man released me I ran toward it and held out my hands. I stood there, my cheeks stinging from the heat, feeling his eyes on me all the while. Then he said something and took me again by the shoulder. We went outside to a shed with a small zinc tub. He indicated that I should remove my clothes. I was frightened and refused. I tried to run away but he was too strong. He was shouting at me, red-faced with anger, as he ripped off my clothing and bade me climb into the tub. I stood there, naked and ashamed, unable to look at him. He filled a big jug with water from a nearby faucet and then he poured it over me. It was like ice and I yelled and wriggled but still he held me, his fingers digging cruelly into my shoulder. He gave me a bar of coarse, smelly lye soap and made me wash myself, then he poured the icy water over me again. When the ordeal was over he gave me a piece of sacking on which to dry myself and I wrapped myself in it, my teeth chattering with cold and fear. And then the door opened and a woman came in.

"She gasped when she saw me, but he quickly explained and she went out again and came back later with some clothing. I put on the *gwailo* clothes. Everything was gray, the undershirt, the flannel shirt, the trousers, the woolen sweater. But the boots were black. And big, with huge nails. I had only ever worn the cloth peasant shoes of China and these were hard and stiff and hurt my feet. They crunched my toes and rooted me to the spot with their weight.

"The woman heated some soup and put a steaming bowl in front of me at the table. I thought I would faint at the aroma. I picked it up and began to drink but she shouted at me. Though I did not understand her words I knew she was saying, 'No, no, you heathen child. You must use the spoon,' and she gave me a long-handled spoon such as I had never seen before.

"The man sat at the end of the table. His eyes never left me and he was smiling a strange little smile. He had fed me and clothed me, but I did not trust him. And I did not like him.

"When I had finished the soup the woman came to me. She folded my hands together and made me bow my head, and then she and the pastor did the same while he recited some *gwailo* prayers. Then the man took me by the shoulder again and we went up the narrow wooden stairs. He opened a door and thrust me inside. I heard a key turn in the lock and I was alone.

"I looked around me. The room was small, the walls were dark, and there were big chests and cupboards in heavy ugly woods. I looked longingly at the little bed covered in a white quilt. In all my life I had only ever slept on the floor on a grass bedmat. I had never even seen a bed like this before. I was exhausted and it lured me to it. But I sensed I was in danger. I could not stay. I ran to the window and looked out. There was a metal pipe running down the side of the wall just outside and for a small agile child it was an easy matter to wriggle through the window and climb down. I was on the ground. I slipped around the side of the house and slid like a shadow back into the trees.

"In a few minutes I was on my way again, hampered by my big boots and my unaccustomed clothing. But I was warm, I had food in my belly, and I felt stronger. And I knew I had escaped some evil I did not understand.

"I walked all that day and all the next night, stopping only to search for food, berries, roots, apples, mushrooms. I would have died happy for a bowl of steaming hot rice-gruel. I had no idea if what I was eating was poison, but I was so hungry I no longer cared. If fate willed it, I would live; if not, I would die.

"The trees thinned out and the landscape became more open. Instead of forest there were undulating grassy hills, meadows, and orchards. I hid myself in the hedgerows by day and walked at night. One morning, as dawn broke, I found myself on the outskirts of a village similar to the one I had seen before. Only this was larger, the houses were bigger, there were flower gardens and stores and all around the hills were strange-looking bushes planted in neat rows. And working in the fields were Chinamen.

"My eyes bulged from my head in astonishment. I thought to myself that this must be the Gold Mountain where the men from Toishan are making their fortunes. I stared around looking for the piles of gold and silver, but all I saw were the strange bushes and the men pruning them. I ran joyously toward them, shouting and waving my arms, and they looked up, exclaiming in astonishment at the little Celestial boy in the big black boots. There were dozens of them and they gathered around as I told my story, and they gasped with horror, cursing the *gwailo* ship's captain as an evil devil and the son of a whore. They told me this was not the Gold Mountain but a place where they grew grapes to make the barbarians' wine. Mostly they worked digging the caves under the ground, but because of the frost they had been sent to look after the vines that day.

"I looked hard at them. They were not dressed in the silks of rich men; they wore the coarse cotton smocks of the peasant. They were tilling fields the way they did at home and digging caves deep underground. Where then was the Gold Mountain? I asked them eagerly. They shook their heads. They had never found it.

"They took me back with them that evening to see their master. They said though I was young, I was strong and could dig harder than any of them. The master was big, like all the foreign devils. His shoulders were broad like the water buffalo's and I thought he could dig harder than all of us. But he wore elegant britches and a jacket of calfskin and he sat like a god astride his beautiful black stallion that danced so impatiently. He owned all the land we could see and now he owned us too.

" 'Put him to work then and we'll see,' he said coldly.

"I went with all the other Celestials to the long house where they ate and slept. A Chinese cook was ladling out bowls of rice and vegetables and the saliva poured into my mouth at its smell. I devoured two bowls and felt that my stomach would surely burst. Then, having no bedmat, I curled up in a corner and slept the way a child should.

"I was awakened before daybreak and with some maize-gruel and steamed bread in my belly followed the others to the caves. The foreman handed me a pick and shovel and we walked down the sloping passage deep under the earth. At the end of the cavern the men began hacking out the rock. In an hour the muscles in my shoulders were burning and my heart threatened to burst. I was covered in sweat and dirt but I dare not stop. I worked alongside the others, matching their every stroke with the pick and then shoveling away the rocks. After a few hours we stopped and they took out their small wooden rice-buckets and ate. But I had no bucket and no lunch and I wandered away so that they would not feel embarrassed and be forced to share their meager meal with me. I sank into a corner and rubbed my aching shoulders. I was exhausted and wanted to cry, but I knew I must keep up with them in order to be given a job.

"A week passed, each day following the other into the tired oblivion of night. But I was young and each morning the ache seemed a little less. And at the week's end I was given my wages. I looked at the few coins in my hand and thought this is the first time I have ever had money of my own, because I did not count the evil captain's silver dollar I had thrown into the sea. And suddenly I knew what I was going to do with it.

"That night after supper the men gathered around as they did every night and took out the cards and the mah-jongg. I took my place in the circle, sitting cross-legged on the floor, and I placed my bet along with the others. I was going to test the lessons I had learned on the ship watching the coolies gamble night after night. Within minutes I had lost all my wages.

"I tried again the following week and the next, and the next, until I learned. And then I began to win. I knew I was clever and could have won all the time but the men had been good to me and I could not take their money. So I quit gambling and saved my wages.

"When the work on the caves was finally over, I followed the other men, working with them in the fields and the orchards, until I finally made my way to San Francisco. They told me the Baptist Church held a Sunday School where they taught the heathen Celestials about their God, but they also taught them English, and so I learned. And I did whatever work I could get." He stopped and looked gravely at them. "And that is how I spent my life until now," he said finally.

"Now we know the *true* Lai Tsin," Francie said compassionately. "I only hope my courage is as great as yours."

"Have no fear, little one," he said in his light, gentle, singsong. "Your courage is even greater than mine."

The night suddenly seemed darker as Francie entered a world of pain. It attacked suddenly and she fought against it, trembling as it abated, knowing it was only lying in wait, like a wild animal, to attack again. The hours passed, and Annie bathed her head and massaged her icy feet. She stoked up the fire and wept in helpless sympathy when Francie screamed.

Dawn came and still no doctor. The day dragged into dusk and then quickly into night. Perspiration beaded her forehead as she fought the pain and Lai Tsin stood beside her and took her hand in his.

Francie looked into his face and saw his strength and felt it flowing into her. She felt a strange sense of exhilaration and suddenly she seemed to be outside her own body. Her mother was beside her, smiling at her with love in her eyes, and she called out to her. She looked down at herself lying in her mother's bed with Lai Tsin holding her hand and Annie crying, and then she saw her own child, a boy, emerging into the world. And she was filled with happiness.

Then she was lying exhausted in her bed with her son at her breast. She smiled with tired contentment. Lai Tsin's strength had saved her, she knew that. Just like it had after the earthquake when she had wanted to die. She was no longer a helpless girl—now she was a mother, she was a woman, and she was strong.

Annie forgot about her boardinghouse nearing completion in San Francisco. She put the past out of her mind and immersed herself in the joy of the new baby, who was named Oliver. He was so like Josh that it transported her back in time to when she was just thirteen and had looked after her own baby brother. And now she would share in raising his son.

She and Francie thought of nothing else but the baby. They marveled at his daily progress, admiring his smallest smile, his soft blond hair, and the beauty of his wide gray eyes. They bathed him, fed him, changed him, and Annie knitted endless little bonnets and jackets to keep out the winter cold. And when Christmas came they decorated a little fir tree with pine cones and scarlet ribbons and lit tiny candles. They invited Zocco and Esmerelda to drink cinnamon-flavored mulled wine and share their feast of roast goose, cooked by Annie to aromatic brown crispness outside and juicy pinkness inside. She made spiced apple dressing and rich brown gravy and a plum pudding stuffed to bursting with a dozen different fruits and nuts, soused in brandy with a lucky sixpence piece, saved from England, baked inside. And the baby gurgled happily in his crib in the cosy firelit kitchen just as though he knew it was Christmas while the pups, Duke and Duchess, gamboled at their feet.

Lai Tsin was not there and they missed him, but he said he must work hard so he could repay the five-percent interest to the Elders as soon as possible.

The New Year came and went and still Annie lingered. "I'll go soon," she kept saying, but then she told herself that Francie and the baby needed her. In February, Lai Tsin wrote that he had repaid his interest. The Elders had listened to his new proposals and granted him a new loan from the rotating credit. He was sailing the following week for Shanghai and it would be many months before they would see him again. Francie read the letter proudly, knowing how long it must have taken him to write it so beautifully and clearly in English. She picked up Oliver and dressed him warmly in his blue coat and bonnet and wrapped him in a shawl. Then she put him in the baby carriage that Lai Tsin had bought him in San Francisco and pushed him down the grassy paths where she had walked with her mother. She gazed happily at the white clouds scudding across the bright blue sky, and asked nothing more from life than to be Oliver's mother.

Annie returned to San Francisco in the spring. "I hate to leave you alone," she said as Zocco piled her baggage into the gig. "But I've put all my money into the boardinghouse and I've got to make a success of it, for little Oliver's sake."

Francie waved until the gig disappeared from sight down the tree-lined drive and she turned back indoors, feeling suddenly lost. She shifted the baby to the other shoulder—he was getting heavier and she smiled, proud that he was growing into such a fine, strong boy.

She wandered around the little house, the dogs trailing at her heels, peeking into empty rooms and lingering in the warm, cheery kitchen. The pies Annie had baked before she left lay cooling on wire racks by the window, the cosy room smelled of vanilla and spices and she could almost imagine Annie was still there. Later that night she sat alone in front of the fire. The baby was asleep in his crib in her room and the dogs sprawled as usual at her feet. The house was still but for the ticking of the clock and the murmur of the fire and it was

so quiet she could amost hear her heart beat. But she wasn't afraid
and she wasn't lonely.

She savored the moment of perfect peace and happiness at her
little ranch, just as she would for each of the next four years, when
she wanted nothing else but to be who she was and what she was,
Francie Harrison, mother of Oliver and friend to Annie Aysgarth
and Ke Lai Tsin.

# Part III

---◆---

# HARRY
# 1911–1918

# CHAPTER 23

## ◆

# *1911*

Harry Harrison walked slowly along California Street past the refurbished Fairmont Hotel, savoring the moment. He stopped and looked across the road at his rebuilt house, and it was as though he had stepped back five years in time. It looked exactly the way it had before the earthquake; the cream stone facade, the white marble steps, the Doric columns and the soaring stained-glass dome. It cost him more than twice as much as the million it had cost his grandfather, but it was worth every cent.

Of course, some things were different: the stables were now garages, there was an elaborate gilt elevator in the hall, and the staircase was onyx instead of oak. But it was the Harrison house all right. He had kept his vow and it stood once again as a monument to the family and their powers of endurance.

Lights glowed at every window and a long red carpet stretched down the front steps and across the sidewalk, lined on either side with liveried footmen awaiting the arrival of his guests. It was Harry's twentieth birthday and everybody who was anybody in San Francisco was coming. Tonight they would know that young Harry was taking over where his father had left off.

He walked across the road and up the steps into his magnificent new house. A footman sprang to open the door and the new butler, Fredricks, stood in the hall, awaiting his orders. Harry looked up at the brilliantly colored glass dome he had commissioned an artist in Venice to design incorporating portraits of the three Harrisons—his grandfather, his father, and himself—with a space where his own son's portrait would one day go. And in ornate gold lettering around the base ran the new family motto he had coined himself, WITH VALOR AND STRENGTH THEY SURVIVE.

He smiled, pleased with himself, running his hand along the smooth black-onyx banister as he leapt two at a time up the midnight-blue carpeted stairs and along the oak-paneled upper hall to his suite of rooms. His valet had run his bath and laid out his evening clothes. A bottle of his favorite Perrier & Jouet champagne was cooling in a silver bucket and he poured himself a glass. At just twenty, he already had a taste for fine wines and gourmet food, as well as an exceptional taste in women. He smiled again as he flung off his clothes and sank into the sandalwood-scented water. He was a young man who knew exactly what he liked and exactly where he was heading. He was a millionaire and the world was his oyster and he intended to enjoy everything it had to offer.

There was just one thing that still troubled him. He had never been able to find evidence that his sister was dead. He had combed the city records a hundred times after the earthquake, but there was no mention of her name and it was assumed that she had perished in the fire along with her lover, Aysgarth, but there was still a nagging little fear at the back of his mind that one day she would reappear to blight his life and bring shame on his name again.

He frowned as he climbed from the tub and the valet handed him his towel. Tonight would be the perfect setting for the long-lost sister to stage her return. He shrugged, telling himself he was crazy, but nevertheless he sent for Fredricks and told him to put guards on every door and to admit no one without an invitation card. He reminded himself that his father would have been here tonight to see the Harrison house in all its new glory, if it were not for Francie. He remembered the vow he had made when they had brought his father home to his final resting place—that he would see his sister dead if it was the last thing he did. If she should ever return, he would keep that vow.

San Francisco's prettiest and most eligible girls had been looking forward to Harry's housewarming and birthday party for months, and they were not disappointed. The wonderful new house was the only private one left on Nob Hill and it glittered like an extravagant Christmas tree. Creamy gardenias in scarlet tubs lined the red carpet and the hall was a bower of velvety, dark crimson roses.

Crowds lined the sidewalks to watch the guests arrive and flashbulbs popped as reporters from all the San Francisco newspapers recorded Harry greeting his guests at the top of his steps for their society columns.

Francie felt oddly calm as she stared at the great house, risen like a phoenix from her father's ashes. The newspapers had been full of Harry's party and the glories of the new mansion, and though she knew she shouldn't, she had been unable to stay away. She half-expected to see her father standing at the portals greeting his guests the way he had done at the last big Harrison party—her own coming-out ball—and she breathed a sigh of relief when he was not there. Even Harmon Harrison had not been able to return from the dead; only his house could do that. And instead, there was Harry.

Harry looked the way their father must have as a young man; tall, broad-shouldered and well-built. With a sensual curve on his lips, he scanned the crowds with light-blue eyes. He looked young and handsome and arrogantly sure of himself.

Francie pulled her hat down over her eyes, pressing closer to the strip of red carpet. The next long, shiny black limousine pulled up in front of the mansion and a silver-haired woman stepped out, her diamonds glittering in the lights of the flashbulbs. It was old Mrs. Brice Leland, and beside her fluttered a young girl in a beautiful lace ball dress and a diamond tiara. Francie gasped. It might have been her five years ago.

Harry kissed their white-gloved hands, waved them grandly into the house and then went back to his post at the door to greet the next arrivals. He should have been greeting his guests inside the great hall, but he was enjoying his starring role. He liked the admiring, envious stares of the crowd and he liked the photographs. He wanted the whole of San Francisco to see him and know that the Harrisons had beaten God at His own game. The house was a temple to his father and to himself and he wanted to make sure they knew it.

A line of limousines stretched all the way down the street, waiting to drive up to the royally carpeted entrance and discharge their passengers—beautiful girls in silks and satins and their handsome young escorts in white tie and tails. It took almost an hour to greet them all and as the last car drove away Harry gave a sigh of relief. Now the party could begin.

He turned one last time to smile at the crowd, *and suddenly his eyes met Francie's.* She pulled her hat lower over her eyes and turned quickly away, but he knew it was her. For a moment he stood frozen with shock. Then he ran down the steps toward her, but she had disappeared into the crowd like a ghost.

He stared blankly at the crowd and they stared back at him, wondering what was going on. He pulled himself together, shrugging his shoulders. He must be mistaken, it was all in his mind, just because he had told himself earlier this would be the ideal setting for Francie's return from the dead. He was being stupid, the girl he had seen was probably someone who barely even looked like her, just the same blond hair and blue eyes . . . *those deep, sapphire-blue eyes.* He shivered as he ran back up the steps. Francie was dead and he hoped her bones and ashes had been scattered to the wind so that no trace of her even remained. Tonight was *his* party, *his* triumph, and he was going to enjoy every minute.

Francie shrank behind the columned porticoes of the Fairmont Hotel, waiting for Harry's hand to fall on her shoulder. She could almost hear his triumphant voice saying, "There you are at last, Francesca." She could feel the coarse fabric and the cold leather straps of the straightjacket cutting into her and see the blank, barred window that would lock her away from life again, just the way they had all through her childhood. Her heart was thudding, shivers ran up and down her spine, and she could hardly catch her breath.

"Are you all right, miss?" a concerned voice asked.

She looked up, terrified, and almost fainted with relief. It wasn't Harry after all, it was the top-hatted Fairmont doorman.

"I just felt faint for a moment," she replied shakily. "Thank you, but I'm sure I'll be all right now."

The doorman eyed her curiously. She didn't look any too well to him, she was pale and her blue eyes looked panicked. He wouldn't normally have allowed a woman to stand here in the Fairmont's entry, but she was beautiful and well-dressed and she was most certainly a lady. "Would you like me to call you a cab, ma'am?" he asked, and Francie nodded gratefully, tipping him lavishly as he helped her into it.

She shrank back into its shadowy interior as they drove by the Harrison mansion. The massive bronze doors that looked fit for a cathedral were closed now, but the crowds still lingered, peering at the lighted windows and listening to the faint strains of the orchestra.

Francie shuddered, wrapping her arms around herself, overcome by a terrible chill. Harry had seen her, he had recognized her, and now she knew he would never rest until he found her.

Back home, at Aysgarth's Boardinghouse, she ran quickly upstairs to Ollie's room. Her four-year-old son was sleeping peacefully, one arm outflung and the other clasped around a worn toy tiger. The night-light shone on his cap of blond hair and his long eyelashes cast curving shadows across his cheeks. She stood for a long time looking at him, her hands clasped to her heart. She told herself she was not a helpless girl any longer, that she was twenty-three years old and a grown woman, she had friends who loved her and this child who was hers to support and cherish. She told herself that Harry could not accuse her of insanity and lock her behind bars. She was her own woman, she had money and friends and there was absolutely nothing he could do to her. But as she turned away there was still that nagging doubt in her mind, and as she closed the door on her sweetly sleeping son she was still afraid.

"It's like old times, Harry," Mrs. Brice Leland told him, as he swirled her around in the first waltz. "How proud your dear father would have been of you. Such a triumph to rebuild this wonderful house. And no doubt when you have completed your studies at Princeton, you will be taking his place on the board of the bank?"

"I have already taken my father's place, Mrs. Leland," he replied, smiling, "as head of *all* his companies. I felt it was my duty to do so right away."

She nodded sagely as the music stopped and he escorted her back to her chair. "A wise head on young shoulders," she told him, smiling approvingly.

Harry danced with all the society matrons, charming them easily. Then he danced with each of the girls in turn. Some were beautiful, some pretty, and others merely attractive. None were ugly. He couldn't abide plain women. But anyway, the girls were too young for him, he liked red-haired older women with knowing eyes and ripe bodies, women who knew what he wanted and how to give it to him. These girls flirted and smiled, but their eyes were clear and innocent, they smelled of scent not sex, and they were after a husband not a lover.

Harry enjoyed his party. He liked the lavish food and vintage champagne, the overwhelming flower displays, the thousands of candles flickering in the giant chandeliers, the gypsy violins and the waltzes, the jewels and the aristocratic names. It would set the standard for all his future entertaining. But when the last guest left, he knew where he was heading.

He had invited half a dozen of his young friends from back East for the party. They were waiting for him in the library, drinking whiskey and laughing as they discussed the evening and the girls. Harry strode into the room and clapped his hands for silence. "I have a surprise for you," he said. "Follow me, gentlemen."

The boys were his age, good-looking young aristocrats with money to burn, and they followed him eagerly into the waiting automobiles, ready for adventure.

Harry took the wheel of the big de Courmont. He drove fast down California Street and turned into Chinatown. Champagne and whiskey flowed in his veins as he zigzagged through a maze of smaller streets, laughing uproariously as the stupid Celestials leapt from under his wheels. He drove down a small, dimly lit alley and stopped outside a red-lacquered door with a small iron grille set in the middle of it. A lantern swung overhead, lighting up the boys' eager young faces. A flap behind the grille suddenly opened and a pair of narrow Oriental eyes surveyed them. Then the door was flung wide and they stepped into another world.

They clustered together, staring apprehensively around. A few Orientals sprawled on low red divans in the dimly lit room, smoking bubble pipes, and the smell of their tobacco mingled with the sharp scent of incense and the sweetness of opium. Harry glanced at his friends, his eyes glittering with anticipation. "I told you it would be a surprise," he said, as the Oriental clapped his hands to summon the girls from the back. "This is my birthday present to *you*, my friends. I've heard a lot about Chinese women and now we'll find out if it's true!"

They laughed uproariously at his nerve, crowding eagerly forward to look at the line of girls. They were all young, pretty, and exotic in tight satin cheongsams slit to the waist. Their smooth hair was long and black and silky, their almond eyes sly and inviting, and their lips painted a seductive scarlet. They placed their hands together, bowing their heads prettily as they were introduced. Harry knew which one he wanted; she was taller than the others, her behind jutted provocatively, and there was a tantalizing gleam in her eyes as they met his. He grabbed her arm. "This one's mine," he said as she led him triumphantly away, leaving his friends to make their own choices.

Her cubicle was tiny with just a brocade-covered divan, a low table with a flask of rice wine, and a carved wooden chair. The red-glass lantern shed a fiery glow and the rice wine sent a matching fire through Harry as it mixed with the champagne and Scotch already flowing in his veins.

The girl took his jacket and hung it carefully over the chair. She unfastened his bowtie and removed his shoes. Harry took another slug of rice wine and she lifted her head and looked up at him knowingly. Then she stood up and slowly unfastened her cheongsam. It slid to her feet with a silken swish and she stood naked before him. She was young and graceful and knowledgeable in sex; she knew how to please a man and Harry knew what he wanted. He wanted her to tantalize him, to tease him, to stretch his nerves and his resistance like a taut, singing wire. He wanted to experience everything and resist the final moment as long as possible, and this willing little Chinese girl knew every game in the book.

And when he was finally finished and lay exhausted on the divan she brought a bowl of warm, scented water and washed his body. Then she brought in a pipe and a little spirit lamp. Harry watched lazily as she scraped up a tiny bead of opium, heated it over the lamp and put it in the bowl of the pipe. Then she offered it to him, saying, "This is the very finest and most costly Chinese opium, master. The poppies were cut at sunrise when the juices flow at their best, and its flavor and power will bring you much pleasure."

She lay on her side next to him and showed him how to smoke it, inhaling deeply and holding the smoke in her lungs. "Try," she whispered, smiling persuasively, "just try it, master."

They shared a pipe of opium and then another, and more rice wine and finally Harry lay back on the divan while she pleasured him again, and he knew he never wanted this night to end.

And the next day, back in his wonderful mansion, if he remembered seeing Francie at all, he thought he must have dreamed it.

Harry's friends slept late and he took his breakfast alone in the big dining hall. No trace of the previous night's party remained except for a bouquet of crimson roses in the center of the table. And no trace of last night's debauchery showed on Harry's face; he looked as fresh and clear-eyed as a baby as he downed fried eggs with deviled kidneys and toast, while he glanced swiftly through the morning editions of the newspapers.

He smiled as he saw photographs of his own handsome face and his wonderful house and beautiful guests splashed across the social pages of every newspaper. THE HARRISONS ARE BACK, the headlines trumpeted over a picture of him standing at the top of his red-carpeted steps with the shiny limousines lined up outside. It went on to tell the story of his father and his tragic death. "But now Harry

Harrison is all set to repeat his father's stunning performance, both socially and in business," it continued. "When young Harry graduates from Princeton, in a year's time, he will take his father's place as head of the multimillion-dollar Harrison business empire. You are looking at a picture of a young man at the pinnacle of life. He has everything life has to offer, youth, looks, money, and assured success. What more can any man want?"

Harry smiled with satisfaction as he sipped his coffee. And then he saw the photograph in the *San Francisco Examiner*. The picture was blurred and slightly out of focus, *but there in the crowd was Francie*. Her hat was pulled down over her eyes, but still he could swear it was her.

Pushing back his chair he strode from the dining room to his study. He picked up the phone and called the *Examiner*'s office and told them to get a copy of the photograph to him right away. Then he sat back in his deep-buttoned leather chair, his hands clasped on the desk in front of him, thinking of what to do.

He remembered the night he had returned from the opera with his father, and the red-faced detective who had been waiting for him with the news about Francie and her lover. He'd taken away his father's gun to stop him from killing her. Now he knew how his father had felt, because if the woman in the picture were Francie, then he wanted her dead.

He got up and paced the study restlessly. Everybody assumed she was dead anyway—she was a missing person, no one would ever even look for her. But how to do it? He thought of the Chinese bordello. It was run by one of the tongs and he knew they had a reputation as hired killers. They would be able to get him the man he needed.

There was a knock on the door and Fredricks appeared carrying an envelope on a silver salver. "From the *Examiner,* sir," he said as Harry grabbed it eagerly.

He peered at the face only half-visible beneath her hat. He knew Francie's face like his own. That was her mouth, that was her hair, he'd swear to it. *And those sapphire eyes that had met his for a fleeting instant had been Francie's.*

Picking up the telephone, he called the chief of police, told him who he was, and asked for the name of a reputable detective agency.

"It's just a small job," he lied, a smile in his voice, "a little matter of security at the bank."

Within minutes he had the name and number he needed, and half an hour later a tall, gray-haired Irishman was employed to find the woman in the photograph. "Right away," Harry told him impatiently. "You've got forty-eight hours."

# CHAPTER 24

◆——

Aysgarth's Boardinghouse was tall and narrow and fronted onto the south side of Union Square. The bottom half of the building was red brick and the top white clapboard. There were apple-green shutters at the long windows, a glossy green front door with a gleaming brass lion's head knocker and a sign in the lace-curtained window to the left of the well-scrubbed stone steps that read, NO VACANCIES.

There were four good reasons for the NO VACANCIES sign: First, the house was immaculately clean in the nicest way; it smelled of lavender and beeswax, not lye soap and disinfectant. Second, it was blissfully comfortable and homey, with bright rugs on the polished elm floorboards. There were deep club chairs in the parlor that a man could sink down into to read his newspaper, and firm beds with good plain white linen and no frills. Third, there was decent plumbing and plenty of hot water and always a good fire in the grate on a cold evening. And fourth, and most important, Annie Aysgarth's cooking was famous.

"Just like your mother made—but better," was what they said about her lamb hotpots with succulent chunks of meat in an herby aromatic gravy with a layer of brown, oven-crisped potatoes over the top. Her simple roast chicken with tiny golden matchstick potatoes and fresh green peas braised with lettuce and pearl onions were what your grandmother should have cooked, and her Sunday roast beef came with real Yorkshire pudding made with the lightest, simplest batter. "Two eggs instead of one," she always said, "plain flour, milk, and just a pinch of salt, the fat heated smoking hot and the batter poured in quickly and cooked in a hot oven until it puffed high and light as an eiderdown." It was served immediately as a course on its own with silky, onion-flavored gravy. And Annie's bread-and-butter pudding was to die for, the plain home-baked bread was buttered and soaked in a beaten mixture of milk and eggs flavored with vanilla, layered with sugar and brandy-plumped golden raisins and broken pecans, then scattered with golden vanilla sugar and baked in a bain-marie for forty-five minutes until it was as lightweight as a soufflé and creamy as a custard.

"You should open a restaurant," her boarders told her admiringly, patting their growing stomachs happily. But Annie didn't want just a restaurant. After four years she had outgrown Aysgarth's and her boarders—she had learned how to run an establishment catering for twenty and now she was ready to take on two hundred. She wanted to open her own hotel.

"With the same standards and the same cooking, though of course I won't be doing it all myself," she told Francie over a breakfast cup of coffee. "But I'm ready to take on the challenge."

Francie's blond head was bent over the *Examiner* and Annie gazed fondly at her. She had thought Francie a lovely girl when she met her, but now she was a beautiful young woman. Her long blond hair waved softly around her face, her candid blue eyes were startlingly dark and long-lashed, and her skin was smooth and creamy. And she was no longer the frail waiflike creature Annie had first known, her body had new curves and she held herself tall and walked with a proud, effortless grace. Annie thought with a pang that Francie was still only twenty-three, she was so young and so lovely. Men looked admiringly at her, she should be able to have her pick of any of them, but she just wasn't interested. She gave all her love to her son, Ollie.

The kitchen door opened as if on cue and the little tow-haired four year old ran in and climbed on Annie's lap. "Annie," he said, smiling cajolingly at her, wrapping his wiry little arms around her neck, "can I have a cookie?" His sweet gray eyes beamed into hers and he looked so like Josh that her heart turned over, but she didn't give in. She said, "It's *'may I,'* not *'can I.'* And anyway, no, you may not. You *may* have an apple instead."

He sighed and pressed himself closer. "Why are you so difficult, Annie?" he complained. "All I want is a cookie."

"You'll have one at teatime with your milk," she promised, smiling fondly at him. "And one day, when you are a man, you'll look into the mirror and see what fine strong teeth you've got, and you'll thank your aunt Annie for not plying you with cookies every time you asked."

Ollie sighed; he knew when he was beaten. Annie looked back at Francie—her head was still bent over the newspaper and she was oblivious to her son's presence. Annie's brows rose in surprise. Francie usually focused all her attention on Ollie, but this morning her thoughts were a million miles away.

"I bet you didn't hear a word I said," she exclaimed loudly. "Your head's been stuck in that newspaper for ages. Whatever's in there that's so fascinating?" Francie looked frightened as she passed the newspaper wordlessly to Annie.

The photographs of the Harrison party covered two pages, with another page detailing the scintillating guest list, the fabulous flower decorations, the expensive champagne, the delicious food served from golden platters by the burgundy-liveried footmen in white gloves, and the amazing rebirth of the Harrison mansion. PHOENIX HOUSE, said the headline over a full-page picture of the mansion. Its portals were flung wide and Harry, in white tie and tails, was greeting his guests. *A San Francisco landmark is reinstated with the year's most magnificent party . . .*

Annie glanced quickly at Francie. She took her hand across the table. "That's where you went last night, wasn't it?" she said compassionately. "You just couldn't keep away."

Francie nodded. "It's worse than that," she said. "I saw Harry."

"Well, Harry's back in town and even though you don't frequent the same places, it's still a small world. Sooner or later you'd have bumped into him anyway, walking down the street or at a corner newspaper stand or in a store."

"Annie, you don't understand. *He saw me. Our eyes met.*"

"Maybe he didn't recognize you. After all, it's been years—"

"Oh, he recognized me all right. And if he didn't, then this will confirm it." Francie pointed to her own face in the photograph of the crowd outside the Harrison mansion.

"There's no mistaking it's you, all right," Annie admitted less confidently. "But I still don't know why you are so afraid, Francie. Things have changed. You're a grown woman, not an underage girl. There's nothing Harry can do to you now."

Francie shook her head miserably. She had been telling herself the same thing all night, but she still didn't believe it. "I know Harry. He never stood up for me against my father, he always felt superior, the great son and heir of the great Harmon Harrison. All Harry ever wanted was to be an exact replica of his father and believe me, he is

—right down to the last drop of hatred. Harry has money and he has power and he'll use them against me any way he can."

Annie stared at her wide-eyed. "Then what will you do?" she asked, suddenly afraid for her.

Ollie climbed from Annie's lap and ran to Francie as she stood up, anxiously clutching her skirt. "Where are you going?" he asked.

She stroked back his hair, managing a smile. "I'm going to see Lai Tsin," she told him.

Lai Tsin's office was at the back of his big warehouse near the waterfront and it was as sparse and neat as the man himself. The walls were lined with shelves of reference books and catalogues; details of monthly tides and sailings were pinned to the notice board and a map of the world was marked with the routes of his current cargoes. A huge iron walk-in safe, to which only he had the key, housed ledgers with details of every transaction he had ever made, the accounts showing his net worth, and a considerable amount of cash, as well as the worn wooden treasure pillow containing a small silken black braid of hair and a faded sepia photo of a young girl holding a fan.

Lai Tsin sat behind a big wooden desk, his fingers flying over his old wooden abacus as he checked long columns of figures. Besides the straight-backed wooden chair on which he was sitting the room contained one other chair, a small stove that he rarely lit because he never felt the cold and a narrow blackwood altar table with two beautiful nephrite jade statues, one of Kwan Yin, the goddess of mercy, and one of the goddess of good fortune.

In the cavernous depths of the gloomy warehouse itself were stored hundreds of thousands of dollars' worth of goods of every sort: silks, laquerware, paintings, rugs, and antiquities from many parts of Asia, as well as more mundane household goods. A second warehouse contained only enormous wooden chests of tea of every sort and flavor. Lai Tsin had taken the money the Elders had lent him and multiplied it a thousandfold, though no one would ever know it because the company did not trade under his name. It was Francie who was owner of the "L. T. Francis Company," but it was Lai Tsin who did the work. It was he who, when he had stopped off at Hawaii on the way back from the Orient, had picked up a bankrupt pineapple plantation for a song and by putting in his own canning factory had turned it into a profitable concern. It was he who had bought the ships' chandlers on the San Francisco waterfront and made it the biggest and the best in the port. It was he who had invested in a rope works in Shanghai and a carpet manufacturer in Hong Kong, in silk worm farms in China and in sheep with the best wool in Australia. It was Lai Tsin who had canvassed the merchants of San Francisco and Los Angeles and Seattle and persuaded them to let him act as their agent, and he who had organized the bigger freightloads that made it possible to cut costs, and he who employed agents to scout for the antiquities and treasures coveted by the Westerners. Lai Tsin had cornered the tea market by importing delicate flavors specially blended for Western tastes. In the eyes of his Chinese contemporaries Lai Tsin was a success, his business had grown by leaps and bounds, he was rich. But for him it was not enough; he had reached a plateau and he knew it was time to move on.

There was a knock on the door and he looked up as Francie walked in. He smiled and said, "You are just the person I need to see." But then he saw her eyes and knew something had happened. He walked over to her and offered her a chair. "Are you cold?" he said anxiously. "I will light the stove."

Francie shook her head. She couldn't wait to unburden herself and the whole story about Harry spilled out, about how she had gone to the house and seen him and now he knew she was still alive, and how afraid she was that he would come looking for her.

Lai Tsin was very quiet for a long while after she finished speaking. If anyone had an answer to her problem she knew it was him, and she waited anxiously for him to speak.

"Harry will see the photograph and he will search for you," he said at last. "You are not yet strong enough to confront him. You must leave San Francisco for a while until he tires of the search and forgets you again."

"I'll go back to the ranch," Francie said eagerly. "Ollie loves it there—"

He shook his head. "There is always a chance he will remember the ranch and go there. No, Francie. You must go far away from here, far from California. You must go to China."

# CHAPTER 25

◆

Harry threw the detective's typewritten report impatiently into his desk. He paced to the window and stared angrily out onto California Street. The fool had been unable to find Francie, but Harry knew she was out there somewhere, he felt it in his bones.

He turned away restlessly. He was irritated and upset; he was supposed to return to Princeton for the spring semester, but he sure as hell didn't feel like it. He was sick of college, sick of San Francisco, sick of thinking about his goddamn sister. He needed a change. He needed wine, women, and song. His spirits lifted as he contemplated the idea, and his mind instantly made up, he raced up the stairs and ordered his valet to pack. They were going to Paris.

He called up Buck Wingate and invited him to accompany him, then he reserved the two best suites on the next liner leaving for France and ordered his private railroad coach to be attached to the Southern Pacific to New York.

Buck Wingate was three years older than Harry. He had graduated from Princeton and was working in his father's Sacramento law practice, gaining experience before continuing his graduate studies in law at Harvard, and immediately after that he meant to enter politics. He was twenty-three years old and had been voted the best-looking man of his year at college. He was tall with dark, wavy hair that grew in a peak on his forehead, steady brown eyes, and a lean athletic body. He swam, rowed crew, played a nine average at polo, and had a golf handicap of seven. But his passion was his forty-foot gaff-rigged sloop, the *Betsy Bee,* which he sailed as often as possible off Newport, where the family had a summer home.

He wasn't sure the trip to Paris with Harry Harrison was exactly his style, but his father insisted he go along "to keep an eye on him."

Jason Wingate had always taken care of Harmon Harrison's legal business and after his tragic death in the earthquake he had continued to keep a fatherly eye on the boy. And not without a bit of aggravation to Buck. He'd had to rescue young Harry from the authorities more than once. His latest scrape was when he'd been caught in a police raid on a notorious New York bordello. "He's just sowing a few wild oats," Buck had told the police, but Jason was worried because Harry wasn't paying too much attention to his studies either and his grades were slipping.

"I'd better take a sabbatical from Princeton, Mr. Wingate," Harry told him. "I need time to get over my father's death and sort myself out."

Buck had raised his eyebrows—it was five years since Harmon had died and he hadn't noticed Harry still grieving. But he said nothing. And now he dutifully packed and joined Harry on board the *Normandie.*

When he looked back on the trip later he knew his instinct had been right, it wasn't his style. Harry Harrison was an arrogant young pup with an embarrassing habit of treating servants like serfs and of throwing money about as though it was going out of style. Buck had been to Europe several times and there were places and things he wanted to see again: Palladio's villas in Italy; Venice by moonlight when the piazzas were silent and empty and he felt he had stepped back centuries in time; the castles on the Rhine and the mountains in Bavaria; the ageless beauty of Paris with the Seine and its romantic bridges and the Louvre full of masterpieces; and the timelessness of London's arcades and squares. There was so much to absorb from Europe, so much to see, to feel. But all Harry wanted to do was party.

Harry insisted they stay at all the grandest hotels. He slept all day and refused to see any of Europe's beauty, except its women. He ate at all the smartest restaurants, drank the oldest wines and the best champagne, and patronized the fanciest brothels.

He bought half a dozen automobiles, a Rolls-Royce, a Bugatti, a Hispano Suiza, a Benz, a de Dion Bouton, and a de Courmont. He had them all specially refinished in the exact color of the Harrison burgundy livery and fitted out in ebonywood and silver. He bought a two-hundred-foot yacht from a tea magnate in England, ordered it to be refurbished from stem to stern and staffed it with a permanent crew of forty. He sent diamond bracelets to women he fancied and sable coats with emerald buttons to those whose favors pleased him.

Buck was no prude, but he watched tight-lipped. Harry's wild oats were on a princely scale, but whenever Buck protested, he just laughed and said he could afford it. And few people, except Buck, knew about his drinking and his taste for opium. Harry was clever enough to keep that to himself. He would just disappear for a night every so often, but he always emerged again the following afternoon, freshly showered and shaved, immaculately dressed and clear-eyed. Whatever he did, it surely didn't show on his face.

The Wingates had had money for three generations, as long as the Harrisons. They owned a fine home in San Francisco, an apartment in New York, and a summer "cottage" in Newport for the sailing. They lived well, but Buck had never seen anyone spend money or pursue drink and women the way Harry did. After a few weeks he had had enough. He cabled his father that he was returning and left Harry to his expensive pastimes.

Left alone, Harry marched angrily into the Ritz bar and at once took up with a crowd of young Englishmen, who were over for a roisterous weekend in Paris. He was bored without Buck's company and tired of the same faces, and when the Honorable Morgan Tilmarsh invited him to visit he accepted with alacrity.

Tilmarsh Hall was a stately pile surrounded by several hundred acres of prime hunting country in Gloucestershire. As Harry sped up the three-mile-long driveway in his racy little Bugatti, a footman in worn dark-blue livery immediately rushed to open the door and take his luggage. "Mr. Morgan is taking tea with Miss Louisa in the small drawing room, sir," the silver-haired butler told Harry. "If you would like to follow me, sir, they are expecting you."

Harry glanced around, impressed as he followed the butler through a raftered medieval hallway four times the size of his own. A fire roared in an enormous stone grate, but the chill of centuries still clung to the ancient stone walls adorned with the antlered heads of long-dead deer. The "small" drawing room was forty feet long, and crammed with chintz sofas and little tables covered with silver-framed photographs of royalty and children. Half a dozen spotted dogs lolled in front of the fire and on the sofas, and as the butler showed him into the room they leapt toward him, almost bowling him over.

"Down, Ace, down, Jack! Rex, Smarty, get down, will you? Behave yourselves for once."

An elegantly booted foot kicked the dogs gently out of the way and a charming English voice said, "I'm so sorry, I'm afraid they're a little overexcited. They were allowed out with the hunt today, you see."

Harry looked up from the dogs and saw the most beautiful girl in the world. "I'm Louisa Tilmarsh," she said, smiling and holding out her hand.

Harry took it, and wanted to hold it forever; he wanted to keep her close to him so he could look longer into that flawless face and bask in her pearly smile and the warm glance from her clear gray eyes. He said, "I'm Harry Harrison. I met your brother, Morgan, in Paris."

She laughed and made a little face as Morgan unfurled himself from the sofa and shook Harry's hand. "Glad you could make it," he said warmly. "You're just in time for tea. Louisa will pour."

"We're just back from a day's hunting," she said, passing a cup and offering a silver dish of hot buttered crumpets. "Do you hunt, Mr. Harrison?"

"Not yet, but I'm sure willing to learn."

She threw back her head and laughed heartily. "Then you'd better get in a little practice. Tomorrow we'll fix you up with a mount and I'll take you out myself so you can get the feel of the land."

She bit into a crumpet, wiping the crumbs daintily from her mouth with long, graceful fingers. Harry couldn't take his eyes off her. Her long, copper-colored hair hung loose to her shoulders and curled in soft tendrils around her face, and she had that wonderful clear-eyed, fresh country-complexioned English look. She was still wearing her riding britches and he thought they clung to her perfect small rump as though they belonged, and her high black leather boots and masculine white silk shirt looked sexy as hell.

At dinner that night she was transformed, in trailing green velvet with a gardenia in her upswept hair. "From our hothouses," she explained when Harry commented on its scent.

Lord and Lady Tilmarsh were rundown aristocrats and very English, but they made Harry welcome and encouraged his interest in Louisa. And when, after a week, he knew he must be polite and leave or overstay his welcome, he could hardly bear to tear himself away.

\* \* \*

"It's incredible," he told Buck back in New York again. "I've never even kissed her and she's the sexiest woman I've ever met."

He couldn't stay away. He forgot about Princeton and he criss-crossed the Atlantic so often that all the stewards on every liner knew him. Louisa was elusive, keeping him at arm's length, something he wasn't used to. On his twenty-first birthday she looked so divinely sexy in her britches and boots and jaunty black bowler with her copper hair tucked into a net, that he finally grabbed her and kissed her. She smelled deliciously of Mitsuko and he was overcome with passion, but he knew there was no chance of an affair, so he asked her to marry him.

The Tilmarsh-Harrison wedding was the event of the 1912 London season. The ceremony was held at St. Margaret's Westminster and was attended by a princess, two dukes, and dozens of lords, as well as three hundred other guests. Louisa looked magnificent in simple white satin from Worth, and the guard of honor outside the church wore hunting pink, forming a triumphal arch for the bridal pair with their riding crops. There was a reception at the Ritz afterward, with a thirty-piece orchestra, a towering five-tier wedding cake, and enough champagne to deplete Krug's reserves for several years to come—all paid for by Harry because it seemed the Tilmarsh's had been rather short of money for a couple of generations.

"Whatever we have we put into horseflesh," Louisa told him proudly. "Our horses are the best Irish bloodstock."

The first night of the honeymoon was spent at the Ritz, and Louisa bathed and changed into a simple white lawn nightdress. She flung herself into bed next to the waiting Harry. "I'm as tired as the dogs after a day's hunt." She yawned, snuggling her head into the pillow and falling instantly to sleep.

Harry stared at her angrily. How could she sleep, tonight of all nights, when he couldn't wait to get his hands on her? He got up again and dressed angrily. He took one last hopeful look at her before he closed the door on his way out, but Louisa was snoring gently and he stomped out of the room and down the elevator, making for London's Soho and some willing woman to assuage his needs.

At noon the next day they sailed down the Thames on his yacht and that evening before dinner he gave her a present. A sable coat with emerald buttons.

"It's wonderful, darling," she said putting it around her shoulders and holding the soft fur against her cheek. "Heavenly."

Harry didn't usually give away sables with emerald buttons until he had had his pleasure and more, but tonight he had it made. Louisa was his. He paced the chilly decks, giving her plenty of time to undress and make herself ready, and then he hurried back to their suite bearing a bottle of chilled champagne.

She was sitting up in bed wearing an ermine-trimmed white satin bedjacket, and she looked expectantly at him with those beautiful, wide gray eyes.

"I'm ready, darling," she said quietly.

"I didn't want to rush you," Harry said eagerly, offering her a glass of champagne.

She shook her head. "No, thank you," she said primly, "I think I'd better keep my wits about me so I know what to do."

He looked at her, puzzled. Of course she was a virgin, but shouldn't she want to lose her head, not keep it?

"I expect it'll be like hunting," she explained brightly, "going over the jumps."

Harry gulped his champagne and climbed into bed with her. He put his arms around her and she lay there quietly. He kissed her and she let him. He stroked her naked body and she stiffened. She lay frozen and silent when his lips traveled slowly across her breasts and her nipples, and gasped horrified as they found her virgin softness.

Harry consummated their marriage that night, but in the next few weeks he realized that for Louisa sex was a boring duty she performed only for the sake of possible future children, and even *they* would take second place to her favorite hunter. His mistake had been in believing that the sexy-looking girl in the figure-hugging britches and boots was the real Louisa. She thought, talked, and lived nothing but horses until he wondered why she didn't smell of the stables in bed instead of Mitsuko.

After a frustrating few months he finally told her that if she ever learned to ride a man as well as she rode a horse, she might be able to keep a husband. But not him.

He played it the English way, he paid for an arranged night of love with a pretty companion in a Brighton hotel. Louisa presented the necessary evidence to a sympathetic judge and was granted a divorce. And Harry returned to San Francisco, only a year older, married, divorced, and several million dollars poorer.

# CHAPTER 26

◆

Francie didn't expect to fall in love on board the S.S. *Orient* en route for Hong Kong. In fact, at first she wasn't even sure it was love. She told herself it was just a shipboard romance; even less than that, it was a flirtation. It wasn't even that, it was just that Edward Stratton was a nice man who had gone out of his way to be kind to a woman traveling alone.

She had been leaning over the deck rail watching San Francisco disappear on the horizon. There were tears in her eyes as she thought of Ollie, left behind with Annie. It was the first time they had ever been apart and she was missing him already and she knew it would only get worse.

The man next to her said, sympathetically, "Too late to turn back now," and she turned to look at him, pushing away the tears with her fingers. He took an immaculate linen handkerchief from his pocket and offered it to her. "Look at it this way," he said, smiling, "ahead lie the Hawaiian Islands and beyond that, China. You have a lot to look forward to."

She nodded, inspecting him cautiously as she dabbed her eyes. He was a confident, handsome older man of medium height with thick, dark hair brushed firmly back. He had bushy black eyebrows and candid, light-blue eyes, he was clean-shaven and he had an English accent.

"Edward Stratton," he said, offering his hand.

"Francesca Harrison," she replied, managing a smile. "I'm sorry. I don't usually cry in public."

He shrugged. "Partings are always difficult."

"Well, thank you for your help," she said diffidently, turning and walking back into the glass-enclosed verandah deck. She half-turned to look at him; he was leaning against the rail watching her and he lifted his hand to wave.

The S.S. *Orient* was a luxury ship and its passengers were a mixture of businessmen and diplomats returning to Shanghai, tea-planters en route to Colombo and rubber-station employees bound for Manila and Penang. Francie's stateroom was luxuriously paneled in walnut with polished brass fittings, soft carpets, and a big bed piled high with downy pillows and covered with an apricot silk spread. There were flowers everywhere, including a posy of lilies of the valley from Ollie; her trunks had already been unpacked and it suddenly began to feel like home.

Before she had left Annie had dragged her, protesting, to the smart Paris House store in San Francisco. "You can't travel halfway around the world without a decent cloth suit and half a dozen evening dresses," she had warned. And tonight as she dressed for dinner in a simple dark-green panne-velvet dress, she was grateful. She piled her hair up in a loose chignon, added a pair of jeweled combs and a dab of jasmine scent at her throat and wrists.

She twisted the narrow gold band nervously on her wedding finger; she had decided for Ollie's sake it would be better to be known as Mrs. Harrison, a widow, and after all, Annie had said encouragingly, it wasn't exactly a lie, she and Josh would have been married had he lived.

But it wasn't Josh she was thinking of as she made her way along the blue-carpeted corridors of the S.S. *Orient* to the dining saloon. The head waiter escorted her to the purser's table and she smiled good evening to her fellow passengers as she took her seat. She looked for Edward Stratton and saw him at the captain's table looking very handsome in a black velvet smoking jacket; she blushed as their eyes met and he smiled and nodded.

She made her way straight back to her cabin after dinner, clutching the brass rail along the companionways as the ship rolled in the Pacific swell. The scent of Ollie's lilies filled her cabin as she lay in bed later, thinking of Edward Stratton and the long voyage ahead, and hardly thinking at all of Hong Kong and Lai Tsin, who would be waiting for her there, and the business she had to take care of.

The next morning after breakfast in bed she went for a brisk walk around the upper deck. The ship rolled in the long gray swell that stretched into infinity and the wind tugged at her hat and took her breath away.

Edward Stratton watched her, an amused little smile on his lips. She was laughing as she staggered against the wind and her pale hair streamed from under her hat in long silken ribbons.

"I'm afraid we're in for some weather, Mrs. Harrison," he called as she looked up at him.

"Worse than this, you mean?" she asked, wide-eyed at the prospect.

He glanced at the sky, full of lowering gray clouds. "The barometer's dropping rapidly, we'll have rain soon and gale-force winds. I'm afraid you won't be seeing many of our fellow-passengers in the dining saloon tonight."

Francie laughed, exhilarated by the storm. "It's exciting, just the sea and the sky and the wind. It makes me feel alive again."

The sky quickly grew dark as night, the wind was howling and the sea had turned a leaden gray as they hurried inside. "I don't suppose you play poker, Mrs. Harrison?" he asked with a smile.

She shook her head and he said ruefully, "No, I suppose not. It's not exactly the sort of thing well-brought-up young ladies learn at school."

Francie thought soberly of how far his idea of her was from reality, but when she remembered the infinity outside, the stormy skies and the wind-tossed waves, she felt as though they were thousands of miles away from real life, and she felt lighthearted and gay. She felt young! Greatly daring, she said, "I could learn, though I don't guarantee I'll be any good."

"Oh, I don't know," he said, throwing her a challenging look as they walked together to the cardroom. "I have a feeling in my bones about you." The green-baize tables were empty and he shook his head. "What did I tell you, we're already losing our fellow passengers."

"Not me," she said confidently as he shuffled the cards and began to deal. His hands were strong and square with tapering fingers and she thought they expressed his personality perfectly: strong and confident, that was Edward Stratton.

They didn't play much poker, but he did tell her all about himself; he told her he was Lord Stratton, that he'd inherited the title at the age of fifteen when he was still an Eton schoolboy. He was a widower, his wife, Mary, had died five years ago, he was forty-two years old with three children aged seven to fourteen. He had a large house in Chester Square in London's smart Belgravia and the family's stately home, Strattons, near Inverness in the far north of Scotland with a stretch of the best salmon fishing river in the country and the most beautiful views in Europe. But Francie didn't tell him anything about herself in return, because she didn't know what to say.

"Shall I see you at dinner?" he asked, looking anxiously at her as she left him, and she nodded, wishing shyly that she didn't blush.

But back in her stateroom she worried about what to tell him. She was an imposter, traveling as the widowed Mrs. Harrison, and she'd bet that if he knew the truth he wouldn't even want to speak to her. She told herself a hundred times she would have supper in her stateroom. She paced the floor watching the clock ticking slowly toward eight. At seven forty-five she gave in. She threw on a slender ice-blue silk dress with a deep V-neckline and long, tight sleeves. She pinned a huge cream silk rose at the shoulder, dabbed the French jasmine scent lavishly at her throat, brushed her blond hair into a shiny knot at the nape of her neck and checked her appearance in the mirror. She told herself nervously that no one could ever accuse her of having dressed to please him; she had gotten herself together in exactly ten minutes and looked as businesslike as any businesswoman could in clinging ice-blue silk. Throwing an aquamarine lace wrap over her shoulders, she made her way to the dining saloon.

She didn't encounter a single other person on her way there and when she walked down the broad stairway into the saloon there were only half a dozen others present, all of them men. Captain Laird greeted her personally. "Please sit at my table, Mrs. Harrison," he said, cheerfully. "There are so few of us left tonight and we'll be glad of your charming feminine company."

The dining room looked forlorn with its empty tables cleared of their glasses and silverware to avoid breakage, but the captain's table was as beautifully arranged as ever, with everything anchored firmly into place. Captain Laird seated her on his right and Edward Stratton sat next to her.

"I thought you weren't going to make it," he whispered with a grin.

Despite herself, she laughed. "I almost didn't," she confessed, although she didn't tell him it wasn't because of the storm; it was because of him.

Captain Laird glanced knowingly at them; he was an old seafaring man, he had captained his own ship for more than twenty years and he had seen everything. He knew the beginnings of a shipboard romance when he saw one and he hoped, in a fatherly way, that young Mrs. Harrison knew what she was doing. Still, Edward Stratton was a gentleman, so he hoped for the best.

Francie was enjoying herself; she sipped a little champagne and nibbled at the caviar, listening wide-eyed to the captain's tales of storms at sea, to the French diplomat's stories of political skulduggery in wicked Shanghai, and to the businessmen's sagas of double-dealing in Hong Kong and Singapore. They were all so sure of their masculine importance and she knew they thought of her as a decorative accessory, of as much value to them and their business world as the roses in the center of the table.

And then Edward turned to her and said, "And what is your reason for going to Hong Kong, Mrs. Harrison?"

"Oh," she replied innocently, "I'm going to buy a ship."

Silence fell around the table as half a dozen pairs of masculine eyes looked up at her.

"A ship, Mrs. Harrison?" Captain Laird asked politely.

"Why, yes," Francie flashed them a dazzling smile. "A cargo vessel. I need it for my business, you see."

"And may I ask exactly what business are you in, Mrs. Harrison?" the French diplomat sitting opposite asked, gazing admiringly at her. In his opinion, women who looked like that didn't need to be in business, any man would be happy to give her as much money as she wanted just to be able to claim she was his.

"I am a merchant, Monsieur Delorges. The L. T. Francis Company. Import and export, to and from the Orient."

The men around the table suddenly looked at her with new respect —they had heard of the L. T. Francis Company and knew it was sound.

"Congratulations, madame," the Frenchman said, "you are a clever woman to be so successful in the face of so much competition."

"I must confess that I have very good advice." She glanced around the table with a faint smile and added, "From a man."

They all laughed and she pushed back her chair and wished them good night. "It was a delightful dinner, gentlemen," she said, smiling. "I enjoyed your company." And picking up her little blue silk evening purse, she bestowed another dazzling smile on them and swept from the room, leaving a hint of jasmine perfume scenting the air.

Edward Stratton watched her go. If he had been the Frenchman he would have said it was a *coup de foudre,* but in his own language he was bowled over. He was madly in love with Mrs. Francesca Harrison.

Edward Stratton had been a devoted husband. After his wife died he had grieved for more than two years, sequestering himself at his Scottish castle with his memories of their youthful love, and their growing years with their young family. Their life together had been a peaceful one where season followed season, each with its predictable round of social events with the same faces they had known since childhood. He had thought their lives would progress on the same happy, even keel as he and Mary grew old together and welcomed their own grandchildren to Strattons, just the way his grandparents had welcomed him. Nothing much had changed in the Stratton family for centuries; life had always been this way: secure, predictable, and uneventful. And that's why Francesca Harrison had knocked him all of a heap.

Sitting alone at the bar after dinner, four weeks out into the voyage, he asked himself, Why? Of course, she was beautiful with that blond, simple, almost classical beauty that overwhelmed him every time he looked at her. And she was unpredictable, one moment shy and insecure, and the next a confident businesswoman. She was a lady, a widow, and a mother, yet she had the innocence of a young girl. And she was a mystery; she seemed to tell him everything and yet when he analyzed it later she had told him nothing but the barest facts about herself and her life. She was beautiful, elusive, and independent. And all those elements added up to the fact that Francesca was *different.*

Edward was a seasoned traveler; he had been around the world many times, he had sailed on great liners and on private yachts and he knew all about the dangers of shipboard romance. He thought of his three children; he was a loving and devoted father and their welfare had always been his most important concern. However much he loved someone he would never remarry without their approval. They came first, that was the way it had always been in the Stratton family.

He smiled as he drained his glass of whiskey, gazing out at the twinkling stars and the crescent moon, imagining it shining down on the gray stone-turreted Stratton Castle, more than seven thousand miles away. How could his children not love Francie as much as he did?

There was just one more week left of the voyage and he meant to spend as much time as possible with her. He had already offered to show her Hong Kong, but she had been in one of her more elusive moods and had put him off. He thought about that, puzzled, because he could swear she was as attracted to him as he was to her.

He lay awake for a long time that night, wondering what was wrong. Finally he decided it was because she had this newfangled idea of being a businesswoman. Probably her late husband's partners did the real work, and if not, once they were married he would find her a good manager to take care of things so she would be free to devote her time to him and the children and Strattons.

Francie was also lying awake, thinking of Edward. The stateroom was in darkness and the smell of the fresh flowers put there that morning by the steward was overpowering. Stifled, she sat up and turned on the lamp.

She told herself for the hundredth time it was just a shipboard flirtation on his part, and that, anyway, nothing could ever come of it. She could only pretend to be the widowed Mrs. Harrison for the length of this voyage and then it was back to reality. A reality Edward Stratton would not like. She thought longingly how too easy it would be just to let him take charge of her life, to be looked after by him. Then she told herself that Lai Tsin had made her strong and yet here she was acting like a weak, silly woman all over again, ready to give it all up simply because she was in love.

The ship's bell struck four and she sighed. Sleepless hours stretched in front of her because the problem she had was unsolvable. Meanwhile she was aware that everyone on board was talking about them. She felt their eyes on them at dinner, she felt them follow her when they walked together on deck and she knew she could not afford to be the object of scandal a second time in her life. There was no answer to her problems. She decided there were only a few days left of the voyage and she would be more discreet. In future, she would keep her distance from Edward Stratton.

The night before the ship docked in Hong Kong the captain gave a gala farewell reception and dinner. For a week Francie had barely left her cabin except to go for an occasional stroll when she was sure Edward would be otherwise occupied. She had taken all her meals in her room and had passed the time with her nose buried in a volume of Dickens borrowed from the ship's library, reading and rereading each paragraph endlessly because her mind simply wasn't on *David Copperfield*. Edward had sent a dozen messages and she had finally written back that she was tired and was resting in preparation for her arrival in Hong Kong.

But she couldn't refuse Captain Laird's special request for her to sit at his table, and she wore her most beautiful dress. The cream chiffon felt like gossamer against her silk-stockinged legs, and the gold lace tunic with its wide, low neckline and long, tight sleeves reached to her knees, so the skirt swirled prettily as she walked. She wore no jewelry, just a fresh cream rose pinned at her shoulder and another in her hair. She squared her shoulders as she walked down the corridor, determined to stay cool and composed as she said good-bye to Edward.

The saloon was festive with red, white, and blue buntings strung from pillar to pillar and stewards in white mess jackets serving champagne.

"Mrs. Harrison," the captain's voice boomed across the room and people turned to stare at her. "Glad to see you back. Feeling better, I hope?"

He kissed her hand gallantly and she smiled, quickly searching the room for Edward, but he wasn't there. She sipped champagne and made polite small talk with the French diplomat who was staying on for the remainder of the voyage to Shanghai. "But tonight is the real farewell," he said, "when our most charming businesswoman departs our ship. I fear without your lovely presence we might sink beneath a wave of boredom."

Francie laughed. He was charming and nice and she felt sure he flirted with every pretty woman who came his way. But still Edward wasn't there.

Half an hour later, when they went in for dinner and he still hadn't arrived, she thought half-angrily that she needn't have bothered dressing up for him, then suddenly she heard him apologizing for his lateness, and he was there, next to her.

"Francesca," he said in a low voice, "I've been so worried about you."

"There's really no need," she said coolly, turning away to speak to the captain.

She thought the dinner would never end as gala course followed gala course, and immediately after it was finished she said a quick good night, and with barely a glance at Edward hurried back to her stateroom. She paced the floor thinking of him, and then, unable to bear her thoughts or her own company any longer, she went out on deck.

All the storms had been left behind as they sailed into the South China Sea and the night was warm and calm. A languorous breeze blew from the land, bringing with it a heavy musky smell instead of the crisp invigorating salt air she had become used to. The sky sparkled with a million jeweled stars and the sounds of the string quartet playing Mozart in the main saloon drifted across the water.

She leaned on the rail searching the darkness for the shores of China, telling herself that this was the end of her little fantasy. Suddenly she felt him beside her and she turned her head to look at him.

"You've been avoiding me," he said quietly.

She shrugged her shoulders delicately. "It's the end of the voyage. Isn't that the usual time for these little shipboard flirtations to break up?"

"Flirtations?" She could see the hurt in his eyes. "It was more than that to me," he said, putting his hands on her shoulders. "I'm in love with you," he said. "I want you to come back with me and meet my family. I want to show you Strattons. I know you'll fall in love with it and then you won't be able to say no to me."

He kissed her and she closed her eyes, feeling the roughness of his chin against her skin, breathing the faint citrusy scent of his cologne. Her body was melting into his with ripples of pleasure; she wanted to run her hands through his hair, to hold him even closer. She wanted Edward Stratton and she couldn't have him. It was as simple as that.

"I must go," she said, pulling herself away from his arms.

"Say you'll see me again," he begged. "I'll be in Shanghai for two weeks and then I'll be back in Hong Kong. Please let me see you, Francesca?"

She shrugged again, hurrying away from him. "Maybe," she called over her shoulder.

The S.S. *Orient* anchored in Hong Kong Bay early the next morning and the smart little white launch from the Hong Kong Hotel sped toward it to pick up its guests and transport them to Pedder's Wharf. Francie felt Edward's eyes on her as she stepped into it and she glanced up. He was leaning on the rail, smart in a tropical white suit and panama hat and so handsome and serious-looking, it tugged her heart. He raised his arm in farewell and she lifted her hand in return. And then she turned her face toward Hong Kong and her real life again.

# CHAPTER 27

The Hong Kong Hotel was on the corner of tree-lined Pedder Street, overlooking the harbor. To the right was the Praya, a long esplanade with the palatial offices of the hongs, the great merchant trading companies. Their house flags fluttered importantly in the breeze and their smart launches were moored in front, ready to transport the powerful taipans to and from their ships. A one-hundred-and-fifty-foot-tall clock tower dominated Pedder Street, though its clock was said to suffer from "indispositions" because of the climate and no one ever set their watches by it. The steep green hills hung behind the waterfront like a painted backdrop, dotted with pines and eucalyptus and huge white marble villas. The blue bay was crammed with ships of every sort: old sea-going junks and enormous white steamers jostled for space with shabby sampans and smart launches, and a line of coolies waited on the jetty ready to haul baggage to the hotels. And behind them, waiting for Francie, was Lai Tsin. He was wearing his usual blue robes and round silk hat and she thought that, for the first time, he looked as though he belonged.

He shook her hand, bowing to her, his eyes smiling a welcome and she could tell he was as glad to see her as she was to see him. He walked with her across the road to the hotel and then left her there, saying he would meet her in an hour's time.

The Hong Kong Hotel described itself as the most commodious and best-appointed hotel in the Far East; it was solidly comfortable in colonial British style with gas-lit bedrooms and bathrooms en suite, hydraulic elevators, Grips restaurant, and a grill-room that served Western-style chops and steaks at any hour. Francie inspected it critically, thinking of Annie's plans for a new hotel, and she thought Annie could do it better. Still, the service was remarkable, her bags were in her suite before she was, and there was an abundance of flowers and fruit and bottled water. The only trouble was that Chinese were not allowed, except for servants.

Lai Tsin had warned her of this and she had immediately refused to stay there, but he had insisted she must. "It is not suitable for a Western woman to stay in a hotel with Chinese," he told her firmly.

He was waiting for her in a black-hooded rickshaw and they soon left the smart paved streets behind, jogging through crowded alleys and up and down hills and steps to a shabby waterfront area. Their rickshaw man wove his way through a maze of narrow lanes behind the docks and stopped in front of a dilapidated gray wooden warehouse. Lai Tsin alighted and held out his hand to help her.

"This is what I have brought you to see," he said, flinging open the door proudly. "Our own godown in Hong Kong. I was fortunate to find it so near the waterfront, because the big trading companies own most of the land. I have bought it in your name, Francie. Look, here are the papers for you to sign." She stared at the papers covered in Chinese writing.

"This is only the beginning," he said excitedly. "The taipans of the big hongs would eliminate us immediately if we were to try to compete with them, it is only because we are small that we have a chance. And it is that very smallness that will be our biggest asset—it will enable us to pick up the crumbs they consider too much trouble to sweep up themselves.

"And if this little godown does not look worthy of the L. T. Francis Company, then only remember this: that from smallness and discretion grows greatness. Our lack of ostentation enables us to act steathily, and steathily we will creep up on our competitors, until one day we shall stun them with our power."

Francie stared at him, impressed. He looked small and fragile, his skin was stretched thin as parchment across his prominent cheekbones, but his black almond eyes sparkled with intelligence and knowledge. He was her mentor, her guide through life, and he knew everything.

Lai Tsin took her hand and led her inside. The wooden shelves were covered in the dust of years and a thin ray of sunlight filtered through a broken pane in the small window. It looked shabby and desolate, but he promised confidently, "The next time you see this it will be filled to overflowing with our wares."

The waterfront was a hive of activity. Everywhere Hakka coolies, stripped to the waist, were carrying, lifting, and staggering beneath burdens more than twice their own weight. Forming human chains, they loaded the little tugs that chugged back and forth to the ships anchored in the deep water bay. Sweat streamed down their backs, it dripped from their furrowed brows into their eyes, but they had no time to wipe it away.

Francie watched curiously, but she didn't notice one of the coolies stop work and stare at her and Lai Tsin. Nor did she see him edge closer, stealing toward them in the shadows behind the mountain of crates.

The coolie was large-boned and desperately thin, his back was bent and there was a permanent frown of anguish on his filthy, sweat-streaked face. He was short and wiry, he kept his head bowed and his face hidden beneath the wide straw coolie hat. He wore his thick, coarse black hair shaved at the front and braided in a queue, and he was dressed in the cheap, black cotton pants they all wore. His skin was burned a dark yellowish brown and only his eyes gave him away; they were the eyes of a Western man, burning with rage and pain and hatred. They were Sammy Morris's eyes and they were staring, stunned, at Francie.

If he had ever prayed in his life it was to see her again. When they had flung him, emasculated and half-dead, into the stinking hold of the filthy Chinese clipper, he had thought he would die. He had *wanted* to die—what was there to live for? To suffer the excruciating pain that racked his bleeding body? To live with the knowledge that Josh was dead? To feel the rats sniffing his blood, gnawing at his limbs, impatiently waiting their turn to mutilate him further? When they had brought him water and rice he had asked them, half-conscious, Why? "You are not to die," they told him. "Those are our instructions." And so, despite his horrific wounds and his wish to depart this world of pain they had forced him to live, in order to suffer the humiliation of poverty and despair, when existence meant a coolie's life, breaking his back for a few *yuan* that bought him only a miserable bowl of Chinese rice morning and evening and a filthy six-by-nine-foot cubicle flimsily partitioned off from a dozen others where he slept nights, and which was rented out during the day to another coolie.

Many times he had contemplated suicide. It would have been so easy to leave his pain behind, to smoke a pipe of opium and then jump into the harbor and let the tide take him, or to climb the bamboo scaffolding surrounding the tall buildings under construction and throw himself off, or to buy a lethal potion from the Chinese medicine shops where they knew all about those things. But in the end, he could never do it. Because one ambition still burned in his shattered, broken shell of a body. He wanted to take his revenge on Francesca Harrison. He wanted her to suffer the way Josh had suffered and the way he was suffering now. She had put him through six years of hell when she had him flung, half-dead, into the China clipper, never expecting him to return. Her big mistake had been in not killing him and shipping him instead to China. It had taken years for him to make his way to Hong Kong. And now fate had given her to him again.

She looked so cool and elegant and aloof, like a queen surveying her subjects, he thought bitterly, his heart jumping with the old excitement. Ignoring the angry shouts of the overseer, he moved from shadow to shadow in their wake. He watched as they climbed into the waiting rickshaw, and as they set off down the street he padded after them, trotting in rhythm with the rickshaw man, but always keeping a careful distance behind.

Despite his crippled back and his terrible wounds, years of work as a coolie had toughened him and he was scarcely out of breath when they turned into Pedder Street. He lingered on the edge of the milling crowds, watching as she stepped from the rickshaw and went into the hotel.

He was very thoughtful as he made his way back to his miserable little rat-infested cubicle later. He bought a bowl of rice and vegetables from a stand on the corner and ate it leaning against a wall, still thinking. And when he went back to his stinking cubicle and lit a pipe of opium, he thanked whatever providence had thrown her into his path. He decided that whatever it took this time he would get Miss Francesca Harrison. He would torture her the way he had been tortured, and then he would be merciful. He would kill her.

Francie had been in Hong Kong a month and at first everything had seemed to be going right. They had found a cargo ship for sale; it was shabby and rusty and not very fast, but it was sound. The purchase was completed within days, an American captain was appointed and a Chinese crew recruited. Now it lay in anchor, empty and waiting for its first cargo. And that was the problem.

The crumbs of business that Lai Tsin had anticipated snatching from the rich hongs' tables had not materialized. They did not do business with Chinese, they told him loftily. And when Francie went to see the taipans, they closed their doors to her, instructing their compradors, the managers, to offer her a glass of sherry and a sweet biscuit and inform her they did not do business with women. Smarting, she had retorted that it was their loss and marched out, but the truth was that now she did not know what to do.

It seemed impossible to penetrate their tight trading cartel, it was all wrapped up and shared out amongst the big hongs, the Jardines, the Swires, and the others.

The rickety godown had been cleaned and swept ready for the bales of silk and cotton, the chests of tea and spices, the precious carpets and the porcelain and jade they'd anticipated shipping, but it were still almost empty. And she knew from Lai Tsin's eyes that he had failed to secure any more business from the hongs. Reassuringly, he said the ship would be filled with his own merchandise, but she knew that there would be little profit in it. Francie's heart sank; instead of being a help to Lai Tsin, she had failed him.

When she returned to the hotel there was a message from Edward Stratton. It said, "I'm back, staying at Government House. Would you please be kind to a poor traveler and have dinner with me tonight?" Francie's spirits suddenly lifted, though she knew she shouldn't see him again. It was an impossible situation, her life was too fraught with complications, while his was as straightforward as A to Z. Yet just the thought of him made her pulse race and she knew she couldn't resist. Sitting at the ornate walnut desk, she wrote a note accepting, and summoned the little pageboy to see it was delivered.

A huge bouquet of flowers arrived for her shortly afterward, tall creamy roses. "I remember you best with these lovely flowers in your hair," Edward's note read, "only they were never as lovely as you. I shall be at your hotel at seven-thirty."

Francie was so nervous, she was ready at six-thirty. She wore the long ice-blue silk dress and tucked a rose into her hair.

She paced the floor nervously until seven-thirty and then with one last glance in the mirror, she picked up her floating blue-green lace wrap and her silk purse and walked slowly to the elevator. She took a deep breath as it descended, telling herself this would be the very last time she would see him. And then the metal grille slid open and he was walking toward her, both hands outstretched and a tender smile on his handsome face, and her heart lurched all over again and all her good resolutions were forgotten.

"You look just the way you did the first time I saw you," he said, taking her hands in his and lifting them to his lips.

She took back her hands quickly and patted the rose in her hair. "It's because of your lovely flowers," she murmured. "You remembered the roses."

She had never realized how intimate a vehicle a rickshaw was until she sat in one with Edward. The black hood closed them off from the view of pedestrians and she felt his arm against hers. "Where are we going?" she asked nervously.

"I'm taking you to my favorite restaurant," he said, smiling at her.

The rickshaw took them farther along the waterfront to a small dock where a sampan waited. She looked at him inquiringly as she stepped into it, but he just nodded and said mysteriously, "Wait and see."

The sun was setting and its fiery red glow silhouetted the black, full-sailed junks dotting the bay. The old woman paddling the sampan swung it around, maneuvering it skillfully to a little platform at the side of a junk, where a flight of steps led up to the deck. Her gnarled toothless face beamed into Francie's and she said something in Cantonese, touching her horny, calloused hand to her cheek and patting her stringy hair.

Edward laughed in reply, tipping her lavishly as they climbed from the sampan.

"What did she say?" Francie asked, shading her eyes with her hand to watch the old woman paddle away.

He grinned. "She said the hairy barbarian lord's woman is very beautiful, but she has too much strength for him."

Francie laughed ruefully. "I'm afraid she made the wrong guess."

"Oh, it's no guess." He took her hand and led her up the steps as dozens of coolies in white smocks and black trousers appeared to welcome them. "These people can read faces the way we read books."

The Chinese junk smelled of tar and rope and salt spray, and they walked to the stern where soft Oriental carpets covered the wooden boards and fat silk cushions were piled around a low red-laquered table. Sticks of incense burned in front of tin figures of the sea goddess, a tasseled red awning sheltered them from the last rays of the sun and there were heavy red silk curtains that could be drawn to shut out the wind or to give them privacy.

In a sudden flurry of activity, the coolies clambered along the rigging, hoisting sails; the anchor was pulled in and Francie sat on her silk cushions speechless with pleasure as they sailed silently across the bay past a dozen tiny green islands dotted with curved-roofed temples. The sun quickly disappeared into the indigo sea, leaving only a faint rosy stain on the royal blue sky and a boy hurried to light the lanterns hanging from tall iron poles, while another solemnly carried in the silver ice bucket with the bottle of champagne Edward had sent ahead. Crystal glasses were filled and as he handed one to Francie he said, "I could think of no one I would rather share this moment with than you."

The sea rippled past like a stream and the wind sang in the rigging, billowing their sails as they watched the sky change to midnight, then to ink. The stars were as bright as their lanterns and he smiled happily at her.

Then half a dozen chattering Chinese appeared bearing steaming platters and they ate their feast, laughing as their ship skimmed over the glossy dark sea.

"Maybe we're destined to spend all our lives on boats," Francie said dreamily, leaning back against the huge soft cushions and gazing upward at the stars. "Liners and freighters and junks . . . permanent travelers of the world."

"Is that what you would like?" he asked, leaning toward her.

She shook her head. His face was so close to hers she could see the little dark flecks in the blue of his eyes. Discreetly, the Chinese removed the dishes from the low table and closed the curtains, leaving them alone in their cushioned lamplit world.

And then Edward's lips were on hers and she wanted him in a way she had never wanted Josh. She wasn't seeking solace or comfort in Edward Stratton's arms, she wanted him the way a woman did.

She pushed him away and sat up, tossing back her loosened hair and quickly twisting it into a knot. With her hair tied firmly back she felt more in control of herself.

Edward was a man of tradition. He knelt in front of her and took her hand in his and said, "Will you please marry me, Francesca?"

She gasped. She was flustered, flattered, tempted. "But I can't," she said. "We've known each other such a short while. . . . You know so little about me."

"That's easily remedied. Come home to Scotland with me, stay at Strattons, meet my children. Bring your son and then we'll all get to know each other. Just say yes, Francie. I've never felt like this before about any woman, not even Mary. She was my childhood friend, I knew her all my life; but you are different." He kissed the hand he was holding. "I feel passionately about you, Francesca. Please say you'll marry me."

She was so tempted she could hardly think straight. "I can't say yes," she said weakly. "But maybe one day I'll visit you at Strattons."

He sighed. At least he had achieved half his goal. "I warn you, I'll ask you again," he said, "over and over until you say yes."

before him as he stepped down th[e]... home ground. Lai Tsin did not lo[o]k and stood at last on his shower of coins in their direction a[nd] their faces as he flung a scrambling, fighting for his largesse a[s] by, but he heard them path to his village, the very same path [h]is feet on the familiar the poor little white ducks on their way [w]hich they had driven in Nanking.                                    ...ver and their deaths

The road was hot and dusty, a yellowis[h] ribbon stretching through the drab, hazy landscape of gray-gr[een] ...ce fields. He saw the children still paddling the big wooden ...wheels, wading through the mud with their heavy baskets, follo[wed by] the water buf- falo, planting the new shoots and praying for a g[ood] crop.

The *fung-shui* grove was on the outskirts of the vi[lla]ge to the west and it was there he went first. He walked slowly, sea[r]ching for the place where the body of his favorite little brother, Chen, had been left for the dogs and birds to take. Even after all these years the terrible night was so indelibly imprinted on his mind that he recognized the very tree, and he knelt before it and bowed his head, offering a prayer to the gods for the soul of his baby brother, who had been considered too young to have one—though Lai Tsin had known better.

After a while, he left the *fung-shui* grove and made his way toward the village. Nothing had changed. To the left was the village lord's reedy pond with the same white ducks and a man tending them. Lai Tsin glanced at him as he walked by, but it was not his father's face. He did not recognize him and so walked on, reminding himself that his father had been an old man of more than sixty years when he had left and that he must be long since dead.

The village of baked-yellow-clay houses rose from the flat, feature- less landscape identical to a thousand other villages along the Yang- tze, but he knew every inch of it. His eyes darted this way and that, seeking out the familiar places, the strange gnarled willow that grew where there was no water, the wooden temple with its carved cor- nices and curved eaves, its red paint worn to a vague brown. There was the same pack of scrawny dogs circling the houses looking for food, the same poor children dressed in their elder brothers' cast-offs, the same tattered red-paper slogans pasted over the entryways and the same desolate little stalls selling minute portions of meat and spices, incense and charcoal. The clay walls that had once enclosed the village were crumbling, disappearing back into the earth from which they came, and many of the small houses stood empty. The

# CHAPTER 28

---◆---

Lai Tsin had returned many times to Nanking in the past few years and every time he had retraced the fateful steps from the waterfront through the alleys of the city, searching for the square where the flesh-peddler sold his wares, but he had never again been able to find it.

He told himself it was a futile quest, that he would never find the man and that he was lucky because it meant that his soul would not be stained with his murder. Because if he ever found him he would surely kill him.

But in all this time and through all his travels in China, seeking the best sources and suppliers for his business, he had never returned to his home village on the banks of the Ta Chiang. Now he knew he could put it off no longer. He must return and exorcise his demons or forever live with a troubled mind.

The long trip upriver on the small shabby steamer was filled with memories and he stood by the rail watching the passing landscape, reliving that other terrible journey. At Wuhu, the stopping point for the steamer, he disembarked and hired a small shabby junk to take him farther upriver to his village. As they approached, he went to the small cabin and dressed himself in the long deep-blue embroidered silk robe that signified he was a man of means and no longer a mere field worker. He put on the stiff new silk hat, but this time the button in the center was not of silk but of precious white jade. He put on his new black leather shoes and then he walked back onto the deck as the junk maneuvered its way to the rickety wooden jetty.

When they saw it was docking at their insignificant little village, people came running to see who it was, staring respectfully at the important-looking man in his grand blue-silk robes. Some kowtowed few people about stopped to stare at him, looking distrustfully at the grand stranger in their midst, and he nodded politely and bade them good day.

The house of his father, Ke Chungfen, was at the very end of the tiny village and his footsteps slowed as he approached it. A child of about three years was playing in the dirt by the door and the sound cf voices raised in argument came from the house. He paused and listened. It was not his father, but it might have been; it was the same haranguing tone, the same violent, careless words, the same harsh threats. He walked to the door and called out the name "Ke Chungfen" and there was a sudden stunned silence. Then a voice shouted, "Ke Chungfen went to his ancestors many years ago. Who is it that calls out his name?"

"It is the son of the *mui-tsai,* Lilin," he replied calmly. "Lai Tsin."

There was a crash from inside and then the door was hurled open and Ke Chungfen's son by his Number One wife stood there, glaring at him. He was short and powerfully built, like his father, and his brutish face had the same discontented scowl; his clothing was poor and patched and his hands calloused from work in the fields. His glowering expression changed as he took in Lai Tsin's prosperous appearance.

"Well, well, Number One auntie's son," he exclaimed, for concubines were traditionally given the honorary title of "aunt." What brings you home after all these years?" He stepped back with an oily smile, waving him inside. "Welcome, welcome, Lai Tsin." Calling his wife, he roughly ordered her to prepare tea for their illustrious visitor. "For I can see you have come far in the world, Lai Tsin," he added. "Of course, it was wrong of you to run away and leave your brothers to take up the burden of the extra work necessary to keep this humble roof over our heads, and care for Ke Chungfen in his final years. But now you have returned to make reparation for such wrongdoing."

"I will not take tea with you, Elder Brother," Lai Tsin told him quietly. "Nor will I discuss my business with you. I am here to ask you one favor, for which I will pay you well. My mother, the *mui-tsai* Lilin, was not granted the honorable burial her ancestors would have expected. They are angry and upset that her soul still wanders far away from them. They have asked me to build her a temple where her spirit will join that of her son, Little Chen, so that she may be remembered on this earth forever, and their spirits may rejoice again in the company of their ancestors."

He reached into his pocket and took out a leather purse. "In here is sufficient money to buy the best materials, and to pay for expert construction. I know about these matters, Elder Brother, and cannot be fooled. I have already purchased the plot of land on the hill sometime ago and in six months I will return to inspect your work. If it is good, then I shall pay you handsomely, and I shall pay you a small sum each year after that to maintain the temple. If you try to cheat me I shall have you run out of this village and cast to the very dogs they gave my little brother to."

Elder Brother nodded his head eagerly, he could hardly believe his luck. "How much shall you pay me, Ke Lai Tsin?" he asked, magnanimously adding "Ke," the honorable family name of his father, to the concubine's son.

Lai Tsin stared at him, remembering the years when he had slept on the grass bedmat at his mother's side in the freezing little room with the ricepaper windows, his belly crawling with hunger and his limbs aching from his work in the fields, while Ke Chungfen and his brothers slept cosily by the charcoal stove covered in padded quilts, replete with rice and meat. He flung a handful of coins onto the earthen floor, watching contemptuously as Elder Brother groveled to pick them up, his lips moving as he counted them gleefully.

"You are generous, Little Brother," he exclaimed, beaming.

Lai Tsin shook his head sorrowfully as he walked to the door. He knew poverty only too well; he understood that it could turn men to demons selling their souls to find food and shelter for their families or opium for the pipe of oblivion. But the man before him had sold his soul many years before for far lesser reasons, and he despised him.

"Do not forget, I shall return to the ancestral temple in six months' time," he called over his shoulder.

Elder Brother bowed his head, dithering excitedly on the doorstep, the money still clutched in his hand. His haggard young wife peeked from behind him as he called, "It will be done, Honorable Little Brother, just as you wished."

Lai Tsin walked to the village burial ground, but though he searched every inch, there was no place marked with Lilin's name and he could not remember its position. Nevertheless he knelt and bowed, touching his forehead to the yellow earth nine times, and in his prayer he told her that soon she would roam the spirit world no longer. At last she would have a home where her ancestors could find her and she could join them in their happiness.

Elder Brother had shouted his good fortune aloud to the village and as Lai Tsin walked back people rushed from their crumbling houses to stare at the rich man in his magnificent embroidered silk robes with the precious white jade button in his hat. "He is a Mandarin," they gasped, "a man of learning and power. He has achieved much for the son of a *mui-tsai.*"

But Lai Tsin ignored them as he strode on toward the great Ta Chiang, turning only once to look back at the village. "Soon," he promised, "all this will be no more. The wind will eat away the walls of clay, the sun will dry the ponds and the drought will wither the rice fields. Then the clay will turn to dust and the wind will carry it away, layer by layer until the Great Ta Chiang rises to cover it." As though already implementing his prophesy, the wind soughed along the arid little road, fluttering the dry trees as he lifted his eyes to the distant hill where his mother's temple would stand. "And then there will be nothing left but the temple to the memory of the woman Lilin and her child. It is as it should be."

Turning, he walked resolutely away. The junk was waiting by the riverbank and he climbed on board, and without a backward glance sailed back to Wuhu and Nanking and Shanghai. And then to Hong Kong and Francie.

Francie was alone with Edward Stratton. She told him about her problem getting enough cargo to fill their big new ship.

"We don't want to steal the hongs' trade—and anyway, that's impossible," she said. "All we want are the crumbs from their tables, the shipments that are too small or too much trouble. We can fill half the ship with our own goods, but it must sail with a full load or we will lose money."

"I'll help you," Edward promised, "but only on one condition. That you come to the governor's reception with me tonight."

She laughed. She knew she shouldn't, but she said yes.

Government House was an impressive white granite building set in its own gardens. Lanterns flickered in the trees, a string quartet played a selection of operatic melodies and the British governor, Sir Henry May, told Francie, laughing, that Edward was a good fellow and she had better hurry and say "yes" and put him out of his misery.

"Everybody's here tonight," Edward told her, scanning the crowd expertly. "All the taipans who have said no to you are going to change their minds tonight. All you have to do is charm them."

It was true. All the men who had sent their underlings to offer her sherry and biscuits were only too pleased to be introduced to her at Governor Sir Henry May's residence. Beautiful women were a rarity in Hong Kong—or at least beautiful *ladies* were, they explained to her. And when Edward mentioned her little difficulty with the family business and the need to fill the ship, they immediately promised to help. Even though they might not have any cargo themselves, there were plenty of the smaller Chinese traders who might need space on a San Francisco-bound vessel.

And when Lai Tsin returned a week later, Francie took him to their rickety godown. She unlocked the brand-new padlock and removed the chain while he looked on, mystified, and then she showed him the shelves filled with bales of goods and wooden crates. She told him the story and he congratulated her on her first big success.

There were two things left for Lai Tsin to do before he returned to San Francisco. The next morning he met Francie and they walked down Des Voeux Road, past rows of tall, important-looking buildings until they came to an empty, weed-strewn lot dotted with ramshackle mat sheds and rickety foodstalls. The aroma of ginger and spices wafted from blackened woks balanced precariously over a dozen charcoal braziers and the high-pitched Chinese chatter competed with the noise of the traffic and the grinding and hammering coming from the building sites across the road. Small children ran underfoot, smiling beguilingly up at them as they pressed a few coins into their hands, and curious faces stared after the beautiful barbarian lady and the Mandarin in his grand blue robes as they paced the length of the lot that Lai Tsin had won from Chung Wu years ago.

They looked at the piece of paper that told the land was his, hardly believing it was true. Nearby was Chater Road and Statue Square, a few blocks behind them rose Victoria Peak with the palatial Government House and above it the green stretches of the botanical gardens and the rich villas of the taipans in the mid-levels. And all around them stood solid, impressive office buildings.

They stared at each other and knew that what had been a simple, cheap plot of land surrounded by wooden godowns and mat sheds when Chung Wu's grandfather had bought it for eighty dollars many years before, was now a prime piece of real estate. "We're standing on a fortune," Francie gasped. "You could sell this tomorrow, Lai Tsin, and retire a very rich man."

He shook his head, his eyes full of the vision of a tall, white, many-windowed building with the name of the Lai Tsin Corporation emblazoned in big brass letters. He saw a geomancer placing it so as to receive the best *fung shui* and he saw bronze lions outside guarding their good joss. He said, "We will not make our fortune from selling. This is the place on which we will build our fortune."

They took a rickshaw down to the docks and then a lighter out into the bay, where the ship had already loaded its cargo and was ready to sail on the noon tide. He pointed to the prow, where the name FRANCIE I had been painted. "It will be the first of our fleet," he said, as they strode the decks inspecting it proudly. "And it is all because of you."

He gave her an envelope and said, "I have a second gift for you which I bought with the first money I made five years ago, and kept it until you were ready. Now it is yours."

Francie opened the envelope, exclaiming in surprise when she saw what it was: the title to a plot of land on Nob Hill, just a block away from her old home on the opposite side of California Street.

Lai Tsin said, "Soon you will be back in San Francisco. You cannot go on hiding forever because of your brother. You can no longer think of yourself as the worthless daughter and the sister forever in his shadow. You will be at the mercy of no one. One day soon you will build your house on proud Nob Hill and show the world your face again. And there will be nothing Harry Harrison can do about it."

Lai Tsin sailed for San Francisco on the noon tide. Francie was to leave early the following morning. She spent her final day with Edward. He took her to the songbird market where thousands of twittering thrushes and canaries fluttered in little bamboo cages to be sold as pets. And Sammy Morris padded softly behind them in his tattered cotton coolie shoes; he followed them through the noisy alleys of Kowloon, past open-fronted stores, little more than holes in the wall selling buckets of squid floating in their black ink, platters of gray shrimp and tanks of silver-scaled fishes swimming exhaustedly to and fro, searching for the freedom that would only come with their death. He lingered while they inspected the stalls of the craftsmen carving chops, the seals that appeared on every document in China, and the calligraphers painting exquisitely on thin rice paper. His burning eyes never left them as they passed the shoemaker and the candlemaker and the women embroidering fine linen. He waited patiently while they dined in a simple teahouse on steamed dim sum and fragrant green tea, and he told himself that if necessary he would wait forever for his revenge.

They took the little tram up the Peak to view all Hong Kong and its islands, watching as the mist rolled in, just like in San Francisco. And they laughed, feeling as if they were almost standing on their heads as they took the tramway back down the steep incline.

Edward glanced briefly at the poor coolie waiting at the bottom of the Peak Tramway, flinging him a coin as he summoned a rickshaw to take them back to the hotel, then looked back at him, surprised as they drove away; he could swear it was not a Chinese face he had seen.

It was their last night together and they dined early in the cavernous dining room of the Hong Kong Hotel overlooking the harbor and its twinkling lights.

Francie knew it was the end. The play was over and the actors had to return to reality.

Darkness fell and the harbor outside glimmered with a thousand points of light. They were silent, each thinking their own thoughts, until she could stand it no longer and she told him she must go.

He took her hand across the table, inspecting the wedding band sadly and said, "Francie, why won't you let me replace this? I'll come with you to San Francisco—"

She quickly shook her head, panicked at the thought of his being in San Francisco. She had to put him off. She shrugged her pretty shoulders and said coolly, "Maybe this was just a shipboard romance after all. In a few weeks you'll have forgotten all about me. I'll just be the woman you met on the S.S. *Orient,* outward bound from San Francisco for the South China Seas."

"It's no shipboard romance," he said vehemently. "You know how I feel about you."

They walked silently to the foyer and he kissed her hand lingeringly, then she left him. She trailed up the curved marble staircase, half-turning, her hand on the banister, to look at him. He was watching her and their eyes locked for a final moment, then she walked on up the stairs to her room.

Edward waited until she had disappeared from sight. Hunching his shoulders disconsolately, he thrust his hands deep in his pockets and strode out into Pedder Street. A movement in the shadows outside the hotel caught his eye and he glimpsed a ragged coolie staring at him, then he melted back into the shadows and was gone. It was odd, but he could have sworn it was the coolie from the Peak Tramway. Shrugging, he turned away, too wrapped in his own emotions to think any more of it. Still, at the back of his mind lingered the faint memory that the face he had seen was not Chinese, but Western.

The next morning as dawn broke Francie stepped into the Hong Kong Hotel's white launch that would take her to the S.S. *Aphrodite,* anchored in the deep water bay. Pedder Wharf and the Praya were a seething mass of coolies and she would have been unable to pick out the one who watched her so intently as the launch sped across the bay to the waiting ship. But Sammy saw her and there was despair in his eyes; she was returning to San Francisco and he knew if he was ever to achieve his revenge he must go there too.

He turned quickly away and made his way through the streets to the docks where he had worked loading the crates onto the small lighters that carried them out to the cargo vessels in the bay. It was impossible for a poor coolie like him to join the crew of a legitimate cargo ship, but he would join up with one of the evil-smelling old trading junks no matter what port it took him to, and from there he would make his way halfway around the world, port by port, ship by ship, back to San Francisco and Francesca Harrison.

# CHAPTER 29

◆

Harry returned to the mansion on Nob Hill that Louisa had never even seen because she refused to leave her horses. He was tired of endless green English paddocks under a sheet of rain. He hoped he never saw another horse—except at the track, and he vowed never to look at another woman in britches. He wanted city streets under his feet again and more urban pleasures.

He decided to turn over a new leaf. He would go to work. The next day he rose at seven-thirty, bathed, dressed, breakfasted exceptionally well to fortify himself, and arrived at the new Harrison Building on Market Street promptly at nine.

The burgundy-uniformed doorman sprang to open the door as the Harrison Rolls came to a stop. He swept off his peaked cap and said, "Good morning, Mr. Harrison, sir. It's good to see you back."

Harry nodded distantly. He had rarely set foot in his own office building, but today he meant to make his presence felt. The double-height ground floor was given over to the Harrison Mercantile & Savings Bank's main branch, though there were a dozen others scattered throughout California. It had tall stained-glass windows and speckled rose-granite floors. The thick, polished-mahogany counters were divided by gilded iron grilles to separate the customers from the clerks, and there was a hushed atmosphere of big-number transactions and serious business deals.

Harry enjoyed walking into his bank and seeing the clerks jump respectfully. He liked the way heads turned to follow him and the whispered admiring comments that "young Mr. Harrison was back." He liked the way the pompous little gray-haired godlike bank manager in pinstripes and tails jumped up, flustered when he strode without knocking into his dark, mahogany-lined, thickly carpeted office.

He liked the way the men at the ticker-tape machines on the second floor, monitoring the financial ups and downs of Wall Street and the European and foreign markets, leapt to their feet, crushing out their cigarettes, waiting nervously for his commands as he strolled through their ranks. On floor after floor, he liked the way everyone, from the lowliest office boys to the managers in charge of the Harrison enterprises quailed under his glance and hung on his every brief word.

And when he reached the topmost floor containing the directors' offices, the boardroom, and his own personal suite, he liked his big office and his solid partner's desk, his leather swivel chair and the walls of important-looking leather-bound books in glass-fronted cabinets, and the view from his tall fifteenth-floor windows. But as he sat in his leather chair and contemplated the view, what he liked most was the sense of *power.*

There was no guardian secretary in his outer office, no one had expected him, but the word flashed through the building like brushfire, reaching the three men in the directors' offices before Harry had even reached the second floor.

Frank Vandenplas, his father's most trusted administrator, was the first to knock on his door. He had just held a conference with his two codirectors and decided quickly on a strategy. He walked in, his hand outstretched, his red-cheeked, gray-whiskered face beaming.

"Harry, my boy," he said, shaking his hand cordially, "I can't tell you how glad I am to see you." He looked sympathetically at him. "And how sorry I was to hear of your divorce. Still," he shrugged his hefty shoulders, "it's a small mistake at your age and easily put behind you. And now you've come to join us at last?"

It was a question, not a statement, and he took a seat looking expectantly at Harry, waiting for an answer. He hoped it was going to be no, because the young pup would cause nothing but trouble, but if it was yes, then he would give him a run for his millions.

"Good to see you, Frank," Harry replied, not meaning it. "And yes, I thought it about time I took up the reins and ran my own company, the way my father wanted."

Frank beamed again. "You could not have given me better news, my boy. Now, where would you like to start?"

Harry frowned. "Since I'm going to be in charge, it's better if you didn't call me 'my boy.' Harry will do." He wanted to tell the old buffoon to call him Mr. Harrison, but he was an old colleague of his father's, and besides, for the moment he needed him. But by God he was going to have these old men jump when he said jump. He'd soon show them who was boss.

"I'd like to know exactly where each company stands financially," Harry said. "I want to know the annual turnover and the profit and the growth patterns. I think that's as good a starting point as any, don't you, Frank?"

Frank nodded. "Correct, Harry," he said smoothly. "I'll have the accountants get their books together and meet you up here in half an hour. Meanwhile I'll send my own secretary to look after you until you have a chance to appoint someone yourself. And my fellow directors will be in to say hello. They're gonna be just as thrilled as I am to know we have a Harrison at the helm again."

Harry scowled. Frank and the two other directors were his father's contemporaries. They had been with the company for forty-five years and he knew exactly what they were like; old-fashioned, cautious, penny-pinching businessmen. Frank was a wily old bastard and Harry knew Frank would make sure to sabotage his ideas before they even got off the ground. *They would have to go.* He would appoint his own retainers, who would work for *him,* and who would carry out his instructions to the letter. Meanwhile, he wanted to see exactly where the Harrison companies stood.

In precisely half an hour the manager of his bank knocked on the door followed by a team of ten accountants and half a dozen office boys loaded with ledgers and box-files, company reports and balance sheets. Frank had drilled them well. "Tell him everything," he had said, "every last goddamn detail until his head spins and he doesn't know which end is up."

After five hours, Harry called a halt. "Okay," he snarled, standing up, his head swimming with numbers and projections. "No more bullshit. Give me the bottom line. Which are successful and which are not?"

"I'm glad to say all the Harrison companies are very successful, sir," the manager said, "particularly the railroads and the steel, though we have high hopes for the oil with the new prospecting in the northern territories."

"The net worth," Harry snarled impatiently, "what's the net worth of Harrisons, goddamit?"

"Three hundred million dollars, sir."

"And my personal worth?" Harry's fingers drummed impatiently on his desk.

"Almost a hundred and fifty million, sir."

He nodded. "Fine. Now you may leave." He waited until they had collected their papers and accounts and statements and filed from his office, then he slumped, exhausted, back into his chair. Goddamn it, all he had asked for was to know what the companies were worth, he didn't need a blow-by-blow account. But by God, he was richer than even he had thought.

But it wasn't enough simply to take over the business his grandfather had started and his father had expanded. He had to do something on his own. Something his father had not created. *This* Harrison had to make his own mark on San Francisco.

He stood and stared gloomily out the window at the newsboys calling the Extra on the street below. Hearst's morning *Examiner* competed in San Francisco with the *Chronicle* and the later editions of the *Daily News,* the *Call* and the *Bulletin.* Harry admired Hearst and his newspaper empire, he was impressed by the Scripps-Howard chain, and he thought deeply about the power and prestige of being a newspaper giant. He thought about how to do it. Money talked—he could always buy the other papers' editors and reporters by bribing them with huge salaries, he could hire away their photographers, install the latest machinery, get his paper out before anyone else's hit the streets, and give the readers what they wanted. And what did they want? A tabloid, he decided, excitedly, and at the cheapest price. *A one-cent tabloid.* Goddamn it, he would be the next Hearst. He would call it the *Harrison Herald,* he'd cover every scandal, every fire, every burlesque star, every murder, *and* show 'em the pictures. And he'd do the same in Los Angeles. In fact, he would make it a policy to open a new Herald in a new city every year, and in ten years he would have beaten Hearst at his own game. He would be "Harrison, the Newspaper King" and his name would be a household word, just like Hearst. He had the money to do it and nothing was going to stop him.

He called back the bank manager and the accountants, but he didn't call in Frank and the other directors. This was his baby and they would have nothing to do with it. He gave his orders: find premises, find the latest machinery, find out costs, get him the names of the top editors and news reporters, not just on the West Coast but in New York, Philadelphia, Chicago, and Washington. Whatever underhanded means it took to do it, find out the operating figures of the rival newspapers. Maybe he could just take over one of them. And just one other thing. He wanted it all done this week.

Smiling, he looked into their astonished faces as he buttoned his jacket and smoothed back his fair hair. "Good afternoon, gentlemen," he said, walking to the door and leaving them, mouths still agape, to do his legwork.

Buck Wingate listened doubtfully when Harry called him to explain his new plans. "I guess we should just be thankful he's doing something other than chase girls and spend money," he said gloomily to his father. But if he thought Harry spent money like water before, it was nothing compared to the sums he began lavishing on the *Harrison Herald*.

He bought a small printing plant on Mission, expanded it into the building next door and installed five brand-new presses and the latest in composing-rooms and darkrooms. He cleared the three middle floors of the Harrison building for the *Harrison Herald* offices and ordered a bewildered Frank to find room for the displaced workers on other floors. He installed a direct private elevator to his office and had that redecorated. He hired away an editor from New York, a night-desk editor from Philly, and stole reporters and photographers and experienced compositors and printers from the other San Francisco journals. He personally designed the *Herald* logo, a sunrise behind a phoenix, which would appear at the top of the front page of his newspaper, and he opened branch offices in every small California city. He spent millions and he got what he wanted: the best. Now all he had to do was sell it.

On the day the first edition was being prepared, he sat in his huge editorial office in his shirtsleeves, his feet on his desk, a cigar clamped between his teeth and a green shade over his eyes, reading every story as it came off the typewriter. Before giving his approval he examined every photograph while the *Herald*'s real editor fumed in his cubicle, trying to make his deadline and get his paper to press. That night Harry threw a huge party at the printing plant. He filled the place with debutantes, movie stars, and playboys, and he himself pressed the button to start his gleaming presses rolling. Champagne corks popped and he watched, satisfied, as the first *Harrison Herald* rolled off the press.

Buck Wingate shook his head. The place was like a society jamboree, not a beat the deadline, kill the competition, hard-nosed newspaper enterprise. He surely hoped Harry knew what he was doing, but he knew it was no good giving him advice. He wouldn't take it.

It seemed this time he was wrong. Harry worked hard. He made promotional visits to all the *Herald*'s offices, he gave speeches at street corners in every little town, extolling the virtues of his new one-cent tabloid, and his face appeared on a daily basis on the front page of his own newspaper. Sales of the *Herald* took off. ONE HUN-DRED THOUSAND DAILY SUBSCRIBERS AFTER ONLY ONE MONTH, his headlines announced proudly. One hundred and twenty-five thousand in two months, one hundred and fifty thousand. . . . Even if it wasn't true, Harry thought it looked good, and besides, people always believed what they read in the papers. Yet though the *Herald*'s stories and pictures were as good as anybody else's, they weren't any better. San Franciscans already had their loyalties to their own news-papers and sales began flagging.

Harry liked to drop in at the office at night, peeling off his jacket and sipping whiskey while he pulled stories off the spike on the nightdesk, issuing them to reporters to write while the night editor glowered furiously at him. The cynical hard-nosed newspapermen mockingly called him "young Harrison Hearst," and stories flew around San Francisco about how he couldn't keep his hands off the women staff and wouldn't take any backtalk from the men. "Fuck and fire, that's all Harry knows how to do," they said.

A new circulation war broke out. Harry's newsboys were beaten up by hired toughs and copies of the *Harrison Herald* were torn and scattered to the wind. Harry vowed to get the perpetrators, but strangely, even the chief of police wasn't able to find out who did it.

Harry went out on his publicity rounds again. He put ads in his own newspaper telling the public that the *Herald* was already ex-panding and that this was only the first in a chain of *Harrison Herald* newspapers across the country.

It was a small item in the financial column of his own paper that caught his attention. It said that L. T. Francis was on its way to becoming one of San Francisco's richest companies, still small but worth watching. It prophesied that with good forward-looking man-agement the merchant company—which had just purchased the first of what promised to be a fleet of cargo vessels—was firmly set on course to becoming one of San Francisco's most successful.

Harry wondered why he had never heard of it. He called Frank and asked him, but he said he had never heard of it either; it certainly wasn't part of the establishment. Still curious, he called the journalist who had written the piece and asked where he'd gotten his information.

"L. T. Francis is really a Chinese company," the man explained, "working out of offices and warehouses on the waterfront. It's all a bit of a mystery—except their success is very much a financial fact. The rumor is that it's some Chinese guy with a Western woman partner. They're in property and shipping and she fronts for him on all the deals. Nobody knows if it's really true, but if it is, it's a clever idea to get around the prejudice."

"A Western woman partner?" Harry echoed thoughtfully. "What exactly does that mean?"

The man grinned. "Your guess is as good as mine, but I have heard her called his 'concubine.' "

Harry laughed. "Sounds like just the kind of story we need for the *Herald.* Tell you what, why don't you dig around a little, find out about this concubine and the mysterious Chinaman. Try to get some pictures and we'll drum up a nice juicy scandal for our readers." He laughed again. "That'll take care of the L. T. Francis Company. Mark my words, you can watch their profits drop to zero the minute a sex-scandal raises its ugly head."

Harry thought no more about it until a couple of weeks later when the journalist came back to him with more information and pictures. He thought the reporter looked at him strangely, but he was more interested in the pictures he offered him.

He stared silently at the photographs. Minutes passed and the man shifted uncomfortably in his chair, but still Harry did not look up. Finally he spoke. "What other information do you have besides the pictures?"

"Not a great deal, sir. The boss is Chinese but he has American papers, probably got them after the quake, same as all the others. He's known locally as 'the Mandarin' because of the long Chinese robes he wears. He is not involved in local Chinese affairs and politics and has no contact with the tongs. He works hard and is said to be extremely clever. The business is sound and growing."

"And the woman?"

Harry's glance was ice and the reporter shuffled the papers nervously. "She's young, has a five-year-old son, lives in Aysgarth's Boardinghouse on Union. As does the Mandarin. And by the way, he's financially involved in that little boardinghouse, too, and I understand that soon there will be an Aysgarth's Hotel."

"Did you find out her name?"

The man cleared his throat. "Er, we understand she is a Mrs. Harrison, sir. And the child's name is Oliver."

Harry's stare was implacable. "A *Chinese* child?"

"I couldn't say, sir. I haven't seen him."

"And you don't know who this woman is?"

"Well, no sir, just that she's Mrs. Harrison."

But looking into his eyes Harry knew that he knew exactly who Mrs. Harrison was, and that his entire workforce now knew his crazy, long-lost sister was the Chinaman's concubine.

"You may go," he said coldly. "Oh, and by the way"—the man turned from the door and looked expectantly at him—"pick up your paycheck on the way out. You're fired."

The journalist stared at him, astonished. Harry was leaning back in his chair, gazing at the photographs of Francie. "You bastard," the man snarled. "You deserve all you get."

Harry ignored him, wincing as the door slammed violently. He spread the photos across his desk and bent over them intently. There was no doubt about it. His sister was living in sin with a Chinaman and their bastard son, just a few blocks away. His hands shook as he shuffled the photos back into a pile, his anger rising like steam in a simmering kettle until it suddenly boiled over. He could stand it no longer . . . he would go and see with his own eyes.

He thrust the photographs into his desk drawer and locked it. Then he called down to the darkroom and told them to destroy the plates immediately. Slamming into his private elevator, he cursed its slowness as it descended sedately to the ground floor. The doorman saluted, but Harry didn't even see him as he strode across the street in the direction of Union Square.

It was a dark, wintry evening and the lamps were already lit. A fire glowed in the grate of Francie's private sitting room, where Ollie lay on the hearthrug, his arm around the dogs, listening intently while Francie told him again all about Hong Kong. She had been back over a year, but he still couldn't hear enough of it. "I'm coming with you next time," he told her authoritatively. "You promised. Besides, I want to see for myself."

"Of course you will. Only now it's bathtime, so let's go." She added, "And I just happen to know that Annie has made brownies this afternoon. Your favorite."

He grinned cheekily at her and her heart turned over. He was almost six years old now, tall for his age with a lanky thinness that belied his appetite for Annie's baking. His gray eyes were as direct and candid as his father's and there was a joyous quality about him that charmed all who knew him. Still, she reminded herself quickly, he was no paragon of virtue, he was an ordinary boy who hated to take baths and tried to avoid his chores. He often came home from school with grazed knees and occasionally bruised fists, and he squandered his few cents' weekly pocket money on marbles and tin soldiers and Hershey Bars. And he was the apple of the boarders' eyes as well as her own.

Francie's mind returned to Hong Kong as she ran his bath, and to the letter from Edward Stratton tucked safely in her pocket. It was exactly a year and three months since they had met. He had bombarded her with letters and cablegrams and even international telephone calls all the way from London, but she had steadfastly refused to see him. Now he had refused to be put off any longer. He was on board a liner to New York and in a few weeks he would be here in San Francisco.

"I insist on seeing you, Francesca," he had written. "Even if you say no, I shall waylay you. Why are you being so stubborn? You know as well as I it was no shipboard romance, and I intend to ask you to marry me again, and this time I will not take no—or any other excuse—for an answer."

"Sounds very forceful," Annie had commented when she showed her the letter. "Sounds like a man who knows what he wants and intends to get it." She'd glanced shrewdly at Francie and added, "And if I were you, love, I'd jump at the chance to marry him. You and Ollie would have a wonderful life, and why shouldn't you? You've done nothing wrong.

"There's no reason for him ever to know what really happened. I'll tell him you were married to my brother and who's to disprove it? Your marriage certificate was destroyed in the earthquake, along with everybody else's." Annie shook her head regretfully. "You're a fool, Francesca Harrison, if you don't say yes."

Francie thought longingly of Edward. She wanted so much to see his dear face, hear his voice, touch his hand. She wanted to marry him more than anything on earth, but she couldn't deceive him. "I'll see him," she agreed at last, "but I must tell him the truth and let him decide. You just can't base a marriage on a pack of lies."

Annie sighed exasperatedly. "You're a fool," she said bluntly. "Do it first and then tell him. Once he marries you he'll never want to let you go."

Ollie was bathed and in his pajamas when the doorbell rang and Annie went to answer it. The man standing on the doorstep said arrogantly, "I'm here to see Francesca Harrison."

Annie stared at him, puzzled; she knew his face but she couldn't put a name to it. "Hurry up, woman," he snarled, and suddenly she knew. "There's no Francesca Harrison here," she said firmly, pushing the door shut.

He quickly put his foot in the gap and pushed it open again. "*Mrs. Harrison,* then, if that's what you call her," he retorted, striding past her into the hall. He turned to look at her. "Tell her that her brother, Harry, is here to see her."

Annie squared her shoulders, glad she didn't have her apron on and that she was wearing her good maroon wool dress. Not that it mattered to Harry Harrison, but at least she didn't look like a servant and it gave her an edge of badly needed confidence. "I'll see if she is at home," she said in a firm voice even though her knees were shaking. "Kindly wait here in the hall."

Harry watched her walk up the stairs. She was small and rounded and attractive, and under any other circumstances he might have fancied her, he had always liked older women. But his mind was on more urgent matters. His anger boiled again as he thought of his sister, here in this very house—flaunting her bastard child and her illicit relationship with a Chinaman right under his goddamn nose. All of San Francisco must have known, except him.

Annie walked into Francie's sitting room and closed the door behind her. She leaned against it, her knees still shaking, and Francie glanced up at her surprised. "It's Harry," she said bluntly. "He's downstairs. He knows you're here."

Francie's eyes grew dark with shock. She stared at Annie and then looked wildly around for an escape.

"You can't," Annie said, reading her thoughts. "You've got to see him. You've got to face him once and for all." She took her by the shoulders. "There's nothing he can do to you, Francie. *Nothing.* Remember what Lai Tsin told you? You are your own woman now. Your brother is not your keeper. You are twenty-five years old. You are *you*, Francie. Face him. And then at last you can get on with your life."

Her round brown eyes pleaded and she gripped her hands tightly together, she wanted Francie to do this so much.

"I can't," Francie said, sounding terrified, and Ollie ran frightened to her side. She flung her arms around him and held him close.

"Yes, you can," Annie insisted. "And you must. Remember Lai Tsin. Remember all the things he's told you. And just think of Ollie, too, think what it would mean for him to be free of the Harrison ghosts."

"What ghosts, Mommy?" Ollie cried, frightened.

Francie looked at her son and knew she finally had to face her past, for his sake. "It's nothing," she said soothingly. "Just grown-up talk, nothing to do with you at all. Go down the back stairs to the kitchen and help yourself to one of Annie's brownies and some milk. There's someone I have to see."

Annie opened the door and Ollie scampered through. Francie glanced down at the ruffled white lawn blouse and gray wool skirt she was wearing, and Annie said reassuringly, "You look fine. There's no need to dress up for the man. Save it for Edward Stratton."

"Show him into your office, Annie," Francie decided quickly. "I'll be down in a minute."

She smoothed back her hair, wishing her hands would stop shaking, but all the old fears had come rushing back. She remembered the loneliness and the pain, the beatings and the barred windows, her father's hatred and Harry's indifference. And then she told herself she was a fool, that Annie was right and that Lai Tsin was right. She was her own woman and to hell with Harry. There was nothing he could do to her. Nevertheless she was still frightened as she walked slowly downstairs and along the black-and-white flagged corridor to Annie's office. Annie was waiting by the door and she looked silently at her, her eyes full of encouragement as Francie went in.

Harry was standing by the desk. He looked just the way he had the night she had seen him at his grand party, tall, handsome, and arrogant, and it didn't take a genius to see that he was simmering with suppressed anger. He glanced contemptuously at her and she lifted her chin, matching his arrogance.

"Why are you here, Harry?" she asked in a calm voice, and Annie, her ear to the door, crossed her fingers and nodded her head encouragingly.

"You may well ask," he retorted, stepping closer to her. "You've finally made your presence felt in San Francisco. What happened to the great death charade, little sister?"

Francie flinched, remembering how Lai Tsin used to call her that. "I think it's better if we forget that we are brother and sister. We have managed to avoid each other all these years, and I have no wish to see you again."

"Nor I you." He grabbed her suddenly by the shoulders, his eyes glaring angrily in hers. "How dare you stand there and coolly say you don't wish to see me? Me—Harry Harrison. When you have done nothing but defile our family name. First you run off with a waiter and now you're some goddamn Chinese's concubine—and with a bastard son, I hear. What goddamn right do you have to bear the Harrison name, I ask you?"

"I must remind you that I have a legal right to use it. It is my name." His fingers dug deeper into her shoulders and he stared menacingly at her. "I should also remind you, Harry, that acts of violence—even by a Harrison—are not so easy to get away with these days. If you lift a hand to me I shall call the police."

He let go abruptly and stepped back a pace. Francie wanted to rub her bruised shoulders, but she didn't want to give him the pleasure of knowing he had hurt her, and instead she faced him calmly, trying to ignore her racing heart.

"There's one thing I'll never forgive you for," Harry said at last. "You killed Father just as surely as if you'd put a gun to his head. It was you he was coming after, you and your lover. He should have been at home asleep in his own bed, not racing down Pacific Avenue after a whore and her man. And now you've given him an illegitimate grandchild—my God, he must be turning in his grave."

"I hope he is. If ever a man deserved hell, he did."

"I guess the boy is the Chinaman's?" Harry said angrily. She made no reply and his anger boiled over again. "Is he?" he demanded, grabbing her arms again.

"If that is what you choose to think," she said quietly.

He dropped her arms, watching her from hooded eyes. "When Father was killed I vowed that if it were the last thing I ever did I would see you dead." He walked to the door, then turned to look at her. "This isn't over between you and me," he warned. "Don't ever think it is. I meant what I said, Francesca."

Annie leapt back from the door as he stalked out and strode angrily down the hall and out of the house. She ran quickly to Francie and threw her arms around her. "You were wonderful," she exclaimed. "So strong and courageous. And what's more, you were right."

Francie sank trembling onto a chair, she felt like crying but she had told herself years ago that there would be no more tears, there had been enough in her life already.

"At least it's over with," Annie said encouragingly.

She glanced up at her, her eyes full of the unshed tears. "Oh, I don't think so, Annie," she said. "No, I don't think it's over. This is just the beginning."

Lai Tsin listened gravely when Francie told him the story of her encounter with Harry and he knew she was right. It was not over. "It will never be over," he said. "But are you going to let that color your whole life? Are you going to sit and wait for whatever Harry might decide to do? Or do you plan to put your problems aside and go on living like the rest of us? Let me remind you, Francie, it is only the young who think of life as being long. As we grow older we think back with regret to those moments we might have enjoyed and that we threw carelessly away. Such moments add up to minutes, hours . . . and finally, years.

"You have much to look forward to in life, Francie. I have tried to teach you what I know, little though it is, to help you become strong. And now the moment is at hand for you to use that knowledge. Your life is your own. You are your own woman. Use your life for your own happiness."

Francie thought of Lai Tsin's words a few weeks later when Edward telephoned from New York. The line was crackly and he sounded a million miles away, but it was his voice all right. "I'm catching the train right now to Chicago," he said. "I'll be on tomorrow's Super Chief and with you in a couple of days."

"A couple of days," she gasped.

"On Tuesday at eight o'clock to be precise," he said with a laugh in his voice. "I only wish it were sooner. Francie, do you have any idea how much I've missed you?"

She blushed, holding the receiver closer as though she could get nearer to him. "Really?" she whispered.

"Do you know what you've put me through all these months? Not letting me see you? Well, now you have no choice. I'm stopping at the Fairmont and I'll be at Aysgarth's at eight o'clock. Promise me you'll be there?"

"I'll be waiting for you," she promised.

"You know what I'm going to ask you?" She nodded as though he could see her. "Please let your answer be yes, Francie. The train's about to leave. I must go. See you Tuesday, my darling."

She hooked the phone back on the wall set, dizzy with happiness. Harry had flown from her mind as though he never existed. Edward was on his way to ask her to marry him and she would say yes. She was Edward Stratton's "darling" and all of their life together was ahead of her, and she didn't plan on wasting a single moment of it.

Edward settled himself in his suite at the elegantly refurbished Fairmont Hotel, then he strolled across California Street to the Pacific Union Club, where he had a meeting with a business acquaintance. The club, which was housed in the old James Flood mansion, was San Francisco's most elite establishment, and tonight it was crowded.

His business was quickly completed and Edward glanced impatiently at his watch; there was still an hour and a half to go before he saw Francie. He contemplated going to Aysgarth's right away and surprising her, but then he smiled and told himself it would not be fair. In his experience women hated to be surprised; no doubt she would be making herself beautiful for him and he would restrain his impatience in the name of politeness. But he could hardly bear the wait.

He sank into a big leather chair, ordered a Scotch from a passing steward and lit a small cheroot. Staring into space, he contemplated the pleasure ahead of him. He had waited a long time. What difference did another hour or so make? But this time he wasn't going to allow Francie to say no. Since he'd met her she had barely left his mind; she was the perfect woman, beautiful and a lady, and passionate—all the things a man could want in a wife.

The man opposite rustled the pages of his newspaper and then flung it disgustedly onto the table, glaring at it as he downed his drink. "Not bad news, I hope?" Edward asked with a faint smile.

"Bad news?" Harry shrugged. "I own that damned tabloid and it's losing money hand over fist. Don't ask me why. God only knows I put enough time and money into it to float a dozen other companies." He glanced moodily at his interrogator, but didn't recognize him.

"You new around here?"

"Just visiting actually. The name's Stratton. Edward Stratton."

"Harry Harrison," he held out his hand and the other man shook it firmly.

"Let me get you another drink?" Harry said, summoning a steward, but Edward shook his head. "Bourbon and branch water," Harry ordered, his eyes restlessly scanning the gloomy, dark-paneled room to see who was around. His nerves were on edge; he was getting bored with his newspaper, bored with San Francisco and the same old faces. He was beginning to think people he knew were looking oddly at him. He suspected they were talking about him behind his back, that rumors were already circulating about his goddamn sister and her son-of-a-bitch Chinese lover. He needed to get away from here for a while, he needed the bright lights and razzmatazz and urban pleasures of Manhattan to set him back on an even keel.

"You're not from New York?" he asked the stranger, and Edward laughed.

"London and Scotland, though I was just in New York on business."

"It's business that brings you to San Francisco, I suppose?" Harry was making polite conversation and he gulped his bourbon, scarcely listening to the man's reply.

"Not really. As a matter of fact, I'm here to get married. That is, if she'll have me. She's turned me down so many times already, I can never be sure."

Harry laughed. "You're lucky. The woman I asked accepted and it cost me a fortune. *And* she was an Englishwoman." He glanced interestedly at Edward. "Is this a San Francisco lady you're marrying?"

Edward beamed. "Oddly enough, she has the same name as you. Maybe you know her? Francesca Harrison?"

Harry stared silently at him. He put his empty glass carefully on the table. He smiled the wide self-satisfied smile of the Cheshire cat and said, "That's not surprising at all, Stratton, since the woman in question happens to be my sister." Edward's expression changed to surprise as Harry continued. "I think perhaps you had better tell me what you know about her, and then allow me to tell you the truth."

"*The truth?*"

Harry lifted a warning hand. "Believe me, Stratton, there are things about Francesca you may never have suspected. Let me fill you in on a few facts."

Edward sat silently while Harry talked; at first he thought he'd met a crazy man, but looking at him—a handsome, well set-up, prosperous fellow, he knew it wasn't so. What Harrison was saying sounded plausible, yet he still could not believe he was talking about Francesca.

Edward stared numbly as Harry concluded triumphantly, "It's the truth, Stratton. Ask anyone in this club what they know of my sister —they'll only confirm what I say. My father kept her locked up when she was a child because even then she did crazy things. She was uncontrollable, but he couldn't bear to send her away to the state asylum. And she repaid him by flaunting her lover in front of him— and now this bastard child." He leaned closer to Edward, staring into his eyes. "Believe me, you are better off without her. She'll ruin you *and* your family, Stratton, mark my words."

A vision of Francesca's innocent blue eyes swam in Edward's mind and he asked himself despairingly if they could mask the wickedness he had just heard described. He thought of his innocent children, home at Strattons. He was a conservative man and he knew he could never risk their happiness and security for his own desires. Disillusioned, he pushed back his chair and stood up. He looked sadly at Harry and said, "Thank you, sir, for your information." And then he turned and walked to the door.

Harry watched him go, still wearing his Cheshire cat smile, savoring his first sweet taste of revenge. He was looking at a broken man.

Francie knew she was looking her best. It wasn't just her wonderful trailing midnight-blue velvet dress, nor the rose in her pale shining hair, it was the inner happy glow that lit her heart-shaped face. She seemed to bubble with suppressed excitement as she nervously checked and rechecked the elegantly set table for two in her sitting room, smoothing the damask cloth yet again, straightening the silverware and adjusting the full-blown cream roses in the crystal bowl at the center. A fire hummed and crackled in the grate, the tall candles were lit in the fluted silver candlesticks, adding their own soft glow and deepening the color of her eyes until they almost seemed to match her velvet dress.

Everything was going as planned; Ollie was in bed, Annie was out, and Lai Tsin was at his office. It was five minutes to eight and in a little while Edward would be here. She ran to the window, peeking through the curtain and laughing at her own eagerness. After all these months of putting him off it was ridiculous that she couldn't bear to wait another five minutes to see him. She walked back to the fire and stood with her back to it, unwilling to sit down lest she crease her dress. She wanted to look perfect for him.

The clock outside struck eight at last and she held her breath, waiting for the bell to ring; Edward was always punctual.

But the bell didn't ring and after a while she walked to the window and pulled back the curtain again, searching amongst the passersby for his familiar figure, telling herself he must have been delayed on business. She inspected the table yet again, turning the bottle of champagne in the silver ice bucket and running through the supper menu in her mind: the beluga caviar she knew he liked so much already sat in its iced crystal bowl on the sideboard; Annie's famous poached salmon waited in the kitchen to be brought up by the maid when she rang, and the *crème brûlée* would follow with the coffee.

Francie sighed. She just wanted everything to be perfect for him because he was such a perfect man.

She glanced at the clock. Eight fifteen. She walked to the window and looked out and then walked back again, puzzled. It wasn't like Edward to be late, at least not without telephoning. Still, things happened, maybe he couldn't get to a telephone right now. Telling herself not to worry, that the food would not spoil and there was no rush, she paced backward and forward across her cosy firelit sitting room, waiting.

By nine o'clock her joyful expression had faded to anxiety and she stared worriedly out the window. By ten she slumped into the chair by the dying fire, her eyes closed, praying for the bell to ring. She jumped up again at eleven when she heard footsteps outside, but the front door opened and closed and she recognized Annie's quick soft step as she walked discreetly to her room. She thought of telephoning his hotel but pride held her back. Surely if he were delayed this long he could have sent her a message.

She didn't count the minutes and the hours after that. There was no use. She knew Edward was not coming. Head in her hands, she asked herself despairingly, Why? She asked herself the same question a thousand times. Hadn't he called her just a few days ago and said he was going to marry her no matter what? Tearless, she paced the floor again. She pulled back the curtains and gazed out at the endless quiet night, watching and wondering. And as dawn fought its way through a pearly-gray mist she sank exhausted back into her chair. She knew that for the second time in her life she had lost the man she loved.

Annie found her there at seven o'clock when she came in to check that the table had been cleared. She stared at Francie huddled in the chair, taking in the elegant, untouched table and the guttered candles. "He didn't come," she said flatly.

Francie's eyes were as dead as the ashes in the grate as she looked at her friend. "It's my fault, Annie," she said wearily. "I should never have allowed him to suggest coming here, I should never had allowed him to think of marriage. I knew it was wrong. You can't build happiness on a foundation of lies." She shrugged. "I don't know what happened, but I know I'll never see him again."

She stood up and trailed wearily to the door. The expensive deep-blue evening gown looked faintly tawdry in the bright morning light, and her shoulders sagged.

Annie said, "Francie, why don't you telephone him, find out what happened? Surely there must be some explanation—"

"We shall never know."

But later that morning two notes were delivered, one on Fairmont Hotel stationery. It read: "Francesca. I have had a long night to think things over and I must come to the conclusion that you were right after all, and it is better that we do not see each other again. Please forgive me." It was signed merely, "E."

The second note was on *Harrison Herald* stationery and told her curtly that Harry had thought it wise to inform her suitor of her background and that he would do anything in his power to stop such a marriage. It was signed, "H. Harrison."

Harry and Lord Stratton were on the same Pacific Pullman train to New York that afternoon. They nodded and Harry smiled, but Stratton did not speak to him and Harry did not see him again for the rest of the journey.

# CHAPTER 30

♦

## *1912–1917*

When he was in New York, Harry always stayed at the Hotel Astor at the corner of Broadway and 44th Street. He liked the location and the luxury as well as the aristocratic connections, and along with Sherry's, Rector's, and Delmonico's, the Astor Roof Garden was his favorite place for an assignation with a woman. The roof garden had flowing streams and sparkling fountains, gushing waterfalls and ferny grottos, flowery gazebos and an ivy-covered arbor. Harry was alone there drinking his bourbon when he saw the red-haired woman. Her companion's back was to him and she glanced across and their eyes met. She dropped her eyes, half-smiling, and then glanced up again at him through her lashes. Harry lifted his glass in a toast.

He called the waiter over and asked who she was. "That's the Baroness Magda Muntzi," he was told.

Harry sent her a note, watching eagerly as she read it. She smiled at him, a discreet smile so that her companion would not notice, but he thought it held promise. He found out where she lived and the next day sent her flowers and another note asking her to have dinner with him. She agreed, and when they finally met, he was instantly smitten.

Magda was Hungarian. She was flamboyant, with his favorite copper-red curls, flashing green eyes, and an uncertain temper. She was older than he was by several years, but she had the kind of body he liked, full of curves instead of the straight up-and-down nonsense that was so fashionable. She had breasts like alabaster, hips that swung when she walked, long tapering legs, and a healthy sexual appetite. She also had a smart apartment, bequeathed to her, or so she told him, by her late husband, and she bought expensive furs and trinkets the way other people bought groceries. Every day.

He forgot about Francie and Edward Stratton. Harry fell so hard for Magda that he paid the price she demanded without question, eagerly financing her forays to Lucille, Mainbocher, Cartier, and Tiffany. He bought a thirty-room house on Sutton Place and then he invited her to marry him and gave her free rein to decorate it. And when she accepted, he forgot about his newspaper and his businesses in San Francisco. He married Magda and for two years played attendent lover to her teasing "mistress" at social events and at nightclubs all over Manhattan.

Two years later, he woke early one morning, full of virile masculine pride, and made love to her. She lay like a stone beneath him until he was finished and then she said coldly, "I'm bored, Harry. I want a divorce." He stared at her, seeing the indifference in her eyes, and then the enormity of what she had said dawned on him. He looked down at himself, still sweating with the glow of his triumphal climax, and at her lying like a marble effigy, her lip curling faintly in contempt. And then he struck her. Hard.

Magda did not cry. She put a hand to her bleeding mouth and bruised eye and said evenly, "That's going to cost you, Harry." And it did. It took another two years and almost half his fortune to buy her silence and save his reputation. She got her divorce, and after the war went to live in Monte Carlo on his money with some phony White Russian count, just one in a long line of lovers, while his fortunes dwindled.

His three years with Magda as mistress and wife had been expensive. The Sutton Place house alone had cost almost ten million by the time she had finished with fancy decorators and important French antiques and Old Master paintings. And even at that price, it had looked like the residence of an exclusive Hungarian whore. Which, he thought disgustedly, it almost was.

When he finally returned to San Francisco, looking a decade older than his twenty-eight years, with the puffy face of a heavy drinker and the world-weary expression of a man who had seen it all, there was a surprise awaiting him. As his chauffeur drove the burgundy de Courmont home along California Street, Harry turned to stare at the new house occupying the long-vacant lot a block down from his own place. "That's gone up overnight," he commented lazily. "Who owns it, do you know?"

The chauffeur refrained from reminding him that he had been away almost five years. Instead he shook his head and replied, "I haven't heard whose house it is, sir." He was lying—he just didn't want to be the one who told Mr. Harrison that his notorious sister had built her house almost dead opposite him and was living in it with her own son—a cute blond kid, as well as a young Chinese boy, and the Chinese millionaire they called the Mandarin. Not that anybody ever visited them there, they seemed to live in splendid isolation, and all their servants were Chinese, so there was no gossip. Still, the woman was surely elegant and she always had a pleasant smile when she passed by. He grinned as he opened the door for Harry to alight and the butler walked down the steps to greet him. The whole city was talking about the house and the Mandarin and his concubine and he thought, "Mr. Harry is gonna be madder 'n hell once he finds out."

Francie's sitting room was on the ground floor, with tall windows overlooking California Street. It was small enough to be cosy and yet large enough to accommodate all her needs, her books, her desk, and the comfortable chairs and sofas she had chosen in pale amber brocade, but it still had that vaguely empty feeling of newness. The house was deliberately unostentatious. It was built of cream limestone in English Georgian style, with a plain facade and a four-paneled black wooden door with a pretty scalloped glass fanlight, and the only marble to be seen was on the front steps and the pastry table in the white-tiled kitchen. The floors were of wide-planked elm, crafted by a master and polished to a pale tawny sheen, and the only paneling was in the library, where it was appropriate. A glorious "flying" staircase seemed to sweep without support to the semicircular gallery on the second floor and tall windows filled the whole house with light. The English architect told Francie it was based on a house in London's Mayfair, and its elegant simplicity was certainly different from the ornate grandeur of her childhood home and Harry's monstrous replica just down the road.

When Edward Stratton left her Francie had not cried, nor had she wallowed in self-pity. She accepted that he had the right to change his mind about marrying her. She would have told him the truth given the chance, but Harry had beaten her to it. Harry had decided her fate for her and her sadness turned to anger and steely resolve.

She had finally built her house and as it grew so did her confidence. The L. T. Francis Company had become the Lai Tsin Corporation and their fleet of ships crisscrossing the world now numbered seventeen, transporting goods for merchants and manufacturers as far apart as Liverpool and Los Angeles, Bombay and Singapore, Istanbul and Hamburg; and their name featured in the shipping charts published in every newspaper in the world.

Lai Tsin had the mysterious knack of being in the right place at exactly the right moment, and though he counted no friends amongst the businessmen of San Francisco and the taipans in Hong Kong, he was no longer treated with the contempt they showed a coolie. He never wore Western clothes and in his long, blue embroidered robe he had a quiet dignity that commanded the grudging respect of the men with whom he did business, and they would have been hard put to think of a single bad deal he had made or any act of injustice he had committed.

From her window Francie saw the burgundy de Courmont drive past and glimpsed her brother's curious face as he turned to stare, but she did not smile in satisfaction. Five years had passed since the fateful night Harry had ruined her life, but to her surprise all she felt for him now was indifference. She watched as the chauffeur held open the door and the butler hurried down the steps while a footman ran to fetch his bags: Harry had never moved a step in his life without a dozen servants to do his bidding and she wondered contemptuously if he even remembered how to put the toothpaste on his brush or how to shave his own face. And with his puffy eyes and the extra padding of weight, he looked a decade older.

She shrugged and turned away, wondering what he would say when he found out that she was his new neighbor, but in truth she didn't really care. There was nothing Harry could do to her now. Her wealth might not yet match his, but if the rumors about his diminishing fortunes were to be believed, his were on the way down and hers were on the way up. There had been stories in the gossip columns about how he'd had to sell off his share of the railroad to pay off his second wife, and everyone knew his newspaper was losing money faster than it was printed. And since he'd fired his father's business colleagues from the board, there were stories of even greater troubles in the Harrison enterprises.

There was a shout from the hall and Francie put Harry and his fading fortunes to the back of her mind as Ollie flung himself through the door with the usual exuberance he displayed on being let out of school. "Mom, can I go to the warehouse with Philip?" he said eagerly.

Francie sighed. "What about homework?"

"Aw, Mom, I'll do it later." He smiled beguilingly at her, and as always, she was reminded of his father. "I promise," he added, giving her a hug.

Now that he was thirteen hugs were becoming a rarity, and raising an eyebrow she asked, "To what do I owe the honor, master Oliver?"

He shrugged. "Oh, I dunno, you just looked sort of *lonely,* I guess. See you later, Mom."

Philip Chen was waiting in the hall. "I'll have him back by six, Elder Sister," he said with a tiny formal bow.

She walked to the front door watching them stride away down the street. Ollie was tall for his age, lanky as a colt, and his thick blond hair flopped untidily over his eyes. They were as gray as Josh's and he had his father's smile—the same one that had just beguiled her into letting him put off his homework—as well as Josh's innocent joie de vivre. Ollie half-ran along the street, his body full of urgency and excitement, while Philip Chen's stride was controlled and deliberate.

Eighteen-year-old Philip was an American Chinese with Western ways. He wore his black hair short and he dressed Western-style, even on Chinese festivals. And that was the way the Mandarin knew it should be. Lai Tsin had wanted him to retain his Chinese background and for most of his life Philip had lived with a Chinese family and attended Chinese school, but each afternoon a tutor had instructed him on the history of America and Europe and on Western culture. He had left school at sixteen and gone to work alongside Lai Tsin, whom he respectfully called his Honorable Father, to learn all aspects of the business. He often accompanied him on his travels to the Orient and the Mandarin treated him as his own son, and there was a great bond of love and trust between them.

Ollie glanced at Philip's serious face as they swung down the hill to catch a tram on Market Street. Philip Chen was his idol. He was small and serious with a pale skin and thick black hair. His slanted eyes were an unusual light hazel brown with an enigmatic expression. He called Ollie "Little Brother," he was silent and mysterious and Ollie never knew what he was thinking, but he guessed it was something important because Philip never seemed to clutter his mind with baseball scores or cigarette cards or the horses out at the ranch. Philip always seemed to be thinking of loftier, more exciting things, like the value of the Hong Kong currency against the dollar and the gross tonnage of the latest addition to the Lai Tsin fleet. And that was one of the reasons Ollie wanted to accompany Philip to the office, because he wanted to learn all about the business. He wanted to travel to Hong Kong with the Mandarin and Philip, he wanted to watch their cargoes being loaded and to sail the South China Sea and visit all the exciting ports of the world.

The other reason was because Philip was his only friend. Money talked and so Ollie attended San Francisco's smartest boys' school, but he wasn't really part of it. Oh, the other guys were okay, he played football with them and they chatted with him all right, but he was never invited to their homes. Sure, it hurt a little, but he knew his family was different and though he was proud of them, sometimes it was tough. And it was always lonely. He tried philosophically to shrug it off, telling himself that next year his mother was sending him back East to prep school, but still it hurt. And when Philip Chen had finally come to live with them, for the first time in his young life he had a friend.

A thin mist was rolling in from the ocean as they approached the docks and Ollie sniffed it eagerly, like a sailor scenting the wind. "You know what, Philip," he said as they pushed open the shabby wooden door, "one day I'm gonna command my own ship. It'll be the flagship of our fleet and we'll call it the Mandarin."

Philip nodded. "If that is what you wish, Little Brother. I myself will remain in Hong Kong and fill your ships with cargo."

"When I was just a kid," Ollie added, "I wanted to be a pirate, but the Mandarin said it was not an honorable profession." He grinned. "I guess it wasn't, but it sure sounded fun."

The warehouse had grown from the first small shed Lai Tsin had bought years ago to a sprawling complex of offices and storage, but it was still just a group of unpretentious tin-roofed wooden buildings on the waterfront, and no one would have suspected it was the headquarters of a multimillion-dollar company, competing successfully for the trade routes of the world.

As usual, Lai Tsin was in his office. He wore the long, plain, dark-blue silk robe he always wore and the simply furnished room was a model of neatness. His plain teakwood desk held his old wooden abacus and a Chinese inkpad and brushes, as well as a Western-style inkstand and pens. In front of him was a neatly squared-off pile of papers and a large red ledger. He looked up as the boys knocked, bidding them to enter.

Philip bowed and Ollie followed suit. He could never remember the Mandarin ever embracing him, even when he was little. Things were always Chinese style with formal rituals and bows, but the Mandarin's eyes lit up when he saw him and he knew he was pleased. "Welcome, Ollie," he said in Chinese. "I hope the pleasure I am gaining from your presence does not mean that you are neglecting your homework?"

Ollie grinned. Shaking his blond hair out of his eyes, he replied, in the same language, "No, sir. I promised Mom I'd do it later."

The Mandarin nodded. "Then since you are here I will set you a little task." He handed him the abacus, instructing him to check the columns on the last page of the ledger. Ollie smiled willingly. The columns were written in Chinese and he knew the Mandarin wanted to test his command of the written language. He had been learning Chinese since he was five years old and was almost as proficient at speaking Mandarin and Cantonese as he was English, but he still had trouble with the written characters. He took the ledger and followed Philip to his own tiny annex next door to begin his task.

Half an hour later a ship hooted somewhere in the fog-bound bay and he glanced at the window, startled as he glimpsed a face peering in. Dropping his pencil he jumped up and ran to look, but no one was there.

"What is it?" Philip asked, following his gaze.

"Oh, nothing," Ollie said uneasily, sinking back into his chair. "I just thought I saw someone at the window, but I guess I was wrong."

Philip went back to his work without comment and Ollie completed his task and then took the ledger back to the Mandarin. He ran an expert eye rapidly down the column of figures and then pointed out his one small mistake. "Your Chinese improves, Ollie," he told him with a smile. "But your mother is waiting and you must keep your promise."

Ollie walked from the offices into the tall, raftered warehouse, wandering the narrow aisles breathing in the aromas of the fresh coffee beans piled in hessian sacks and the tea whose fragrance permeated even the wooden chests used to store it. He smelled the fresh peppercorns and the cinnamon, the ginger and cloves, dreaming of the far-off foreign countries they came from and where one day he would sail in his ship as commander of the Lai Tsin fleet. The warehouse was his favorite place, because if he closed his eyes he could almost believe he was sailing the Indian Ocean or the Andaman Sea, in the lee of some exotic island where the tamarind and lotus bloomed and adventure waited.

Outside on the street it was cold and the damp, clinging mist quickly swirled away his dreams of sunny southern islands. He quickened his pace, hurrying to keep warm. He knew the way to the tram station like the back of his hand and the fog did not trouble him though it muffled his footsteps eerily and he suddenly fancied he heard them echoing behind him. Remembering the face at the window he looked apprehensively over his shoulder, but the street was quiet and there was only the wall of gray mist. Unnerved, he broke into a run, breathing a sigh of relief as the brightly lit tram clattered into view, and he swung himself safely on board, heading for home.

# CHAPTER 31

◆

The faces around the boardroom table of Harrison Enterprises Incorporated were serious as Harry took his seat. He glanced scornfully at them and their waiting accounts and financial reports, drumming his fingers restlessly on the highly polished mahogany and ordering his secretary to fetch him some coffee immediately.

"Well, gentlemen," he said, giving them the temporary benefit of his full attention. "Let's get this over with."

"There's a great deal to discuss, Mr. Harrison," the chief accountant said reprovingly. "We must take the opportunity, while we have you in San Francisco, to go through the accounts of each of the companies and decide what must be done. As you know, sir, some of them, including the *Herald,* are doing badly."

"How badly?" Harry demanded, leaning back in his big leather swivel-chair and sipping his coffee.

"The *Herald* has been losing steadily since its inception, Mr. Harrison. Its losses currently amount to thirty million dollars."

Harry glanced at him, startled. "Thirty million? How can that be?"

"You were away for five years, sir. And you left orders that it should continue with full staff and top production no matter what happened. Also," he reminded him, "on your instructions, all your shares in the Union Pacific Railroad were sold and the money applied to your divorce settlement from the baroness."

Harry sighed. "Goddamn gold-digging bitch," he said succinctly.

Pouring more coffee he listened with half an ear to the saga of disasters afflicting the Harrison enterprises: the new oil fields into which he had poured gallons of money had remained obstinately dry; the steelworks production had been decimated by strikes; the sugar plantations in Hawaii were burned by laborers sick of living on the pittance Harrisons paid and angry that their demands for better pay went unheard. The list went on and on until he raised an angry hand and demanded to know why nothing had been done to put a stop to the oil drilling and the strikes and the rest.

"We did keep you informed of these matters, sir," the chief accountant chided, "but you were away for so long, and after Mr. Frank and Mr. Wallis went, well sir, there was just no proper management. If you'll forgive my saying so, Mr. Harrison, a company with so many diverse areas of operation needs a firm hand at the helm. Otherwise . . ." He shrugged graphically, holding out the sheaf of reports with their long columns of red ink.

Harry was silent. He glanced away from the papers showing his companies' losses and said, "What about the bank?"

"I'm glad to be able to tell you the bank is sound, sir," the accountant said with a rare smile. "The public have retained their belief in the stability of Harrison Mercantile."

Harry nodded, relieved. "Okay," he said, folding his arms, "so what's the current state of play?"

"Overall, sir," the accountant said, peering at him over the top of his gold-wired half-glasses, "Harrison Enterprises are down one hundred and eighty million in four years. That leaves a net worth of one hundred and twenty million."

"Well, goddamit, man, that's not so bad, is it? I thought you meant the Harrisons' were going under!" Harry breathed a sigh of relief as he stood up to go.

"As I told you, Mr. Harrison," the accountant said agitatedly, "several of the companies are in deep trouble. Even though the overall picture still shows a profit, the net worth of your companies is less than half what it was when your father died."

"Is it, by God?" Harry paused uncertainly near the door and then he walked back to the table. "And what about my personal worth?"

"On the whole sir, your investments have proved sound. Though, of course, with the marriages and the yacht and the houses and cars and your general high expenditure, well, I'm afraid that it is down considerably too." His gaze wavered under Harry's beady eyes.

"How much?"

His sharp voice made the man jump and he answered quickly. "Sixty million, sir. Less than half what it was."

Surprised, Harry stared at him, wondering if it could really be true. Could he have gone through so much in so few years? Well, he supposed, as the man said, with the houses and the yacht and the marriages and the settlements, he must have. Finally worried, he thought about his ailing companies and decided he had better take charge again.

"All right, gentlemen," he said, sitting down again in his leather chair and shuffling the sheaves of financial reports lying on the table in front of him. "Here's what we do. First we close down the *Herald* —as of tomorrow."

"May I suggest Friday instead, sir?" the accountant asked eagerly. "The money is already committed this week and it would not look good for Harrison's *financial* image if we closed down right away. Rumors, you know," he added vaguely, but Harry got his point.

"Okay then, Friday." He picked up the next report. "We'll sell the sugar plantation," he decided briskly. "Those goddamn Chinese laborers are more bother than they're worth."

"It's not a good time to sell, sir," the accountant objected. "If we came to some reasonable agreement with the workforce—"

"Sell," Harry repeated coldly. He went through report after report, ordering which were to be sold and then he told them that with the proceeds, Harrisons would be entering into the commodities market, dealing in futures of metals, coffee, cocoa, and rubber. "There's no future in manufacturing," he told them briskly. "I intend to set up an office on Wall Street and move the base of our operations there."

The sea of stunned faces around the table stared after him as he left, but Harry had a ninety-five percent holding in Harrison Enterprises and there was nothing they could do. His word was law.

On the Friday that the final edition of the *Harrison Herald* was published a copy was delivered personally to Harry at his home. He opened it as he took his breakfast, devouring eggs and bacon and sausages with his usual hearty appetite, until he saw the lead article on the front page. His face paled and his appetite shriveled as he read it.

THE LAI TSIN CORPORATION'S TRIUMPHANT PURCHASE OF THE LATEST AND FASTEST CARGO VESSEL IN THE WORLD, the headline announced over a photograph of Francesca and her son on her latest ship. It went on to describe the company's successes and then in bold type at the end it said, *"The partners in the Lai Tsin Corporation are the Chinese Ke Lai Tsin, known far and wide as 'the Mandarin,' and Miss Francesca Harrison, sister of the owner of the* Harrison Herald,

FORTUNE IS A WOMAN

*Harry Harrison, and daughter of the late Harmon Harrison. It is understood that Miss Harrison and the Mandarin enjoy life together in their delightful new mansion atop Nob Hill, not one block from her brother's, though it is known that she and her brother have not spoken for many years. Mr. Harrison has not commented on his sister's success in business, but the rumors of his own financial decline are rife amongst his companies, as evidenced by the imminent closure of this newspaper."*

Harry flung the tabloid to the ground with an oath. He stalked to the telephone and dialed his office at the *Herald*. "Fire that bastard, whoever he is," he shouted into the phone.

There was a chuckle on the other end and then the voice said, "Aren't you forgetting, Mr. Harrison, you've already fired all of us."

Harry stormed from the phone, raging and cursing. This was the final straw. He'd find a way to get Francesca—and her goddamn Chinese lover. He'd see them both in hell.

Sammy read the article leaning up against the noisy bar of a Barbary Coast saloon. He was wearing a shabby woolen jacket and pants and a worn collarless blue shirt he had acquired from the Church Army charity in Liverpool, England, the previous year, on just one of the many stopovers in his long, backbreaking, tedious journey to San Francisco. He had not been able to afford the extra sixpenny piece to purchase an ancient cast-off overcoat, and that winter, while he waited for a ship that would take him on as a stoker or a deckhand—anything that would get him one more step closer to California and Francie, he had thought he would die of cold. But he had refused to give in. He couldn't. Not yet.

During that long winter in England he had thought many times of going back to Yorkshire to see his mother, but he didn't even know if she was still alive and anyway he was sure the police would be on to him in a flash. But the main reason he didn't go back was because he did not want his mother to see what he had become; a nothing, the lowest of the low. Not even a man.

He counted the coins in his pocket, ordering another drink and thinking about his next moves. It hadn't been hard to find out all about Francie Harrison; she was the most notorious woman in San Francisco, living openly with her Chinaman on top of Nob Hill. And they said she had a son, too—Sammy had seen him with his own eyes, though only at a distance—and it was then he had come up with his plan. He'd kept watch on Francie for weeks, he knew her movements and he knew that on Thursdays she went out for a few hours in the late afternoon. And that would be the time he would strike.

The bartender glanced anxiously at him as he passed him the drink; even in this rough area this guy looked wild with his lined yellow skin and hungry eyes. His back was permanently hunched and he looked as if for two pins he'd run a knife into you. Stepping discreetly into the back, he telephoned the local precinct and told the cops he had a suspicious-looking character in his bar. He glanced at Sammy as he returned and their eyes met. The bartender looked quickly away, nervously whistling an off-key melody. With an intuition learned from years of practice, Sammy sensed trouble; he downed his whiskey, threw a final menacing glance at the barman, and hurried outside.

The police understood the rarity of a call from any Barbary Coast saloonkeeper and sped to the scene, but by that time Sammy Morris was long gone, back to whatever hole in the wall or doorway would shelter him for another cold night.

# CHAPTER 32

◆

Lai Tsin devoted his life to his work. He traveled frequently to Hong Kong and each time he returned to his homeland he journeyed up the Yangtze River to visit the ancestral temple Elder Brother had built according to his strict instructions.

Elder Brother was growing fat on the monies he received from him monthly, but at least now Lai Tsin had the satisfaction of seeing that his child was no longer ragged and his wife's face was less haggard. The exquisite little gilded wooden temple had been built on the hill in the most favorable *fung-shui* position, sheltered in the curve of two adjacent hills and fronted by the winding slow-flowing river on the plain below, so that it received the best *ch'i,* or cosmic breath. It was immaculately maintained, though Lai Tsin doubted his brother had much to do with it, and he always managed to slip a little extra money into the poor wife's small hand, earning her undying gratitude.

Lilin's ancestral temple was small, the eaves and cornices were intricately carved and it was painted a deep vermillion that glowed like a flame on the distant gray-green landscape. When the evening sun glinted from the curving green-tiled roofs, turning the gilded eaves to burnished gold, the villagers and the river-travelers stopped to stare at its beauty and offer a prayer for the happiness of the spirits of Lai Tsin's mother and her children.

When he returned to San Francisco he summoned nineteen-year-old Philip Chen to his office and in the Mandarin Chinese they always spoke together, he said, "In two years I have taught you all I can about our business. I have decided the time has come for you to go to Hong Kong. Now we are ready to show the big hongs our power, to show them that we are here to stay and no longer need the crumbs from their tables." He placed the deed to the plot of land in the expensive central district on the desk in front of Philip and said with just the faintest touch of triumph in his voice, "Now we will build our headquarters in white granite to match theirs, with our golden name showing proudly to all of Hong Kong. You are to sail on your namesake ship, the *Philip Chen,* next week and you will take with you all the responsibilities and honor of your new position as comprador of the company." He looked affectionately at his son and smiled. "You will be the youngest comprador in Hong Kong. Many will try to scorn you and to cheat you, but I know that my trust in your abilities and your loyalty will not be misplaced."

Philip's voice shook with excitement as he realized he was to be the manager of the huge company. He thanked Lai Tsin and said, "Honorable Father, the honor you bestow on your lowly son is overwhelming. I will do everything in my power to uphold the interests of the company and to guard its face against the wiles of the big hongs and their jealousies. I will do my best to ensure that good joss remains with us and I will use my brains and my hands and as many hours of the day or night it takes to achieve the honor you have so generously given me."

Lai Tsin nodded, satisfied. "Then let us go visit your Honorable Number Two mother," he said, as the kindly Chinese woman with whom Philip had lived in the years following the earthquake was called. "We shall tell her of your success."

Lai Tsin's discreet black automobile with the Chinese driver was waiting outside to take them to Chinatown. Sammy Morris watched as their red taillights disappeared from sight, then he limped the couple of blocks to the nearest bar and placed a telephone call to the Mandarin's residence on Nob Hill.

The Chinese houseboy answered the phone, took the message, and delivered it to Ollie. The Mandarin had requested Ollie to meet him at his office as soon as possible; he had something important to show him.

Ollie glanced up from his homework, pleased. He knew he should tell his mother, but she had not yet returned from Annie's and there was no time to lose—the Mandarin had said as soon as possible. Flinging on his coat, he made for the door.

It was six o'clock on a cold February evening. Darkness had come early and already the moon was rising and the wind had swept the sky of clouds, leaving it clear and spangled with stars. Ollie hurried down the hill to the tram and from there he walked the last few blocks to the waterfront. He stopped for a few moments to admire the crowded merchant ships silhouetted against the sky before turning down the narrow street leading to the offices. He stared at it, puzzled; the building was in darkness, there wasn't even a light in the Mandarin's window. He tried the door but it was locked and he stepped back, wondering if he had come too late.

Sammy's footsteps were as soundless as a barefoot coolie's. Ollie did not hear him as he sprang from behind, thrusting an ether-filled pad over his nose and mouth, rendering him senseless in a mere few seconds.

Annie's new hotel was small but very chic, with seventy palatial rooms and a dozen richly appointed suites. It had the comfortably old-fashioned feel of an English country house, yet everything was of the latest design, from the showers to the heating, the elevators and the lamps, and of course, the food was exquisite, a more cosmopolitan version of her good plain food using the best seasonal ingredients, perfectly cooked and presented.

For Annie, running it was child's play. It was what she had always done, only more of it. Her days were busy and every night she enjoyed dressing in her best and going downstairs to personally greet her guests, sharing a little conversation and maybe a glass of champagne before seeing that they were seated for dinner and leaving them with a few recommendations from the menu she had drawn up herself.

Aysgarth's Hotel ran at ninety percent occupancy and the restaurant was one of the most famous and popular in the city. Money was flowing into Annie's personal coffers and she had good reason to feel pleased with herself. She worked hard; her guests needs came first; her hand-picked staff were well paid and happy; and she was already talking with the Mandarin about opening a second hotel in New York and another in Hong Kong.

She glanced affectionately at Francie across the tea table. She thought that for a woman in her early thirties who had gone through all she had in life, there wasn't a single line on her face. She still wore her heavy blond hair long and pulled back in a chignon and she had become one of San Francisco's smartest women, always immaculately turned out in clothes ordered exclusively from Paris, though she had never been there in her life. And though she owned few pieces of jewelry, what she had was impressive, like the rope of creamy nickel-sized South Sea pearls she always wore and the enormous Burmese ruby ring that matched her soft woolen dress.

"Quality," was the way Annie would have described her friend, and she didn't just mean the Yorkshire interpretation of "aristocratic," but the deeper sense of Francie's quality as a person. Annie knew that her days were filled with business meetings and her precious time with Ollie. Francie was a loyal friend and a loving mother; she gave everything she was to others and left little over for herself. But Edward Stratton was long gone and it was time for Francie to meet other people.

"Other *men*, you mean?" Francie retorted when Annie mentioned it to her. "You must be dreaming, Annie. You forget who I am. Who do you suppose would want to be seen with the notorious Francie Harrison?"

Annie sighed exasperatedly. "I'm still not sure it was a good idea, you living with the Mandarin—it only adds to the gossip."

"Well, at least it gives them something concrete to talk about," Francie said carelessly. "What do you suppose they hate most—that he is Chinese? Or that he's a man?"

Annie shook her head and poured more tea. "You've given them a double-header."

Francie shrugged. "Anyway, I'd better get back and check on Ollie and his homework." She laughed, her eyes softening with affection as she thought of him. "You know him, he'll do anything to get out of it." As she kissed Annie good-bye she said, "Will you join us at the ranch this weekend? And *no*, I just don't want to hear you are too busy again. This hotel takes up your entire life."

"That's the way I like it," Annie replied firmly. "And I'll think about the ranch, Francie. We've a full house this weekend, there's the Republican Party meeting and you know how demanding those politicians can be."

"Well, I can't blame them for choosing to stay at Aysgarth's. It must be the loveliest hotel in the world."

Annie smiled modestly. "Oh, I don't know, maybe in Paris there's another." She laughed and added, "But they'll not beat my food, even in Paris."

Francie walked back up the hill from Aysgarth's. She hated taking her car for such short distances, and anyway she could use the exercise. It was seven-fifteen when she got home and the houseboy greeted her in the hall with the news that master Ollie had been summoned to see the Mandarin. Surprised, she telephoned the office and when there was no reply she assumed they were on their way home and went upstairs to tidy herself for dinner.

Fifteen minutes later she came back down, smiling as she smelled the delicious aroma of ginger and chili coming from the kitchen; the Chinese cook doted on Ollie and each night he prepared special dishes for him.

A few minutes later the phone rang. She was in her bedroom and she grabbed it quickly and said, "Ollie?"

The man on the other end of the phone laughed, a short ugly sound that held no humor. "Ollie's here with me, Francie," he told her. "Down at the warehouse."

"Who is this?" she demanded, suddenly frightened.

"Don't you know? Don't you remember? Well, no, I suppose you wouldn't, would you? After all, you thought you'd finished me off years ago. But here I am, back from the grave, Francie, haunting you just the way Josh haunts me."

Francie's face paled. She gripped the receiver so tightly, her knuckles showed white. "Sammy Morris," she whispered.

"Ollie's waiting right here for you, Francie. Why don't you come and get him. *Only, don't bring any of your bastard Chinese hatchetmen this time. And no police either. Or you know what to expect.*"

The line went dead and she stared numbly at it for a second, then she threw down the receiver and ran for the door, flinging her coat over her shoulders as she went. Ollie was in mortal danger—he was alone at the warehouse with Sammy Morris. She turned and ran back again, grabbing the small pistol from the drawer by her bed. The Mandarin had given it to her for her protection years ago when the tongs were warring with each other and he had felt she might be in danger. Now she meant to use it on Sammy Morris.

The narrow street in front of the warehouse was in darkness and Sammy had left the boy where he lay while he'd quickly broken a window and groped his way to the office. He'd drawn the window shade and found the telephone, turned on the light and called Francie, so choked with bitter excitement at the sound of her voice he could barely speak. But his real triumph had come when he'd realized how terrified she was and he had laughed out loud. Didn't they say the way to a woman's heart was through her children? Well, this time he had Francie's heart and he was going to mangle it to pieces. Only then would she know how he felt about Josh.

He found his way to a side door, pulled back the bolts and went back outside to get the boy, cursing as he stumbled in the darkness. Picking up the unconscious lad he threw him over his shoulder and carried him into the office. He flung him roughly into the chair and stepped back and looked at him.

The dose of ether had been a heavy one, he'd wanted no trouble and the boy was still unconscious. His head was tilted back and his gray eyes were half-open. And as he looked at him Sammy's face paled. He was looking at the young Josh. He clutched his head in anguish; one part of his mind was telling him this was Josh's son, the other was refusing to accept it. He was flung backward in time, back to Montgomery Terrace with his best friend, Josh; he would do anything for Josh, and Josh would do anything for him. Stabbing pains shot through his brain, his blood pulsed so hard he felt his head would burst and he suddenly fell, senseless as the boy, to the floor.

The smell of kerosene revived him, stinging his nostrils, choking him and he sat up, coughing. The room was in darkness again and he reached out to touch Josh, glad he was still there. His best friend had not left him after all. He lifted his head, sniffing the air, sensing danger. There was a flash of white light and the warehouse behind him suddenly exploded into orange flames. He stared numbly at it for a few seconds and then he dragged himself to his feet. The whole place was burning, the flames were leaping toward him, throwing strange shadows over the boy Josh's face and he knew he had to save him.

He lifted him onto his shoulder and staggered back down the corridor into a wall of heat. A pall of black smoke crawled toward him and he ducked his head, fighting against it as it filled his lungs. There were only a few more yards to go, a few more steps to safety. The boy's weight grew heavier and his knees buckled. He couldn't breathe but he knew he must go on, he must save Josh this time. And then the black smoke filled his lungs and his head and he knew no more.

Harry was preparing to leave. His valet had packed his bags for an extended trip abroad and the chauffeur was waiting with the de Courmont ready to drive him to Union Station. Time was passing. The train would leave within the hour, yet Harry was still pacing up and down the vast hall peering every few minutes at his wafer-thin gold fob-watch. It was another expensive self-indulgent gift to himself, but he was in no mood to admire it. He stared hard at the telephone on the table across the hall, willing it to ring. He was still boiling with rage at the newspaper article about Francie and himself and now he was waiting to learn if his first act of revenge had been accomplished.

He thought about his plan, reminding himself how clever it was of him to use the Mandarin's own people against him. The hired tongs should have done their work by now, but they were late in calling and he wondered anxiously if something had gone wrong. Surely they wouldn't dare take his money and welsh on their deal?

He resumed his pacing as another ten minutes ticked by. His valet, waiting by the door, reminded him that the train would leave in half an hour.

"I know, I know, goddamn it," he snarled. And then the telephone rang. He leapt across the hall and snatched up the receiver. A faint smile crossed his face as he listened to the man's garbled report.

Still smiling, he put down the receiver without a word and walked to the door. Revenge felt very sweet.

From the cab driving to the port, Francie saw the red glow in the sky ten blocks away. Then she heard the wail of the fire engines and saw the flashing lights of the police cars as they sped past them.

"Looks like trouble ahead, lady," the cabbie said.

She felt that first fateful tug of dread. "Hurry, please hurry," she begged. A policeman stopped the cab two blocks from the warehouse. Ignoring his protests, Francie leapt out and ran toward the blaze. A second policeman grabbed her and she turned, screaming at him to let her go. "My son is in there," she cried. "I must find him . . . help me, oh *please* help me." Fighting her way out of his grasp, she ran into the street leading to the offices. The heat came toward her in great waves. She stopped, stunned by the fiery inferno. The whole complex was ablaze. Flames leapt from the windows. The corrugated tin roofs had already buckled and melted.

Lai Tsin, summoned by the police, saw Francie from the top of the street and ran toward her. Taking her by the shoulders, he helped her away. Shaking with terror and shock, she told him about Sammy's call and her fear that Ollie was in the warehouse. He shook his head in disbelief.

When Lai Tsin tried to guide her to his car, she pleaded that she had to stay with Ollie. But finally she climbed in and sat beside him, quiet and biddable as a child. In her state of shock, she reminded Lai Tsin of the night when he'd first met her. Now he was driving her back to her own home on Nob Hill and if what she had said was true, tragedy had struck a second time.

He put his arm tenderly around her waist, helping her up the stairs to her room. He summoned the servants to put her to bed and a doctor to give her an injection to make her sleep.

"Whatever shall I do?" she cried, as the Mandarin sat by her bedside, waiting for the sedative to take effect. Her eyes were wild with horror and her face ashen. He shook his head slowly, not knowing what to say. "Leave it all to me, Francie," he said gently. "I will find your son for you."

But as her eyes closed under the influence of the drug, for the first time in many years Lai Tsin felt fear in his heart.

The fire was so fierce it gutted the entire complex, though the firemen managed to prevent it from spreading to the adjacent buildings. By midnight it was all over. There was nothing left of the warehouses with their treasure troves of goods. Later, when the ashes were cool enough, the firemen discovered evidence that the place had been deliberately torched, doused from end to end with so much kerosene it had exploded into flames and been virtually gutted within minutes.

Later that morning they confirmed that the remains of two people had been found in the ruins, one a man, and the other an adolescent boy.

Lai Tsin's face was bitter with sorrow as he mounted the stairs to face Francie. She only needed to look into his eyes to know the truth and she watched him silently. He reached out for her and she thrust him away. She flung herself onto the bed, screaming and flailing her arms in a rage of despair. "Harry did this," she cried in a strangled wail, her face awash with tears. "I know it was him. *He* killed Ollie— not Sammy Morris. It was all a ruse to get him there."

She looked piteously up at Lai Tsin and he sat down beside her and for the very first time in their relationship he put his arms around her. She felt small and fragile, sobbing on his shoulder. He could find no words to comfort her and his own tears ran unchecked down his face as he shared her sorrow. And Lai Tsin knew he had failed Francie. He had made a terrible mistake by not letting the hatchetmen kill Sammy Morris all those years ago. Because if Sammy hadn't kidnapped Ollie, he would be alive now.

On the train to Chicago, Harry read the headlines in the morning papers and his satisfied smile changed to a gasp. He told himself nervously that he hadn't meant to kill the kid. How in hell was he supposed to have known he was there? They'd told him the Mandarin had left and the place was locked up for the night.

He reread the report uneasily. Then, tightening his tie he walked down the train to the dining car. But somehow breakfast didn't taste very good that morning. So he hurried back to his private compartment and ordered a bottle of bourbon and some branch water. A few hours later, he summoned his valet and told him to cancel the week's stay in New York and to book them on the first ship leaving for Europe—anywhere in Europe. Until the speculation died down he wanted to put as many miles as possible between him and San Francisco.

# Part IV

---◆---

# BUCK

# CHAPTER 33

◆

## *1927*

Buck Wingate was in the Wall Street branch of his law office, waiting for Harry. It had been nine years since he had last seen him. That had been when he had refused to act as his attorney in a libel suit he was planning after the disastrous fire that killed Francesca Harrison's son. The newspapers had been full of rumors about a mysterious telephone call luring the boy to the empty offices and the police had confirmed that the fire had been set deliberately. But it was the barely veiled references to Harry's animosity toward his sister that pointed the finger at him. And they had also printed a rumor that Francesca Harrison had accused Harry of killing her son. From a safe distance in his new Monte Carlo villa Harry had expressed his shock at the tragedy and just for the record, proved that he had been on board a train on his way to New York the night it occurred and knew nothing about it until he'd read it in the papers.

The stories had filled the nation's journals for weeks. There were photographs of Miss Harrison and her "close friend and business partner," the Mandarin, at the funeral. Francie's face had been hidden beneath a heavy black veil and she had been clinging to the Mandarin and her friend, Annie Aysgarth, looking as if she were about to faint.

At the time Buck thought he would not have put it past Harry to have had a part in it. When he'd come to see him about a libel action Buck had told him bluntly, "If you take the matter to court they'll dig up every bit of scandal and dirt they can about both you and your sister. And since your own past is not exactly squeaky clean, my advice to you is to let sleeping dogs lie."

"What do you mean—my past?" Harry blustered. "I've nothing to be ashamed of." Buck's steady eyes met his and he added uncertainly, "I mean, I had nothing to do with this fire, nothing at all—"

"Drop it, Harry," Buck said evenly.

"Goddamn it, I thought you were my friend," Harry toppled his chair as he got to his feet. "If that's a friend, then I guess I'd better get myself another attorney."

"I guess so, Harry," Buck replied coldly, "because I sure as hell am not gonna touch it."

The next he'd heard of Harry was the phone call this morning asking to see him. He said he had questions about his father's estate.

The Wingate and Wingate law practice was an old and established one; Buck's entrepreneurial grandfather, a poor immigrant from Ireland, had made his first small fortune at the age of twenty trading furs in Alaska. Then, bored with the freezing north, he had turned to building railroads and then to grain. Finally, he was rich enough to satisfy his own high standards and he grew bored again. An orphan with little education, he endowed a small midwestern college with a new library. In return they allowed him to enroll as a student at the age of thirty-two. He amassed credits quickly, the way he'd amassed his money, and he graduated with honors, summa cum laude, a mere two years later. Then he'd applied to Harvard Law School.

When he received his Doctor of Law degree, he left the world of commerce behind and devoted himself entirely to his new profession. He married the daughter of another rich speculator, hoping she would give him a brood of sons to staff his newly founded law firm. But only after three girls did she bear a boy—his son, Jason. Jason followed in his father's footsteps, expanding the law firm from Sacramento to San Francisco and New York. Now Jason's only son, Buckland Aldrich Wingate, had inherited the firm. But Buck's passion was politics, not law. He'd left most of the practice in the hands of his partners while he served as senator for California. He was on several important senate committees, particularly in the trade sector, at which he was an expert.

Jason Wingate had died a few years ago, but his tall, gray-whiskered presence was maintained in the full-length portrait on the wall in Buck's New York office. Looking at him now he remembered how much his father had despised Harry Harrison—and he knew he had good reason. Still, the Wingates had looked after the Harrison legal affairs ever since they'd started and he must do his duty.

Harry was late, as usual. When he finally sauntered into his office,

Buck thought he looked heavy, but his face was sun-bronzed and still handsome and he was wearing an impeccably-cut Savile Row suit and a conservative French silk tie. He was clean shaven and he wore his receeding fair hair slicked back. He looked as immaculate as an excellent valet could make him. Even the soles of his shoes shone from the layer of polish applied each night. Buck smiled cynically; he knew the real Harry who lurked behind that English-gentleman facade.

"Morning, Buck," Harry said, offering his hand and smiling genially as though nothing had happened and they had seen each other just the other day. "Sorry to have missed your wedding, but I was in Monte Carlo at the time. Or was it London?" He shrugged. "I forget. Still, how is your wife?"

"Maryanne is well, thank you, Harry." He watched as Harry's eyes swiveled to the silver-framed photograph on his desk. Harry's brows shot up. "I heard she was a stunner, Buck, but you sure did yourself proud. Money and looks—and an old aristocratic family. An unbeatable combination, I'd say."

"Would you, Harry?" he replied dryly. "And what about your own marriage prospects?" He knew all about Harry's escapades with follies' stars and movie actresses. He hoped he wasn't about to indulge himself in another expensive misalliance, because he knew he could not afford it.

"Ah, the hell with all women I say," Harry retorted bitterly. "I'm here because I need your help. I suddenly find myself in a small financial predicament and I need to raise cash. Of course, it's only temporary," he added quickly. "You know how the commodities market's been behaving lately. I've taken a bit of a beating on cocoa futures and I thought maybe it was time to open up the rest of the trust fund." He smiled winningly. "Kind of an emergency, Buck. You know how it is."

"From what I recall the second half of your trust does not become available until you are forty. And you have a few years to go yet."

Harry heaved a theatrical sigh. He lit a cigarette and leaned lazily back in his chair. "Surely we're not going to let four years come between me and my money? My father would have wanted me to have it if I needed it. And I do need it, Buck. Now."

"That trust is watertight until you reach the age of forty. That is the way your father wanted it. I'm afraid there's absolutely nothing I can do about it."

Harry sighed again, contemplating the glowing end of his hand-made Egyptian cigarette. "I had a feeling you'd say that and I've thought about what I would do." He looked at Buck, smiling. "I can always borrow against it, can't I?"

"At exorbitant interest rates."

Harry drew on his cigarette and blew a perfect smoke ring into the air. "I'm sure the Harrison Mercantile will be pleased to offer me the loan of a few million at a very favorable interest rate."

Buck leaned forward, his hands clasped on the desk in front of him. "Look, Harry, banks have their rules, too, you know. As you are the bank's owner, I'm not at all sure of the legality of what you are suggesting. I'm advising you to watch your step."

Harry laughed, but he was not amused. "Well, thanks a lot, fella. That's just about all the advice I've had from my old family lawyers in years. Still, we won't allow these things to get in the way of our friendship, shall we? We've known each other since we were kids, Buck. Remember that trip to Paris all those years ago? God, that was fun, wasn't it? All those wonderful sexy French women in those racy bordellos? I've never forgotten it, have you?"

"I've never forgotten your escapades in Paris."

Harry laughed as he stood up to leave. "What are all these rumors I hear about you being a potential Republican candidate?" he asked casually, turning at the door to meet Buck's eyes. "Sounds like a great idea. With Maryanne Brattle at your side, how can you fail? Choate, Princeton, Harvard Law—the perfect wife and the perfect family man. I'll be the first to congratulate you." He smiled his smile and said, "Sorry we couldn't do business together today. Maybe some other time, eh Buck? In fact, how about inviting me out for a weekend sometime soon? I'd love to meet Maryanne and the kids." He waved airily as he left, leaving the door ajar. Buck sighed. Harry Harrison never changed.

Maryanne Wingate used her Washington house for political social-izing only; New York was where she chose to *live*. Her friends were there, her children went to school there and it was where she re-treated when the "provincialism" of Washington got on her nerves—which was four days out of each week.

The Wingate's apartment on fashionable Park Avenue covered three floors, though Maryanne had had part of one floor removed to create a grand baronial hall with a stairway that swept downward in two perfect curves from a central gallery. She'd had the walls lined with French limestone and hung with ancestral portraits and massive silver sconces and she liked to keep a fire glowing in the twenty-foot stone chimney from the first cool day of autumn to the first warm day of spring. Her well-bred King Charles spaniels were usually to be found sprawling in front of it. She would laughingly tell visitors she was just a country girl at heart, and that if she had to pay the price of helping Buck in his career by being in the city, then she would just make her apartment look like her beloved girlhood home. She was only sorry she couldn't bring her horses too.

The three dogs lifted their noses in the air, waving lazy tails as Buck walked by, but they didn't run to greet him as they did with Maryanne; they were her dogs and no one else's and they knew it.

Maryanne refused to keep a butler, saying it was either "too old hat or too new-rich." A uniformed parlor maid took Buck's coat and told him that madame was expected back soon.

Behind the grand hall was a regal drawing room and the library, with its collection of rare books and ancient maps, and beyond that the kitchen. The first floor contained his and Maryanne's rooms, each with its dressing room and bathroom, her own personal sitting room and his study.

Buck took the lefthand sweep of stairs two at a time and then ran easily up the next flight to the nursery floor. Six-year-old Grace Juliet Margaret Brattle Wingate, known as Miffy, glanced up with a discontented smile as he came in. "Oh, hello, Daddy," she said.

There was a grumbling undercurrent to her tone that Buck knew only too well and he grinned wryly. "Hello, Miffy. Is that the best you can do to greet your poor old father?" He walked toward her, his arms outstretched, and she smiled reluctantly as she walked into them and he hugged her. "Really, Daddy, you're so exuberant," she chided, copying her mother's words, and he laughed.

"And you sound like your mother. So? What's the matter with my girl?"

She looked at him guardedly and he thought how pretty she was. She had her mother's straight dark blond hair, pinned at the side with a gold barrette, and Maryanne's rather large mouth and her dark-lashed green eyes; she was tall for her age, coltishly long-legged and she could turn on the charm in a minute if she wanted something. But he guessed she didn't at the moment because there was a distinct whine in her voice as she complained her mother had said she must get dressed and come downstairs and say hello to their dinner guests that evening.

"I don't want to," she said fractiously, "they're all so goddamn boring."

"I'm glad to see they teach you the finest English language at Miss Beale's very expensive little school," Buck said sarcastically.

"I don't want to," she repeated obstinately.

Buck frowned. He knew Maryanne wanted to show off her pretty daughter to their visitors; she would have had liked Jamie there, too, but five-year-old Jamieson Alexander Buckland Wingate had succumbed to an attack of the mumps and had been banished to their country house in New Jersey with his nurse. They were entertaining several influential politicians and businessmen, and after dinner they were expected to declare their allegiance to Buck personally as well as to the Republican Party in the big, somber library.

Buck had worked hard for the party, campaigning tirelessly in the last presidential election, and Maryanne had worked even harder, entertaining lavishly, always the perfect political wife, mindful of their public position. There were no stains on Maryanne's character; all the Brattles' lives were open books. They had been in and out of the Senate for generations and now they had put all their powers behind Buck's career. At forty he was poised to make the transition from senator to presidential candidate.

He quickly decided it would do his spoiled little daughter no harm if she were to put on the pretty, and no-doubt expensive, dress her mother had bought her and act nicely to their guests.

"What'll you give me if I do?" Miffy demanded sulkily.

"What will I give you? I'll give you the moon, the stars—"

"Really, Daddy, I'd rather have a brand-new sailboat."

He sighed. "There's no romance in your soul," he said as he departed, thinking again she was just like her mother.

He peeked into Maryanne's room on his way down the hall. They'd had separate rooms ever since their first child was born because she'd decided she preferred it that way. "After all, we can still visit, can't we?" she'd said with a winning smile, the very same smile he saw in his daughter's face when she wanted something. The lamps were lit and Maryanne's maid was bustling about putting away the clothes she had just cast off and flung to the floor en route to her bath. A waft of scented steam came from the pink Italian marble bathroom. He strode to the door and called out, "Can I come in?"

"Oh, must you, Buck? Shouldn't you be getting changed for dinner? They'll be here in forty minutes."

He walked in and looked at her, lying back in the vast tub of perfumed water. Maryanne would never use anything as vulgar as bubblebath no matter how expensive; she used scented oils specially prepared for her by French perfume experts in Grasse and they had concocted a subtle innocuous scent of lilac and wildroses that was her trademark.

"What is it, Buck?" she demanded crossly. "I'm late and there's a lot still to be done." Stepping from the tub, she stretched out a dripping arm and said, "Hand me the towel, will you?"

He passed it silently to her, thinking that Maryanne naked had been the biggest disappointment of his life. She was one of those women who looked stunning in clothes, but out of them she was small-breasted and sinewy. Socially she was always charming, always well-dressed and he had never once heard her raise her voice. She was a good if rather distant mother to his children. He still occasionally made love to her, but he was not in the least bit in love with her. Oh, he had been in the beginning; he had admired her striking looks and her forceful personality that some called bossy, and he'd liked the effortlessly confident way she rode a horse and the way she strode into any room as though she owned it. Maryanne had generations of aristocratic breeding behind her and it showed.

As he watched her patting dry her long smooth legs, he guessed that it had just been a mutual admiration society—one that he had mistaken for love. In the seven years they had been married their relationship had never drifted into casual affairs on either of their parts the way so many other couples they knew had; instead they had channeled their energies into politics. Maryanne did not want sex with a stranger, or even her husband; all she wanted was to see him advance in his career and maybe ultimately to enter the White House.

"You'd better get dressed," she told him, gliding into a white silk robe. "I thought I would keep the food simple tonight—you know these politicians, all they ever want is steak, steak, steak. They alone could keep Chicago in business. And I decided on the Château Leyoville Las Cases, they know a good claret when they taste it. The 1870 port has been decanted and—oh my goodness, just look at the time. Buck, will you please go and bathe. . . ."

He said, "I saw Harry Harrison today."

She glanced quickly up at him. "Trouble?"

"He's been nothing but since his father died—and probably before. He wanted to get at his trust fund and I had to say no."

"Quite right," she said briskly. "From what I read about him, he'd spend it all on rather squalid women anyway."

Buck sighed as he left her in front of the mirror trying on a diamond necklace and debating whether she should wear her pearls instead. As he walked back along the hall he wondered whether it was all worth it.

He was ready and waiting on the dot of seven-thirty, the fire was blazing, the dogs were snoozing picturesquely in front of it, and Maryanne looked suitably regal in the long-sleeved red silk with a heart-shaped neckline that showed off the magnificent Brattle diamonds. "I thought I'd better remind them who they're dealing with," she whispered, smiling as she adjusted his black tie. "My, we make a handsome couple," she added with satisfaction.

A dozen influential men and their wives had been invited for dinner, and the leader of the House of Representatives and his wife were the last to arrive. "I bring greetings from the White House," he told Maryanne, kissing her soft cheek. "President Coolidge says his grandfather knew your grandfather."

"Indeed he did," she agreed. "I believe they were at school together."

She saw to it that the men were served their favorite whiskey, even though she disapproved of it before dinner. The ladies were offered champagne. And then little Miffy made her entrance, curtsying shyly as she was introduced. Unerringly, she picked out one of the most important party contributors and climbed onto his knee, looking up at him with her mother's engaging smile. For a moment Buck wondered whether Maryanne had coached her, but then he told himself he was being mean.

Dinner was Maryanne's idea of a simple meal: soup, fish, beef, chocolate dessert and cheese, perfectly chosen for the company, perfectly cooked and perfectly served, and accompanied by some of the most beautiful wines France had to offer. Immediately afterward, she swept the ladies off the the drawing room, where they chatted about their children and their country houses and their husband's sailboats, while Buck escorted the men to the library, where they sat on deep leather sofas in front of the roaring fire, sipping glasses of fine old port and discussing the future. By eleven that night several of the large tycoons said they would contribute generously to the party now, and in return, Senator Buckland Aldrich Wingate III, would watch out for their interests. And when the time was ripe, they would support him should he choose to run for president. It would take many more years and a lot more effort, but Maryanne had got what she wanted. For now.

# CHAPTER 34

◆

Annie drove her little Packard roadster along the leafy lanes of the Sonoma Valley to the de Soto Ranch. Over the years, Francie had bought more and more land encircling her original forty acres until now it stretched farther than the eye could see, four hundred and thirty acres dotted with shady oaks and stands of silver birch. Tended by Mexican cowboys, contented golden Jersey cows grazed in the pastures. On either side of the ranch house itself lay neat rows of vines interspersed with roses that at this time of year were into their second fragrant blooming. Francie planted the roses because pests attacked them before they attacked her precious vines, and she inspected them every morning so that she could take fast action, but Annie suspected she loved the flowers so much she would have planted them, bugs or no bugs. There were new outbuildings too: cottages for Zocco and the housekeeper, as well as workers' quarters and the small winery.

The years since Ollie's death had been ones of quiet seclusion for Francie, but they had been fruitful. Annie could hardly bear to think of the first terrible months after the tragedy; Francie had seemed to shrink into solitude like a small, wounded animal seeking a quiet place in which to find her own death. Waking and sleeping, she had endlessly relived the night of the fire in her mind, until they were afraid she would lose her mind.

She had retreated to the ranch, the place where she always went to lick her wounds, and for two years she never left it. Zocco and his wife took care of her, though she barely spoke to them. She went nowhere and saw no one. Though Annie's own heart had been broken by Ollie's death, she finally could bear it no longer. She'd driven to the ranch in a fury of despair and stormed through the door;

Francie had been sitting in the rocking chair by the kitchen stove with Ollie's dogs at her feet and she'd lifted her head indifferently to see who was there.

"Here," Annie had said, snatching a shotgun from the rack on the wall and flinging it onto the table. "Why don't you just get it over with instead of putting us all through the agony of dying slowly? I'm sick of it, Francie Harrison. And I'm sick of seeing your sorrowful face. We loved Ollie more than we'll ever love again, but he's gone, and you are young and able-bodied and now you're rich, probably richer than you even know or care about. There are dozens—no, hundreds, maybe thousands of poor, sick, needy children back there in San Francisco who need people like you. But if you would rather die than help them, then do it now and put us all out of our misery once and for all."

Stamping her foot she burst into tears. "Oh God, what have I said. . . . how could I be so cruel. I didn't mean it, Francie, truly I didn't. . . . I don't want you to die—only please, please, come back to the land of the living."

Francie had stood up and walked to the table. Annie's brown eyes widened and her hand flew to her mouth with a little gasp as Francie picked up the shotgun Zocco used for killing the rapacious blackbirds. Frozen with terror, she watched Francie break open the barrel and check it. Francie's eyes met hers; she clicked the barrel back in place and then she'd pointed the gun at her; seconds had passed. Then she flung the gun back on the table and said calmly, "That shows how much you know about ranching, Annie Aysgarth —the chamber's empty."

Annie had hurled herself on Francie. "Oh, thank God, thank God," she'd gasped, "I didn't mean it, honestly I didn't. It's just that I didn't know what to do."

Francie had glanced out the window at the sun slanting off the stable roof, and linking her arm in Annie's she casually said, "Let's go for a walk to the stables and check on Ollie's horse. The poor thing's been neglected for far too long."

Annie had watched admiringly as she petted the gray that had been her son's favorite. Her desperate impetuous action had carved the first chink in the ice of Francie's despair. She was on the long, slow road back to life again.

That year Francie and the Mandarin established the Oliver Harrison Memorial Foundation, through which they helped sick and needy children, but it was Francie who ran it. And it was Francie who every week visited the new annex they had donated to the Children's Hospital, bringing toys and games, and books that she read to the small patients. She sat for hours at the bedside of the desperately ill and comforted the distraught parents. And it was Francie who helped rehouse the poorest Chinese families and rescued the youngest children from their slavery in terrible sweatshop factories. She provided textbooks for schools and scholarships to enable immigrant children to attend college. She worked tirelessly for months on end, though she was careful always to keep out of the limelight and her name rarely appeared in the newspapers. And when exhaustion finally overcame her she always returned to her beloved ranch again.

The vineyard was her new passion and Annie smiled as she drove past the acres of neat rows. Francie's vines were manicured to the peak of perfection and though her production was small, a mere three thousand bottles, the soft red wine was good.

"Good—but not good enough," Francie told her later as they strolled through the vineyard together. She stooped and picked up a handful of the rich, dark earth. "Look at this," she demanded indignantly. "Can it be any better in France? We have the same sunshine, the same rain, the same sheltered slopes. So why can't I produce a burgundy as good as theirs?"

Her blue eyes were flashing with the old fire and Annie laughed. "Ask the French, not me."

"I may just do that. One day." Annie knew she was joking because she never went anywhere anymore, and she said, "Then before you venture so far afield, why don't you come to my party next week?" Francie stared off to the horizon and she added quickly, "It's about time you did something to please yourself—and me, for a change. Good works are all very well, Francie Harrison, but it's time you got out and about a bit more and met some people."

Francie looked thoughtfully at her. Annie was always busy, she had dozens of friends and hundreds of acquaintances; she was a queen bee of the smart hotel world and everyone wanted to know her. With a sudden lonely pang, she envied her. She said quickly before she could change her mind, "All right then. I will."

Annie looked so astonished that it made Francie laugh. But later as she packed her bags for the trip, she was more than a little apprehensive. Her life was as cloistered as a nun's. San Francisco had grown from the small town of her youth to a bustling city, and sometimes, driving home from Aysgarth's after dining with Annie, she would stare enviously at the noisy crowds thronging the sidewalks outside the cafés and theaters, feeling like a little girl with her nose pressed to the window again, as real life passed her by.

This week the President was giving a large ball to thank the Californians who had worked in the party's behalf. The city was packed with out-of-towners and hotel rooms were at a premium. Over the years Annie had played host to many of Washington's politicians, and before the ball she was holding a small champagne reception for her favored customers, one of many held that night.

"My own inaugural reception," she told Francie excitedly as they waited in the private drawing room for her guests. She patted her expensive bronze lace dress anxiously. "Do I look like the First Lady of the hotel world?"

"You look perfect," Francie reassured her, and indeed she did. Her glossy brown hair was arranged in smooth waves and her brown eyes shone with excitement. The bronze lace suited her creamy complexion and its low square neck showed off her full bosom to advantage. She wore a choker of five rows of small emerald beads with matching drop earrings and a large topaz ring. "I don't want to compete with their diamonds, love," she confided to Francie. "After all, I'm still the hired hand, aren't I?" And then she laughed uproariously as she thought of the prices she was charging them for the privilege of staying at Aysgarth's.

But Annie was never mean; it was nothing but the best for her invited guests: vintage Roederer champagne—the very same that used to be served by the czar of Russia; impeccable caviar from Persia; the finest wild salmon from Scotland; and morsels of delicious lobster from the coast of Maine.

"We shall not be served finer in the White House itself, Mrs. Aysgarth," the President told her, beaming. The room was full of pretty women, but Annie was the center of attention and her Yorkshire accent and boisterous laugh could be heard over the noisy buzz that marked a successful party.

Francie stood near the door, her champagne glass clutched nervously in her hand, answering politely when she was introduced by Annie and wishing she had never promised to come. She had never in her life attended a party like this and she felt like a fish out of water.

Maryanne Wingate's expert eyes rested on her momentarily, registered the fact that she was unknown and passed quickly on in search of more important prey. But Buck's eyes lingered. He thought she looked lovely but remote and unapproachable, as though she had erected an invisible fence around her that said "keep away." Her floating gray chiffon dress was as discreet as a cloud, and the pearls were worth a small fortune. He walked across to her and said, "You look as though you are about to bolt out the door. Is the party that bad?"

She glanced at him, startled. "Oh, no, not at all. It's a perfectly lovely party."

He held out his hand. "I'm Buck Wingate."

She shook his hand so quickly he scarcely felt the pressure of her fingers. "Francesca Harrison," she murmured, blushing.

It was his turn to look startled. "But I know your brother," he exclaimed. She froze, her eyes grew distant, her mouth tightened, and she did not reply. "My father was your father's lawyer," he said, realizing he was getting deeper and deeper into the mire. "I mean, that's the only reason I know him, because of his trust. My firm handles it."

She nodded and said icily, "I see."

"Miss Harrison," he said, though he had no idea why he should be making such an effort to set the record straight, she meant nothing to him, nor did her brother. "I did not choose your brother as a client, I inherited him. You know, the sins of our fathers . . . ?"

He smiled winningly at her, breathing a small sigh of relief as she smiled back and said, "Please don't apologize for knowing Harry, Mr. Wingate. It's your misfortune, not mine."

He nodded, searching to change the subject, but in the back of his mind he was running through what he knew about her. Wasn't there a Chinese lover and the multimillion-dollar corporation? And of course, the tragic death of her young son in the fire. Her past certainly didn't show in her flawless face and he thought again how beautiful she was. "What brings you to a political party like this, Miss Harrison?"

"Annie Aysgarth is an old friend. She wanted to show off her guests to me."

"That sounds like Annie, she enjoys a bit of praise—especially for her Yorkshire puddings."

Francie laughed. "They're the best—and probably the most expensive puddings this side of Yorkshire. But there's more to Annie than that."

"I daresay there is. I've known her for about ten years now. How come I've never met you before?"

"Oh, don't you know?" Her tone was faintly contemptuous and he raised his eyebrows questioningly. "I'm San Francisco's worst-kept secret. The notorious Harrison sister living in sin with her Chinese lover on Nob Hill, right opposite her illustrious brother, Harry. Nobody ever talks about me, Mr. Wingate, except behind my back."

"Buck?" Maryanne took his arm and he turned quickly.

He said, "Maryanne, this is Miss Harrison."

She nodded. "Indeed?" she said cuttingly, not offering her hand. "How do you do, Miss Harrison." Without waiting for a reply, she said, "Buck, I'm afraid we must leave or we shall be late for the ball." Then she swept through the door without so much as a glance in Francie's direction.

Buck stared angrily after her. "Forgive my wife," he said bitterly, "she sometimes has worse manners than her six-year-old daughter."

Francie shrugged, her face expressionless as she turned away. "Please do not concern yourself, Mr. Wingate."

He watched her as she walked gracefully across the room toward Annie; her cloudlike dress floated around her slender body and the lamplight caught her shining hair and her wonderful pearls. And he thought she looked the loneliest woman in the world.

Francie knew she couldn't go through with it; she waited until the reception was over and then told Annie she had a headache and was going home.

Annie glanced sceptically at her. "Well, at least you showed up. I guess it was a start. Let's take it from there, shall we?"

Annie was surprised when Buck Wingate called her the next morning and even more surprised when he asked about Francie.

She had known Buck for a long time. His primary residence was in Sacramento, but he stayed at Aysgarth's whenever he was in San Francisco, which was several times a year. At first she had been suspicious of him because she felt any man as handsome and charming as he was had to be up to no good, but Buck Wingate did not play around; he was a good husband even though his wife was a cold fish. He had been involved in politics for years, he was one of the country's youngest senators and a big future was already being predicted for him by men important enough to influence such things. So why was he calling and quizzing her about Francie Harrison?

"Maryanne's gone back home," he explained casually, "but I have to stay here for a meeting. I'm going to be at loose ends and since you are the only woman in San Francisco that I thought might take pity on me I called to ask you to dine with me tonight. And Miss Harrison as well, of course," he added rather too quickly.

"I'm a busy woman," she told him, "but I'll see what I can do." Putting down the phone she threw on her coat and hurried over to Francie's. She leaned against the door, her arms folded across her chest with a knowing smile on her face. "So, Francesca Harrison, what did you say to Buck Wingate that's got him so smitten?"

"Smitten?" Francie blushed the way she used to when Edward Stratton's name was mentioned. "You must be wrong. He told me he knew Harry and I was very rude to him. Then he introduced his wife and she was very rude to me."

"Maryanne Wingate is rude to everybody unless they can do her some good," Annie said bluntly. "And rude or not, Buck Wingate would like the pleasure of our company for dinner tonight—without his wife. And he would probably like it even better if it were without me too."

"Then you'd better tell Mr. Wingate that I cannot accept his invitation." She looked exasperatedly at Annie. "Oh Annie, don't I have enough trouble without Maryanne Wingate's husband?"

"You do," Annie agreed. "I just thought you would like to know that the world has not passed you by. If Buck Wingate is interested, other men will be too—if you gave them half a chance."

But Francie just shook her head. She wasn't like ordinary people and she knew it. Marriage and happiness were simply not her fate. Nevertheless, it was Buck she was thinking about on the long drive back to the ranch.

The image of the lonely woman in the cloud-gray dress stayed with Buck for a long time. He was a busy man who never did anything by halves. He devoted himself to his work and senatorial responsibilities and tried to avoid the endless round of the entertaining that Maryanne insisted was "all for your career, darling." He had entered politics as an idealistic young man and though those ideals had been tempered by reason and circumstance, he was and always would be a "man of the people, and for the people." He hated Maryanne's parties and social climbing, though sometimes he had to admit it was necessary.

Their house on K Street in leafy Georgetown was always full of committee ladies having lunch, or important visitors taking tea, or influential politicians at one of the "intimate" candlelit dinners for which Maryanne was famous. "Can you believe it, darling," she exclaimed to him, laughing, "people are actually trying to bribe my friends for an introduction in the hopes of being invited. Isn't it amazing?"

Buck looked at her presiding over his polished Georgian dining table with the gleaming eighteenth-century silver Paul Storr candelabra, the vermeil service plates, the carved crystal wine goblets, and the lavish but understated flower arrangements, and he knew she was in her element. But there was not one man at his dinner table that night he could call his friend and he suddenly felt as lonely as the lovely woman in the cloud-gray dress.

"Let's invite *friends* to Broadlands for Christmas," he said impulsively to Maryanne when their guests had gone. They were in her bedroom and her maid was hanging up the taffeta dress she had worn. Maryanne slipped on her rose-colored peignoir and sat down at her dresser, smiling at him in the mirror as she creamed her face. If there was one place she really loved it was her childhood home, bequeathed to her by her grandfather. "Why, of course, darling, what a wonderful idea. Christmas in the country with the children and friends, what could be nicer? I'll draw up a guest list tomorrow and instruct the housekeeper to prepare everything."

"It'll be good for us to be together with the children," he said seriously. "I see far too little of them these days."

She sighed. "That's true, darling, but there simply isn't room in this tiny house and anyway they are much better off with the nurse and the governess and staying in their same schools. And we are always so busy . . ." She sighed again, stretching her arms over her head and yawning. "And I'm always so dog-tired at the end of the day I just don't know where I'll get the energy to face the next morning."

Her eyes met his in the mirror and he saw emptiness in them and wondered sadly what had happened to their marriage. Their lives were arranged around his work and her ambitions for him. If it were not for the children and his political career he would be tempted to ask her for a divorce right there and then. Instead he said quietly,

"Good night Maryanne," closing the door softly behind him as he left.

New York in the couple of weeks before Christmas was Buck's favorite place. He liked the strolling Santas ringing their bells outside the stores and the smell of roasting chestnuts from the peddlers on the street corners. He liked the frosty nip in the air that made him tighten his fringed cashmere muffler and brought memories of childhood winters, skating on the frozen duck pond and tobogganing on an old tin tray down the steep slippery slopes at Strawberry Hill, his maternal grandparents' home in New England where his family had spent all their Christmases. He stared wistfully at the clockwork trains and magic sets and wooly animals in the windows of the toy store at the corner of Fifth and Fifty-ninth Street, remembering all those long-ago Christmas mornings with the fire roaring in the grate, the snow falling outside, and mysterious presents still to be unwrapped. He remembered the laughter of family and friends and children and the smell of good things cooking in the big kitchen, wishing himself back in time, wishing he could start all over again.

The last person Francie had expected to see was Buck Wingate. She stopped for a moment to watch him, a half-smile on her face, debating whether to say hello. She had just decided she had better not when he turned and caught her eye.

"Do you remember me?" she said shyly. "Francesca Harrison—we met at Annie Aysgarth's party in San Francisco." She held out her hand and added with a smile, "You looked like a little boy with your nose pressed longingly against the windowpane."

He stared at her, surprised. She was wearing a narrow cream cashmere coat with a huge fox collar and a small cloche hat, her cheeks were pink from the cold and her eyes were the most incredible, deep pansy blue. He thought she looked wonderful. He smiled ruefully. "Was it that obvious? I was just recalling memories of Christmases past." He took her hand, feeling the warmth beneath the soft beige suede glove. "Of course I remember you." He didn't say, "How could I ever forget?" but his eyes did, and she looked away, flustered.

"What are you doing in New York, Miss Harrison?" he asked, letting go of her hand. She told him that she was in town to look at a property for the Lai Tsin Corporation and to do some Christmas shopping.

He glanced at the gaily wrapped parcels she was carrying and said ruefully, "It surely looks as though you're more successful at it than I am. I still haven't found anything for Maryanne—my wife."

Francie thought of Maryanne, so cool and sure of herself. "Jewelry?" she suggested.

He shook his head and grinned. "Another pair of earrings and she would be mistaken for a Christmas tree ornament." Francie laughed and he thought, surprised, how different she looked when she was happy.

"I know what *I'd* like for Christmas if I were your wife," she said, still smiling. "I just saw it in a gallery and fell in love with it."

"Why don't you show me?" he asked, eager for her company.

They walked companionably across Fifth Avenue and around the corner to the little gallery. In the window was a small portrait by Morisot of a blond child, her face serious and her eyes dark with wonder. Francie sighed. "Don't you think the artist has captured the essence of childhood?" He thought again of all those wondrous childhood Christmases and knew she was right.

"I'm afraid it's not exactly Maryanne though," he said regretfully. "Maybe I'll just get her the gray pearls after all." He glanced up as the first flakes of snow began to fall. It was four o'clock and the sky was already dark. "At least let me invite you for tea," he said eagerly, "to thank you for your help?"

She tilted her head consideringly. "I really shouldn't, I still have so much to do."

He'd bet she didn't have a single important thing to do at four o'clock on a Thursday afternoon before Christmas. He said authoritatively, "I won't take no for an answer," and took her arm, hurrying her back across Fifth and into the new Sherry-Netherland Hotel.

The café was busy with smart shoppers relaxing after their afternoon's labors. The sound of their high-pitched chatter mingled with the violins of the quartet and the tinkle of silver spoons against fine china and the giggles of overexcited children being treated to ice-cream sodas and chocolate cake.

Francie thought tremblingly of Ollie; Christmas was always the hardest time and that's partly why she was in New York, to get away from her memories, but it wasn't always possible to succeed. She thought sadly that he would no longer have been a child—he would have been a young man now and maybe he would have been taking her out to tea instead of Buck Wingate.

He said quietly, "I can see you find Christmas lonely too." She looked at him, her eyes dark with sadness, and he wanted to put his arms around her and tell her it would be all right again one day, but of course he couldn't—and it wouldn't. Nothing could ever compensate her for the loss of her son.

"The children are having such a good time," she said with a smile. "Look at them enjoying all those forbidden treats."

"And what shall *we* treat ourselves to?" he asked gaily. "That fabulous chocolate cake? Or a mountainous ice-cream sundae? Cherry cake? *Millefeuille?* Or are you the cucumber sandwich type of woman?"

Francie laughed, swinging out of her dark mood. "If you want to know the truth I'm a toasted muffin type of woman," she confessed.

"Then muffins it shall be." He gave the waiter his order and then said, "You see how much I'm learning about you in just a few hours? I know you're buying property in Manhattan, and what you'd like for Christmas, and what you like for tea—better be careful or soon I'll know all your secrets."

She laughed again. "But I don't have any secrets—not anymore. My life is an open book, everybody knows everything about me."

He shook his head. "No, oh no. I'll bet there are very few people who know the *real* Francesca Harrison."

Francie glanced nervously at him; he was too perceptive by far. Looking into his steady brown eyes, she told herself they were getting into deeper waters than they should for two casual acquaintances, but she couldn't help noticing the little lines of laughter around his steady brown eyes and the way his dark hair waved slightly and that there were already touches of gray at his temples. Annie had told her Buck Wingate was too handsome for his own good and it was true.

Then the waiter brought tea in a silver pot and hot toasted muffins oozing wickedly with butter, and he changed the subject to his work. He told her he had loved the world of politics since he was just a kid, and that first the Senate had taken over his life, so he never had time to think of anything else. He told her he hardly saw his children anymore and that he was going to spend Christmas with them in the country and that he was afraid they would treat him like a stranger.

"And where are you spending Christmas?" he asked when the muffins were finished and the final cup of tea had been drunk. "Oh, I'll be at my ranch with Annie and Lai Tsin," she told him. And then she met his eyes. She had never felt the need to define her relationship with the Mandarin to anyone before, but now she said, "Lai Tsin is my friend."

Buck nodded. "I envy him your friendship," he said quietly.

She wouldn't let him take her back to the Ritz Tower, where she was staying, and once again he watched her walk away from him, threading her way through the crowds. He watched until she disappeared and he thought maybe he had it all wrong and it was he who was the lonely one after all.

A few days before Christmas a beautifully wrapped parcel addressed to Miss Francesca Harrison was delivered to the house on Nob Hill. She couldn't wait to open it, ripping off the scarlet ribbons like an excited child. Inside was the small painting she had admired in the New York gallery and a card from Buck Wingate that said, "This was meant to belong to you. I shall be thinking of you at Christmas."

Francie ran her fingers lovingly over the carved frame. She held the painting at arm's length and looked at it and it was just as beautiful as when she had first seen it. She thought of Buck going to the gallery and buying it for her, of him writing the note—*thinking of you at Christmas,* it'd said. And then she shook her head and told herself it was far too expensive a gift, that he shouldn't have bought it and of course he wouldn't be thinking of her at Christmas at all. He would be with his family and friends at his wonderful country house three thousand miles away and it might as well be a million.

She went to her desk and wrote him a note thanking him for his thoughtful and extravagant gift and saying that in return for his generosity and kindness she was donating sackfuls of toys and Christmas cheer to a dozen needy orphanages across the country in his name, and that she knew he would enjoy thinking of the pleasure he had given them on Christmas morning.

And then she took the beautiful painting and placed it on a little gilt easel on her bedside table where it would be the last thing she saw every night before she went to sleep.

Christmas at the Wingates' country house, Broadlands, was a traditional but elegant affair. There was a vast fir tree trimmed by the staff with gilded pine cones and lit with tiny red candles, mountains of expensively wrapped gifts, and log fires in every room. Maryanne had invited her brother with his wife and children, and a dozen important Republicans and their wives. "I can't tell you how pleased they all were to be invited," she told him happily. "This was such a *good* idea of yours, darling."

Spending Christmas with a bunch of politicians was not Buck's idea of "friends" at all. On Christmas morning he shook his head gloomily as Maryanne handed out the expensive, tasteful little trinkets she had bought, and the children squabbled over their toys. His fingers touched the little note in his pocket from Francie Harrison; he didn't need to read it again, he'd read it so often he knew it by heart. He thought of the orphan children she had sent gifts to and he smiled, and he thought of her having Christmas at the ranch with her friends, just as he had said he would.

# CHAPTER 35

———◆———

The Lai Tsin Corporation headquarters in Hong Kong towered a lofty fifteen stories. The best geomancers had studied the site carefully and made their pronouncements and the white granite, many-columned building stood at a slightly off-angle to the street with its main doors also placed off-center to prevent the good *ch'i* from escaping. Eight broad marble steps, a lucky number, led up to massive red-lacquered doors, which were guarded by a pair of fierce bronze lions. The magnificent reception hall was paved in different-colored marbles and decorated with columns of malachite, wonderful mosaics, statues, and carvings. Lai Tsin's office was not tucked away on the top floor, but at ground level off the main hall where he could be easily accessible to all who wished to see him, from the grandest taipans to the humblest worker, and it was as simple as his first office in the warehouse in San Francisco.

True, the walls were not old wooden planks anymore, they were of plaster laquered his favorite dark plum. His desk was not made of teak but of ebony wood, and there was no ugly old iron safe lurking in the corner because he no longer needed it, since there was now a safety vault in the basement. But it was still as neat as the old one with the Chinese inkpad and brushes, the Western inkstand and pens and the sheaf of papers lined up neatly on his desk.

More than ten years had passed since Francie was last in Hong Kong and this time she stayed with the Mandarin in his white villa overlooking Repulse Bay. The exterior was neoclassical in style but inside it was Chinese with pierced window screens, exquisite black-wood furniture, and a carefully chosen collection of ancient wall hangings, calligraphy, porcelain, and paintings. Francie had created the house on Nob Hill, but this was Lai Tsin's heritage.

He studied her carefully over dinner one evening. She had been in Hong Kong for over a week and he had shown her the wonderful headquarters, the fleet of ships—no longer just shabby steamers bought cheaply from Swires but the latest from the shipyards of Japan and the fastest in the world. He had shown her his mansion and all his treasures and now he said humbly, "Everything you see is yours, Francie. Without you, I would be nothing."

She looked at him, shocked. "Surely it's the other way around."

He was silent while the soft-footed servants removed their dishes and placed small fragrant pots of tea in front of them.

"Tomorrow we shall journey to Shanghai," he said, "and from there we shall sail upriver to my home village." She looked at him astonished because in all these years he had never suggested such a trip, and he added, "I would like to show you my village and the ancestral hall of Lilin, so that you may better understand what I have to tell you. I travel there twice each year to remind myself of my humble beginnings, lest I forget that the luxury surrounding me is merely temporal. I go to cleanse my heart of acquisitiveness and to refresh my soul." He paused, then added, "It is important that you come with me."

He looked down at the bowl of tea in front of him and she watched him, puzzled. She had never seen him like this before, nervous and unsure of himself. "Of course I'll go with you," she said. "I am honored you wish to show me these things."

They sailed for Shanghai the next morning and when they got there they boarded Lai Tsin's shiny white steamship, the *MV Mandarin*. As they sailed upriver Francie hung over the rail, exclaiming at the sights, but Lai Tsin remained strangely silent.

When they reached Nanking he took her ashore and they walked together along the same streets he had once run through with his young sister, fleeing from the flesh-peddler. Francie heard the depths of grief in his voice as he spoke of Mayling and she guessed each time he took the journey he still hoped he might find her, even though he knew in his heart it was impossible.

The broad river flowed on, sometimes between high banks ten times as tall as their little ship, and sometimes so flat that only the reeds showed where the river ended and the land began. As they approached the little jetty nearest his village, Lai Tsin changed into his embroidered blue robes and put on his hat with the button of rare white jade. The beautiful white ship edged its way to the rickety wooden jetty and the smart sailors leapt to tie her up.

A crowd gathered as the gangplank was lowered and Lai Tsin and Francie stepped on shore. Astonished, they stared at the strange barbarian woman with the pale hair and eyes of piercing blue fire, turning away their heads in fear because they had never seen a *gwailo woman* before. Many of them kowtowed before such important personages, as they walked amongst them and Lai Tsin gave them coins from his purse. And then with Francie by his side, he set off on the long familiar walk to his village.

On the way he pointed out all the things he had mentioned when he told her his story the night Ollie was born: the duck pond glowering like a sheet of steel under the gray skies and the sleepy white ducks, the endless gray-green rice fields and the children working in them, the desolate *fung-shui* grove where the body of Little Chen, with his merry eyes and his face as round and flat as a pancake, was left in a wicker basket for the birds and the dogs to take, and in the distance, glowing like an icon on the hill, the vermillion ancestral hall of Lilin.

The yellow-clay walls circling the village were now only a pile of stones and rubble and many of the tumbledown dwellings stood empty. Only Elder Brother's house had strong rice paper in its small windows and a charcoal brazier sending smoke into the cold air. Elder Brother's young wife had quickly swept the outside when she glimpsed them from a distance and now she lurked timidly behind her husband in the doorway, for the Mandarin never set foot over their threshold. Her eyes grew wide with astonishment as she saw the barbarian woman walking at the Mandarin's side and Elder Brother shouted an oath. "Will the *mui-tsai*'s son never cease to bring shame on the name of Ke Chungfen, bringing a *gwailo* to his family home." But he said it softly enough that Lai Tsin would not hear and cease paying him the money that filled his rice bowl each night and replenished his flask with rice wine more frequently than it should.

His young wife ran from behind him and knelt before Lai Tsin and the barbarian woman. She touched her forehead to the ground and said, "Welcome, welcome Honorable Younger Brother Ke Lai Tsin, and welcome his Honorable Guest."

Lai Tsin smiled gently at her, and taking her hand he helped her to her feet, thanking her for her kind welcome. Elder Brother bowed stiffly, trying his best not to look at the barbarian woman, yet his eyes were drawn to her. He had never before in his whole life seen a *gwailo* woman and he thought she must be the ugliest creature on earth, with eyes of such terrifying blueness they must be a devil's and hair so pale she must surely be a hundred years old.

"Welcome, Younger Brother," he said, smiling at Lai Tsin and ignoring Francie. "We have expected your visit and you will see that the ancestral hall of Lilin is swept and kept clean. The gilding was worn away by the big winds of the winter and I was forced to spend money to replace it. Each week Number One wife goes to pay her respects to your ancestors and you will find everything as you would wish it."

"Thank you for your report, Elder Brother," Lai Tsin replied. He turned to Francie and said in English, "This is the second son of Ke Chungfen by his Number One wife. The others have long since left to find work in the cities, but he is lazy and he drinks too much. His little wife has a good heart and she would be better off without him, but she is Chinese and she will obey the traditions and stay with him, even though he beats her and treats her worse than a servant. That is the way it still is in China."

Francie smiled at the girl and she ducked shyly out of sight again behind her loutish husband. Lai Tsin handed a small leather purse to Elder Brother, who bowed and quickly thanked him, his harsh expression changing to an oily smile again.

The villagers had gathered and stood watching at a respectful distance, but they shrank back as they turned and walked past them, some hiding their faces from Francie's gaze, fearful that the Mandarin's companion was a devil.

They walked together along the path that ran through the rice fields and the merry-eyed children came running, unafraid of the *gwailo* woman because she was with the Mandarin and he always gave them coins and small presents from his pockets.

Together they climbed the rocky path to Lilin's ancestral hall and when they reached it Francie gasped in admiration. The vermillion walls shone like satin from the dozens of coats of paint carefully applied—coats of lacquer, each layer rubbed thin with glass paper before the next was applied, until it shone like the richest satin. The pierced carving was of the finest workmanship and the handmade tiles on the curved roof were an opalescent green. Inside the walls were inlaid with lacy patterns of mother-of-pearl and a marble slab inscribed in gold bore the names of Lilin and her two dead children.

Lai Tsin lit sticks of incense in the little bronze holders and kowtowed many times. Then he said to Francie, "I have brought you here because I can no longer live with the sins on my conscience. All I ask is your patience in listening to my story. I will tell you the two truths and then you may judge me as you wish." He took a deep breath and said, "Let us sit together in my mother's house, and I will tell you the deepest secrets of my soul."

She looked again at the tablet on the wall that was all that remained of Lilin and her children, and at Lai Tsin's gentle face and sad eyes and she said, "My dear friend, whatever is in your soul you may share it with me. Have no fear of my judgment, for who am I to judge others? And there is nothing you can say that would ever destroy our friendship and the love I have for you."

"We shall see," he said quietly.

The story was a long one and when he had finished there were tears in her eyes. Her heart ached for him and she put her arms around him in a loving embrace. "Thank you," she said quietly. "Everything you have done was only for good. I am honored to have the friendship of such a person."

They left the temple and walked back down the rocky path together, the dark, delicate Mandarin in his sumptuous robes and the tall, blond barbarian woman in her simple pleated blue skirt, back to the beautiful white steamship that would take them on the same journey Lai Tsin had taken all those years ago with Mayling, and which he would never take again.

# CHAPTER 36

◆

Francie sailed from Hong Kong for Europe the following week. She was to meet Annie in Paris, and then go in search of vines for the ranch. The British ship was filled with families returning on home-leave and the pallid hard-drinking men from the upriver rubber plantations in the jungles of Malaya who boarded at Singapore, and the sunburned tea-planters picked up at Colombo, as well as the usual sprinkling of foreign diplomats and businessmen.

As taipan of one of the richest hongs, Francie was seated at the captain's table along with the most important passengers, and she played her role perfectly. Each night she dressed discreetly but beautifully in one of her Paris dresses. She put jeweled jade ornaments in her high-piled blond hair, wore her wonderful pearls and her delicious jasmine scent. She smiled at her fellow guests and she spoke charmingly to them when they spoke to her, but she never encouraged their admiring glances and she never lingered after dinner. As she swept from the dining saloon back to the solitude of her stateroom, the men speculated about her in hushed tones but none of them ever made advances to her, because everyone knew she was the concubine of the great taipan, the Mandarin Lai Tsin.

Francie knew what they thought and she did not care, she only wanted to be alone. The ship steamed across the Indian Ocean, calling at Bombay and Port Said en route to the Mediterranean. Francie's spirits began to rise as she surveyed the lovely pine-fringed shores of southern France and she wished enviously that she had time to linger in the pretty little resort of Nice, where she disembarked. But she had a reservation at the Ritz in Paris, and Paris was the city she had always dreamed of visiting, ever since she was a child learning French from her governesses.

The manager showed her personally to her suite overlooking the rue Cambon; he knew her importance and her wealth and there were vases of tall red roses, bowls of fresh fruits, and a bottle of excellent champagne to greet her. She inspected her new quarters, thinking of Annie as she tested the perfect bed springs and inspected the fine linens and the impeccable bathrooms. Annie was considering opening a hotel here and she would be arriving in four days. Meanwhile, she was on her own with all of Paris as her playground and without wasting another second she left excitedly, guidebook in hand, to inspect its wonders.

Buck was driving to the American Embassy from the Elysées Palace, where as head of an important trade mission he had just had a meeting with the President of France. He was in his favorite city in the world, he'd been there exactly three days and he hadn't had a moment to enjoy it. But his bags were already packed and in an hour he would be back on the boat train on his way to Cherbourg and the liner *Normandie,* sailing that evening for New York. He gazed longingly out the window of the chauffeured limousine. The last time he had been in Paris was with Maryanne and all she had wanted to see was other important people.

He wanted to stroll leisurely across the city's beautiful bridges, not drive quickly over them, and to stop to admire the vistas instead of glimpsing them fleetingly from a car window; he wanted to linger on her chestnut-lined boulevards and browse in her fabulous museums. He wanted to drink the wine and eat long leisurely meals and admire her beautiful women. *And by God, he was going to.*

At the embassy, he quickly canceled his sailing, said good-bye to the ambassador, sent his bags over to the Crillon and strolled at a leisurely pace through the Place de la Concorde. He took a seat at a sidewalk café and ordered a Pernod, contemplating his freedom. He was alone in Paris and for once his time was his own. He glanced at the woman on his right absorbed in her guidebook and his heart jumped. Her back was toward him but he would have known her anywhere. It had been almost a year since he'd had tea with her in New York, and he still carried in his wallet the note she had sent him thanking him for the painting. He'd been to San Francisco several times since—more often than was strictly necessary for business, always in the hope of seeing her, but Annie Aysgarth had been as closed-mouthed as a sphinx; she'd always told him vaguely that

Francie was traveling or at her ranch. And now, six thousand miles away in Paris, fate had sent her to him.

She looked as beautiful as ever in an amethyst-color wool jacket braided in black; her short skirt showed off her slender black-stockinged legs and her hair was tied back with a large black silk bow.

Feeling his eyes on her, Francie turned and saw him. "Oh," she said. Her heart lurched and she dropped her guidebook in confusion. "Buck Wingate. What a surprise." She bit her lip, blushing like a girl as he picked up her book, took her hand in his and lifted it to his lips, French-style.

"I couldn't ask for a better one," he said, smiling into her eyes. "You look about nineteen years old with that bow in your hair, and lovelier than ever."

She laughed. "There's something about this city that makes a woman *feel* nineteen again. It must be something in the air—or maybe it's just the Pernod. But what are you doing here?"

"Oh, business." He grinned. "As a matter of fact, I'm playing hookey. I should have been on the *Normandie* sailing for New York tonight and suddenly I just couldn't bear the thought of it. I've been in Paris three days and I haven't been to any of my favorite haunts or eaten in any of my favorite bistros. So—I canceled the sailing, checked into the Crillon, and met you. Now, Francie Harrison, if that is not fate, I don't know what is."

She thought how nice he was, and how handsome; again she noticed his eyes crinkled at the corners when he laughed, and that his hair was a little grayer at the temples, and he was tall and lean and devastatingly attractive. She said cautiously, "I admit we seem destined to meet on street corners."

"Ah, but that's because it's impossible to meet you anywhere else. I've tried, but Annie Aysgarth won't let me near you."

Francie's heart skipped another happy beat; she couldn't deny the little crackles of electricity between them. She knew she should say good-bye to him right now but she'd not felt like this since Edward. And besides, she was alone in Paris, the loveliest and most romantic city in the world.

She met his eyes and said conspiratorially, "Annie won't be here for another four days," and they both laughed.

"Would madame care for a guide?" he cried. "I am at your service. We'll start right away." He held out his hand and she took it feeling like the girl he had said she looked instead of the mature woman she was. She let herself be swept happily into a taxi to inspect some of the wonders of the Louvre, and then on to Notre Dame, where they heard a choir sing a soaring anthem beneath the glowing light from the famous rose window, and then on to browse through the piles of secondhand books at the *bouquineries* lining the banks of the River Seine, stopping occasionally in their breathless whirl to drink reviving rich black coffee out of small thick white cups. And when he asked her where she would like to go for dinner she said unhesitatingly, "Maxim's," and he said, "Maxim's it is."

She dithered in front of her closet in an agony of indecision, lifting out dress after dress, holding them anxiously up against her, gazing in the mirror then tossing them onto the bed. Finally, she decided on an ankle-length dinner dress of deep aquamarine crepe de chine, cut on the bias so that it just skimmed the body. The long, tight sleeves were cut into points at the wrists and she clipped a pair of leaf-shaped diamond pins at the corners of the wide square neckline. She swept up her hair and pinned it with the jade combs, then she took it down again and tied it back with a ribbon the way he'd admired it that afternoon. And when she was ready she looked at her reflection in the mirror and knew she had dressed to please him.

She kept him waiting ten minutes while she prowled her suite in case he thought her too eager, and then she went downstairs to meet him. He was waiting in the foyer and she thought, breathlessly, that he must surely be the handsomest man in Paris, and he looked adoringly at her and made her feel like the loveliest woman in the world. The maître d' at Maxims knew a pair of lovers when he saw one and he sat them in a discreet booth and immediately suggested champagne.

Francie gazed happily around the famous restaurant and its glamorous patrons and thought that if she hadn't met Buck Wingate she would have been dining alone at her hotel. "I can't believe my luck meeting you," she said impetuously. And he looked steadily at her and said, "Nor can I." The sexual electricity crackled like lightning between them and she glanced shyly away.

They drank a toast to Paris and ate tiny Belon oysters from a silvery bed of ice and tasted morsels of each other's dishes. He told her about his trade mission and she told him about her visit to Hong Kong, but she didn't tell him the Mandarin's secrets—or her own. Instead she tasted his white-chocolate mousse and her eyes rounded with pleasure, making him laugh. She thought it must be the champagne fizzing in her veins that made her feel so frivolous and light-hearted. In all her life she couldn't ever remember laughing like this with a man before, not even with Edward.

She glanced idly around the crowded restaurant. There wasn't a single person she knew and she turned to him, one eyebrow raised. "I wonder what people would say if they saw the Senator from California dining at Maxims with the notorious Miss Harrison?"

He took her hand across the table and said quietly, "They would say he's a very lucky man."

"And what would Maryanne say?"

He thought for a while and then he said seriously, "Maryanne and I do not love each other, I doubt we ever really did. I've thought of asking her for a divorce more than once. In fact, the last time was on Christmas morning. Remember? I said I would be thinking of you?"

She nodded and he said, "Well, I was. Oh, in theory all the right Christmas elements were there, the tree, the log fires, the gifts, the squabbling children and the so-called friends, but like our life together it was all an expensive facade. It was all such a sham I wished I were anywhere else but there." Her blue eyes were gazing into his and he said softly, "I wished I were with you."

She was silent and he took her note from his pocket and unfolded it. It was creased and worn and he held it out to her and said, "Remember this? I've carried it around with me ever since. And believe me, I've asked myself a thousand times, Why? But it's only now that I think I have the answer."

He put the note on the table in between them and he said quietly, "Francie Harrison, this may sound crazy, but I'm afraid I must be in love with you."

Their eyes locked; she felt calm and elated at the same time. When she had met him in New York she had refused to admit the possibility that the spark they had felt could be anything so wonderful, so irrevocable as "love" and now she shook her head. "How can it be possible, we hardly know each other?"

"Time has nothing to do with it."

"Then maybe it's just the magic of Paris . . ."

He took her hand and kissed it. "It could be Detroit . . ."

"Then how do we know it's *true*?"

He kissed her fingers again and little tingles ran down her spine. "You don't question fate, you take what it offers and are glad."

She looked at him frightened, and said, "I must go."

He called the waiter and took care of the bill. Then they walked from the elegant restaurant hardly noticing that people turned to watch the handsome couple, speculating on who they were. She was silent in the cab on the way back to the hotel, aware of his eyes on her. She was afraid; she had only known two men in her life and she didn't know if what she felt was love or not. She thought of what he had just said about not questioning fate and when he walked with her to the gilt-caged elevator at the Ritz, she said, "Do you think people would talk if I asked the senator to my suite for coffee?"

He shrugged and took her hand. "Let them," he said happily.

The silk-shaded lamps had been lit in her elegant rooms and the bottle of champagne still waited in the ice bucket. He opened it and poured her a glass, then filled his own and lifted it and said, "I have another toast, Francie. To love."

She drank the toast and then she put down her glass and took his hand and walked with him into the bedroom. The heavy brocade curtains were drawn across the tall windows and the lamplight cast a golden glow across her face as she looked at him. "I don't know what to do," she said helplessly.

"You don't need to know, my darling," he said, folding her in his arms.

He thought that undressing Francie was like unfolding the petals of a flower, each layer of soft rustling pastel silk sliding from her body until she was naked, and her shyness touched his heart and her beauty, his senses. He took her in his arms and held her close, he caressed her velvet skin and she clung to him. She loved the feel of his body against hers, his lips on her eyelids, her hair, her throat. She clung passionately to him as he entered her and felt him trembling in her arms as he made tender love to her.

"I can't bear to leave you now that I've found you," he said later as they lay still languorously entwined. "I think all my life I must have been looking for you." He tilted her face to his and said quietly, "Don't ever go away."

"Shhh"—she put a finger softly on his lips—"you mustn't say that." She struggled from his arms and sat up, pushing her long tumbled hair back from her face as she looked at him. "Let's just take this little time together and be happy."

She was sitting with her arms clasped around her knees, her long blond hair fell across her shoulders, covering her beautiful breasts with streamers of gold, and her troubled blue eyes were fixed seriously on him. He thought how unaffected she was and how unaware of her own beauty, and he compared her quickly with Maryanne's artifice, her false smiles and chilly dismissal, and he knew he could not give her up. "I don't care," he said, snatching her back into his arms, "I only want you."

He was holding her close and she felt loved and protected, even though she knew it was all impossible, it should never have happened. But she never wanted to move from his arms, from this bed, from Paris. . . . She pushed the cold reality of who she was and who he was to the back of her mind. She would take her happiness while she could, however fleeting. "Just for now, Buck," she said happily. "Just for these few days."

"Forever," he promised, covering her face with passionate kisses. "I'll never let you go." And as he made love to her again she hoped just a little bit, in her heart, that it might be true.

They couldn't bear to leave each other's side. He sent for his bags from the Crillon and moved into the suite next door to her at the Ritz and her sumptuous bed became the center of their little universe. Every now and then they ventured forth, sipping Pernod in Left Bank cafés, exploring the narrow streets of Saint-Louis-en-l'Ile, arguing over paintings in art gallery windows and dining in tiny candle-lit bistros where monsieur *le patron* was chef and madame, his wife, the waitress, and where there was nobody to notice them as they lingered over a glass of red wine, holding hands and gazing into each other's eyes without any thought for the future.

And in those long evenings she told him about her life, holding nothing back, waiting for his judgment of her. He looked lovingly at her and said, "My poor Francie, you've had to be so strong. I hope life will never be so harsh to you again."

On their final night he watched as she combed her hair. It gleamed like satin and he ran his hand wonderingly across it and said, "Promise me you'll never cut it. It's like a treasure trove of gold."

Francie's clouded sapphire eyes met his in the mirror. "I promise," she said sadly.

He was leaving at six to catch the boat train and then the liner back to America, but both of them knew it was more than that, and that at six o'clock he was going back to reality. They lay sleepless in each other's arms savoring each precious fleeting minute, but the separation loomed over them and Francie told herself desolately it would be forever.

"I can't leave you," he whispered as the time grew near. "Don't you understand, Francie? My life with Maryanne is false, she doesn't care for me and I don't care for her. I've never felt like this about any woman before. I didn't know there could be such happiness. Please say you'll stay with me. I'll get a divorce and we'll be married; just tell me yes. We'll buy a pretty little house in Washington and I'll look after you and love you forever."

Her whole being yearned toward him, she could almost taste the delicious new life they would share together. She thought that because his life with Maryanne was meaningless then just maybe it was all possible. But then she remembered Buck was a public figure—he was a man heading for the top and a scandalous divorce would wreck his career. And she was a scandalous woman.

She covered his mouth with tender kisses, stifling his words, counting their final minutes together, and when the time came for him to go she cowered naked in their bed as he packed his bags, telling herself she mustn't cry and that she should be glad for the happiness she had been given.

His bags were in the hall and she heard him instructing the porter and then his footsteps as he walked back to her bedroom. He stood in the doorway, his eyes devouring her. He looked the way he had when she first met him, handsome, well-dressed, powerful—a man with a future. She knelt on the tumbled bed, the sheet covering her nakedness, waiting for him to say good-bye. He walked toward her and wrapped the silken strands of her hair around his hands like golden chains as she tilted her face to him. "This isn't the end, Francie," he promised, his eyes burning into hers. And then he strode quickly away.

Annie stared suspiciously at Francie. There was a hectic flush on her usually pale cheeks and a nervous air about her that was different. She had dragged her from one Paris couturier to another, buying recklessly at Patou and Lelong, Molyneux and Chanel, and now they were sitting in Madame Vionnet's dove-gray salon while models paraded sinuously in front of them. There was nothing there to suit Annie's rounded figure. Vionnet made sleek, easy, graceful clothes in clinging crepe de chine and supple satins, but they were perfect for Francie's tall, streamlined body and long legs, and Annie shook her head, marveling as Francie ordered a dozen dresses in different colors. "Where on earth are you going to wear all these things?" she asked. "You go to Hong Kong once every few years, and when you're in San Francisco you are working hard for your charities and the rest of the time you spend on the ranch. I hardly think you'll be wearing Madame Vionnet's sugar-plum slipper satin to tend your vines?"

Francie shrugged and gave her a too-brilliant smile. "Oh, I don't know, they're all just so pretty," she answered vaguely, but she knew she was buying them because Buck would have loved her in them. It was impossible to put him out of her mind and impossible not to think of herself as part of his life. She had received a cablegram from him every day since he had left and they all said the same thing: "I love you." She was playing with fire, but if Buck ever came back to her she would not be able to send him away again.

Annie said suspiciously, "You haven't met a man, have you?" and Francie blushed. "I see," Annie laughed, pleased. "Then why haven't you told me about him?"

Francie bit her lip, staring embarrassed at her hands. "I can't."

"That means he's married." Annie sighed. "Oh dear, Francie, what have you gotten yourself into now?"

"Annie, it's Buck Wingate." The news brimmed from her lips. "It's like a miracle. I mean, love *can* be a miracle, can't it? It's not like with Edward when I just fell slowly in love with him. This is *Love,* Annie." She almost shouted the word, and the vendeuses and the models turned to smile—love was love in any language. Francie dropped her voice to a conspiratorial whisper as she told Annie quickly about her whirlwind affair.

"And you sent him away?" Annie asked, amazed.

"I sent him away," she repeated, her blue eyes searching anxiously for approval.

"Then why all the new clothes? It seems to me you might be expecting him back again."

"Yes . . . no . . . oh, Annie, I don't know. If he came back . . . oh, what should I do?"

A vendeuse interrupted with the account for Madame Harrison to sign, and then they left the salon and strolled thoughtfully down the avenue together. "Buck fell for you the minute he saw you at my party," Annie said. "I knew it even if you didn't. But everything's against it, Francie, it's not just Maryanne, it's his career. You realize he would have to give it up if he married you?"

Francie hung her head, she had hoped against hope that Annie would pull an answer out of her practical bag of tricks, but there was none. A man's work was his life. "I know," she said sadly, "that's why I sent him away. I can't let him throw away a brilliant future. Oh, but Annie, what if he comes back again?"

Annie looked compassionately at her. "Let's just wait and see, love, shall we?" she said.

They spent the next few days looking at hotels for Annie and she decided the French had their own style and she declined to compete, and then they took the train to Bordeaux. They visited half a dozen châteaux and tasted a hundred wines and bought new vines for Francie's ranch, but still she couldn't forget him, and she hurried Annie back to Cherbourg and onto a liner to New York a week earlier than they had planned.

In San Francisco she hung all her beautiful Paris dresses in the closet and waited for him to call. A week passed, then two. She told herself she wouldn't call him, she must not. After three weeks she steeled herself to the fact that it was over and left, heartbroken, for the ranch.

The weather was cold and windy but the sky was a clear hard blue. She put on her riding britches and flannel checkered shirt and flung an old navy wool sweater over her shoulders. She saddled up her favorite Appaloosa and rode over the hills with the cold wind tugging at her hair and stinging her cheeks, but she welcomed it—anything to take away the ache of new loneliness.

Hours later she rode the tired mare slowly back again, wishing she had never met Buck Wingate. And then she turned into the courtyard and there he was.

She was off the horse and in his arms in an instant. "You shouldn't be here," she said, her voice muffled against his shoulder.

"You're wrong," he said. "This is where I belong." He held her at arm's length, looking at her. "You won't send me away again?"

She shook her head. "I can't. But I'll never take you away from your wife, Buck. Or your career. I'll just be happy to see you, whenever we can."

And she thought as he held her close, that for all the Mandarin's teaching, she was still only a weak and helpless woman when it came to love.

# CHAPTER 37

## ◆

## *1930*

Maryanne Wingate was a busy woman, she was rich and spoiled and used to having things her own way, but she wasn't a fool. She suspected Buck was having an affair and at first she said nothing, supposing it would pass, as these things did. Not that she was worried: she told herself men needed the sort of women they had affairs with, women they paid for in small trinkets or cold hard cash, not *her* sort of woman. And she knew the Bucks of the world *never married* women like that. Her position as his wife was inviolate, but as months passed and the weekends away began to grow more frequent and the door between their bedrooms remained firmly shut, she began to get frightened. A casual affair was one thing, but a major indiscretion would be a disaster.

She thought angrily of all the time and effort she had put into furthering his career and decided she was going to get to the bottom of things. She called a very discreet detective agency and had her husband followed. She was shocked at the speed with which she received her answer—it seemed Buck hardly bothered to cover his tracks. And she was even more shocked when she found out the name of her rival.

She fumed silently for days, pacing like a maddened panther around her room. Buck was away again—at the ranch with *her.* He'd been going there for over a year now and she thanked God that at least the ranch was at the back of beyond and they weren't flaunting their relationship in front of all San Francisco. She remembered seeing Francie Harrison at that party and she thought angrily that she was beautiful, and with a reputation like hers she wasn't surprised Buck had fallen for her. But now if she wasn't to lose everything she had worked for, she had to do something about it.

\* \* \*

Francie lived for their weekends at the ranch, it was their home—hers and Buck's: her room was now their room, his clothes hung in her closet and his riding boots stood in the hallway next to hers. His nervous black thoroughbred shared the stables with her Appaloosa mare, his books filled her shelves, his papers filled her desk, and his shaving things her bathroom. It was exactly two years since they had met in Paris and she was more in love with him than ever, her whole world revolved around the stolen hours he spent with her. She had kept her promise to herself that she would never ask for more, only now things were different. She needed him.

It was Friday evening and he was on his way from San Francisco. She paced the shady front porch gazing hopefully down the driveway, sighing happily as she quickly counted her blessings: she had this beautiful ranch with her dairy cows and her cattle and her precious vines; she had her wonderful house in San Francisco, and her charity work; she had wealth and two good friends, Annie and the Mandarin; she had a man who loved her and now she was having his child.

Her face clouded as she thought about her beautiful Ollie; she would gladly have given everything she had if she could have brought him back, the circumstances of his death were too painful to bear and she kept them in the back of her memory, but he was always in her thoughts, and she and Annie often talked of him. She remembered the night he had been born, here at the ranch, with only Annie and Lai Tsin to help. And now she was to have another fatherless child.

Her happiness drained quickly away as she faced the facts. She would never have asked Buck to divorce Maryanne for her own sake, but now there was his child to think of. She sank down into the porch swing, closing her eyes as the old familiar loneliness crept over her, wondering what to do.

Buck saw her as he turned the bend in the drive in the little Ford and he honked the horn, sending birds whirring excitedly from the trees and setting the dogs barking in the stables. He swung into the courtyard with a squeal of tires, leapt from the car and strode up the steps to the porch, marveling that his heart still gave a little lurch when he saw her. She stepped into his arms and they hugged each other tightly. "It's been too long," he murmured into her soft hair, "a month since I've seen you." They walked hand in hand into the house and he glanced around appreciatively; the ranch was the one place he knew that never seemed to change. Oh sure, an extra room was added here and there, a new painting was hung on the parlor wall, maybe new curtains at the windows, but the heart of the place never changed. The polished elm floorboards shone, the window-panes glittered in the sunlight, big bunches of wildflowers were crammed into innumerable vases and the house smelled of honey-suckle and lavender and Hattie's cherry pies baking in the kitchen.

"God, I love this place," he said, his voice full of yearning. "Every time I'm here I ask myself why I ever leave." He poked his head in the kitchen door and called, "Hi, Hattie. What's for dinner?"

"Hi, Mr. Buck. Why, it's nothing but southern fried chicken and fried bananas, just your fav'rit, that's all."

Her face split in a wide grin and he grinned back. "That's why I love ya, Hattie, you surely know the way to a man's heart."

"*Some* men's hearts," she sniffed, going back to her stove, but she was smiling. Hattie was Francie's housekeeper and she approved of Mr. Buck, "Marry him, Miss Francie," she said firmly and often. "He's the best thing ever happen'd to you."

"But he's already married," Francie protested and Hattie would sniff disparagingly and say, "A man can get a divorce, cain't he? And you're as good as married right now—'cept in the eyes of the Lord."

"You're right, Hattie," Francie had said wonderingly. "We are as good as married." And she often consoled herself with that thought in the long days and nights when Buck was in Washington—with Maryanne.

He stripped off his clothes and headed into the shower, singing tunelessly at the top of his voice and Francie laughed. "Guess what?" he called.

"What?"

"I've got something for you. It's in my bag."

Her eyes lit up. "A present?"

"It's special, very special." He stepped into the bedroom, a towel wrapped around his loins. "I hope you're gonna like it."

She opened his bag, staring at the small gold box and then at him. "Go on, open it," he said gently. His smiling eyes were fixed on her face as she untied the ribbon and lifted the lid. It was a perfect miniature portrait of Ollie. It was exactly the way she remembered him and she burst into tears.

"Oh God, Francie, I'm sorry." He sat beside her on the bed staring anxiously at her. "I had it copied from the photograph you keep in the bedroom. Annie has the same photograph and she lent it to me. I thought the artist had caught his expression so beautifully, I really thought it would please you. Oh God, Francie, I didn't mean to upset you."

She shook her head, her eyes still brimming. "It *is* Ollie, and that's why I'm crying. It's just the most wonderful, wonderful present."

Somehow the time didn't seem right to speak of the new baby and the next morning she watched sadly as Buck hurried back to San Francisco. She knew he was staying at Aysgarth's as usual and she waved good-bye to him again, envying Annie who was free to speak to him and even dine publicly with him without causing a scandal. The ranch felt lonely and impulsively she decided to return to San Francisco too.

Harry Harrison saw her car pull up outside her house later that day. He was just leaving and he stood at the bottom of his steps watching as she strode quickly indoors without glancing his way. She wore a simple jacket and skirt and she drove an unpretentious Ford, but she had the easy confident air of a woman rich in her own right, which, goddamn it, she was.

He fumed silently about her as he walked to the Pacific Union Club, thinking about the Lai Tsin Corporation and how, thanks to the Mandarin's astute business brain, it had only been mildly affected by the stock-market crash while he himself had damn near gone under. He supposed by most standards he was still considered "rich," but not by his own. Thanks to decent management—again not his own—the Harrison Mercantile Bank had survived, but he was no longer chairman of the board and had little say about its day-to-day affairs and he certainly couldn't touch its assets; but his commodities brokerage business had taken an irreversible beating and his investments had disappeared like melting snow.

He had what was left of his trust fund and his remaining blue-chip stocks but his major investment, the phosphate mines in South America, were not coming through as promised. Still, he was certain they would soon, if only he could hang in; one day he would recoup the Harrison fortune and he would be like his grandfather and stash it away in gold bars in the bank vaults where nobody could touch it. Meanwhile, his father must be turning in his grave, seeing Francie flaunting her ill-gotten gains and her illicit relationship with that damned Chinese.

The club was crowded but his restless eyes immediately spotted Buck Wingate in conversation with a couple of prominent San Francisco businessmen and he strolled over and slapped him on the shoulder.

"Afternoon, Buck," he said genially, nodding a greeting to the other men. "I can see you're busy right now but I'd like a word with you later, if I may?"

The last person Buck wanted to see was Harry, but his firm still handled his trust and he had no choice. "I'll be back at Aysgarth's around five," he said coldly. "Why don't you call me then."

Harry nodded. He'd caught the chill in Buck's voice and it angered him. As he turned away and ordered himself a bourbon he asked himself what goddamn right Buck Wingate had to be so goddamn superior when *he* was the client, goddamn it. The Wingates had made a fortune handling the Harrison affairs over the years. Wingate had just better remember that. He sat brooding over his drink thinking that first it was Francie looking so goddamn superior and then Buck, and he asked himself who the hell they thought they were?

Buck was in San Francisco alone and Annie was surprised when later that day she saw Maryanne Wingate walk into the lobby and speak to the desk clerk. She knew she wasn't expected because when Mrs. Wingate accompanied her husband they always requested the royal suite. She noted that even after her journey, Maryanne looked uncreased and coolly beautiful in a lipstick-red coat with a wide, silver-fox collar and a matching fur hat.

"Mrs. Wingate, what a pleasant surprise," she said. "We weren't expecting you this time."

Maryanne looked at her coldly. She knew Annie Aysgarth was Francie Harrison's friend and that she probably knew about her and Buck. "I decided to surprise my husband," she said with an innocent smile. "The poor man travels so much, and I know he misses me. A man under constant pressure the way he is needs the support of his wife, don't you think?"

Annie nodded pleasantly, but there was something about Maryanne's smile that sent little warning bells ringing in her head. "I'm sure you're right, Mrs. Wingate," she said, "though I wish I had known because I would have kept your favorite suite. I'm afraid it's already taken. Perhaps the Knaresborough will do instead? It's not quite as big, but it has the same view across the square and the gardens."

"Whatever," Maryanne agreed uncharacteristically quickly. "Just move Mr. Wingate's things in there along with mine."

As she escorted her to the lift Annie had the feeling in her bones that something was up; normally Maryanne would have refused to take anything smaller. She was just too easy, all sweetness and light as she made small talk about the weather.

Maryanne treated her to another of those cold, innocent smiles. "I think I'll take a rest, Miss Aysgarth. Could you see that I'm not disturbed? The maid can unpack for me later. If you could just quickly send up some tea, I'd be so grateful."

As soon as Annie had closed the door behind her Maryanne flung off her bright red coat and fur hat. She took her keys from her alligator purse and unlocked her big leather valise; she took out a simple black coat, shaking it from mounds of tissue paper her maid had packed it in, and took a wide-brimmed black hat from one of the hat boxes.

She hurried into the bathroom and quickly applied face powder and lipstick, she brushed her short blond hair and then tucked it beneath the black hat. There was a knock on the door and she swung guiltily from the mirror, but it was just the maid with the tea and she called out to her to leave it on the table. She waited until she heard the door close again and then she put on the black coat, checked her appearance in the mirror again, picked up her purse and walked to the door.

She looked quickly up and down the empty corridor and then she ran to the emergency exit and pulled open the fire door, hurrying down the drab concrete staircase, counting the floors until she was dizzy. When she reached the bottom she glanced quickly around and then hurried out through the back exit. It was the first time in her life she had ever left by the servants' door and she pulled her black hat low over her brow, praying no one would see her as she turned on Taylor Street toward Nob Hill.

The climb was a steep one and her heart was thudding as she walked along California Street looking for Francie's house. When she saw it she stopped for a moment to collect herself and then she strode firmly up the steps and rang the bell.

Walking back from the club, Harry glanced with surprise at the woman ringing his sister's doorbell. There were not many visitors to the Lai Tsin residence, but there was something eerily familiar about the woman in black. Moving stealthily into the shadows he watched as the door was opened by the Chinese houseboy and the woman spoke to him. The boy held the door wider and she turned and glanced quickly right and left before stepping inside. Harry gave a low, surprised whistle. What the hell was Maryanne Wingate doing visiting his notorious sister? Whatever it was she was up to no good. It wasn't like Maryanne to lurk on anybody's doorstep *and* she had been dressed in what amounted to a disguise, with her coat collar turned up and that hat pulled down over her eyes.

Intrigued, he hurried back to his own house. He stood at the first-floor window, watching, telling himself he must be mistaken, it couldn't be Maryanne. But he waited until she came out again to make sure.

Francie was in her room when the houseboy told her Mrs. Wingate was waiting downstairs to see her. She stared speechlessly at him; her stomach leapt with shock and then tightened sickeningly. "Mrs. Wingate?" she repeated, hoping he had made a mistake.

He nodded solemnly. "Mrs. Wingate, Miss Francie. She's waiting in the hall."

Francie got slowly to her feet; she knew there could only be one reason Maryanne Wingate was in her hall. She looked down at her short pleated blue wool skirt and her simple white blouse, wondering wildly whether she should change into something grander to meet her rival. Then with a quick shrug she said, "Show Mrs. Wingate into the drawing room, take her coat, and tell her I shall be with her in just a minute."

She sat trembling at her dresser, staring at her own frightened face. Then she brushed her long smooth hair and tied it back with a velvet ribbon. She added a touch of jasmine scent, took a deep breath, and walked to the door. She hesitated, her hands pressed against her belly and the still-invisible roundness that was Buck's child, and then she opened the door and walked slowly down the beautiful curving stair-case.

Ah Fong, the houseboy, opened the drawing room door for her. Maryanne was standing by the window looking out across California Street. She glanced up and the two women stared at each other, sizing each other up.

"Mrs. Wingate?" Francie said politely, but she did not offer her hand and neither did Maryanne.

"I'll come straight to the point, Miss Harrison," she said. "Of course you know why I am here." Francie said nothing and Maryanne paced from the window to the marble fireplace; her glance traveled slowly over the luxurious room with its Oriental carpets and works of art. "You have a beautiful home, Miss Harrison," she observed coldly, "and as you are a very rich woman I shall not insult you by asking if it was my husband's money that paid for all this luxury."

Francie's chin tilted warningly but she said nothing and Maryanne continued.

"It is well known," she said in her calm cool voice, "that men of my husband's age often succumb to"—she hesitated, searching for exactly the right words—"a *'crise de coeur.'* Their lives are so full of work and pressures and family and they suddenly need a change. A sexual affair is very soothing to a man's ego, Miss Harrison. Sometimes I think they are even vainer than women." Her smile was almost conspiratorial as she looked at Francie. "But then, I'm sure you know how they are just like naughty children really."

Her gaze hardened as she looked at Francie in her simple skirt and blouse, unmadeup and with a ribbon holding back her blond hair. "I must admit you are not what I expected," she added. "I had thought someone more flamboyant, a notorious woman who enjoyed the intrigue and suspense of an illicit romance." She looked away and paced back to the window.

Francie stared at Buck's wife: she was beautiful, there was no denying that; and cold, there was also no denying that; and in her impeccable gray wool day dress she looked every inch the lady.

"What is it you want to say, Mrs. Wingate?" she asked, surprised at how calm her own voice was when she was churning inside with fear.

Maryanne swung around from the window. "I am here to appeal to your intelligence, Miss Harrison. I do not want to know the sordid details of your relationship with my husband, but there are things about him that you ought to know. *That you must know.* For *his* sake. Tell me, have you ever considered his children?"

Francie's heart jumped, there was no way Maryanne could know that she was pregnant, even Buck didn't know yet. . . .

"They are still young, Miss Harrison, and they have a right to expect their father's presence as they grow up. They need his help and guidance"—her eyes pierced Francie—"to say nothing of his support. How do you think this scandalous affair would affect them?" She paused for a moment, letting her point sink in and then she said, "Of course, I shall not speak of the hurt this has inflicted on me, but I will mention something more important—not only to me, but to Buck. And to our country." She sat down on the edge of the chair opposite Francie, her hands clasped around her shapely knees, her eyebrows raised in interrogation. "Does he speak to you of his work?" She didn't wait for an answer, just shrugged and carried on. "No, no of course he wouldn't, I'm sure you had other things to talk about. Then I must tell you that his work means everything to Buck. He is a *dedicated* man, a political animal through and through. He *lives* for politics. You have known him such a short while, how could you possibly be expected to understand these things? But, you see, I have known him all my life, his father used to bring him to my home when he was just a boy. We were a family of politicians and Buck rarely bothered to play with us children. Oh no, he was always hanging around the library, listening to them talk. I guess he absorbed politics by osmosis—through his skin, and I must say my family encouraged him. And as he grew up they saw he had a big future ahead of him. *Take politics away from Buck, Miss Harrison, and you might as well stick a knife into his back.*" She paused again to let her words sink in. Francie stared at her, mesmerized. "A scandal like this"—she shrugged, lifting her arms expressively outward and up— "a scandal like this affair would finish him in politics."

Francie looked away from her, down at the pattern on the carpet. "I understand," she said quietly.

Maryanne sighed. "I hope so, Miss Harrison. I do hope so. For Buck's sake, not my own." She paused, a gleam of triumph in her eyes. "Buck has a brilliant political future in front of him. The political world is Buck's oyster. It just wouldn't be right—for any of us— to jeopardize that."

Francie's heart sank, she thought of the child she was carrying and realized how wide the gap was between Buck's life and her own. Their time together at the ranch, which she had thought so real, was just play-acting, and reality was the man with the brilliant political future ahead of him, married to the perfect woman who gave him children who had the right to bear his name. She looked at Maryanne Brattle Wingate, so confident of her "rightness," confident of her life, of her claims on her husband, and she knew she could never ask Buck to give it all up. She would never be the one to put the knife in his back and take away all the things he had worked so hard to achieve.

There was sadness in her eyes, but her voice was calm and quiet as she said, "Thank you for coming to see me, Mrs. Wingate. I realize how hard it must have been for you. Of course I shall tell Buck that I do not wish to see him again."

Maryanne couldn't hide the triumph in her voice as she got to her feet and said, "And, of course, I'm sure I can rely on your discretion. You know how important it is for him."

"Naturally." Francie walked with her to the hall. She watched as Maryanne put on her coat and hat and then she said quietly, "Ah Fong will show you out." She left Maryanne and walked up the beautiful flying staircase to her room and lay tearless on the bed.

She heard the door close downstairs and she stared at the ceiling, imagining Mrs. Wingate hurrying down the front steps and back down Nob Hill, back to her husband and their wonderful future. And as the bitter tears flowed she asked herself why fortune treated her so harshly. And she felt again the way she had when she was a child, when her terrifying father towered over her, the strap in his hand. It was then that she had first realized that it was a man's world and she was merely a woman.

# CHAPTER 38

◆

Annie watched with astonishment as Maryanne Wingate hurried across the lobby to the elevator, tapping her foot impatiently as she waited for it to appear. She watched her step inside, glancing nervously around until the doors closed and she was swept upward out of sight. Maryanne had often stayed at Aysgarth's over the years and in all that time she had never seen her look the way she did now, in that anonymous black coat and hat, scuttling through the lobby of her elegant hotel like a guilty wife.

Annie shook her head. Something was wrong and she wished she knew what, because that feeling in her bones was growing stronger.

Fifteen minutes later, Harry Harrison entered the hotel. He walked up to the desk, told the clerk Mr. Wingate was expecting him, and asked the name of his suite. Annie stared suspiciously after him as he took the elevator. She asked the desk clerk where he was heading and was stunned when she heard it was the Wingates' suite. She went into the elegant drawing room and took a seat near the entrance, where she could monitor everyone who came or went, and then she ordered tea and settled back to wait.

Maryanne was just stepping from the shower when the doorbell rang. She knew it must be room service with the coffee she had ordered and she called "Come in." Coffee was her only vice, and she really needed a cup now. This afternoon had been quite a strain, though she knew she had handled it supremely well. "Leave the tray on the table," she called out, patting herself dry with a soft peach-colored towel with an inch-thick pile. She had to give Annie Aysgarth credit, whatever her background was she knew "the best" and she provided only "the best"; even in towels. She hummed a little tune as she slipped on her blue velvet robe and pushed her narrow aristocratic feet into matching velvet slippers embroidered with a family crest that she had specially made at an exclusive men's shop on Jermyn Street in London. She was still humming happily to herself when she emerged from the bathroom and came face to face with Harry Harrison.

"My God," she said, startled, "how did you get in?"

"I rang the bell, you called 'come in,' so I did. Sorry I startled you, Maryanne, but Buck said to meet him here about five-ish. I guess maybe I'm a little early."

Maryanne sighed. She didn't bother to pretend she was pleased to see him; Harry was not one of her favorite people. In fact, Harry was nothing but trouble and why Buck even bothered with him was beyond her comprehension. The doorbell rang again and this time it was the waiter with the coffee; he placed it on the table and left.

Maryanne glanced at Harry with annoyance. She had wanted to be alone when Buck came in, she wanted to surprise him with the new, sexier woman she was about to become—for his sake, not hers. As she poured coffee, she thought with a little smile how good it was for one's ego to vanquish a mistress and reclaim one's husband, it was almost worth going through it, it made her feel so good. "Coffee?" she asked, holding out the cup to Harry.

"Thanks, Maryanne." He sat opposite her on the sofa, admiring her with his eyes and she stared haughtily back at him.

"Why do you want to see Buck?" she asked.

He sipped the hot coffee, regarding her more thoughtfully, and then he said, "I'll tell you why, if you'll tell me exactly what you were doing at my sister's this afternoon."

She felt the color drain from her face; he had caught her completely off guard and she set down her cup with a trembling hand. "You must be mistaken," she said, frantically gathering her scattered wits back together. "I don't know your sister. Ah, one moment, I tell a lie." She held up her hand and tilted her head back, thinking. "Yes, I did meet her once, at a party Annie Aysgarth gave. We were introduced, I believe." She shrugged delicately as if it were too unimportant to recall.

Harry was enjoying himself and he smiled. "My butler saw you, too, and my houseman," he lied. "And even under that hat"—he waved at the black coat and hat lying with her purse on the chair where she had thrown them—"even under that hat, there was no denying it was you. I wonder," he said, putting things as delicately to her as she had to Francie earlier, "I wonder if dear, devoted, upright Buck has developed an intimate acquaintance with my notorious sister."

He laughed at her shocked face. "Right in on one, I'd say," he chortled, setting down his cup.

"You're talking nonsense, Harry, just as you always do," she said icily, but her voice shook just a little, and he was the sort of man who noticed those details.

"Oh I think not," he said, still smiling. "Not after what the detective report said."

She stared at him aghast, her face the color of chalk. "The detective report?"

He patted his pocket, smiling gently. "You must remember to keep your door locked, Maryanne, and not to invite just anybody in without first seeing who they are. You never know, it might be a thief. And your purse was just lying there, so temptingly open. . . ."

Maryanne glanced at her purse and then at him; she closed her eyes, feeling sick. "You bastard," she said quietly.

"Oh, I don't know," he said easily. "I don't mean any harm. All I want is a little help—from you and Buck. Just a word or two in the right place, that's all, maybe to your father and the right banker—you know the scene. I have these phosphate mines, you see, down in South America, and I need a little financial backing. Look upon it as an investment, Maryanne. That's all it is—an investment. Because one day soon this mine will supply the world with phosphates and it'll earn you a fortune."

"I already have a fortune," she told him coldly.

He shrugged as he stood up to leave. "Tell you what, I'll let you talk to Buck for me," he said, strolling toward the door. "I'm sure you know what to say to him better than I do. I'll just leave it in your capable hands, Maryanne."

She looked murderously at him smiling at her from the door, and he patted his pocket holding the detective's report meaningfully. She could hear him laughing as he walked down the hallway, as though life were just one big joke. And she knew this time the joke was on her.

Buck was in the lobby waiting for the elevator as Harry stepped out. "Harry," he said with surprise.

"Sorry I missed you, Buck," Harry called as he stepped around him on his way to the exit. "I'm in a bit of a rush. But I spoke with Maryanne, she'll tell you all about it."

Buck turned to watch him, a puzzled look on his face. *"Maryanne?"* he said.

Annie hurried across to him. "Oh, Buck, I'm afraid Mr. Harrison's gone and spoiled your little surprise. Mrs. Wingate told me she thought it would be nice if she joined you. I've transferred you to the Knaresborough Suite on the same floor."

They looked at each other for a moment. Annie had often met Buck with Francie at the ranch. She understood about their affair and she never let the fact that she did not approve affect her liking for him as a man. But they never spoke of it between them.

He nodded as he stepped into the elevator. "Thanks, Annie," he said wearily. It had been a long day and he was too beat to speculate on just why Maryanne had chosen to join him in San Francisco, or what Harry Harrison wanted.

But Annie suspected why Maryanne was there and she was not in the least bit surprised when Francie's houseboy, Ah Fong, arrived a short while later with a note marked "private and personal" to be delivered to Senator Wingate when he was alone.

Annie Aysgarth took the note and called Buck on the phone and asked him to please come downstairs to see her.

He wondered what she wanted, but Maryanne bet she knew why. He didn't come back for hours, and when he did he acted like a crazy man.

She watched him warily as he prowled from room to room; his eyes were blank with pain and she thought, relieved, that she had just been in the nick of time. If only that swine Harry had not seen her, everything would have worked out perfectly. Still, all he wanted was money and her father could always put a good thing or two his way, and Buck need never know. But the look of triumph in his loathsome face had made her uneasy, and with Buck acting like a madman, she had better watch out he didn't do something stupid. Like go back to Francesca Harrison.

Buck stared out the window; San Francisco was wreathed in one of its sudden white fogs but he scarcely noticed. He felt torn apart inside. When he had read the letter Annie gave him he'd said disbelievingly, "No, it can't be true." And then he had looked at Annie's grave face and he had known it was. He'd reread Francie's note again and again. *"I cannot live like this any longer,"* she said, *"with only half a life—and lately it has been even less. I realize it is wrong to take you away from your own world, from your children, and from your work. I have the right to make this decision, Buck, and it is final. I do not want you to question it or try to see me. All I want is to be left alone to build my own life again. I have loved you and been happy, but now it is over. . . ."*

He'd stalked out of Aysgarth's, up Taylor to Nob Hill. He'd pounded on Francie's door until the houseboy answered. He had never been in her home before and he stepped into the hall and stared around looking for her. "Where is she?" he demanded. "I must see her." And when the boy told him she was not there he strode disbelievingly from room to room calling her name.

"Miss Francie's not here," the boy repeated, frightened. "She has gone away, not to the ranch. . . . away somewhere, for a long time. . . ." He waved his arms vaguely while Buck had stared at him helplessly, then he knew it was true. Francie had written him out of her life forever.

Now he turned from the window and stared suspiciously at his wife. "Why did you come here today, Maryanne?"

"Why, to surprise you, darling." He stepped toward her, his eyes wild with pain and anger and she said nervously, "Is something wrong?"

He stood close to her, his hands clenched at his sides and she saw the effort with which he was controlling himself. His whole body trembled as he said, *"You did this, didn't you, Maryanne? You went to see her."*

She turned her head away, avoiding his eyes. "I don't know what you mean.

*"Yes, you do!"*

"You have your children to think of," she retorted defensively. "And everything you've worked for, your future—"

"Is it really *my* future, Maryanne? Or is it yours?"

He took her chin in his hand, tilting her face up, forcing her to look at him. "I won't forget," he said quietly.

She saw the defeat in his eyes and knew she had won and she said solicitously, "It's all for the best, Buck darling. I was only thinking of you. After all, I am your wife."

He let go of her. His marriage was an empty shell. Francie had left him. A glittering future stretched ahead, but he no longer cared.

He looked at Maryanne, elegantly beautiful in clinging blue velvet.

She was his wife and the mother of his children, she was protecting her own. But the distance that had always existed between him and Maryanne now lay like a coiled, venomous serpent between them.

"Buck . . ." she cried as he walked past her to his room and closed the door.

Maryanne sank onto the sofa with a little sigh of relief. It was over. She thought of the look of pain in his eyes and told herself it surely couldn't be that bad. Tomorrow, like one of the children with a badly scraped knee, the pain would be gone and he would feel better. And they would just pick up the pieces and life would go on as if nothing had ever happened.

Lysandra was born with the dawn on a beautiful spring morning in Dolores de Soto Harrison's lovely old carved bed. Annie was at Francie's side and the Mandarin was also there to share her joy.

He held the infant wrapped in her pretty white shawl and his black eyes shone with happiness because Francie had a new child to give her love to.

"A beautiful little girl," Annie exclaimed joyfully. "Oh Francie, this old ranch will be a happy place again."

"It surely will, Miss Francie," Hattie said, peering at the child's tightly shut little face. "She's like a rosebud in the mornin' before the sun opens her petals."

Francie smiled. "I'm afraid I'll never have a whole bouquet though, Hattie," she said. Then she looked wistfully at the Mandarin. "I just wish Buck could see her. I wish she had her father's name."

He placed the baby carefully back into her arms. He bowed and said, "I am an old man. I cannot take the place of her father, but I will guard her as if she was my own grandchild. I will teach her everything I have learned and share your pleasure in watching her grow."

Francie looked at her dearest friend; it was true he was old, even he didn't know his true age. Somehow he seemed smaller, his shoulders were stooped but his face was strong, his eyes still glowed with the same energy and there was a wonderful dignity about him. She thought of all he had done for her throughout her life: everything she was, every triumph large and small was because of him. Lai Tsin had been her only good fortune and now he would be her child's.

She said, "Would you give Lysandra your name? It is an honorable one and it will make me very proud."

The Mandarin's eyes widened, first with astonishment and then with pleasure. He took the baby's tiny, perfect hand in his and he kissed it. "Dearest Francie," he said, his voice charged with emotion, "you have bestowed upon your old friend the greatest honor of his life. I was a worthless peasant, I had nothing, no wealth, no family, and no love. And now I have all three. I have a name to be proud of and a grandchild to bear it. I am the happiest person in the world."

The Mandarin was Lysandra's beloved grandfather for seven years and in all that time Francie kept her promise not to see Buck again, though she thought of him every night and followed his career in the newspapers. She didn't see him until after the Mandarin died, in 1937, that same fateful week of Harry's party.

*Part V*

---◆---

# FRANCIE
## 1937

# CHAPTER 39

◆

## *1937*

*Wednesday, October 4th*
Lysandra Lai Tsin leapt out of bed on the stroke of half-past six the morning after the Mandarin's ashes had been scattered on the sea, because even though she was sad, she still could not bear to miss a single minute of the day. She always awoke with the same joyous expectancy that maybe something wonderful would happen and usually it did, whether it was an "A" in math, or sleeping over at her friend Dorothy's house, or even just her favorite chocolate cake after supper. Lysandra enjoyed life and she met it head-on every day, and she never, ever expected anything bad to happen to her.

That was why it had been such a blow when her grandfather had died, because the two of them had been very close and she just never expected anyone she loved ever to go away.

But today was a new day. The sun was shining and she was filled with her old optimism and bounce as she ran to the bathroom and quickly washed her face and brushed her tangled blond hair, braiding it lopsidedly and tying it with a piece of scarlet yarn, Chinese-style. Then she inspected herself in the mirror to see if she looked any different, decided it was just the same old face and the same round blue eyes and she had not turned into a mature raging beauty overnight after all. Slamming the door behind her and whistling cheerily, she ran along the wide semicircular gallery overlooking the big hall to Francie's room.

She tapped on the door, waiting for the usual, "Come on in, baby." Ever since she was little, as soon as she had awakened, she had evaded her amah's grasp and run to Francie's room to climb on her bed and share her morning tea and toast. Francie liked her toast simply buttered, but Lysandra always slathered hers with the peach preserves put up every summer by Hattie, the cook-housekeeper at the ranch. Then she and Francie would walk down the street for their usual daily swim in the Fairmont Hotel's pool. Francie said it was the only thing the Fairmont had over the Aysgarth Arms, but personally Lysandra preferred the glossy silver-and-green art deco cocktail bar at Aysgarth's to the Fairmont's canopied swimming pool.

But today there was no reply from Francie's room and she opened the door and peeked in. With an "oh" of alarm she saw the towering four-poster had not been slept in. The blue brocade curtains were still drawn, the lamp still burned and the Morisot portrait of the little girl on the gilt easel on the bedside table glowed like an icon in the soft light.

Lysandra glanced around, calling Francie's name as she inspected the dressing room with its crowded closets, and the mirrored bathroom with its shelves of scented powders and lotions. But Francie wasn't there and she felt a sudden misgiving. She had lost her beloved grandfather and now she had lost Francie too.

She ran along to the end of the long galleried hallway to the Mandarin's room, hesitating before opening the door and going in.

Lai Tsin's were the only Chinese rooms in the big house, and Francie, who understood these things, had supervised their decoration herself. The first room was his study. Its walls and ceiling were lacquered a beautiful glossy red. Two walls held rows of heavy leather-bound books and a simply carved blackwood altar table stood against the wall nearest the door. The white azaleas he had favored bloomed in a pot near the window and a filigree iron lantern decorated with scarlet tassels hung over the low central table, around which were grouped the big square-backed slippery wooden chairs Lysandra had always complained were so uncomfortable.

She ran to his bedroom and peered in, but the austere white room looked as it always had. There was just a low Chinese wooden bed with a padded bedmat, a little charcoal brazier in the fireplace and tall windows with pierced Chinese screens and plain rice-paper shades. The Mandarin's bedroom was bare of all decoration and it was empty.

Lysandra ran back along the gallery, down the stairs and across the hall, slipping and sliding on the polished wooden floorboards as she flung open the door to Francie's sitting room. She heaved a great sigh of relief. Francie was curled up on the sofa fast asleep. "Oh," she exclaimed, "there you are after all."

Francie opened her eyes and stared bewilderedly at her. She

glanced around the little sitting room, at the dead ashes in the fireplace and the lighted lamp and drawn curtains, as though she was reseeing them after a long journey and she shook her head wearily. She supposed she must have fallen asleep but her dreams of the past had been so troubled she still felt exhausted.

"It's after six," Lysandra said impatiently. "And you're still dressed from yesterday. Didn't you go to bed at all?"

Francie stretched her arms over her head, smiling. Lysandra still looked such a baby with her hair braided all wrong and her sweater on inside-out. She was always in such a hurry, she never had time to bother with boring things like dressing properly.

"Did you brush your teeth?" she asked automatically as she did every morning, and Lysandra shook her head guiltily.

"I forgot. I'll do it after breakfast." She ran to Francie and gave her a hug. "I couldn't find you. I was frightened," she whispered. "I thought maybe you'd gone away too."

Francie hugged her back. "I'd never go away without telling you." Then she smiled and said, "I've got a great idea. Why don't you and I go to the ranch? I dreamed about it last night, about picking grapes for the new wine, and riding the horses for miles and miles and making pancakes. I think we need a little holiday and I'll just bet Cookie and Mousie will be real happy to see you. If we leave right away we could be there in a couple of hours."

Lysandra's face lit up as she thought of the ranch and the dog and the cat—and her pony. She clapped her hands together, whirling delightedly around and around the room. "I just knew something nice would happen today," she cried.

Watching her, Francie smiled. She was just a little girl and it was so easy to make her happy. But she wondered worriedly what would happen as she grew up and realized she was pretty Lysandra Lai Tsin, maybe the richest girl in the world with power over a business empire that employed thousands and earned millions of dollars. She sighed; it was not going to be easy. Lysandra was rarely still, she enjoyed life and action and the idea of her presiding over a boardroom table was remote. But the Mandarin had chosen her and he had never been wrong.

The de Soto Ranch and Winery was a lot different from the tumbledown clapboard buildings scattered over a few humble acres that it had been the first time Francie had gone there with her mother.

Over the years, she had purchased all the tracts around until now it covered four hundred acres. The old wooden ranch house was still at the core, but it had been expanded and two new wings formed a courtyard, with a long galleried porch running all around. There were three big barns next to the graceful arched stucco buildings of the winery, and beyond were the workers' dormitories and cookroom. To the right of the house lay the new stables and next to that was the cottage where Zocco, the Mexican ranch-hand, lived with his wife.

Zocco was in his seventies now and was as brown and gnarled as an old oak tree. His children were grown and had children of their own, but he still worked a long day, supervising the stables and giving the ranch-hands a hard time if they failed to meet his standards of spit and polish. He still rode the perimeters of the ranch, mending fences and sleeping under the stars the way he had when he was a young man, and his arthritic hands still had the featherlight touch on the reins that they had when he taught Francie to ride as a child. His wife, Esmerelda, cooked for the employees who tended the vines as well as for the dozens of migrant Mexican workers who came each October to pick the grapes.

Hattie Jeremiah was big and beautiful, with skin like the smoothest, plumpest black grapes. A bundle of energy, she ran the main house with a glint in her eye that told she would stand for no nonsense, and a reluctant smile that told you well, maybe she would. She was waiting on the front porch as they drove down the long, winding blacktop road bordered with Francie's favorite golden poplars. "There you all are at last," she said grumpily, her arms folded across her ample chest. "I thought you was never gonna get here."

Lysandra jumped from the car almost before it had stopped and bounced up the steps into Hattie's arms for a kiss. "Guess what?" she confided, wriggling away like a slippery eel. "I don't have to go to school for three whole weeks."

"Is that so?" Hattie called after her as she leapt back down the steps and headed full speed for the stables. "Well then, young lady, you sure are just in time to help pick the grapes and do a little work for your keep."

Her eyes met Francie's as she walked toward her and a look of understanding and affection passed between them. "I'm sorry, Miss Francie," she said, tears spilling over her round cheeks. "I know it was expected, but knowing somebody's gonna die don't make it any easier to bear. I never knew a Chinese before but I had nothing but respect and admiration for the Mandarin." She sniffed back her tears and added, "And love, too, because he was the kindest, most honorable man I ever knew." She put her arms around Francie and held her close and then added, "Not that I've known any honorable men 'ceptin' the Mandarin anyways. All the others were just a bunch of bums, in my opinion."

Francie laughed. "Sometimes I think you might be right, Hattie," she agreed, remembering when a few years after Hattie had come to work at the ranch, she had suddenly disappeared, returning a year later with an infant in her arms and a disillusioned look in her eyes.

"I done wrong, Miss Francie," she had said bluntly. "Now I'm like you, with a kid on my hands and no man to be his father. I'd like my old job back if it's still goin', and I promise you this child ain't gonna disturb you none. He'll just be as quiet as a mouse."

Lai Tsin had been listening and he had told her that children were not a disturbance, they were a blessing, and he had built her a cottage where she could raise her boy. He had gone to the local elementary school and high school, and now Hattie's boy, Jefferson—named after Thomas Jefferson, the famous president—was a sophomore at the University of California, Berkeley, majoring in science. He planned to go on to medical school and Hattie said proudly he was the first member of her family even to finish high school, let alone college. She said most of 'em couldn't even read or write properly, and now she had a son who was gonna be a doctor. And she would have done anything for Francie Harrison and the Mandarin. Anything they asked.

"Miss Annie telephoned 'bout half an hour ago," she said as they walked into the house. They were followed by the houseboy, Fong Joe, carrying the luggage, and Lysandra's amah, Ah Sing, in her black smock and trousers carrying her bedmat, her padded quilt, her tea kettle, and her incense sticks. These she would use to light the little shrine to the kitchen god, which she always placed by the stove, even though Hattie grumbled about it.

"She said you didn't tell her you was comin' out here, but she somehow guessed and she said to call her back right away."

The lithe ginger cat, Mousie, was lying in the hall in a patch of sun and he waved his tail lazily at Francie as she passed by. An appetizing smell came from the kitchen. "Lysandra's favorite," Hattie explained, "honey-baked beans, fried chicken, and chocolate fudge pie."

Francie laughed as she walked down the hall. She had come home and she felt better already. The door to her room stood wide, the windows were flung open to catch the warmth of the sun and it smelled of fresh air and lavender-polished wood. The old armoire in the corner held the few clothes she needed: her riding britches and cambric shirts, a few warm sweaters, a fringed suede cowboy jacket, and the long, flowing Chinese silk robes she liked to wear in the evening.

There was a pine dresser, a comfortable old chair, and a faded blue braid rug. The old carved oak bed that had been her mother's was spread with a patchwork quilt stitched by Zocco's wife twenty-five years ago. It had been her mother's room, and her own son and daughter had been born there and every time she walked through its door it brought back memories. Some wonderful, some terrible. But that was the way her life had always been.

Buck woke late the morning after Harry's dinner party. He glanced irritably at his watch. It was ten-thirty and he'd hardly slept, he'd tossed and turned, checking his watch every hour until five when at last his weary eyes had closed and he had dozed off. He had been thinking of Francie; he hadn't seen her in over seven years, but he'd noticed the light in the windows of her house last night and had read the news of the Mandarin's death in the papers. He knew how much she cared about him and he couldn't get the thought of her, alone in her big house, out of his mind.

He thought of the years that had passed, Francie leading her own very private life and him leading his very public one. The truth was that he no longer had a private life. He and Maryanne kept up the pretense "for the children's sake," she'd told him earnestly, but the children were Brattles and cool as their mother. They went to the "right" schools and made the "right" friends and went to all the "right" parties, and they respected their father from a distance.

He wondered again why Maryanne had insisted they go to Harry's dinner last night. "His name still counts for a lot in San Francisco," she had replied imperturbably when he'd asked her. "He can still be a lot of help to you, Buck."

"I can't see exactly why I need Harry Harrison's help," he'd replied dryly.

She had patted her immaculate hair and said, "Just trust me, Buck. Don't I always know best?" And she had smiled that cool superior Brattle smile that annoyed him so intensely.

He climbed tiredly out of bed. He called room service and asked them to send coffee and the morning papers, then he stepped into the shower and turned the water to cold. The icy jets snapped him awake and he toweled briskly dry, threw on the terrycloth robe and walked through to the sitting room just as the coffee arrived. He poured himself a cup and glanced at the *Examiner*. THE RICHEST LITTLE GIRL IN THE WORLD was the headline over the top of a photograph of a child in a summer-print dress:

> "Seven-year-old Lysandra Lai Tsin inherits a million-dollar empire from the man she called her grandfather, the Mandarin Lai Tsin. Her famous mother is, of course, Francesca Harrison, whom the child resembles strongly."

There was a lot more about Francie and the Mandarin and her past, but Buck wasn't reading it. He looked at the picture of Lysandra and he thought of Francie and the seven years that had passed since she had sent him away, and he knew he was looking at his daughter.

The cup of coffee lay forgotten on the table; he put his head in his hands and groaned aloud, "Oh, Francie, *why* didn't you tell me? Why?" He thought of all she must have gone through, bringing up the child alone and the scandal she had faced, and then he thought of Maryanne, sleeping the sleep of the righteous in the room next to his. He looked at his watch: it was seven o'clock, still early, but he couldn't wait. He picked up the phone and called Annie Aysgarth.

She answered promptly. "Buck," she said with surprise. "Is something wrong? Do you have a complaint?"

"I've seen the morning papers," he said abruptly.

Annie said, "Then you've beaten me to it, love. I've not had time yet. What's in there that's so important?"

"A photograph of seven-year-old Lysandra Lai Tsin."

There was a little silence and then Annie said in a quiet voice, "I see."

He could almost hear her thinking and then she said, "Give me five minutes; then come and have breakfast with me, up here in the penthouse."

Annie had been up since six, she had already bathed and dressed
and dealt with the morning's mail, the day's menus, the chef, the staff
complaints, and her general inspection. Now she powdered her nose
in front of the silver dressing-table mirror that once belonged to the
wife of an eighteenth-century grandee and for the first time since she
had owned it she didn't marvel that she, Annie Aysgarth from Montgomery Street, owned such a beautiful, expensive object, because
right now she was wondering what she was going to tell Buck about
Francie.

The bell rang, and taking a deep breath she went to answer it. As
she let him in she thought that like good port, Buck got better with
years. But she also noticed he looked too lean, his thick dark hair was
streaked with gray, there were tired lines imprinted on his handsome
face and a weary look in his steady brown eyes.

He kissed her cheek and she said bluntly, "You look as though you
need a good breakfast, Buck Wingate. Doesn't that wife of yours feed
you anymore?"

He shrugged and took a seat opposite her at the heavy glass-topped
table, watching as she poured orange juice from a big crystal jug.

He said, "Lysandra Lai Tsin is my daughter, isn't she?"

Annie looked at him. "You're putting me in a very difficult position, Buck."

"It's all right, you don't have to answer. I know it's true. Just tell
me *why* Francie didn't want me to know. I would have looked after
them, cared for them. Francie was everything to me." His eyes
searched hers, and he added softly, "She still is."

Annie looked at him and she saw an unhappy man; she thought of
Francie and Lysandra, and then she thought of Maryanne Brattle
Wingate and weighed the balance. She had always been a woman
who spoke her mind and now she didn't hesitate. She told Buck the
story of Maryanne's visit to Francie, that Francie had not wanted
him to give up his career for her, and that she would never have used
the fact that she was having his child as emotional blackmail.
"Francie's not like that," she said fiercely, "she's an honest woman."
She didn't add, "unlike Maryanne," but he knew she was thinking it.

"She set you free," Annie said simply, "no strings and no ties. Free
to do whatever you wanted. To fulfill your political destiny."

She filled the coffee cups, watching sympathetically; she could almost read the thoughts rushing through his head and she wasn't the
least bit surprised when he finally said, "I must see her, Annie."

She nodded, "She's gone to the ranch with Lysandra. They left early, they should be there by now." She gulped down her coffee and stood up. "There's a phone on the desk. I must be on my way to see what my staff are up to." She smiled at him and said, "For what it's worth, I told her she was a bloody fool to send you away." Then she hurried from the room, leaving him alone.

Francie's number at the ranch was imprinted on his memory and he dialed it, hearing it ring and imagining her running to answer it, the way she always did.

"Hello," the voice on the other end almost sang the greeting, but it wasn't Francie's.

"Hello," he replied cautiously. "Is Miss Harrison there?"

"Sure, I'll just call her. . . ."

There was a clatter as Lysandra dropped the receiver onto the table and he heard her shouting, "Mom . . . it's for you," and distantly a voice say, "Who is it?"

"Some man," Lysandra called and he smiled at the irony; he was her father and yet to her he was just "some man" on the phone for her mom.

"Hello?"

His heart jumped and his pulses raced in the same old way as he said, "Francie, it's Buck."

Francie leaned against the wall for support, closing her eyes. She was swept back in time, all that existed at that moment was Buck's voice on the end of a telephone wire. She said, "You don't need to say your name, I would have known."

"It's been so long," he said quietly.

She sank onto the little rush-bottomed chair by the table. "Why are you calling me, Buck? It's against our rules."

"*Your* rules, Francie. Not mine." She was silent and he said quickly, "I spoke with Annie, she said I should call you. I'm here now, in her apartment. I saw Lysandra's photograph in the *Examiner* this morning. *My daughter*'s photograph."

Francie sighed. "Did Annie tell you?"

"She didn't have to. I knew."

"She's a lovely girl," Francie said, pressing a hand to her chest, trying to quiet her racing heart, "she knows nothing about—about us, and I don't want her to."

He heard the dismissal in her voice and he said urgently, "Francie, we must talk. Please, there are things we must discuss. I must see you."

She thought of all the years that had passed, and of how much she loved Lysandra, and how much she still loved Buck and she didn't think she could bear to see him, even though he surely had a right. Now that he knew about his daughter.

"Francie, I have to leave tomorrow morning. I have meetings here all day, I'll cancel them and come out to the ranch—"

"*No.*" She didn't want him to meet Lysandra, it would be too painful to see them together. "I don't want you to cancel anything for my sake. I'll come back to San Francisco. I'll be there by this evening. Where shall I meet you?"

He thought quickly. "Come to Aysgarth's, to Annie's penthouse at eight. And Francie . . . thank you."

She put down the phone with trembling hands. Lysandra stared curiously at her. "Who was it, Mommy?" she asked. "Was it someone nasty? You look so upset."

Francie looked at her startled, she shook her head and smiled. "Oh no, he wasn't nasty at all. He's—an old friend, that's all."

"An old friend? Then how come I don't know him?" Lysandra cocked her head enquiringly to one side, just the way Francie did when she asked a question, and she laughed.

"Because you are only seven years old and 'old' friends are much older than that." A sudden little thrill of excitement flashed through her veins as she thought of Buck and she threw her arms impulsively around Lysandra and hugged her. Then she picked up her basket of flowers and carried them into the kitchen and began putting them into vases just as though nothing had happened, but all the time inside she was shaking at the thought of seeing him again.

Harry awoke, still angry with Maryanne. As he sat down to his usual substantial breakfast he asked himself who she thought she was to act so superior last night, when if it were not for him she would be just another wife of a political has-been. And she had been damned cagey when he'd asked her about the extra investment for the oil drilling in New Mexico, sighing and rolling up her eyes and asking exactly *when* the wells were going to spout the black liquid gold that was supposed to recoup their investment?

He mulled matters over in his mind as he dug into his favorite deviled kidneys and fried eggs and decided that the balance of their relationship was all wrong. Maryanne acted like the superior one, like she was in charge and he was an employee, like she was the Brattle goddess and he was just the dust beneath her chariot wheels. It was time dear Maryanne was taught a lesson.

He called her after breakfast. It was eleven-thirty and she yawned and said irritably, "Why are you calling, Harry? I only saw you a few hours ago at your dreadful party. Who *were* those movie people? I had a hard time explaining to Buck exactly *why* we were there."

He didn't bother to explain that the reason she and Buck were there was to boost his credibility when he went to Zev Abrams and the others and asked them to invest in his oil drilling operation. "Of course, Buck is already in," he would tell them confidently, and he knew now they would believe him; after all hadn't they just had dinner with him at his house?

"You and I need to talk, Maryanne," he said smoothly.

She leaned back against her pillows, groaning. "My God, what now, Harry? I'm a busy woman."

"But never too busy to see me."

She held the phone away from her ear, staring at it with surprise, as though she were looking at his face. She thought worriedly that Harry was becoming very insistent, pushy even.

"Can't you tell me over the phone?" she asked plaintively.

"No. I must see you. Tonight at eight o'clock. At my place," he said briskly.

"I can't do that. What would I tell Buck?"

"Tell him you're dining with an old school friend. In my experience with women and excuses, that one always works."

"Indeed," she said icily.

"Eight o'clock," he said and put down the phone.

Maryanne replaced the receiver and lay back against the pillows, wondering what she was going to do. Harry was becoming a problem and problems had to be dealt with, though she didn't quite know how. She sighed deeply; right now there was nothing she could do. Harry had her exactly where he wanted her and he knew it.

# CHAPTER 40

◆

Maryanne breathed a sigh of relief when Buck told her he would be busy that evening, at least it saved her the embarrassment of finding an excuse to slip out for half an hour to see Harry. "Don't worry about me, darling," she said, still smarting at the idea of Harry demanding, no, *ordering* her to go see him. "I'll have room service send something up." She yawned delicately. "I'm tired, anyway."

Buck glanced at her, surprised she hadn't asked where he was going, but communications between him and Maryanne were reduced to businesslike basics these days. He watched her powdering her pretty nose, peering at herself in the mirror of the little gold-and-platinum striped Cartier compact with her initials in rubies that he had given her for Christmas years ago. He had married a cold, ambitious, self-seeking woman who would have happily traded her entire family to become First Lady. He shrugged, he didn't care anymore. A touch of warmth crept into his chilled heart as he thought of Lysandra, his newly discovered daughter, and Francie whom he would see again in just a few minutes.

Maryanne lazed in her peach satin robe on the flowered chintz sofa, watching as he shrugged on his overcoat and walked to the door. "Bye darling," she called, blowing him a kiss. The expression in her eyes changed to anger as he flung a cold good-bye over his shoulder and closed the door.

She glanced at her watch, there was no time to waste, she must dress and get over to Harry's and back again before Buck returned. It occurred to her that she did not know how long Buck was going to be or where he was going, but there was no time to brood on that now. She dressed quickly in a black wool-crepe dress, black suede pumps, and an emerald green cashmere cape lined with mink. She had decided fur linings were a good idea since it wouldn't be good to look too ostentatiously rich publicly right now, with Buck being presented as "a man of the people." She picked up the little black clutch purse, stuffed the key, her ruby-initialed Cartier compact, her lipstick, her lizard-skin address book, and a white linen handkerchief into it, and then hurried to the elevator. The front lobby was crowded and she glanced quickly around, then swung unnoticed through the revolving doors.

Annie was in the Dales Lounge greeting her guests as usual before going to the dining room to check that everything was in order. But tonight her guests only had half her attention. She had let Buck into her penthouse apartment and left him there and now she was watching for Francie. Finally she saw her hurrying through the crowded lobby at a few minutes after eight. From a distance Annie watched her take out her key, and step inside the little private elevator. As the gilded metal gates swung closed Annie heaved a worried sigh. She hoped she had done the right thing.

Francie closed her eyes as the elevator wooshed silently upward to the twentieth floor. The gates swung open, she opened her eyes, and Buck was standing there, looking at her.

"Francie," he said, his eyes full of love.

"Buck." She stepped from the elevator and held out her hand politely, searching his face. "You look the same, just a little older."

"*Seven years* older," he reminded her. He couldn't have described what she was wearing but it was blue and it brought out the color of her eyes, and at a time when every woman had bobbed her hair she still wore hers long, swept back with jeweled combs into a sumptuous heavy golden swathe at the neck.

"You didn't cut it," he said, remembering her promise and she shook her head.

"I would have hated it if you had," he said. "I always think of you like this."

Their eyes locked and the same old feeling swept over her. If she had ever doubted that she would love Buck Wingate till the day she died, now she knew for sure. But he was another woman's husband, an important man. A "man of the people," the press were calling him now.

"I shouldn't have come," she said nervously. "There's nothing for us to say, Buck."

"Yes, there is." He caught her hand in his and held it against his cheek, then he kissed her fingers gently. "I feel as though time has been frozen, that we are back where we were. That life is just a simple matter of you love me and I love you."

She pulled her hand away. "But that's not true, is it? Time hasn't been frozen and life is never that simple. I've made a life for myself now. I have my work, my charities, and my daughter. I don't need any more secrets and lies. I just want peace of mind."

She walked to the long white sofa by the window and sat down before her knees collapsed from under her. Her heart was pounding and all she really wanted to do was to hurl herself into his arms, but she couldn't. She had Lysandra to think of. She clasped her hands loosely around her knees, leaning forward, watching him.

"Maryanne went to see you, didn't she?" he asked.

She shrugged, "And if she did? She was right."

"Why didn't you at least call me, speak to me . . . ?"

He looked desperate and she wanted to take his hand and tell him it was all right, nothing had changed. "I was pregnant. You were married, you had your children to consider. And your career. I had to make the decision."

"*Your* decision, Francie. Not mine. There were two of us involved. Surely I had a right to half the votes?"

His eyes pleaded with her and she sighed. "I'm not here to talk about you and me, Buck; I'm here because of Lysandra. She doesn't know you are her father and I don't want her to know. I told her her father left us before she was born and she accepts that. She's still only seven, but she asks questions and I tell her what you were like, that you would have loved her. I can't expect her to understand now, but maybe when she is older, when she is a woman herself, then she might."

Buck thought of his two children, so immersed in their own lives he rarely saw them, and of this new daughter whom he was forbidden to see and he threw his arms wide and cried, "What is it I'm doing wrong? My life is nothing, I have nothing—"

"Oh, Buck, don't say that. Please don't say that." She looked at him, shocked.

"It's true," he said bitterly. "When I met you in Paris, I told you my life was a facade, a sham. Nothing has changed."

"You have your work," she said. "A brilliant future, everybody says so. . . ."

He shrugged, and she got up and walked toward him. He held out his arms and she stepped into them and he held her close, his head resting against hers. Their bodies fitted together with the easy familiarity of lovers, she could feel his heart beating, feel his breath on her hair, the strength of his arms around her. It was as though the gates of paradise had reopened and allowed her in, just for a few moments.

"Come back to me, Francie," he murmured. "Let's start all over again. I love you, I've always loved you."

She wanted with all her heart to say yes. She stepped back and looked at him. "Tell me one thing, Buck. If I had asked you to make that decision seven years ago, if I had asked you to give it all up, your wife, your children, your career, and your glittering future, to marry me, what would you have said?"

He hesitated, his eyes fixed on hers. "I can't lie to you," he said quietly. "I just don't know."

She nodded sadly; it was the answer she had expected.

She picked up her coat and put it over her shoulders. "Please don't try to see Lysandra," she said quietly. "It wouldn't be fair to her. Or to me. Or even," she managed a half-smile, "to yourself."

"Francie," he grabbed her shoulder urgently, "please don't go. I don't know what I'll do without you."

"Everything will be all right, Buck," she said, "we'll just go on doing whatever we've been doing all these years." And then she pulled herself from his grasp and stepped quickly into the elevator. The little golden mesh gates closed, shutting him out of her life again. Their eyes met longingly through the grille as the elevator slowly descended and he disappeared from view.

Harry had given the servants the night off; he wanted to be alone with Maryanne. The fire was lit in the oak-paneled library and a decanter of fine French brandy waited with two wafer-thin crystal glasses on the lamplit table behind the dark-green leather Chesterfield sofa. When the doorbell rang he answered it himself and Maryanne looked at him surprised.

"Where's your butler?" she asked, stepping over the threshold into the hall.

"The poor fellow had to go visit a colleague in the hospital," Harry lied, "so I gave him the night off." He took her fur-lined cape and flung it carelessly across a Jacobean carved oak chair, and Maryanne looked at him suspiciously.

"And your wonderful footmen, Harry? Or at least a maid?"

"Well, of course, in these terrible times, 'with the memory of the Depression still so close in all our minds,' " he said, quoting her, "I thought it better not to keep footmen any longer. I simply hire them by the night whenever I need them. And the maids come daily. They worked hard cleaning up after last night's dinner party. I told them I would answer the door and let my guest in myself so they could leave early."

Maryanne's eyes narrowed. "And since when have you become so generous?" He was wearing a fashionable velvet smoking jacket and that satisfied smile and she didn't trust him an inch. She followed him into the library, taking in at a glance the cosy fire, the soft lights, and the two waiting glasses.

"Sit here, Maryanne, by me," Harry said, patting the sofa.

Ignoring him, she walked to the big wing chair by the fire and sat down. "Brandy?" he asked, fussing with the decanter and the pretty glasses.

Maryanne hesitated, she rarely drank but now she needed something to steady her nerves. Harry was up to something and she didn't know what. "Thank you," she said in her calmest voice.

He handed her the glass and took his and went to stand in front of the fire, looking at her. "It's good to see you again, Maryanne," he said. "We so rarely see each other alone."

She glanced up at him, her hackles rising, there was just something in his tone that sent a shiver up her spine.

"To be quite correct, Harry," she said quickly, "we *never* see each other alone. And quite honestly I don't know why I'm here alone with you now." She glanced at her small diamond wristwatch and said briskly, "Perhaps you can explain quickly, Buck will be expecting me back."

He smiled and took a sip of the perfect brandy, savoring it slowly. "Relax," he said jovially, "you and I know there's no real hurry. After all, Buck's hardly going to miss you, is he?"

"Exactly what do you mean by that?" She put down her glass, watching him warily.

"Maryanne, we are such good friends, there are no secrets between us, are there? I must say I can't understand Buck, neglecting a beautiful woman like you. But then he's always been dedicated to his career—apart from the little 'episode' with my dear sister of course.

We both remember that vividly, don't we, Maryanne? And naturally I have been most grateful for your help."

"You want more money," Maryanne said flatly.

He nodded. "That—as well." He put down his glass and came to stand in front of her and she looked warily up at him. "You know I've always admired you, Maryanne," he said, reaching down and taking her hand. "You are a beautiful woman; you're wasted on a man like Buck, you need someone to teach you what life is all about, someone to melt the ice around your heart and unlock your secret juices—"

"Don't be a fool, Harry," she said shortly. Her face burned with disgust. She stood up and attempted to step past him, but he grabbed her arm and pulled her roughly to him. Her eyes opened wide with horror as he pressed his lips on hers, running his hand down her spine, across her buttocks, caressing her, the other hand holding her closer with a vicelike grip.

For the first time in her life things were out of her control and Maryanne was frightened. When he finally took his mouth from hers she screamed at him, "Let go of me, you bastard, I'll have you arrested, I'll have you thrown in jail for this."

"Of course you won't," he said easily. "Think of the scandal. I need hardly describe the headlines." He scooped her up into his arms and carried her, kicking, across to the sofa. "Don't you dare touch me, Harry Harrison," she warned as he lay her down and knelt beside her, "If you do I shall scream."

"Scream away," he said confidently, "there's no one to hear you. And besides, it adds to the excitement. Maybe that's what it takes to get to you, Maryanne? A bit of rough-and-tumble." He slapped her suddenly across the face and she gasped, staring terrified at him. He ran his hand the length of her body and she watched in horrified fascination, as though it was an insect crawling over her.

She shuddered as he began to unfasten the row of tiny satin-covered buttons at the neck of her dress. "Don't touch me," she warned him. "I'll give you as much money as you want—"

"Of course you will," he muttered, opening her dress and exposing her small, silk-covered breasts. And then his head sank to her bosom.

Maryanne knew he was mad, crazier even than his sister. She looked wildly around for a weapon; the heavy cut-crystal brandy decanter was on the sofa table just above her head. She stretched her arm upward, her fingers searching for a grip. Suddenly she had it and as Harry lifted his face from her breast she smashed the decanter down as hard as she could on the back of his head.

The decanter was tougher than Harry's head; it didn't break. Brandy flowed pungently into the cut and Harry groaned and staggered to his feet.

He put his hands to his head. Blood poured from the wound and he stared murderously at her. She stared back, too terrified to move. He reeled to the fireplace, clutching the mantel, still looking speechlessly at her, then his knees buckled and he fell heavily onto the stone hearth.

Maryanne looked at him, stunned. The big longcase clock in the corner ticked on and the logs on the fire crackled and spit, but Harry did not make a sound. She quickly pulled her dress over her naked breasts, wrinkling her nose at the smell of brandy, then she stood up and stepped cautiously toward him. He was lying on his side, the back of his head was a splintered mass of blood and bone and she made a little face, sickened. Taking courage, she felt his pulse. She breathed a sigh of relief, it was fast but Harry was still alive.

"Oh my God," she said, frantically buttoning her dress. "Oh my God, I'd better call an ambulance." Then she thought of Buck and the scandal and saw her whole life in ruins. She shook her head violently from side to side—she could not allow this to happen, she just could not! She glanced wildly around again as the clock struck nine. Nine o'clock already. She only had Harry's word for it that the servants were out, they might come back any minute. She wondered frantically what to do.

The logs settled into the grate amid a shower of sparks and one rolled to the very edge. It lay smoldering dangerously on the brink and Maryanne stared, hypnotized, as it fell. Somewhere from the maze of fear in her mind came a cool, clear thought. The whole room reeked of brandy, Harry had been drinking, he had fallen and hit his head. . . . All it needed was a delicate little push with the toe of her black suede shoe and the log was touching the expensive Aubusson rug, not two feet from where Harry lay. It smoldered for a moment and then there was a red glow and then a tiny yellow tongue of flame.

With a terrified cry she fled from the room, slamming the door behind her. She ran through the marble hall to the door, then remembering her cape she ran back again. She flung the cape over her shoulders with the dark fur on the outside in the hope she would not be so visible. Then she opened the door and stepped outside.

She looked up and down the street, but the night was dark and cold and it was deserted. She ran down the steps, flinging herself around the corner out of sight of that terrible house, hurrying as fast as she could in her high-heeled black suede pumps back to Aysgarth's. As she turned into Union Square she slowed down, smoothing back her hair and wishing she could powder her nose and put on her lipstick so she would appear more normal. And then she realized she had left her purse behind at Harry's.

She thought of the log on the rug and her purse lying on the big wing chair near the hearth and she told herself reassuringly it surely would have burned by now. Clutching her fur cape closer she strode into Aysgarth's and hurried across the lobby to the elevator, praying it would be waiting empty on the ground floor. She was in luck, it was, and she stepped inside, ignoring the bellboy who said a cheerful good evening as he pressed the button, leaning against the wall waiting for it to waft her to safety.

Maryanne hid her face in the cape collar as the elevator sped upward. She ran down the corridor to the Knaresborough Suite, only realizing when she got to the door that her keys were still in her purse. And her purse was at Harry's. Her heart sank, it meant she would have to go back down and explain to the desk clerk that she had been out and had lost them. The service elevator pinged to a stop at the end of the hall and a waiter appeared with a tray. She breathed a sigh of relief as she sped toward him, he would have keys and could open her door, she was saved after all.

She was in her suite within minutes and running a hot bath, as hot as she could bear, pouring in lavish amounts of her expensive French bath oil. She stripped off the ruined dress, wrinkling her nose again at the smell of brandy as she rolled it into a ball and threw it into the wastebasket. She tore off the ecru silk slip and ripped it to shreds and threw it in with the dress. Then she climbed into the tub and lay back with her eyes closed letting the sweet-scented water wash away the vile imprint of Harry's hands.

She was still there half an hour later when Buck came in.

"Is that you, darling?" she called in her usual calm voice.

"Yes." He stood in the doorway looking at her and she glanced gratefully at him. He looked so strong and handsome, just like his photographs in the newspapers. He was her husband and now nothing could harm them. She had made it all right again. Vaguely from a

distance in the street below came the urgent sound of bells and sirens.
"What time is it, darling?" she asked as he turned away.

"Nine-fifteen."

"Must be a fire somewhere," she said with a lazy smile as she lay
back again and closed her eyes. There had been plenty of time for the
house to get well alight and if there was anything left of loathsome
Harry, it would be unrecognizable by now.

# CHAPTER 41

◆

Francie was lying sleepless on her bed when she heard the fire engines coming up the hill. Her mind was still full of Buck, of how he had looked, the new tired lines on his face, his eyes pleading with her. And of how she had felt weak again with love for him, how much she longed to stay with him, to show him his beautiful little daughter, to have him back in their lives again. But she had called Annie and told her what happened and said she never wanted to talk about him again. Just so she couldn't change her mind.

The fire engines clanged noisily past then screamed to a halt and she sat up, startled. She ran to the window and stared down the block at Harry's house. Flames were leaping from the windows and she closed her eyes, thinking she must be dreaming, but when she opened them it was true. The house, that great monument to the Harrison name, was burning. Again.

For the second time that night she was swept back to the past; this time more than thirty years ago after the earthquake, when she had watched her father's house burn along with the rest of California Street. Letting the curtain drop back over the window, she wondered what Harry would say now?

With a stab at her heart she remembered the night Ollie had died in the fire. She had always known Harry had something to do with it and this was a small revenge. Only she didn't want revenge, she just didn't want to think about Harry ever again.

She pressed her face to the pillow, trying to shut out the sounds of frantic activity outside, but it was impossible and she got up wearily and went downstairs to the kitchen to make herself some tea.

Ah Fong was in the hall with the front door wide open, staring wonderingly at the blaze.

"Mr. Harrison's house, Miss Francie," he said, gesturing excitedly at the scene. She went and stood beside him. The street was jammed with fire trucks and dozens of firemen were pouring streams of water at the flames in the windows while men on ladders tackled the roof.

"Did they get everyone out?" she asked anxiously, thinking of the servants.

An Fong shrugged. "They say no one was there."

Francie made her tea and took it back upstairs, but she didn't drink it. She lay on her bed, thinking of the night of the earthquake and the great fire. And Josh. And of one of the secrets the Mandarin had told her at Lilin's temple. And she knew now she had to tell Annie. When dawn came she got up and pulled back her curtains and looked out at the wreckage. The Harrison house was a blackened shell. She stared at it waiting for some reaction but she felt nothing, neither pleasure nor triumph. It simply did not matter to her anymore.

Annie called her first thing. "They say Harry's house was burned. Is it true?" she demanded.

"It's true. It looks exactly the way it did after the earthquake."

"It's taken thirty years for fate to take its revenge," Annie said bitterly, "and nobody deserved to lose everything more than Harry."

"Are you busy today?" Francie asked suddenly.

Annie thought of the million and one things she had to do and said calmly, "I don't have to be."

"I need to see you."

There was a silence and then Annie said, "I'll be there in an hour."

Francie was waiting for her in the hall. "Don't bother taking off your coat," she said. "We are going somewhere."

"To meet Buck?" Annie asked, stepping into Francie's little black Ford.

"I told you I don't want to talk about him," Francie said abruptly. "It's just not meant to be, Annie. The man's life is on a different course from mine." Annie nodded sadly as she added wearily, "I'm on my own, Annie, and that's the way it's always been. Last night, seeing the house burn brought back memories of Josh.

"You remember the night of the Mandarin's funeral?" she said as they drove down the hill. "When I said you didn't know all the truth? Well, now I shall tell you. I couldn't before, Annie, because it was his secret, but I want you to remember that what he did, he did for love. I'm taking you to see something and then I shall tell you what happened."

They drove south of the city to the little clifftop graveyard and she showed Annie the carefully tended plot with Josh's name on it, while she told her the Mandarin's story of how he had taken him from Sammy and tried to help him, but it had been too late. And why he had not let them see Josh before he died.

Annie's face was sad but she shed no tears. "I'm glad," she said simply. "I couldn't have borne to see him like that. He was right, we had done our mourning and it was time for life again."

They sat side by side, warmed by a faltering sun, gazing out to sea remembering Josh, and as they left she said, "It's a grand place, Francie. Josh would have loved it."

The Extra was being called by every newsboy on the streets when they drove back through San Francisco late that afternoon. "*What* did they say?" Annie gasped, rolling down her window the better to hear. Francie shook her head, it was rush hour, the streets were crowded, and she was concentrating on her driving.

"Harry Harrison Dead in Blaze," the newsboy yelled, running alongside the traffic and thrusting a copy of the *Chronicle* at them as Annie handed over a coin.

Francie swerved to a halt at the curb. Her stunned eyes met Annie's and she said, "Can it be true?"

"It's true all right." Annie shook open the newspaper and they bent their heads over it together, reading how Harry Harrison had died in the blaze that had gutted his house the previous night.

Francie shook her head. "I can't believe it," she said, wonderingly. "The same way Ollie died. Surely it's God's vengeance."

"If Harry really was responsible for Ollie's death, then it's vengeance of some sort," Annie agreed. She glanced anxiously at Francie, who looked pale and strangely calm. "Are you all right, love?"

Francie sighed deeply. She patted Annie's hand and said, "All these years since Ollie died I've wanted to kill Harry, and now he's dead. It's all been wiped out in a single night, Annie. It's like a gift, but it's not one that brings happiness."

* * *

She dropped Annie off at the hotel and then drove back home, turning her head to look at the house that had become Harry's tomb, just the way it had for his father. The ruins were cordoned off and half a dozen police officers stood guard, watched by a curious crowd of onlookers as well as a coterie of newspaper reporters and photographers. Their faces turned to look as she drove by and Francie nervously decided to use the servants' entrance around the back.

She called hello to Ah Fong and the Chinese cook on her way through the kitchen and they told her the reporters had been hanging around all day, waiting for her. She went to her small sitting room, walked to the window and stood looking at the activity across the road. She wasn't glad Harry was dead; she wasn't anything. Just tired.

She flung herself into a chair and kicked off her shoes, rereading the newspaper article. *"An autopsy is being carried out, but a forensic report has already established beyond doubt that the remains are those of Mr. Harrison."*

She flung the newspaper from her and leaned her head on the cushions, her eyes closed. Harry was dead and Buck had gone back to his own life, and she would go back to hers. Tomorrow she would ride her acres with Lysandra and tend her vines and chatter to Hattie as though nothing had happened. And that's the way it would be from now on.

She tossed and turned all night, it was impossible to sleep, there was just too much on her mind, Josh and Buck and Harry, and she was up and bathed and dressed by seven. She walked wearily downstairs to the morning room. The table was set for her solitary breakfast and the morning paper lay folded by her plate. She poured herself some coffee and opened it up and read the headlines about Harry again. Only this time they said, "HARRY HARRISON—MURDER."

With her stomach churning, she read. *"Though his body had been almost totally destroyed in the fire, the autopsy had been able to ascertain that Mr. Harrison had not died in the flames. He had died before the fire even started, of a fractured skull. The remains had been found facedown and the police confirmed that the injury could not have been sustained in a fall, but by a deliberate blow to the head. No suspects were being named at this time."*

She flung down the paper and called Annie. "They say somebody killed Harry," she blurted. "Oh, Annie, who could it be?"

"Any one of a hundred people, I should think," Annie replied briskly. "I felt like it myself more than once. I guess he just pushed somebody too far and that was it. And I can't say I blame them."

Despite herself Francie laughed. "Did I ever tell you you were good for me?" she asked. "You always manage to put things in perspective."

Annie said, "Thanks for yesterday, Francie. I feel much happier knowing where Josh is, and about his last days. I've got a lot to thank the Mandarin for too."

Francie smiled. "I hear the doorbell. I hope it's not the reporters again. I'd better go."

She sipped her coffee, listening as Ah Fong padded across the hall to answer the door. She heard a man's voice and Ah Fong padded back again. "Miss Francie," he gasped, his voice shaking, "it's the police. Three of them, Miss Francie. They say they must see you. Right away, they said—"

"Very well," she replied, puzzled, "show them into my sitting room." She supposed they must want to ask questions about Harry since she was his only living relative, and she tidied her hair in the mirror and walked across the hall.

The three men turned to look at her, one uniformed police officer and two in plainclothes. They introduced themselves as Detective Inspector Walter Sinclair, Detective Sergeant Charlie Mulloy, and Officer Stieglitz of the San Francisco Police Department.

She asked them to be seated and the two detectives complied, but the police officer stood by the door and she looked at him surprised. She took a seat opposite the burly plainclothes detectives and asked, "I assume this is about my brother, Harry? How can I help you, gentlemen?"

Inspector Sinclair took a little notebook from his pocket. "Is it true, ma'am, that you are Miss Francesca Harrison? And that you are the sister of the deceased, Harmon Lloyd Harrison, Jr., commonly known as Harry Harrison?"

"Of course it's true," she replied, surprised. "You already know that."

"Just a formality, miss," Detective Mulloy said quickly.

"Miss Harrison, how would you describe relations between you and your brother?"

Francie glanced scornfully at him. "I hated my brother, everyone knows that. And he hated me. It's been well-documented in every newspaper in the county."

"It has been said," the inspector said, looking her straight in the eye, "that you blamed Mr. Harrison for the death of your son, Oliver, in the Lai Tsin warehouse fire several years ago."

"My opinions and my private life are my own," she retorted angrily. "And now would you mind telling me exactly *why* you are here?"

He cleared his throat, glancing down at his notes again and then back at her. "We have witnesses to the fact that you were heard to say you wanted to kill Harry Harrison for what he had done to your son."

She looked at his beefy red face and his narrow blue eyes and suddenly realized what he was getting at. "You can't seriously be suggesting that I had anything to do with my brother's death," she exclaimed.

The inspector cleared his throat again, glancing at Detective Mulloy. "Would you mind, ma'am, telling us where you were between the hours of eight and nine on Wednesday night?"

Francie stared at him. They were asking for her alibi, just the way they did in gangster movies, and on Wednesday night she had been with Buck Wingate in Annie's penthouse and she could never tell them that. But if she told them she was home alone, here in her own house, they would suspect her of Harry's murder.

She thought quickly and said, "I—I was at Aysgarth's Arms. I spent the evening with my friend, Annie Aysgarth."

The two detectives exchanged significant glances and Mulloy said, "I already checked the staff on duty that night at Aysgarth's, ma'am. There are witnesses to the fact that Miss Aysgarth was around most of that night, first in the Dales Lounge and afterward in the dining room. She stayed late and dined alone and later she was seen talking to guests in the lobby."

His eyes met Francie's frozen gaze as he stood up and said quietly, "I'm afraid, ma'am, it is my duty to arrest you on suspicion of the murder of your brother, Harmon Lloyd Harrison, Jr."

Francie looked numbly at him and then she said, "It's not true. I didn't kill Harry. I only lied to you because I knew if I told you I was home alone you would think I could have done it. This is all a mistake."

"If you'd like to put on your coat, miss, we'll take you down to the precinct and talk about it there." He nodded to the uniformed police officer. "Escort Miss Harrison upstairs to get her things, Steiglitz," he said, and Francie knew she was their prisoner.

She walked slowly upstairs to her room, too numb to think straight. She put on a dark-plum coat and a matching hat, pulling the little spotted veil over her eyes as she walked back to the door. Steiglitz followed her back down the stairs, past the frightened cook and the wailing Chinese maids and Ah Fong, who said with tears in his eyes, "I get Miss Aysgarth, Miss Francie. I call her for you right now. She always knows what to do."

Detective Mulloy opened the door and Francie stepped out into a barrage of flashbulbs. She stared at them, startled, and then the detectives gripped her arms and hurried her into the waiting police car and drove her away.

# CHAPTER 42

◆

*Friday, October 6th*

Buck had left the hotel early on Thursday morning. He was at Stanford University, where he had just given a talk, when he heard the news about the fire, and in Sacramento when he heard that Harry was dead. Later he was shocked by the report that said Harry had been murdered.

It was late Friday evening when he returned to San Francisco. He had planned on returning to Washington first thing in the morning. There was no reason to stay, his work was done. He'd had a hard day with stops at more than a dozen large and small towns. He'd shaken hands with local dignitaries as well as with "real people." He'd barely had time to snatch a bite and when he walked into his suite at Aysgarth's all he wanted was a shower and bed.

"Is that you, darling?" Maryanne called from her room and he wondered wearily for the thousandth time who she thought it was. She emerged looking immaculate in a dark-green dress, her blond hair waved sleekly across her well-shaped head, and she was smiling at him.

"Poor darling," she said soothingly, "I know you must be exhausted. Let me fix you a drink." She went to the table and poured him a whiskey with one ice cube, the way he liked it. He sank tiredly into the chair and she sat opposite him on the sofa, swinging her foot gently, still smiling.

"I thought we might have supper up here," she said. "Just something light. I know you're too tired to cope with much."

"If you like," he said, uncaring, absently watching her foot swing to and fro. "What's happened to your shoe?" he said suddenly. "It looks worn at the toe."

Maryanne glanced down at her black suede pumps and her face turned pink. She had just thrown the shoes into the closet after she had come back from Harry's and she'd slipped them on now without even looking. "Damn," she said standing up and hurrying to her room to change them, "they are dusty, aren't they? I'll have the valet clean them tonight."

"What happened to Harry?" Buck asked suddenly.

"Harry? Oh, isn't it shocking? The poor man got burned up in his own house and now they think it's murder." She hesitated; she realized he didn't know Francie had been arrested and she wondered whether to tell him, but decided against it. They were leaving first thing in the morning. She knew he was too tired to turn on the radio and if she kept the newspapers away from him with luck he wouldn't find out about it until they were safely back in Washington.

"I suppose," Buck said, staring reflectively into his drink, "that Harry was the kind of man a lot of people would be happy to see dead."

"Well, we certainly shan't be staying for the funeral," she said briskly. "I'm sorry about Harry, but I must get back to the children, I'm away from them far too much."

Surprised, he glanced at her. She saw the children as infrequently as he did and it was by her own choice. He finished his drink and went to take a shower and when he came back the room-service waiter was wheeling in a trolley. Maryanne disappeared quickly into her room. "Take care of things, will you Buck," she called hurriedly.

"Good to see you, Senator." The man smiled while arranging the dishes. "Though I guess you must be real cut-up about your friend, Mr. Harrison."

"It's sad news," Buck agreed, signing the bill.

"I wonder, did Mrs. Wingate ever find her keys, sir?" he asked solicitously. "I sure looked everywhere for 'em that night, all along the corridor and the elevator, sir, but no sign of 'em."

"Her keys?"

"Well sure, yes sir. Wednesday night when she came in, she said she had lost them. It's all right though, you tell her not to worry. Mrs. Aysgarth always has plenty of spares. These things happen, don't they, sir?"

"I guess they do," Buck replied, wondering vaguely where Maryanne had gone on Wednesday night.

He tipped the waiter, said good night, and poured himself another drink, staring moodily out the window, wondering if Francie was home, and what she thought about her hated brother's death. She must be glad, he thought, even though she would tell herself it's a terrible way to feel. He thought about calling Annie to ask, but Maryanne came back into the room just then, and anyway he didn't have the right.

"Consommé," she said, lifting the lid of a tureen and inspecting it. "Roast quail for you and lobster salad for me. You look dreadful, darling. Come and eat, it smells good."

He sat opposite her, watching as she ate her salad, listening to her chatter of what they would do next week in Washington, of the parties where they had to appear and of the dinner she was giving for the British ambassador. The telephone rang and she stopped in mid-sentence.

"I'll get it," he said, walking across and picking it up.

"Sorry to disturb you, Senator Wingate," the voice on the phone said. "Detective Sergeant Mulloy here, sir. I'm sure you know about the fire at Mr. Harrison's? I'm sorry, Senator, I know he was a friend of you and your wife. In fact, that's what brings me here tonight sir. It's our job to sort through the ruins, searching for a reason for the fire, really, and for anything that might have been saved. Well, it turns out something rather valuable was found in the ashes, sir, and the butler identified it as belonging to your wife. It's a little powder compact with her initials on it. The servants said you and your wife had dined there Tuesday night, sir, and I guess she forgot it."

"Thank you," Buck said automatically.

"We cleaned it up a bit, of course, sir," the detective sergent said. "I think you'll find it's all right. Even has the powder still inside. It's amazing how some things survive a fire and others don't, you'd be surprised what we find: toys, shoes, wristwatches. . . . It never ceases to amaze me."

"Yes," Buck agreed.

"I'll send it up then, Senator, and if you could just sign the receipt for me and send it back with the boy, I'd be very grateful."

"Don't bother," he said. "I'll come down and get it."

He could feel Maryanne's eyes on him as he walked to the door and he said, "There's someone who wants to see me downstairs."

"But your supper—"

The door closed behind him and she pursed her mouth angrily, wondering what was so important.

Buck collected the compact from the officer and signed the receipt. He slipped it into his pocket and walked out into the street; he needed to be alone with his thoughts. He walked rapidly through the square along Geary and up Nob Hill. A crowd still lingered round the cordoned-off ruins of the Harrison house and he stopped and stared. He remembered how he had dined in that house just four nights ago; his hand closed over the little powder compact in his pocket and he ran his thumb over the ruby initials MBW, thinking, puzzled, of Maryanne. A picture of her came into his mind. She was sitting on the flowered chintz sofa in a peach peignoir and she was powdering her nose. *She had been using this compact.* It was the night he saw Francie again, the same night Harry's house had burned. *The night Harry Harrison had been murdered.*

He gripped the little gold compact so hard it buckled. He saw in his mind the concerned face of the room waiter asking if Mrs. Wingate had found her keys; he had let her in, he said, on Wednesday night. . . .

"Senator Wingate, sir?"

He turned quickly to look at the uniformed police officer. "Can I help you, sir?" the man asked.

Buck shrugged, "Thanks, no. It's just that I knew him, it's a shock. . . ."

"Surely, sir. I'm sorry about that, Senator Wingate. I guess you'll feel better though, sir, now they've arrested the woman. Between you and me they are pretty sure she did it."

Buck unclenched his hand from the compact as relief sagged through him, he was crazy to think what he had been thinking. Of course it was one of Harry's women, some poor rejected girl. . . .

"Everybody knew how he and his sister hated each other," the officer continued. "That Harrison family's been feudin' for more than thirty years. She always claimed he killed her son and I guess it was only a matter of time before she got her revenge."

Buck stared at the man, his face blank with shock. "What are you saying? Who has been arrested for Harry's murder?"

"Why, his sister, sir." The officer looked concernedly after him as Buck turned on his heel and strode away.

He almost ran back down the hill to Aysgarth's, head down, hands in his pockets, his mind full of horrifying images of Francie being arrested, Francie terrified and alone, Francie in jail for Harry's murder. A murder he knew for sure she had not committed.

Maryanne was sitting on the same chintz sofa wearing the same peach peignoir she had last Wednesday night. She looked up from her book and gave him a relieved smile. "Darling, I've been so worried about you," she said. "Where on earth have you been?"

He took the jeweled compact from his pocket and held it out to her. "I've been to get this," he said, his voice tight with anger.

She looked at the compact and then at him. "Oh my goodness," she said shakily, "I wondered what had happened to it. Did I drop it downstairs somewhere?"

"You left it at Harry's," he said evenly. "On Wednesday night."

"On Wednesday night? Don't be ridiculous, we were at Harry's Tuesday, not Wednesday," she said flustered.

"*We* were at Harry's Tuesday. *You* were at Harry's Wednesday. The night you lost your keys and the room waiter had to let you in. Remember, Maryanne?"

She pushed a nervous hand through her immaculate hair. "Wednesday? Surely you're wrong. Wasn't I here, alone with you?"

"What was going on between you and Harry?" She put up a protesting hand and he said, "No. Don't lie to me. I want to know what you were doing there."

She shrugged her slender shoulders, defeated. "Harry was blackmailing me," she said quietly. "Over you and his goddamn sister. I've been paying him off for years—oh, not from my own purse, so to speak, but managing to get nice little deals put his way. . . . through my family and you, Buck, though you never knew it." She glared furiously at him. "It's all your fault, if you had never had that stupid little affair none of this would have happened." She looked up at him, her eyes hard. "She's threatened him all these years, he told me so. And now they've arrested her for his murder. And if she hadn't killed him then one day he would have killed her. They're two of a kind."

"Francie didn't murder Harry," he said, grabbing her roughly by the shoulders.

She smiled at him, that girlish innocent smile she could do so well. "Why, of course she did, Buck. You just don't want to believe it. Harry told me himself she had accused him of killing her son in a fire. Don't you think this was the perfect way to get her revenge? Another fire? It's quite biblical really, an eye for an eye, a fire for a fire—"

"You lying, scheming little bitch," he said, letting her go.

She dropped thankfully back onto the sofa, thinking Buck really looked quite frightening with that wild gleam in his eyes. "It's all so long ago, Buck," she said in a coaxing conciliatory voice. "You finished the affair and that was that. And after all, I'm the one who's had to pay the price." She shuddered delicately. "Harry was such a . . . such a scoundrel. . . ."

"I did not finish with Francie," he said stonily. "You did it for me. Just the way you tried to manage the rest of my life. I didn't want to leave her, I loved her—"

She latched quickly onto his use of the past tense of the word "love." "Well, there you are then," she said. "You loved her, it's all over, and now she's gotten herself into this mess. I'm sorry, Buck, but we can't let it affect our lives, not now with so much at stake."

He stood quietly, his hands in his pockets, looking at her and he knew the stakes had gotten too high for Maryanne. He thought of the cool impervious beauty he had married and of his alienated children, he thought of his brilliant future and knew it was just ashes. Maryanne had burned their lives away just the way he knew she had burned Harry's house on Wednesday night.

He turned and picked up his overcoat. "Where are you going?" she said, clutching her silk peignoir to her throat, frightened.

"I'm going to see Francie. I know she didn't do it—she has the perfect alibi. She was with Senator Buck Wingate Wednesday night—while you were at Harry's."

*"No! No! It's not true."* He walked to the door and she ran after him, tripping over the hem of her peignoir.

"You've always been a woman who got what you wanted," he said, "but not this time, Maryanne."

"I did it for you, Buck," she screamed, clinging to his arm. "I did it for you . . . for *us*."

"Whatever you did, you did for yourself," he said bitterly, "just the way you always have. Only now you have to live with it."

She watched aghast as he strode through the door. A little sob escaped her lips and she put her head in her hands, trembling. After a while she pulled herself together and walked into her room. She sat at her dresser, staring in the mirror at her disheveled hair and her own frightened eyes, thinking of how nearly she had brought it all off. She knew Buck would have been in the White House one day and she contemplated the power, the prestige, the acclaim that would have been hers. She would have had it all if it were not for Buck's stupidity. She wondered what he would do about Harry and decided she wouldn't worry about that; it was only Buck's word that the compact hadn't been left behind on the night of the dinner party. There was no way he or anyone else could prove anything. She was safe. And when he came back this time she would make him pay for it. She would surely make him pay for all he had put her through this week.

She combed her hair and powdered her nose, changed her torn peach peignoir for the blue panne velvet robe and lay down on the chintz sofa to wait for him.

The desk sergeant jumped hastily to his feet when Senator Buck Wingate walked in and asked to see the police chief. "Surely, sir . . . Senator Wingate. I guess he'll be home, Senator. I'll call him for you, right away, sir."

Buck waited fifteen minutes in a cluttered brown office. A green-shaded lamp burned over the desk, mountains of files spilled from the shelves and there were two old wooden chairs with the brown paint peeling off.

"Senator Wingate. Good to see you, sir. What can we do to help you?" The police chief was a burly man with an intelligent face, red from hurrying.

Buck took a seat. He looked steadily at the police chief and said, "I'm here about Francesca Harrison."

"The Harrison case?" He looked surprised.

"I'm here to tell you that Miss Harrison did not commit that murder, Chief Rawlins. She couldn't have. You see, she was with me that night."

Rawlins drew in a surprised breath; he saw and heard a lot in his job—scandals were scandals, but this was a big one. He sighed, thinking sex could really screw up a guy's head; whether he was a senator or a janitor, it was all the same. But this was an important man, a very important man. And his wife's family were almost royalty, if this country had such a thing. . . .

"Are you sure you want to say this, sir?" he suggested delicately, offering a way out.

"I'm certain. Miss Harrison is innocent and I am prepared to sign a statement saying she was with me. If necessary I will go to court and stand as her witness."

Rawlins shook his head quickly. "That won't be necessary, Senator, of course not. I'm quite prepared to release Miss Harrison on your say-so. There would be no need for any statement sir. No one need ever know." He looked at Buck and smiled, thinking cynically that his sort always got to keep their cake and eat it too.

Buck said briskly, "I want to make that statement, Rawlins. And I want it released to the press. I want everyone to know that Miss Harrison is not being let off this serious charge on a mere technicality. I want them to know without a shred of doubt that she is innocent. What I don't want is to leave any suspicion the media can build into another scandal she doesn't deserve."

The chief looked nervous. "I'm just worried about your own situation, Senator. How's it gonna look for you?"

Buck shrugged. "I've thought of all the implications, Chief Rawlins."

"If you'll just write your statement then, sir, I'll witness it. Then I'll send the sergeant for Miss Harrison. She's in an interview room down the hall."

The terrible vision of Francie in a grim prison cell dissolved in his mind and he picked up a pen and quickly wrote his statement. He signed it firmly and the chief read it and added his own signature as witness.

There was a knock on the door and the young sergeant held it open and Francie walked in. Her head dropped and her eyes were dark with fatigue and shock; he thought she looked like a frightened fawn. She looked from him to the police chief, saying nothing, and he knew that even now she was prepared to protect him and his family and his political career. His wonderful career that he had sacrificed their happiness for.

He smiled at her, his face full of love. "It's all right, Francie," he said. "Chief Rawlins knows you were with me the night Harry died. You're free now."

She looked at him, then she lifted her chin proudly. "Free?" she said. And he knew what she was asking.

"Yes," he said, taking her arm and putting it through his as they walked from the cluttered, drab office. "We both are," he told her, smiling.

Maryanne read the sensational story of Francie Harrison's release in the *Examiner* the next morning; and the announcement, under his picture, of Senator Wingate's rumored retirement from politics.

White with anger she tossed the newspaper to the ground and stamped on her husband's handsome face, then she called the maid and ordered her bags packed. She dressed carefully in her silver-gray woolen dress, her mink-lined cape and matching hat. She added a touch more lipstick than usual, checking her appearance in the long mirror. Then she went downstairs to face the press camped in the street outside Aysgarth's, waiting for her.

"Mrs. Wingate," they shouted, surging toward her as she walked down the steps to the waiting limousine. "Mrs. Wingate, what do you have to say about Francie Harrison and your husband? What about his resignation, Mrs. Wingate—?"

She turned, one foot in the limousine, and gave them a plucky little smile. "Gentlemen, gentlemen," she called amid a flurry of flash-bulbs, "thank you for your interest, but I am sure you can appreciate that this is a purely personal matter. And of course, we Brattles never talk of such things outside the family." And with a final brave little smile and a wave she stepped into the car and was driven to the airport where she took a plane to New York to consult her lawyer about a divorce.

Annie Aysgarth watched Maryanne from the top of the steps as she gave her farewell performance as Senator Wingate's beautiful wife and she sighed with relief when she finally left. Between them, Harry Harrison and Maryanne Wingate had conspired to wreck the lives of those around them. Maryanne and Harry were alike: they were both selfish and unscrupulous, they took without giving and they stopped at nothing. Not even murder. Now Harry was dead and Maryanne had created her own personal hell and she would have to live with it.

The reporters and photographers had disappeared, eager to scoop the story of Maryanne's dramatic departure, and Annie walked down the steps into the street and turned to look up at her hotel. She had created this place, and all the others. Aysgarth's was her own world and she loved it. She had shared in Francie's children, just the way she had with Josh when he was small and though she had never had a husband and a child of her own, she was fulfilled. She ran back up the steps into her world. Through all the tragedies, fortune had smiled on her and she was a happy woman.

*   *   *

Francie and Buck were at the ranch. There were so many things to be said between them that would never be discussed. They didn't need to. He had said it all when he had told her they were free.

Buck had not resigned immediately after the scandal broke. "If I do, they'll either think you are guilty—or I am," he told her. "You'll see, we'll be a nine-days wonder and then a new scandal will take our place. Besides, they have to figure out who they're going to appoint to replace me. I can't just leave all those people who are depending on me up in the air."

Of course, he was right. He was well-liked in Washington and when he tendered his resignation a month later, the political columnists were eager to sing his praises. "The world of politics loses a good man," they said. "But it's by his own fair choice and not any puritanical pressure. While it is hoped he enjoys his retirement and his new life, the Republican Party would be foolish to let him go entirely and the word is that he is available in an 'advisory' capacity, which his boundless experience more than qualifies him for."

When he'd finally met Lysandra he had taken her in his arms and kissed her and told her he was the old friend of her mother's she had spoken to on the phone. He'd crouched down so their eyes were on a level and she had stared silently at him, then she said, "You're the one, aren't you? You are my father?"

Francie had gasped, afraid of what she would say next, but he had smiled gently at her and said, "That's true, Lysandra. I hope you'll forgive me for not being around for the first seven years, but you see, I didn't know about you."

"Are you gonna stay around now?" she asked wistfully, her head on one side.

"If your mother will let me," he replied with a glance at Francie.

And Lysandra had slipped her hand into his and said confidently, "Oh, she loves you all right. I can tell."

Now they were the best of friends and Francie watched them walking along the rows of vines. Buck was bending toward Lysandra, who was showing him something, probably explaining how they were pruned for the winter. Lysandra always knew about everything.

Buck looked up and caught her eye. "She's teaching me all about growing vines," he called. "Didn't I always tell you I wanted to run a winery?"

Francie remembered he had, all those years ago, and she laughed as she went to join them. She just wished though that the Mandarin, who had changed her fortunes, could have been there to share their happiness.

# Part *VI*

◆

# *LYSANDRA*
## *1963*

# CHAPTER 43

◆

## *1963*

*Hong Kong*

Lysandra Lai Tsin had more than fulfilled the destiny the Mandarin had bequeathed her. She was president of Lai Tsin International and a beautiful woman in a man's world, though she was careful never to exploit that fact. She wore formal, almost severe suits of dark cashmere in winter and creaseless silk in summer. She kept her shoe heels sensibly low, even though she had long shapely legs to show off, and wore her rippling pre-Raphaelite corn blond hair swept up at the sides with a pair of antique jade combs from her fabulous collection. Her skin was creamy and flawless, she had her mother's startling sapphire-blue eyes and her full mouth was painted a bright fuschia—her only makeup and her only concession to femininity. But even her enemies—as well as those who respected her—admitted Lysandra did not need makeup: not with *those* looks. And *that* money. And *that* power. And no one who ever got close to her ever forgot those cool, enigmatic blue eyes nor the faint, almost invisible scent of her, like the clean early morning scent of a summer garden with the very faintest hint of lilies.

She was alone in her office atop the spectacular new thirty-story Lai Tsin Building between Connaught and Des Voeux Roads, though the company's official business address was still the old godown on the seedy waterfront where the Mandarin had first started. When the new skyscraper had replaced the Mandarin's first headquarters Lysandra had insisted that all the great things he had shown her so proudly as a little girl, the malachite columns, the mosaics and the carvings, were preserved and incorporated into the startlingly modern new reception hall. And the great bronze lions still presided over the front steps, keeping out the bad *ch'i.*

It was seven-thirty P.M. The sun was just setting over Victoria Bay, painting the sky orange and gold, and the gray water and bustling little ferries a gay carnival pink. Lysandra had been in her office as usual since seven-thirty that morning, and now it was silent but for the ticking of a tiny jeweled clock and the muffled noise of traffic in the street far below. She rarely left her office during the day—people always came to see *her*, and if there was a lunch meeting it was always in her private dining room on the thirtieth floor, which had the reputation of being the gastronomic equal of the best restaurants in Hong Kong. And Lysandra had the reputation of being one of the city's toughest businesswomen.

"The old man knew what he was doing when he chose her to run the company," the Hong Kong taipans acknowledged with grudging admiration. "You can't put anything over on Lysandra Lai Tsin. Nothing gets past her eagle blue eyes and she has an instinct for a deal that can only be called supernatural. Or good *fung shui*."

They said that Lysandra had started her career when she was still just a child of ten years.

In November of 1941, Lysandra had been on her annual visit to Uncle Philip Chen and his family—and forever afterward Buck was to blame himself for his lack of foresight. Although there was a war in Europe it was business as usual in Hong Kong: the harbor was crowded with cargo vessels and Pan Am flying boats came and went regularly from the U.S. Buck was still well-liked in Washington, though he had resigned from the Senate. He'd wanted to spend his time with Francie and devote himself to expanding the ranch and the winery, but Washington still lured him and occasionally he found himself called upon in an advisory capacity.

He had been asked to go to Hong Kong on a three-week mission by the War Department under the guise of being an observer for a proposed trade delegation. There was no reason to believe America or Americans were under any threat and the Japanese were not acting belligerently across the borders in China. And Lysandra had cajoled and pleaded, her blue eyes filled with longing. "After all," she'd said wistfully to Francie, "Hong Kong is my home, too, or it will be one day." A look of sadness had filled her eyes as she added, "Besides, it's what Grandfather Lai Tsin wanted me to do."

It was the look of sadness that did it. Francie's eyes had met Buck's and she'd sighed. "It's true, the Mandarin did want you to visit Hong Kong each year."

Lysandra had flung her arms around her mother's neck. "Please

Mommy," she murmured, "please let me go. I'll be safe with Buck, you know I will."

Buck had grinned and said, "I can't argue with that."

So Lysandra had gone with him and after only three days in Hong Kong, Buck came down with typhoid, spent two weeks in the hospital and was shipped home on a stretcher. It was decided that Lysandra should stay on with Philip Chen and that his wife Irene would personally escort her home in a couple of weeks' time. Weak and debilitated, Buck had agreed it was better than accompanying a sick man on a stretcher. And then things happened too suddenly for anyone to act.

On December 7th the Japanese simultaneously attacked Pearl Harbor and crossed the Shenzen-Hong Kong border. Kai Tak Airport was heavily bombed and the runways put out of action and less than three weeks later, on Christmas Day, 1941, Hong Kong surrendered. Philip Chen quickly removed the secret and important documents from the Lai Tsin headquarters, including those from the Mandarin's personal safe, to which only he and Francie held a key, and hid them under his kitchen floorboards. It wasn't the best hiding place in the world, but it was all he could do.

Francie was crazy with fear for Lysandra and the Chen family. Pale and thin and still weak from his illness, Buck held her close while she wept bitter tears at her foolishness in letting Lysandra go.

"It's my fault," he said, tight-lipped with the effort of controlling his fear for his beloved daughter. "I took her there and it's my responsibility to get her back. I'll get her out of there if it's the last thing I do." He'd left for Washington the next day.

For the first time in her life Francie couldn't bear to be at the ranch, it was full of Lysandra, the walls and tables were filled with her photographs, her clothes brimmed from the closet and her books from the shelves, and her dogs followed at Francie's feet. All her young life was here, this was where it had begun . . . and for all she knew it might already have ended. Terrified, Francie fled to Washington and Buck. His name still counted in the nation's capital, he knew everybody who was anybody. If strings could be pulled to find Lysandra, Buck would find the right ones.

Philip Chen watched the British soldiers being marched off to prisoner of war camps in Kowloon. Like many other Chinese he ran beside them, giving them what food and money he could hastily lay his hands on, helping carry a weary young soldier's heavy pack until a brutal Japanese guard began to harangue him, beating him and the soldier to the ground with the butt of his rifle. As he pulled himself to his feet and walked away, he glanced back at the young soldier still lying in the road; he had not been so lucky. After that Philip knew what to expect from the Japanese captors.

Notices appeared informing all foreign civilians to report to the Japanese officials, ready to be sent to internment camps near the sea at Stanley; only Chinese were free to remain. Philip spoke urgently with his wife, Irene. They were responsible for the safety of the Mandarin's appointed heir, Lysandra, whom they loved like their own child, and they decided immediately they must hide her, whatever the risk, until the war ended. Ah Sing, Lysandra's amah, watched them worriedly. She adored her young charge and now she sensed danger. Her love was as fierce as any mother's for her Number One daughter.

That afternoon Philip Chen was summoned to Japanese headquarters. The man who interrogated him through an interpreter was arrogant and to the point. He ordered one of the guards to deliver a fierce blow to Philip's head for failing to bow to the Imperial Japanese invader. His small eyes gleamed in triumph at his own power over the influential comprador of one of Hong Kong's most important merchant houses.

"Tomorrow," he said, "at eleven hundred hours, the Imperial Japanese Army will take over the headquarters and assets of the Lai Tsin Corporation. We request that your taipan accompany you to this meeting so that his signature may be obtained for the documents relinquishing all his rights to the Imperial Japanese Government."

Anger flared in Philip's eyes, but he controlled it; he guessed their spies knew little about the Lai Tsin Corporation except that it was rich, and they coveted its assets and its ships, many of which thanks to the Japanese bombardment now lay beneath the waters of Hong Kong harbor. And he also guessed they did not know about Lysandra. "The taipan was in San Francisco at the time of your invasion," he said contemptuously. "He will not be available to sign such documents."

The Japanese officer's cold eyes met his. "We have information to the contrary." His voice rose to an angry shout. "Our informant is very reliable. A Chinese. We know the Lai Tsin taipan is here in Hong Kong and we shall expect him to be present tomorrow at eleven. Failure to do so will invoke serious reprisals, Mr. Chen—for you and your family."

Philip felt his eyes boring into his back as he was marched back out by the guard, and he hurried home a very worried man. Even in such a short time, the Japanese Kempeitei, the military police, had achieved a reputation for brutality that matched the German Gestapo's, and he knew he could expect the worst. He was a rich and important man in Hong Kong and he lived in a beautiful house in the mid-levels. He was a target and he knew it.

"We'll smuggle her into China to some remote village where she can hide," he told his anxious wife, but she said it was impossible.

"She's so blond and with those blue eyes there is no disguising her as Chinese. Even if we sent her with Robert," she added, her normally sweet face frowning with worry as she glanced at ten-year-old Lysandra and fourteen-year-old Robert, listening to what was being said.

"I'm not going without Lysandra," Robert said stubbornly. He was a tall, bespectacled, studious boy and Lysandra had always suspected he did not like her, so she glanced at him surprised when he added, "I'm staying to look after her."

Philip shook his head. "We have to get her out of here immediately, before they come looking for her."

Lysandra looked quickly from Irene to Philip and realized that because of her they were in terrible danger. "What do the Japanese want from me?" she asked, puzzled.

"They have requested the taipan be brought to our offices tomorrow to meet the general and personally sign the order relinquishing all claims to the company and its assets."

"And if I do not?"

He shrugged, "There will be 'reprisals.' "

The Japanese occupying forces had been around long enough for Lysandra to know what that meant, and she thought quickly of what her mother would have done.

"Okay, then it's simple. I shall go into our offices tomorrow and as taipan of the Lai Tsin Corporation I'll sign the order. And then when we win the war we'll take it all back again."

Philip smiled at her cockiness, she was just a little schoolgirl and she thought she could take on the Japanese warlords. "You may be taipan, but until you're eighteen your mother is 'acting head' of the company. A document signed by you, as a minor, would be worthless."

"Then that's even better, isn't it? They'll think they've got what they want and they'll leave you alone."

"I can't let you do it, it's dangerous. You don't know what they're like, Lysandra, they are without conscience or mercy."

She weighed his words carefully: all she knew was the Japanese would show no mercy to Uncle Philip and Aunt Irene and Robert if they hid her and she did not appear at the offices the next day. "As taipan of Lai Tsin," she said, sticking her chin in the air and looking Philip Chen straight in the eyes, "I'm giving you my first order. Tomorrow at eleven hundred hours you will escort me to our headquarters, where I shall sign the document for the Japanese."

Philip Chen had loved his "Honorable Father," Lai Tsin, well. He had transferred that love and loyalty to his Honorable Granddaughter, Lysandra; he thought of Francie and Buck and knew he could not expose her to such danger. "They are expecting a man," he said, casting his mind around quickly for a substitute. "We'll find someone to go in your place."

"No!" Lysandra's voice was imperious. "My grandfather gave the responsibility to me. I shall be the one to sign the document." Her face crumbled and she suddenly lost all her bravado. She ran to her uncle and from the comfort of his arms cried, "Don't you see, it's the only way. You are my family, I love you, I can't let them hurt you."

"When they see she's just a child," Irene said reassuringly, "they'll leave her alone." But Ah Sing shook her head as she turned away and that night she lit incense to all the gods she could think of, praying Irene was right.

Lysandra was awake early the next morning and she ran from her room to Robert's, next door. He lifted his head from the pillow and looked sleepily at her, searching for his glasses. "What is it?" he asked, alarmed. "Have the Japanese come for us?"

"No, no." She shook her head and her blond hair flew. "I just want to ask you something." She leaned forward conspiratorially, "I just realized that by the time I'm old enough to run Lai Tsin, your father will have retired. Robert, please will you be my comprador when you are older?"

He found his glasses and stuck them on his nose, looking at her. "I planned on being a brain surgeon," he said. "I don't think I'd be much good as a comprador."

Lysandra heaved a sigh. "Promise me you'll think about it," she pleaded. "The Mandarin always said I would need every friend I could get."

Philip was taking no chances and after breakfast Robert and his mother were sent to stay with friends in Kowloon. From there they would adopt the disguise of a peasant woman and her son and be taken under cover of darkness through the New Territories and across the border into China, where they could hide. Tears stung Lysandra's eyes as she kissed them good-bye, wondering when she would see them again, and she watched anxiously from the window as Philip first walked the length of the street alone, checking to see if he was being observed. When he was sure the way was clear he waved Irene and Robert out through the servants' entrance and down the alley behind the building, watching until they were out of sight.

As eleven o'clock approached, Ah Sing helped dress Lysandra in her best blue cotton, white ankle socks, and black patent Mary Janes. Even though it was a hot day she put the beautiful deep-blue silk robe, embroidered in gold and crimson, over the top. The Japanese had already annexed every motor vehicle in Hong Kong, so, accompanied by Ah Sing, who refused to leave her side, they made their way by rickshaw to the office.

The staff had been warned of the visit of the Japanese general and they were standing nervously about in the lofty, pillared reception hall. They stared in amazement as Philip Chen walked through the door with little Lysandra Lai Tsin in her Mandarin's robe, quickly forming a line and bowing respectfully as she walked past, and in turn Lysandra bestowed a regal nod and a smile on each.

The Mandarin's office at the back of the hall was exactly as he had left it; no one was ever permitted to use it and it was cleaned and polished each day by the most trusted workers. His Chinese inkpad and brushes, his silver inkstand and pens and his old wooden abacus were arranged on his ebony-wood desk, just as though he might appear at any moment to use them. Lysandra stared at his portrait hanging on the wall opposite the window and she smiled tremulously at him. Like her, he was dressed in his Mandarin robe and he looked as wise and kind as she remembered. Her knees were shaking and her palms sweating with fear as she sat in a thronelike antique blackwood chair behind her grandfather's desk, waiting for the Japanese general, and more than anything she wished her mom and dad were there.

Seeking courage, she glanced again at the painting of the Mandarin, remembering the time he had first brought her here, and she knew he would have expected her to be strong in adversity, the way he had always been.

Philip Chen stood behind her chair to the left and a dozen men, the heads of all the departments, lined up alongside him, while Ah Sing crouched in a corner, fingering the sharp kitchen knife hidden beneath her black smock, ready to kill anyone who tried to harm her beloved Number One daughter.

At precisely eleven o'clock there was a sudden commotion of shouted orders and the sound of booted feet marching across the marble hall. The door was flung open and the Japanese general stood there, surveying them.

Lysandra noticed quickly he was as short as she was, and slender with a little pencil moustache and narrow slanting eyes. Unlike the soldiers his uniform was perfectly tailored; his brass buttons glittered and his jackboots shone and a long cape lined in scarlet was flung across his shoulders. Behind him were half a dozen guards, rifles at the ready, and a young lieutenant who was to act as his interpreter.

The general swaggered into the room, tapping his stick against his palm; he looked at Philip Chen and at the managers bowing their heads respectfully. He stared at the Mandarin's portrait. And then he looked at the blond blue-eyed child sitting in the blackwood throne behind the taipan's desk of one of Hong Kong's greatest companys. The fawning half-smile he had deigned to bestow was replaced with a glance of such fierce anger, Lysandra closed her eyes so she would not have to see it.

He screamed something and the Japanese interpreter repeated it nervously in the flawless English he had acquired when he was studying at Stanford University in California. "The general asks what kind of joke this is that you are playing on the emissary of His Imperial Majesty? He warns you that the reprisals will be severe and instructs you to bring forward the proper taipan of the House of Lai Tsin immediately."

Lysandra pulled herself to her tallest, she tilted her chin in the air exactly the way her mother, Francie, did when she was angry, and said, "Tell the general I am the taipan of the Lai Tsin hong. It is I who shall read the documents he has brought and decide whether they shall be signed."

The general's angry slitted eyes were fixed on her as the interpreter relayed the news and this time she did not look away. She noted with satisfaction that his face turned from scarlet to purple as he tried to decide whether he was being made a fool of.

He looked murderously at Philip Chen, barking still another question at the interpreter. "The general asks your name and why is it the great Lai Tsin hong has a child at its head?"

Lysandra nodded gravely. "Tell the general I am Lysandra Lai Tsin. On his death my Honorable Grandfather, the Mandarin Lai Tsin, left me in sole charge of his empire. You have already met my comprador, Mr. Chen, and these men are my managers. Tell the general that I am the only person with the power to sign his papers, and that I take sole responsibility for my company and my employees."

The general listened to the interpreter; his glance was still uneasy, he realized that if this was a trick all of Hong Kong would soon know about it; he would be a laughingstock and his loss of face would be so bad as to possibly demand his death.

"Ask the girl where is the chop, the Great Seal of Lai Tsin?" he demanded.

Lysandra took the red sandlewood box inlaid with gold from the drawer and removed the carved jade seal. "Here it is," she said, laying it on the desk in front of her. "And now will you tell the general that I wish to see his papers at once."

Her blackwood throne was high and slippery and she wriggled forward, hoping he would not notice her feet failed to reach the floor. The general stared angrily at her; he ordered the interpreter to ask her who her mother was and where she lived? And when he heard the answers he knew she was who she claimed to be.

Burning at having to do so, he clicked his heels and bowed briefly to her before handing her the document, while the interpreter explained that she was turning over her company to be "managed" by His Imperial Majesty, Emperor Hirohito's emissaries. She must affix her signature and the chop and then her comprador and all her managers must also add their signatures to the document. The assets of the company, including this building and all the vessels currently at anchor in the harbor, would be annexed from this moment.

Lysandra turned again to the portrait of her grandfather. Then she looked back at the arrogant Japanese general and then at Uncle Philip and the other silent men and she knew she had no choice.

Using the Mandarin's own brushes she wrote her name in the

exquisite Chinese characters he himself had taught her. The seal was applied and the deed was done.

Replacing the seal carefully in its box, she stared fiercely at the waiting Japanese. She pushed back her chair and stood up. "Tell your general he now has what he wants and these offices are his; we shall leave." Her glance collected Philip and the heads of all the departments as she led them from the Mandarin's office without another word.

The general stared after her as she strode past him, her blond head held high. Her black patent Mary Janes and white ankle socks peeked from beneath the richly embroidered silk robe and she clutched the box with the seal of the House of Lai Tsin firmly in her small hands.

For once in his career he had nothing to say and the interpreter looked nervously away, unwilling to witness such a deep loss of face lest the general take his anger out on him.

"She will not get away with this," the general muttered, shuffling the documents she had left on the desk, and his voice shook with anger as he repeated ominously, "She will not get away with this."

A short while later Philip Chen and each of the managers were arrested by the Kempeitei and taken to the Supreme Court building to be brutally interrogated and tortured, and a few weeks later they were imprisoned and put to work as laborers, rebuilding the runways at Kai Tak. Lysandra Lai Tsin was taken into custody and sent to Manchuria, where she was kept in confinement with other important prisoners. A few months later, she was spirited away by Chinese patriots, and after a long and hazardous journey through Russia, arrived in neutral Finland. The first person she saw as she stepped off the flimsy little aircraft was Buck and she fell into his arms, tears raining down her taut, tired little face. "Oh, Buck," was all she could say between the choking sobs as he held her close, his own tears falling onto her tangled, unkempt hair.

"It's okay, little one," he'd murmured. "You're safe now! Soon you'll be home with Mommy." And he thanked God he'd been able to keep his promise to Francie.

They flew secretly to London and from there to New York and a rapturous reunion with Francie. But Lysandra's adventures were kept secret for fear of reprisals on Philip Chen, until after the war when he was released and reunited with his family.

Outwardly, Lysandra's life returned to that of a normal schoolgirl, but the experience had left a permanent stain on her soul that made her feel different from her young friends. Francie tried to get her to talk about it, but somehow she just couldn't tell her mother and she kept the savage images of fear locked away in some secret compartment of her mind, never to be looked at again.

It was Annie who finally broke the barrier. Lysandra had gone after school to have tea with her in the penthouse, an event which she loved both for the feeling it gave her of floating above the city and the fabulous cakes made by Aysgarth's Swiss pastry chef—of which she was allowed to choose exactly two.

"Two cakes are enough for any growing girl who doesn't want to get fat," Annie said briskly, though she herself had grown substantially plumper. Pouring tea into wide blue china cups, she passed one to Lysandra and said, "Your mother's worried stiff about you, you know that, don't you?"

Lysandra stared blankly at her. "Mom's worried? About what? What have I done?"

"It's what you haven't done. You've scarcely mentioned the prison camp and what happened to you."

"I don't want to think about it," Lysandra exclaimed, staring at the chocolate eclair on her plate. It suddenly didn't look as appetizing as it had just minutes before.

Annie said gently, "You know, love, sometimes the only way to get rid of a bad memory is to talk about it, confront it. Then you can say 'The hell with it, I'm rid of you forever!'"

Lysandra stared doubtfully at her. Annie was her godmother, but she was also her friend. She talked straight and never pulled her punches, she wasn't afraid to tell her when she thought she was out of line and she was never stinting in her praise whenever she deserved it. Annie was always impartial and never judgmental and she had the knack of being able to make her see both sides of a question. She never provided the answer, but somehow she showed her how to find one, and now Lysandra recognized that what Annie was saying was true.

She stared silently at her, her blue eyes frightened. Annie had grown stouter and more solid as she grew older. Her hair was gray instead of shiny brown, but her big shrewd eyes were the same and they were filled with affection and pity.

"I just didn't want to upset Mommy and Buck more than I had already," Lysandra murmured, twisting her hands together agitatedly. "I know they blame themselves for letting me go, but it was me, Annie. I was the one who insisted it would be all right. Buck was going and I wanted so badly to see Uncle Philip and—and everything. I put everybody's lives in danger, the Chens', Buck's . . ."

"And your own," Annie said softly. Leaning forward, she took Lysandra's hot, tightly gripped hands, unlocking them and holding them firmly in her own cool, smooth ones. And suddenly the whole story spilled out about how scared she had really been under the facade of cockiness the day she had signed the Japanese document, of her terror when she had seen Irene and Robert disappear into the night and she had realized she might never see them again, of her sense of desolation alone in the Japanese prison and the despair of not knowing what had happened to Philip. When the Chinese came for her she thought they had come to execute her.

"Everybody thinks I was so brave," she murmured through her tears, "but I wasn't, Annie, I was scared all the time."

"Of course you were, sweetheart," Annie said comfortingly. "Only a stupid person wouldn't have been." She listened to Lysandra's tales of the daily brutality she had witnessed, the beatings and the screams that came in the night, of the scuttling of rats and the smell of vomit and latrines. And though Annie's face was impassive, inside she was hurting for the child.

"And all the time I thought about Mommy," Lysandra said. "I thought how worried she must be. I cried myself to sleep every night thinking of her and Buck, and of you, Annie. I pretended the dogs were curled on my bed the way they do at the ranch and that I could hear the rustle of the wind in the orchard and the whinny of the ponies in the stables. I tried to block all the bad things out and sometimes it worked and I dreamed I was home again."

"And now you *are* home, child, you really are. And that's what you must remember, not the bad stuff. War is evil and it was partly your own fault you were caught up in it, but your mother and Buck were also to blame for giving in to you. You've all suffered for it, but now it's over and you can pick yourself up and get on with real life. Just the way your mother had to when she was a girl, not that much older than you are now. And let me tell you something," she added fiercely, "don't ever say you were not brave, because you were, Lysandra Lai Tsin. Any good soldier will tell you that he is afraid when he confronts the enemy and goes into battle. And you were as brave as any good soldier."

"Do you really think so?" Lysandra asked tremulously.

"Damn right I do," Annie said, a smile spreading across her still-pretty face. "Now, let's have some more tea, shall we?"

But that conversation stayed a secret between Annie and Lysandra, and afterward, whenever any newcomer arrived in Hong Kong he was always told, "Better watch out for Lysandra Lai Tsin, she's inherited the old man's balls as well as his empire." And they would chuckle as they recounted the story of the schoolgirl taking on the Japanese general and causing him such a terrible loss of face.

Within four years, the Lai Tsin ships were sailing the world once again and the great company had retained its power. Lysandra fretted away her four years at Vassar, longing for Hong Kong. She knew her fate was different from that of the society girls she met. Oh, she wore the same pastel cashmere sweater sets, the pearls and the saddle shoes, but all they wanted was to meet Mr. Right and get married and have babies and she was Lysandra Lai Tsin, taipan of one of the richest companies in the world. She looked eagerly forward to facing her responsibilities. "It's sort of like you're Mr. Rockefeller," one of the girls told her wonderingly when she finally left Vassar for Hong Kong.

Francie and Buck flew over with her and the Chen family were at the airport to greet them.

"You never change, Philip," Francie said, hugging him. "You still look like the serious bespectacled young man who used to help Ollie with his homework."

"Would that the gods had been kinder and Ollie was still with us," he said gently. "But you, Francie, you are not a day older and even more beautiful."

She shook her head ruefully. "Even I can't ignore the white hairs, Philip."

"Wisdom arrives with the white hairs, and wisdom enhances beauty."

"Careful," Buck laughed. "I won't be able to keep up with all these Chinese compliments."

"It's true though." Lysandra looked admiringly at her mother, as slim and chic as she had been twenty years ago. Her full, cream silk shirt and little navy jacket showed off her still-small waist, and she wore a shady-brimmed navy straw hat with a silk gardenia pinned to one side. "Mom gets even prettier as she gets older."

"And so does Aunt Irene," she said, hugging the diminutive Chinese woman, equally smart in a red shantung shirt dress with the newly fashionable full skirt. "And no white hairs either," she added admiringly. Then she hugged her again, and said, "Oh, am I glad to see you."

Only Robert was different. He was standing back waiting for his elders to greet each other and Lysandra thought how grown-up he looked. "Robert," she said, hurrying over to him, both hands held out to take his. "You look . . ." she paused, assessing him while he smiled down at her. He was tall and broad-shouldered, his horn-rimmed spectacles half-hid his blue eyes and he had the same thick shock of black hair. But there was something else about him and she hesitated, still searching for the right words. There was an air of confidence, as though he knew exactly where he was going in the world—but then he always had. "You look 'distinguished,' " she said with a grin, "like a famous neurosurgeon."

He laughed. "And you look exactly the same, only even skinnier."

"I am not," she cried indignantly. "I am fashionably slender." She laughed. "Dammit, you always knew how to get a rise out of me." She put her arms around him and hugged him. "Are we still friends?"

"Always," he promised. "You can count on me."

The taipan had come to claim her rightful heritage and there was a celebration party in the grand hall at the Lai Tsin headquarters that week. After the long formal dinner Francie watched her daughter proudly as she stood up to make her speech. She looked very young in a deep-blue cheongsam, but she spoke in flawless Mandarin, promising to guide the company as surely and firmly as her grandfather, telling them that she prayed one day she would be as wise as he, but that meanwhile she would need their help, and that the Lai Tsin hong would continue to be known for its fair and just business throughout the world.

"Oh, Buck," Francie whispered, clutching his hand with a pang of misgiving, "I only hope the Mandarin knew what he was doing. She's so young, shouldn't she be out enjoying herself like other girls her age?"

"Lysandra isn't 'other girls,' " he whispered back. "The Mandarin molded her when she was still just a kid. Plus she's got your backbone and determination and this is what she wants. And believe me, should the day ever come when she decides she doesn't want it, she'll be just as determined and sure of her decision."

"I hope you're right," Francie whispered.

A week later she and Buck returned to California. "I'll miss you," she told Lysandra as she said good-bye.

"Not half as much as I'll miss you," her daughter said, hugging her tightly, tears springing to her eyes. She watched as Buck and her mother climbed the steps to the plane, choking back the lump in her throat as Buck put his arm around Francie and they turned to wave to her. She thought how perfect they looked together, as though they belonged, and she was glad for their happiness. But as the plane disappeared into the clouds she knew her life was to be different from theirs. Her destiny was not as any man's wife, but as taipan of Lai Tsin.

She worked for a year at Philip Chen's side, learning all he could teach her. She took books home to study at night and worried about the time wasted attending weekend swimming parties at the country club or dancing with endless young men who always seemed so much younger and more carefree than she was, at parties at the Peninsula Hotel. Behind her pretty blond facade was a very serious young woman determined to live up to the demands of her inheritance, and nothing was going to stand in her way. And then, when she was just twenty-two, she met Pierre d'Arancourt.

He was forty and very distinguished-looking. His black hair had a silver streak at each temple, his nose was properly arrogant and his mouth sensual. He was lean and tall and his shoulders were broad, and he was different from any of the boys she had met. She first saw him riding in a visitor's race at the Happy Valley Racetrack.

"Who is he?" she asked, her eyes wide with interest, immediately placing fifty dollars on him to win.

"Oh, that's Prince Pierre," someone told her casually. "He shows up every now and then in Hong Kong when he's bored with Paris or New York or Buenos Aires. He's French, with an old title, but brought up mostly in Argentina—that's why he rides so well, I guess."

"I guess," she breathed, lifting her binoculars to watch as he rode to win.

He was at the dance given that night at the Government House and she noticed that he had noticed her watching him and she looked shyly away. In all her twenty-two years she had never had a boy-friend—oh, she'd been out on plenty of dates but she had never had a real boyfriend. She knew her mother worried about it, but Annie understood it was the wrong time in her life. She had to work hard and beat the game first, and though no one realized it, behind her cool facade she was an insecure young girl who knew nothing about love.

Pierre was so much older than she was, she didn't know exactly how to respond when he came over and introduced himself and asked her to dance. She thought that he was even handsomer than Buck, and she listened entranced to his tales of his ranch in Argentina and his apartment on the Avenue Foch in Paris and the family château in the Loire. His life sounded cosmopolitan and glamorous, peppered with exotic names from the theater, movies, and society, and light years removed from her own cloistered, single-minded existence.

"And what do you do with yourself all day, out here in Hong Kong?" he asked, somehow managing to make it sound boringly provincial, and when she told him that she worked hard learning to run the company she had inherited from her grandfather, he laughed. His dark eyes were filled with mocking amusement at the idea as he said, "Well, maybe we should do something to change all that. You're far too beautiful to be wasted on mere business."

No one had ever called her beautiful before and Lysandra smiled breathlessly at him, saying nothing. She had been forced to leave him then and join her own party for supper, but she glanced his way often that night.

The next morning alongside her breakfast plate was a bouquet of tiny, perfect yellow rosebuds and a note, saying he hoped he would see her again. She put the flowers in water, remembering with a little frisson of excitement his dark eyes looking into hers and his deep voice telling her she was beautiful. Her head was in a whirl all day thinking of him, hoping he would call, but at six-thirty he still hadn't and she drove disappointedly home to her small apartment in the mid-levels. Ah Sing flung open the door, her face wreathed in smiles, and as she stepped inside, Lysandra saw the place was filled with flowers; roses and orchids, jasmine, peonies, and little tubs of creamy gardenias. The scent was overpowering and the message clear: Prince Pierre was very interested in her blond beauty and not her business brain.

The phone rang, and when she picked it up it was him. "Thank you for the flowers," she said breathlessly. "I've never seen so many in my life, you must have ransacked every florist in Hong Kong."

He laughed and asked her to dinner at the Peninsula Hotel and she caused raised eyebrows among the "colonials" in her sea-green brocade cheongsam and high-piled blond hair. "They forget my heritage is Chinese," she told Pierre, proudly. She wore one of his gardenias at her shoulder and he told her he would never smell its wonderful scent again without thinking of her. "Gardenias were made for you," he said, as she smiled, excited to be in the company of the handsomest man in the room. When he took her home he kissed her hand on the doorstep and she watched as he strode back to his waiting car; he turned to wave and she kept the memory to dream about in bed that night.

The next evening when she returned from the office there was a small parcel wrapped in scarlet paper and tied with shiny ribbons waiting for her. She read her name, written in his own writing, and hefted the parcel excitedly from hand to hand wondering what it could be. Then she ripped it open and stared in delight at the exquisite little jade fan, carved so finely it resembled a piece of lace. But the card he had written enchanted her even more: "I found this on Hollywood Road. I thought of you in your Chinese cheongsam, and knew it belonged to you."

She called his number excitedly. "It's much too extravagant a present," she told him, laughing, "but I can't bear to give it back. I shall just have to buy you something in exchange."

"I never accept presents from women," he said, suddenly cold.

She replied, flustered, "Oh, I didn't mean anything wrong, I just— well, I guess I just wanted to make you as happy as you made me."

"That's all I ask in return," he said gallantly. "And one more thing—have supper again with me tonight."

Lysandra thought of the dinner she was supposed to attend that night and knew she would cancel it. He took her to a Chinese restaurant in Kowloon and she wore cool-blue linen and carried her exquisite jade fan, wafting it gently to and fro in the sultry air as he entertained her with stories of his family, who went back all the way *before* Louis, the Sun King, who was the only French king Lysandra knew much about.

She dined with him the next night and the next, and her pretty little apartment was filled with so many fresh flowers it was like an exotic garden. And each night he gave her a different gift: jade combs studded with pearls and yellow diamonds—"the color of your hair," he told her; a pair of gold-embroidered silk slippers with curled-up

toes said to have belonged to the Dragon Empress Cixi that he
"thought would appeal to her"; and last—because she forbade anymore, a glorious jeweled egg, reputedly Fabergé, that he said he'd
bought from an old Russian emigré eking out his last days on a
pittance in a tiny apartment surrounded by czarist treasures.

Philip and Irene Chen soon heard of Lysandra's new suitor and
the word about him was not good. "It's only a flirtation," Irene
guessed worriedly, "but she's so young and inexperienced. I hope she
doesn't do anything foolish." And she wished Robert were there to
give her a friendly word of warning, but he was doing his internship
in Georgetown.

Lysandra took Pierre to see her grandfather's old mansion on Repulse Bay, now a fabulous museum. She showed him the towering
Lai Tsin building and her merchant ships in the harbor. And when
he took her in his arms and kissed her and whispered words of passion in her ear, she eagerly agreed to marry him.

"Let's keep it to ourselves," he said jubilantly. "We'll throw a big
party later in Paris for all my friends."

She thought guiltily of her mother, who would have so loved to be
at her wedding, but Pierre's enthusiasm for his plan just swept her
along and she was so much in love she thought only of him. The next
day he chartered a yacht and they sailed to Macao, where Lysandra
Lai Tsin became the bride of Prince Pierre d'Arancourt in a quick,
very private ceremony in the lovely old Portuguese church. She wore
a dress of red lace, the Chinese wedding color, and carried a bunch of
scarlet roses, and she was so in love she forgot all about being the
president of the Lai Tsin Corporation; all she wanted to be was
Pierre's wife.

She sent a quick cable to Francie and Buck in San Francisco signing it "Princesse d'Arancourt," and they wired back their shock and
demanded she bring her new husband home immediately to be inspected and approved. But Pierre wanted to go via Europe and they
took the presidential suite on the first Messageries Maritime French
liner bound for Marseilles.

Pierre was not a very tender and considerate lover, but Lysandra
had no one to compare him to, and she just assumed his quick, take-
it-or-leave-it attitude was normal. She didn't for a minute suspect he
found her inexperience a nuisance and her youthful adoration boring.
She was just so enamored she only saw how handsome and debonaire

he was and noticed, jealously, how other women watched him with predatory eyes.

Pierre was not unfaithful to her until they reached Paris. He spent a lot of time on the phone in their suite at the George Cinq, where they were staying because his apartment on Avenue Foch was "being redecorated"—though anyway he said he planned to sell it and buy a larger one. He sent her alone to the couturiers to buy clothes. "You can't go on wearing those dreadful cheongsams," he told her disparagingly, and she gazed at him, hurt, remembering how he had liked them. She didn't know where he spent his afternoons and they seemed to dine early in their suite most nights and then he would leave her, telling her he had to visit his ailing grandmother, or that he was playing cards with his friends, or he had to travel to Deauville to sell the polo ponies he bred at the Argentine ranch.

They had been at the George Cinq for two months when she found the note from his mistress in the pocket of his robe and even though it was written in French she knew enough to understand it was not a casual affair, it had been going on for years, and she gasped with shock when she saw her own name mentioned . . . "the rich Chinese concubine who is keeping you in the manner to which you have always aspired to become accustomed," it said. The scales of love fell from her eyes and she looked at the truth. She thought of her mother and the stories of how she had been "the Mandarin's concubine" and remembered how much they had hurt her, and anger flared in her blue eyes, turning them to steel.

There was a rap on the door and when she called "come in" she was surprised to see the manager. "Princesse, forgive my intrusion," he said, looking embarrassed, "but I think there must be some oversight on the Prince's part. It is the bill, Madame, we have presented it several times and the Prince promises to pay, but so far"—he shrugged—"nothing. I myself have brought it to you, Madame, in the hope that you might personally take care of this small matter to all our satisfaction."

Lysandra stared at him and her heart sank; it was all clear to her now. She thought of how Pierre had wooed her with his charming words and gifts and then she thought of the Mandarin and what he had said to her all those years ago in Hong Kong, when she was seven years old and his business acquaintances had showered her with a treasure trove of presents.

*Remember,* he had said, *the gifts are not because these people are your friends, but because you are a Lai Tsin.*

Pierre had not married her because he loved her; he had not married Lysandra. He had married the Lai Tsin fortune.

She signed the bill and the manager thanked her effusively, backing out of the salon and closing the door gently behind him, and a short while later a bottle of the best vintage champagne was delivered to her with his compliments and apologies for having disturbed her.

Lysandra wasted no time: she called the maid and instructed her to pack all her things. Then she took a pair of scissors and went through Pierre's closets systematically snipping his beautifully tailored jackets to shreds, leaving a jumbled heap of flannel pinstripes and chequered cashmere rags on the floor. Her bags were waiting and she put on her new blue Dior matching dress and coat and then she opened the bottle of champagne and drank a toast to the Mandarin, her grandfather, whose wise words would from now be indelibly printed on her brain and whose advice she would always follow. She emptied the rest of the champagne over Pierre's expensive silk ties and ordered her bags sent downstairs. Then she went to the airport and caught the next flight out to New York, and from there home to San Francisco, to cry on her mother's shoulder.

Gossip has a short fuse and the explosive story of how Prince Pierre had found his clothes snipped to shreds on the floor of a Paris hotel suite he had not even paid for, and that Lysandra had cut him off without a shilling, made its way back to Hong Kong before her. And it was added to the fund of Lysandra Lai Tsin stories that made up her legend by the time Matt Jarrad met her, thirteen years later.

The sun had completed its descent into the South China Sea and Lysandra turned from her office window with a sigh; Pierre was only an unpleasant memory now, she had divorced him quickly and her attorneys had crushed his attempts to claim part of the Lai Tsin fortune. It had been a nine-day wonder in the international newspapers, nothing more, but it had left her wounded.

Robert Chen had returned to Hong Kong to work in the hospital there and now he headed up the neurological wing funded by Lai Tsin. He was her friend and confidant, and he, too, was married to his work, so they understood each other. She devoted her time to the company, only occasionally dating men whose backgrounds she knew and with whom she had business in common, but she never had allowed herself to fall in love again. Until Matt.

It was late. She turned from the window, picked up her purse from her desk and strode quickly to the door. She nodded good night to her secretary, who breathed a sigh of relief and picked up the phone to alert the waiting chauffeur that Madame was on her way down.

Lysandra stepped into the waiting dark-green Rolls, gazing blankly out the window at the crawling traffic as she headed homeward. "Home" was a sprawling, luxurious white "cottage," half-hidden behind hedges of oleanders and jacaranda on elegant Po Shan Road, and for a single brief year she had shared it with Matt, not caring what the taipans of Hong Kong or anyone else thought.

Matt was an adventurer, she'd known that when she'd met him. He was handsome and easy-going, an artist who traveled the world with a single ancient beat-up leather satchel containing his few shirts, an extra pair of jeans, and his precious paints and brushes.

She had met him at an exhibition of his paintings at a smart new gallery on Nathan Road. She and everyone else had been dressed to the nines in sequined chiffon and black tie, but the artist had turned up in faded jeans and a badly cut, collarless white shirt. He had a tall, rangy body, dark-red hair still wet from the shower and gray-green eyes that seemed to see right through her self-contained facade. His generous mouth turned up at the corners in a half-smile as he watched her sizing him up.

"Sorry about the shirt," he said. "When I saw how smart the gallery was and the words 'champagne and canapes' on the invitations, I dashed to the tailor around the corner and had him run up half a dozen of these in an hour." He grinned, his eyes lighting with delight. "I've been living in a hut on a beach in Bali for the past year; I guess I'm just not fit for society anymore. I've forgotten all the rules."

"You don't look like a man who obeys rules, anyway," she said.

Their eyes met for a long moment and then he said, "I guess you could say that's true."

She lingered longer than she normally would at such an affair and as the crowd thinned out he came to her and said, "Stay awhile. Have supper with me."

He looked searchingly at her and her heart jumped almost to her throat; she had never met anyone like this, a free spirit, a man who lived by his own rules.

She took him back to her lovely house on Po Shan Road and fed him scrambled eggs and champagne and when he touched her cheek and then kissed her she knew that what she was feeling was new. He asked her about her life and she told him about her family and then about Pierre. "I've never met a man yet who didn't think of my money as soon as he met me," she said challengingly.

He looked at her coolly and said, "Well, I guess you have now, Miss Moneybags. All I can think of is that your skin is like new cream and your eyes change color from aquamarine to sapphire in the candlelight, and that your hair should be tumbling down your back, not confined with jeweled combs. You're a pre-Raphaelite maiden and I don't want your money. All I want is to paint you."

She looked at him astonished. "You don't want to make love to me?"

He grinned and took her face between his hands. "That as well," he admitted.

That had been a year ago; a year of passionate lovemaking and passionate fights because she had kept her personal vow to devote her life to running the Lai Tsin Corporation, and maintained her strict business regime, leaving the house at seven-thirty each morning, often not returning until eight or nine at night. He would be there waiting for her, his lanky body propped against the verandah rail, a glass of whiskey in his hand, and champagne—her only drink—waiting in the silver bucket, beaded with icy drops. She had told herself sternly she wasn't going to give up *what* she was—*who* she was—for any man, and each night the distance seemed to grow between them.

"Drop it," he told her one night. "Let it all go, Lysandra. The company doesn't need you on a day-to-day basis, those guys could run it standing on their heads. Live your own life—be a woman for a change." He looked at her with those quiet, gray-green eyes and said, "Marry me, Lysandra."

She shrugged away his proposal, dwelling angrily on the fact that he thought the Lai Tsin Corporation could manage without her. *Her* —its dedicated taipan. He'd waited for her answer but she hadn't given him one and he turned away with a wry smile, and she thought nervously that his eyes looked sad.

He had left her just as easily as he'd met her. "Where are you going?" she'd asked, puzzled, as he'd flung his few possessions into the battered leather satchel.

"Away," he'd replied quietly.

"Away?" Her eyes were wide with the question.

"Away from you, my love," he'd said, with his endearing lopsided smile.

And then he'd slung his bag over his shoulder and with a final glance from those quiet gray-green eyes he'd turned and walked out of their bedroom, out of the beautiful white house on the smartest road on the Peak, and out of her life forever.

The Rolls turned into the driveway and she stepped quickly from it and into the house. She glanced as she always did at the verandah, half expecting to see him there waiting for her, but of course he wasn't, and she walked disconsolately through to her bedroom. *Their room,* as she always thought of it now, but without the clutter of his paints on the bathroom sink, and his watch—bought for a few dollars from a Cathay Road street vendor—lying on the bedside table, without his sweater tossed over the chair and his books on her shelves, the house felt like a silent tomb. No one would be coming, there was no need to dress, so she showered quickly and changed into a soft gray cashmere robe.

Ah Sing, who was really too old to look after her any longer but held an honorary position over the servants, came bustling into the room. Her face was as crumpled as a pickled walnut, her gray hair was scraped back from her wrinkled brow and she still insisted on wearing the traditional black smock and baggy pants of her profession. "It's come, Young Mistress," she said in Chinese, delving into the capacious pocket of her black smock. "Didn't your Old Mother tell you it would?"

"Old Mother" was the honorary term for an amah, but it also denoted the love Lysandra felt for her. Puzzled, she looked at her. "What has come, Ah Sing?" she demanded, a touch impatiently; she was tired and had so many things on her mind.

"The letter you've been expecting all these months." Ah Sing brought the postcard from her pocket at last and held it out to her. "There you see. It's from him. Am I not right?"

Lysandra took the postcard with a trembling hand; it was from Australia, a beach somewhere near the Great Barrier Reef. There was just a thatched hut, a strip of golden sand, and a ripple of white surf on an azure sea. "The only thing missing is you," it said on the back.

Her heart jumped the way it had when she'd first met him and her legs threatened to give way. "He can't mean it, Ah Sing," she said quickly. "Can he seriously expect me to give up all this and go live on some desert island? Or at least *this* month it's a desert island. Next month it might be Katmandu or New Guinea or Venezuela."

Ah Sing put a gnarled hand on her shoulder and said quietly, "Your Old Mother is not wise enough to guide you in these things. All she knows is Number One daughter is not happy. And if all the money in the world cannot make Number One daughter a happy woman, something is wrong."

Lysandra thought for a long time about what Ah Sing had said. She turned Matt's postcard over and over in her hands, pressing it to her cheek, to her lips. She paced onto the verandah and stared down at the lights of Hong Kong. She thought of her mother and Buck and how happy they were. They had met Matt on their last visit six months ago. "He's different," Francie had said, smiling.

"Too different, perhaps," Lysandra had replied.

He'd got on famously with her mother, and even Buck, who since Pierre had monitored her potential boyfriends with suspicious eyes, had said, "That's an honest man, Lysandra, a rarity these days."

*Maybe too honest,* she thought ruefully now. She realized her life was at a crossroads and she didn't know which way to turn. Her thoughts turned to the Mandarin and the time he had brought her to Hong Kong when he had been an old man and she was just a child, and now she remembered what he had said about the "truths."

"I shall not have the honor of knowing you on your long journey through life into womanhood," he had told her. "I am giving you everything you could wish for on this earth—riches, power, and success—in the hope that your life will be blessed with happiness. I have told you everything, Lysandra, with the exception of one Truth. This Truth is my secret. This Truth is written down and locked away in my private safe in my office in Hong Kong. Only if despair overtakes you and your path in life seems unclear must you read it. And if that day should come, Granddaughter, then I pray you will forgive me and that my Truth will help you choose the right road to happiness."

Lysandra ran from the verandah to her bedroom. She threw on a pair of jeans, a white cotton shirt, and tan cowboy boots. She snatched up her car keys and ran to the garage and drove her little sapphire-blue Mercedes 500 SEL convertible down the misty Peak roads, back to Central.

The night security man at the Lai Tsin building recognized her immediately and let her in, and she took the elevator to the thirtieth floor to her office. She took down the framed Chinese scroll hanging in front of her tiny private wall safe, quickly dialed the combination and removed the manila envelope she had transferred from the Mandarin's old safe when the company had moved to its new building. Then with trembling hands she opened the letter he'd said she must never read unless she needed to know the truth. And sitting behind her own desk, the way he had as head of the great Lai Tsin hong, she read what the Mandarin had to say:

"To my granddaughter, Lysandra, my great-grandchildren, great-great grandchildren, and so on into infinity, the beloved ones, whom I shall never see. This letter will come to you from beyond the grave, since my allotted time is long past. It is my ardent wish that it may never be read but if fate decrees it must, then so be it.

"I will tell you the true story of Mayling. But to do so I must first reveal the Untruths. Let me explain it to you now.

"Mayling was thirteen years old and Lai Tsin was nine when they were sold by their father. The selling of women was big business in the Chinese provinces. Men made fortunes abducting young girls who would then be sold and resold many times. Despite her harsh life and the violence of her father, Mayling was a joyful, happy little girl with merry dark eyes. Her hair fell a smooth glossy black to her waist, and she wore it braided, the way all Chinese girls did. Sometimes she would fantasize about how she would look when she became a woman, and she would comb her shiny hair and sweep it into a bun, stabbing it through with blades of straw in place of ornamental jade combs to keep it in place. She would pretend she was wearing a beautiful silk cheongsam, and saunter elegantly up and down, imagining she was a great lady, the Number One wife of a rich and kindly man, with servants to care for her and children of her own to play with. Sadly, it was only a dream.

"When the flesh-peddler tore Mayling away from her brother that night on the junk at Shanghai, her whole life changed. And when he took her to his cabin and touched her secret places she screamed so much he struck her across the face. And still she screamed. He put his hands on her throat, contemplating strangling her, he was so angry, but then he remembered how much he had paid for her and thought greedily of his profit. There were a hundred other girls he could have who would cause less trouble than Mayling, and besides, if he sold her as a virgin his profit would be even higher.

"He struck her a few more blows around the head to teach her a lesson, then he flung a piece of sacking over her and carried her, wrapped like a dead dog, off the junk and into a sedan chair.

"Mayling's ears were still ringing from his blows, her head was bursting with pain and she lay stunned on the floor of the sedan chair as it jogged through the streets of Shanghai. She prayed for escape, but it was not to be. The sedan stopped and the man flung her out onto the dark street. He dragged her by her pigtail inside a dark building and down an ill-lit passageway. In the room at the end an old man was sitting at a table. He had a wizened face and eyes so narrow, Mayling wondered how he could see, but she still felt his appraising stare.

"The flesh-peddler jerked her pigtail, forcing her to stand taller. He prodded her flesh with his fingers, extolling her qualities and especially her virginity, until she blushed with shame. The old man behind the desk named his price and the flesh-peddler harangued him as a thief, but after much shouting a bargain was struck and he left her alone with her new owner.

"Mayling cowered back against the wall, but the man did not touch her. Instead he bade her to follow him and she was too frightened not to obey. He led her down some steps into a cellar and left her there, bolting the door so she could not escape. Mayling sat on the steps in the dark, crying. A rat rustled past her and she screamed and leapt to her feet, but nobody came to save her. She thought of her brother and knew she would never see him again. She was alone in an evil world she did not even understand.

"When the cellar door finally opened again, she was too stupified with fear to cry or scream anymore, and she followed the man obediently into a waiting mule cart. Her hands and feet were bound and she was covered with straw and the cart moved slowly out of the city streets into the countryside.

"Mayling did not know how many hours it was before the cart stopped and she was bundled out again, but she saw they were on the outskirts of a large village. The driver took her to a wooden hut and thrust her through the door and bolted it. She heard a sound and peered into the darkness. A dozen pairs of eyes looked at her. She shrank back with a cry of fear and a girl's voice said gently, 'Do not be afraid, little sister, we are his prisoners also.'

"Someone came toward her and took her hand, Mayling could scarcely see her it was so dark, and though the girl's hand felt rough her voice was gentle. 'But you are so small,' she exclaimed, 'and still with a pigtail. You are only a child.'

" 'I am thirteen years,' Mayling admitted, clinging to the girl's work-roughened hand.

"She heard her sigh. 'I myself am fifteen,' she replied quietly. 'I was abducted from my village. And the other girls, too, though some were lured away from the rice fields with promises of employment as servants in rich households in the city, and some were sold by their fathers because they did not want to pay for a dowry and a wedding feast. We are all worthless females and now who knows what is to become of us?'

"She took Mayling to sit beside her and offered her rice from a small bowl. Despite Mayling's despair and her aching head she craved food, but she knew it was all the girl had and she politely took only one mouthful. The other girls generously offered her their bowls and from each one she took a single mouthful, bowing respectfully and thanking them. Then exhaustion overcame her and she lay down with her head in the older girl's lap and slept.

"They were awakened by men brandishing whips, commanding them to get on their feet and go outside. Mayling followed the others. It was dusk and a cold half-moon peeked over the straggling trees that ringed the small town, glinting on the smooth, deep, dark river that flowed nearby. The men ordered them to remove their smocks, but the girls hung their heads and refused until they felt the lash of the whips and then, screaming, they did as they were told. The men prodded them into line, laughing mockingly at their shame as they tried to cover their nakedness. They twisted their arms behind their backs and tied their wrists so tightly that the slightest movement cut deep into the flesh. Then the evil old one hung a placard with her price around each girl's neck, and urged on by the whips, they forced them down the road to the village.

"Mayling walked last in the line, her head bowed and tears stinging her eyes, grateful for the darkness that hid her nakedness. But the road outside the village was brightly lit with a dozen lanterns. A stall had been set up selling rice wine, and groups of men, already half-drunk, turned to stare as they approached. The girls stumbled and hesitated but the stinging lash sent them forward again, down the middle of the road, past the silent gaping men. Then with a sudden gutteral roar of lust they lunged at the screaming girls. Those who tried to run were lashed unmercifully and they stood, trembling, while the men examined them.

"Mayling wanted to run and hide, too, but like an animal at the slaughterhouse she was rooted to the spot with fear. Men walked past her, eyeing her naked immature body and laughing. They pinched her flesh and felt her most secret places with their dirty hands, checking on her virtue, spitting contemptuously into the dust at her feet as they haggled furiously over her price. Mayling's head sank onto her chest, her shame was so deep she wanted to die. A tear trickled down her cheek into the corner of her mouth and it tasted as bitter as she felt. A filthy middle-aged Hakka peasant bargained shrilly for her, laughing toothlessly as he made his deal.

"Mayling's eyes met her new friend's for a second before she was dragged away. The girl's eyes were dark with sympathy, expressing the pain and sorrow of women who for centuries had been subservient to men, to be used and abused, to be bought or to be sold. She shook her head and whispered good-bye as the Hakka dragged Mayling away. He threw her still naked into the back of his bullockcart, covering her with filthy straw. Then he drove her to his wooden hut in the fields.

"The Hakka was a cruel, ignorant peasant, his body stank and his teeth were rotting in his mouth. He took her as he would an animal, leaving her dumb with shock and pain, covered in her own blood and vomit.

"The next day he put her back in the bullock-cart and sold her to another peasant for a profit. This one was younger, but no less ugly, no less cruel. He, too, had meant to have her for a single night and then sell her, but he enjoyed his new 'child bride,' he liked her glossy black hair and her budding breasts, and he liked the way she screamed whenever he took her. He was on his way to Shanghai, taking a ship from there to America and the Gold Mountain. He decided his new little 'child bride' should go with him. When he tired of her he could sell her. There were few Chinese women in America and she would command a good price. He shaved the front of her head like a boy's and braided her hair into a queue. He dressed her in a coolie's smock and trousers and told her if she ever spoke a word to anyone he would kill her. And then he took her with him onto the ship.

"The voyage took four months and was very hard. Mayling sat

silently at her captor's side, afraid to speak. She was the only female on board and she knew what would happen if the men found out about her, or if the peasant decided to sell her to them. She longed to drown herself in the merciful sea, but he never let her out of his sight until the captain ordered her to be his cabin boy and then she had to endure his drunkenness and abuse.

"When the typhoon struck she prayed the ship would be wrecked, but fate was not that kind. And when the storm came up off the coast of Mendocino she leapt into the sea with the others, thinking that finally she would be reprieved and allowed to die. But as she sank beneath the icy waves, deep inside her was the ancient instinct for survival. She kicked frantically to the surface just as the god of providence sent a piece of driftwood floating past her. She clung desperately to it, gasping for air, staring around her at the heads bobbing in the water. Suddenly the peasant was beside her. He grabbed at the driftwood, kicking her away, cursing her. 'You are worthless,' he screamed, prying her desperate fingers from the wood. 'You are only a girl. Your life means nothing.'

"She heard the roar of a great wave as it surged toward them, then she was engulfed in dark, icy water, her lungs were filled, they were bursting, she was choking, she was dying. There was a great pain all over her body as she was flung onto the shore and the wave receded, leaving her on a scrap of shingle at the foot of a cliff. She heard a cry and looked behind her. The peasant was striding from the waves. In the glow from the phosphorescence she could see his face, livid with rage—and behind him the sea surging outward as though drawn back from the shore by some giant force.

"Mayling scrambled to her feet and began to run, clambering up the side of the steep cliff, clinging to the rocks and little ledges. Her feet slipped on the loose stones and her hands were bleeding. She heard him behind her and looked down. He was running across the strip of shingle and she sobbed with fear, she knew soon he would catch her and he would kill her. She wished she had drowned with the others rather than be killed brutally by him. The sea roared ominously and the peasant turned and looked behind him, puzzled. The ocean had receded a long way, leaving a strip of shingle fifty yards wide, but now it gathered itself together into a single towering wave and roared toward the shore, higher and higher, faster and faster. It hurled itself onto the rocks, engulfing the peasant.

"Mayling clung to her ledge on the cliffside, staring down as the wave receded again, but there was no one. The peasant had gone along with all the others. Only she had survived.

"Too frightened to move she waited for the ocean to come and claim her, too, but it was suddenly calm, as glassy as a summer lake under the moon.

"Mayling clambered up the cliff. She rested that night and then began to walk. She lived on fruits and berries and what she could steal and kill with her own hands. The nights were cold and when she came to the little wooden chapel she curled up on the bench and slept. The pastor who found her was red-faced, sly-eyed and blustering, full of phrases of 'the Lord.' She understood not a word, except that when his hand fell on her shoulder, he was another man. He took her to his cottage. He lived in a community of bleak, hard-eyed men and women and he told them piously he was saving the heathen by taking her into his house, 'the Lord's house.' That night he made her kneel beside him while he drank whiskey, intoning long, loud anguished prayers. And then he did to her what all the other men had done.

"She was clothed like a boy in foreign devil's clothing and kept locked indoors. Despairing, she climbed from the window and made her escape. Much later, to her surprise, she came across a group of Chinese, working in the fields and she hid behind in the trees, watching them. They were Chinese, but they were also men, and she was afraid. The coolie had told her what a price she would fetch from the men once he got her to the Gold Mountain, and she knew he was right. But her belly was churning with hunger, she was dropping with exhaustion and she knew she could go on no longer. She could find a quiet place in the forest and curl up under a tree and wait for death to take her. But then she would never see her little brother again, and she so longed to see him. . . . There was only one thing she could do.

"She thought over the idea carefully. She was already wearing boys' clothes, even though they were foreign devil's clothing. She was young and still undeveloped enough to pass as a boy. The coolie had shaved her head at the front, and with her long queue she looked just as they did.

"Mayling took a deep breath. She knew that if she were to survive in this world, she must live as a man. She must become Lai Tsin.

"Beloved one, for two years Mayling worked alongside the men from Toishan. Every day was an ordeal because every day she thought she would be discovered. She was young and slender and looked like a boy; she was careful always to keep her body modestly covered, but each month, now that she was a woman, became an ordeal of concealment. The work was brutally hard but she did not complain. She watched the men carefully. She learned to talk like a man, to act like a man, to think like a man. Mayling lived like a man until she no longer remembered what it was to be a young girl, only what it was like to suffer abuse at the hands of men.

"When the work finally came to an end she drifted off with the others, through the many fertile valleys of California to Santa Clara, San Joaquin, Ojai, and Salinas, picking cherries and almonds, lemons, oranges, and lettuces, and when the season finished and winter approached, she went to the big city. She took whatever small jobs came her way, but mostly she paid for her food and shelter from gambling.

"San Francisco was big and frightening, but her heart lifted when she saw Chinatown. The streets had a familiar look and so did the temples with their golden dragons and the smell of incense, the voices, the faces, and the shops with their scrawled slogans wishing prosperity and long life. The smell of spices was familiar, as were the pigtailed children in gay clothing, the fortune-tellers, and the teahouses.

"She stared enviously at the girls, feminine in their cheongsams and padded jackets with flowers in their hair, then looked sadly at her own work-toughened hands, comparing her large feet, heavy boots, and long stride with their tiny delicate ones and their feminine little steps. She listened to the high chatter of their voices and her own rough monosyllabic words copied from the men, and she longed for their dresses and their hair combs, their feminine shoes and chatter. She longed to be a girl again, like them.

"On an impulse, she went into a Chinese store and squandered her precious money on a bright silk smock and trousers, pretending to the shopkeeper she was buying them as a present for her sister. She bought shoes and combs for her hair and took them back to her tiny cockroach-ridden cubicle behind a dry-goods store. She tore off all her foreign devil's men's clothes and looked at herself naked. She was almost sixteen years old and her body was still a girl's with small high breasts, narrow waist, and slender adolescent hips. She filled the tin bucket with cold water and washed herself carefully all over. Then she put on the silken smock and trousers. She slipped her feet into the precarious curved-soled shoes and unbraided her hair, coiling it into a smooth bun at the nape of her neck and fastening it with the combs.

"She peered at her reflection in the dirty windowpane and saw a miracle. She was no longer the peasant Lai Tsin, she was sixteen-year-old Mayling again. She practiced walking around the room in her strange wobbly shoes, wincing at the pain because she had become used to her big flat boots. Then plucking up her courage, she ventured outside onto the street, hardly daring to look at anyone in case they were staring and laughing at her. She walked slowly to the little shop in the alley nearby where the photographer took pictures of the Chinese to send home to their relatives. He barely looked at her, just gave her a scalloped paper fan to hold and told her to sit very still. There was a blinding flash and it was all over.

"Mayling went back to her room. She took off the clothes, folded them, and put them carefully away, because she was so used to being Lai Tsin she no longer knew how to behave as a girl and she was afraid.

"Back in her man's disguise, she found a job working in a gambling hall, serving drinks, cleaning tables, washing floors. Any menial job was hers. And at the end of each week when she received her few dollars' wages she would spend the night at the tables, and sometimes she would win and sometimes not, because these gamblers were cleverer than the peasants she had learned from. And every Sunday without fail, she attended the English classes at the Baptist Sunday School. She had a roof over her head, food in her belly, and she looked for no more.

"Wu Feng, the Chinese who ran the gambling hall, paid rent to a *gwailo* landlord and each week the man would call to collect his money. He was a young man, tall, with pale-blue eyes, thick curly hair, and a beard, and Mayling's eyes were often drawn to him as she served him rice wine. By now she spoke enough English to understand when he asked her for wine, or how old she was and where she was from. The man's voice was soft and his eyes often lingered on her but she did not feel afraid because to him she was Lai Tsin. She was a 'man,' like he was.

"Then one week he did not come to collect his rent but sent a message asking Wu Feng to have the money delivered to him. 'Lai Tsing can bring it,' he told Wu Feng, giving him the address.

"Mayling was very frightened at leaving Chinatown and she hurried along Market Street, her head down, afraid to look at the faces of the foreign devils. The landlord's house was a grand one. It had five white steps leading up to its shiny black-enameled door and she hoped her boots were not soiling the pristine marble as she nervously rang the bell.

"A Chinese houseboy in a white jacket and white cotton gloves opened the door. He grinned slyly at Lai Tsin. 'Master waits for you upstairs,' he said, giving her a little shove toward the red-carpeted staircase.

"Mayling walked hesitantly to the stairs and then turned to look for him, but he had disappeared. With a nervous sigh she walked to the top of the stairs and called out the landlord's name. It was a famous name in San Francisco and she could see the man was rich, richer than she had ever dreamed of anyone being. She stared at his *gwailo* treasures, the silk carpets, the huge, dark paintings, the silver urns and crystal vases as she waited, uncertain, what to do.

"She heard him call, 'Come in here,' and walked down the corridor toward his voice. He was sitting behind a big desk. She bowed and he stood up and walked to the door and locked it. Mayling blinked in surprise, but then she remembered this was a transaction of money; obviously he would not want his servants to see or overhear.

"She took the parcel from her secret pocket and laid it on his desk. 'Wu Feng's rent, honorable sir,' she said in her soft, rough voice. He perched on the edge of his desk, his arms folded. He looked at her for a long time and then he laughed.

" 'Thank you, Lai Tsin,' he said, still smiling. 'And how would you like to have that money back again? Your own money this time, in your own secret pocket?'

"She gasped, her eyes grew round at the thought, but she asked, puzzled, 'What can Lai Tsin do to earn such a sum?'

" 'Do you really not know?' His voice was deep with a rough throaty eagerness. His hand shot out and gripped her shoulder. Mayling gasped, she had heard that sound in a man's voice before, she had felt that grip of steel, felt the hands that trembled with passion. But this man thought she was a boy. 'No, sir, no. You don't understand,' she cried.

"He laughed as he held her squirming in his grip, 'What don't I understand, little boy?' he asked, amused. 'Don't I understand the glances you send me each Friday when I come to Wu Feng's? Do I not understand the language of your body, the languorous look in your eyes, the movements of your hands and your buttocks? Of course I do. You and I understand each other perfectly, little Lai Tsin. I want what you can give me, and you want what I can give you.' He took the money from the desk and thrust it at her. 'Take it. I'm a generous man to those who please me.'

"Mayling twisted from his grasp and he laughed as she ran for the door. Of course, it was locked. She turned slowly to face him. 'You do not understand,' she said again in her halting English. 'I am not Lai Tsin. I am Mayling. I am a girl.'

"He shook his head, laughing. 'That's a good one,' he chortled, his face pink with merriment. 'A girl in sheep's clothing!' And then he pulled her roughly to him, thrusting his hand between her legs. He looked at her, surprised, and then with a roar of laughter he commanded her to take off her clothes. Mayling was shaking with fear and humiliation. She shook her head, she would rather die than do what he asked. But her masquerade had inflamed his passions, she was both boy and girl and he shook with desire as he threw her to the ground. He pulled at her clothes and lay on top of her, fumbling and cursing as he forced himself into her, trembling with passion for the few minutes it took to satisfy his bestial urge. Then he stood up. He buttoned his pants. He walked back to his desk and sat down, smoothing back his hair and straightening his cravat. 'You may go now,' he said coolly, 'and I don't want to see you at Wu Feng's again. Do you understand? I don't ever want to see your face again.'

"Mayling stumbled to her feet. Her body was defiled with his sticky semen and she trembled with disgust and anger as she covered herself quickly and walked to the door. It was locked and he tossed the key across to her and said, 'I don't know what kind of game you're playing, but I warn you, it's a dangerous one. Other men would not be as kind to you as I was. They would kill you for such a deception.'

"Mayling closed the door quietly behind her. She walked slowly back down the beautiful staircase and through the grand hall. From the corner of her eye she caught a glimpse of the sly, grinning Chinese houseboy as she let herself out of the door. He ran after her, grabbing her shoulder. He whispered, 'Mr. Harrison is a generous man, give me half what he put in your secret pocket and I will not tell about you.'

"She looked blankly at him. 'Mr. Harrison?'

" 'My boss,' he said impatiently. 'Harmon Harrison, the big banker. He's the most powerful man in San Francisco.'

" 'I did not take any money,' she said pushing the Chinese houseboy out of her way and running down the steps. The name meant nothing then to Mayling. Only many years later was she to realize who he was.

"She did not know how she managed to walk back to Chinatown, but when she got back to her little cubicle, she stripped off her clothes and scrubbed her body with icy water and coarse soap until it stung. Then she put on her girl's smock and trousers and lay down on her bedmat, wondering what to do. She longed with all her heart for her mother and her little brother, and she burned with hatred for all men. But when all her tears were spent, in the end she knew there was nothing she could do. She must continue her deception. Except no man was ever going to touch her again, and if any tried, she would kill him.

"The next day she found herself a new job as a coolie carrying vegetables and live chickens to market in two straw baskets slung over her shoulders on a bamboo pole. And at night she worked in another gambling hall, a smaller, seedier place run by the tongs, with opium divans in the back and men with hatchets tucked into their belts at the tables. She did not care, she scarcely even noticed them. All she wanted was the dollars. And then a few months later she found she was pregnant.

"She was ignorant in such matters and by the time she realized that the hated Harmon Harrison's child was in her womb it was too late to do anything about it, even if she dared. She worked until it was no longer possible to hide her condition and then she found herself a different room. She became Mayling again, in her silken smock and long smooth-coiled hair.

"An old Chinese woman, experienced in birthing, came to help her, though Mayling had to pay her too much because the woman despised her for having no husband. She did not know what to expect and thought the pain of birth would destroy her mind, but in the end the child was born. A small, pale-faced, wailing boy.

"After a while the old woman completed her tasks and left Mayling alone. She looked at her baby, wrapped in a shawl beside her on the bedmat. He was tiny, with dark hair and dark eyes, and he did not look in the least bit like the foreign-devil landlord. He looked Chinese, like her. And he looked as helpless and frightened by his new world as she was. Her heart went out to him and at last she picked him up and began to feed him.

"When the boy was two months old Mayling knew she would have to return to work. She thought and thought about what to do and knew there was only one answer. It had always been the custom in China for families with too many mouths to feed to give away one or two of their children to less fortunate, childless couples, and now Mayling found a family for her son. They were middle-aged and had given up hope of ever having the pleasure of their own baby and their eyes lit with happiness when Mayling handed them her boy. She promised she would send them money every month for his welfare and then she turned quickly away, her eyes burning with unshed tears.

"Mayling went back to being Lai Tsin. She returned to her work in the fields and to the gambling. Her life was solitary, for she dared call no person her friend. She stayed alone and every month she sent money for her child, though she never tried to see him in all the long, slow years.

"Time passed and one day the couple sent a message that the son was now eighteen years old and had become betrothed. Mayling immediately sent all the money she had to help pay for his wedding, but she was not invited as a guest. The next year she was told that a son had been born and she rejoiced in their happiness. She realized that she was now a grandmother, though she guessed she was only about thirty-four years old. She went back to her work, drifting between the fields and the gambling, a solitary figure on the Chinese landscape.

"On the day of the great earthquake Mayling was on her way back to her little cubicle on Kearny Street. She had gambled until dawn and when the paved street suddenly rose under her feet and hurled her to the ground, her first thought was that the gods were angry with her for all her sins and at last had come to seek their revenge. She crawled into a doorway as the world collapsed around her, and when the earth stopped shaking and the buildings stopped trembling she opened her eyes onto a scene of devastation. She immediately thought of her son and her grandchild and her heart trembled like the buildings as she thought of what might have happened to them.

"She leapt to her feet and ran through the crowded, broken streets to the house where they lived. It was no longer there. Neighbors were frantically shifting beams and chunks of masonry, digging with their bare hands in the rubble while a small half-naked boy sat on the sidewalk, solemnly watching them. Mayling ran to him and took his hand. He held onto her tightly, looking up at her with trusting black eyes. Someone cried out that they had found them, the old couple and the young one, still in their beds. The chimney had fallen in on them and they had died instantly. The child's small bed in another room was untouched.

"Mayling walked through the rubble and looked at the face of her dead son. It was the first time she had seen him since she gave him away when he was just two months old, and her heart mourned, for he was young and handsome and had much to live for. She told the neighbors she would look after the child. They quickly found him some clothes, and with one last long glance she left her son again for the last time.

"So you see, Beloved Ones," Lai Tsin wrote, "Mayling's story is Lai Tsin's, and Lai Tsin's story is Mayling's. When Lai Tsin met Francie Harrison on Nob Hill he told her the boy was an orphan he had rescued from the earthquake. It was only part of the truth. That boy was also his real grandson, Philip Chen. And the grandson of Harmon Harrison. It was always my sorrow that I could not admit he was of my own blood, but it was already too late. Too much time had passed and I had my new identity, but in my heart, Philip Chen was always the beloved son I never knew.

"I am telling you the truth now, Lysandra, because as a woman you are vulnerable not just to others, but to yourself. I was forced by circumstance to deny my womanhood in order to survive. And all my success, all my wealth, and my power as a taipan were never enough to compensate me for its loss.

"You will read this only when there is need and I counsel you now, dear granddaughter, to remember that first you are a woman. Do not deny your happiness in your search for yourself. Be strong and adventurous. Seek your own life wherever it might take you. To be a woman is your fortune. Use it wisely and with compassion and love."

Bitter tears rained down Lysandra's face as she replaced the Mandarin's letter in the envelope. Her heart burned with pity for Mayling and her terrible secret and her suffering, and she wished with all her heart she might turn back the clock and give a new start to the poor terrified Chinese child who had, through circumstance, become "the Mandarin."

She thought for a long time about the sadness of Mayling's life and the sacrifices she had made in order to survive. And her message was as clear to her as it had been to Francie, all those years before.

"Be strong, be your own woman."

Lysandra took the manila envelope and drove back to Po Shan Road. She went to her room and looked at herself in the mirror. She saw a thirty-two-year-old woman, still beautiful and desirable, but already with lines of strain around her eyes and mouth. She saw the years stretching emptily in front of her, with more success and more money and her biological clock ticking desperately away and she knew Matt was right—the Lai Tsin Corporation could go on without her. But she could not go on without him—not any longer.

She sent a prayer of thanks to the wise Mandarin for pointing the way to happiness. She took a small bag from her closet and packed it quickly with the few essentials needed for life in a thatched hut on a beach, then added a large bottle of her favorite gardenia perfume. Then she took the letter and walked to the fireplace, and lit a match; and as she watched Mayling's secret disappear in a quick flutter of flame and blue smoke, she felt closer to the Mandarin than she ever had before.

She called Philip Chen and told him what she had decided and asked for his help. "You know you always have that," he said quietly. He knew Matt and liked him and he didn't question her decision, and she was glad for that. She thought of what Lai Tsin had told her and said, "Philip . . ."

"Yes?"

She hesitated, the phone clutched to her ear. "Oh, nothing. Except, I just wondered if you ever knew just how much Lai Tsin loved you . . . ?"

"He loved me like his own son, I know that."

His voice was calm, without any underlying meanings, and she said quickly, "Well, I just want you to know I love you, too, Philip. And I want to thank you . . . for everything."

"Good luck, little one," he said quietly. "Our thoughts will be with you. I'll do what I can to guide the company until you appoint a successor."

She sat for a while staring into space thinking of Philip, and Lai Tsin and Harmon Harrison. Then she shook herself back to reality and made a few calls to the important men who helped run the company. And then she called Robert.

He laughed when she told him. "You should have gone with him when he asked you, I told you that."

"Robert, do you think maybe I'm too late? Will he have fallen out of love with me by now?"

"No chance. Any man who falls for you is in for a life sentence."

"I hope you're right."

There was a silence and then he said abruptly, "I've got to rush, I was supposed to be at the hospital fifteen minutes ago. Good luck, Lysandra."

"I'll be in touch," she said a little wistfully, as she put down the phone again, feeling as though she were cutting off a whole part of her life.

She glanced at her watch as she gave the operator the number at the ranch; it was three in the afternoon in California. Buck answered and his cheery familiar voice suddenly brought a lump to her throat.

"How are you, baby?" he demanded. "Everything okay?"

"Oh, Buck, I'm in love," she said with a sob.

"Are you gonna cry about it?"

She sniffed. "No—no, I'm just happy, that's all."

"It's Matt, I hope?"

"Yes."

"Well, honey, he's a great guy, an individual; you surely won't have a run-of-the-mill routine life with a man like Matt."

"Then you approve?"

He laughed, "If I have to—and you promise to invite us to the wedding this time."

Lysandra felt herself blushing, "I turned him down the first time . . . I may have to ask him."

His laugh boomed down the line again. "You always were a girl who went after what she wanted. Good luck, baby, and remember, take care of yourself."

Francie got on the line and Lysandra caught her silent anxious vibrations across the thousands of miles of crackling cable and ocean as she told her her decision. "I guess I've always been looking for what you and Buck have, Mom," she said, "and this time I think I've found it. I just had to find out the hard way that love demands a lot from you. It has to come first."

Listening, Francie gazed abstractedly at the view through the open doors leading to the courtyard. She could see a pair of horses running in the paddock and the hillsides with their neat rows of vines interspersed with roses. The turbulence of her earlier life seemed light years away from the happiness and tranquillity of the present. She ran her hand worriedly through her hair, trying not to think of the disaster with Pierre. Matt was different, she knew that, and despite his itinerant lifestyle there was something solid about him. He'd been strong enough to walk out on Lysandra when she had been determined to call the tune, and she had given him credit for that because she knew how much he loved her. Still, she hoped he was the right one. "How can you be sure?" she asked.

"Oh, Mom." Lysandra's voice held amusement. "How can you, of all people, ask me that? How did you and Buck know? Pierre flattered me into believing I was in love. But Matt is reality—for better, for worse. Besides, I opened the Mandarin's letter." She paused. "Mom, did you know what was in it?"

Francie sighed. "Yes, I knew. He took me to his old village and showed me the Temple of Lilin. But I gave my word to respect his secret—all his secrets—Lysandra, and I couldn't tell even you."

"Oh, Mom, he was so brave. He sacrificed so much and bequeathed us more than just his success and wealth. He bared his soul so he could help us—and now I'm taking his advice. I have to hurry, Mom, I've a plane to catch, so wish me luck, won't you?"

"Of course I wish you luck, darling, and happiness too."

Francie smiled as she walked out onto the porch where Buck was waiting. She sat beside him on the sofa and took his hand.

"She said she only wants what we have," she told him. "Do you think she's doing the right thing?"

He looked at her with love in his eyes, seeing the same beautiful woman he had met all those years ago. "You betcha," he said, smiling.

And early the next morning Lysandra Lai Tsin was on a plane to Australia, and Matt.

# EPILOGUE

◆

Many years later, when a beleaguered China opened her doors to the world again, Lysandra and her husband Matt took a shabby black-sailed junk upriver from Shanghai, past Nanking and Wuhu, sailing up the broad yellow Yangtze through the high gorges and past low-lying reedy banks, retracing her beloved Mandarin's fateful journey. On the way, she told Matt the story of Mayling and her brother Lai Tsin, of Little Brother Chen and the beautiful *mui-tsai* Lilin, who was their mother. But she did not divulge the Mandarin's secret, not even to the man she loved and the man who was the father of her three children, who had brought her more happiness than she ever believed possible.

They stood together at the rail as the junk edged its way to the bank, where an old wooden jetty dipped drunkenly into the river and coolies in high-necked blue Mao jackets leapt to fasten the thick mooring ropes. The flat land cowered like a beaten yellow beast under a lowering gray sky and the road that led to the Mandarin's old village was now little more than a track.

Holding tightly to Matt's hand, she ventured down the narrow clay path, gazing around her, searching for the places she felt she already knew; but the flat steely pond was dry and choked with reeds and no longer home to a thousand pretty, doomed white ducks; the rice fields had reverted to marshland and the *fung-shui* grove where Little Chen had been left to the birds and the dogs was but a few barren, leafless trees. The walls that once encircled the village had long since crumbled, there were no more hungry dogs roaming in search of food, and all that was left of the houses were a few piles of yellowish stones.

Lysandra shivered as she looked at the scene of desolation; there was nothing here to remind her of the Mandarin and she turned sadly away, wishing she had never come.

They took the overgrown path through the rice fields and suddenly saw on the hill in front of them, like a flame against the gray-gold landscape, the vermillion ancestral hall of Lilin. They scrambled breathlessly up the rocky path until they stood before it and even though its lacquer was faded and its gilt long since gone, they saw it was very beautiful.

They went inside and there, sitting cross-legged on the floor, was an ancient holyman. He was so old, his fragile bones could barely support their meager covering of flesh. His face was skull-like with a wisp of pointed, gray beard and his eyes seemed even older than the rest of him, steeped in knowledge and alive with goodness. Instinctively, Lysandra bowed to him.

He was sitting on his grass bedmat wrapped in his worn saffron robe and she sat beside him and addressed him in Chinese.

"Honorable Elder, I am sorry to disturb your peace with my humble presence, but I am here to pay my respects to my honorable ancestors."

The old man's eyes searched her features, but he did not question what she said. "Their spirits will be glad you have come," he replied in a thin, reedy voice.

"Tell me, holyman," she said. "All life has gone from this place. Why are you here?"

"Honorable Daughter," he replied gently, "I came across this small temple many years ago on my travels, and each time I pass this way I am drawn again to its peace and its beauty. Each time I stop and pass a few hours or a few days here, I do not know how long for I am so old I can no longer remember the passing of time."

"Then you remember this place Honorable Elder," Lysandra said eagerly. "You remember the village? And what happened to it?"

He nodded. "Even when I first came the village was poor and the village lord was stern and greedy. Drought followed upon drought each year, withering the rice fields and drying out the pond. The young people eluded the greedy lord's cruel grasp and ran to the cities in search of a better life. Great changes came to China and the village was abandoned. The houses crumbled and returned to dust and the winds came and blew away their dust. Then one year the great Ta Chiang rose and covered the land and there it remained until the summer, when it crept back into its bed and the drought began again. Each winter the Ta Chiang comes closer and stays longer and longer, and very soon all that will be left is the hill with the ancestral hall of the woman Lilin and her children."

Lysandra thanked him for his story and then she lit the sticks of fragrant incense she had brought with her and knelt on the floor and prayed, kowtowing many times to the spirits of her loved ones.

She said good-bye to the holyman and placed an offering in his bowl. A cool soft wind stroked her pale hair, touching her cheek gently as she turned for one last long look at the temple built by Mayling for her family, glowing like a beautiful scarlet beacon on its hill, and she smiled. "She knows," she said contentedly to Matt. "She knows I was here to say 'thank you.' "

The wind filled the sails of the shabby black junk as it pulled away from the riverbank on its return journey, sighing across the flat desolate landscape, carrying away the dust and the earth layer by layer, until very soon nothing would remain but the vermillion temple on the hill.